The
TOWER OF
GEBURAH

A Fantasy

John White

INTER-VARSITY PRESS
DOWNERS GROVE
ILLINOIS 60515

InterVarsity Press is the book-publishing division of Inter-Varsity Christian Fellowship, a student movement active on campus at hundreds of universities, colleges and schools of nursing. For information about local and regional activities, write IVCF, 233 Langdon St., Madison, WI 53703.

Distributed in Canada through InterVarsity Press, 1875 Leslie St., Unit 10, Don Mills, Ontario M3B 2M5, Canada.

ISBN 0-87784-560-3
Library of Congress Catalog Card Number: 78-6363

Printed in the United States of America

18	17	16	15	14	13	12	11	10	9	8
94	93	92	91	90	89	88				

To Miles (who flattered my reading
with wide-eyed attention),
Leith (who fell asleep on
me a couple of times) and Liana
(who scorned to listen,
but who sneaked down to my study to
devour the manuscript
in solitude).

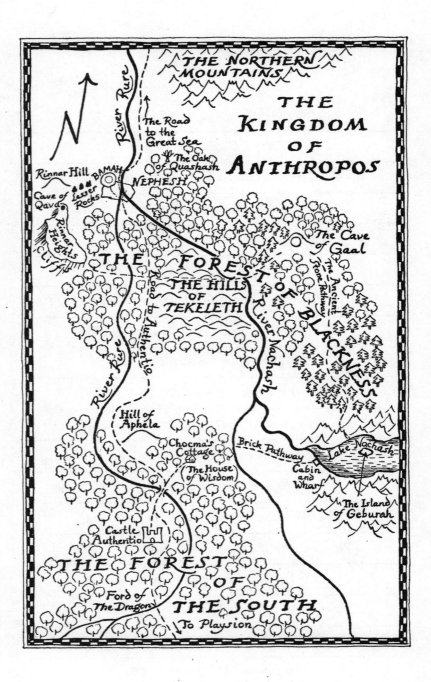

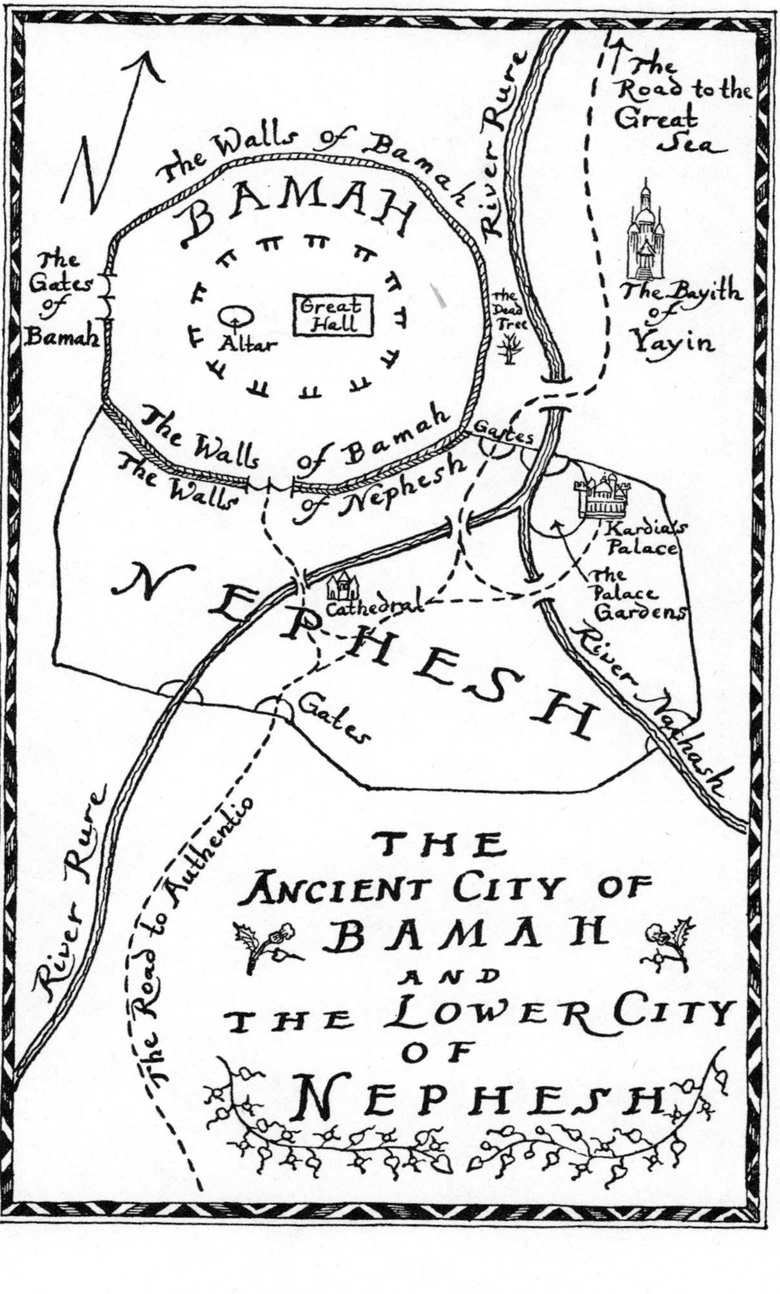

N

The Walls of Bamah

BAMAH

The Gates of Bamah

Altar   Great Hall

River Rure

The Road to the Great Sea

The Dead Tree

The Bayith of Yayin

The Walls of Bamah

Gates

The Walls of Nephesh

NEPHESH

Cathedral

Kardia's Palace

The Palace Gardens

River Nathash

Gates

River Rure

The Road to Authentio

THE
ANCIENT CITY OF
BAMAH
AND
THE LOWER CITY
OF
NEPHESH

I
The Forbidding Attic

Maybe they shouldn't have been there at all. Wesley, the oldest, was more touchy than the other two about getting into trouble. Not that they often did—at least, no more than most kids their age.

But still, something felt vaguely wrong about it. Wesley actually said so, and Kurt closed the door because it seemed safer that way even though there was no one else in the house. Consciences are funny things. All three of the children had tried the door previously and had found it locked. But today it was open. "Mrs. Janofski won't get here for a couple of hours yet," said Lisa to reassure herself that they wouldn't be found. Mrs. Janofski was to look after the three while Uncle John was away. The weekend promised to be interesting.

At lunch time Uncle John had left for the airport by snowmobile to take the first plane flying east to Toronto. A three-day blizzard had immobilized the city, wrapping its streets in soft white snowdrifts up to ten feet deep.

The kitchen windows at Uncle John's were half covered with snow. The back door could not be opened. But Mrs. Janofski who lived right next door would come over for the weekend to keep house for them. ("We could have looked after ourselves," Wesley had grumbled, but Uncle John had insisted.) So, as I said, the weekend promised to be interesting, though none of them knew *how* interesting, indeed how very frightening it was to prove.

"Look at the TV sets!" said Kurt wonderingly, staring around. "I wonder why he keeps them all here?" Kurt was the youngest and a TV addict. All three children stood together on the old, worn carpet in the middle of the room and stared about them. It was a plain room, with not a stick of furniture except for the five television sets. Two sets stood like sentries on either side of the attic window below a sloping ceiling. The other three were against the opposite wall of faded, old-fashioned blue wallpaper. They reminded the children of what you see in secondhand stores on North Main. The whole room was drab and dingy, and a layer of dust covered the televisions and the windowsill.

"I wonder if any of them work." Lisa, the middle child, said what was on everyone's mind.

Wesley stepped toward the window and looked out onto Grosvenor Avenue below. "You get a terrific view from up here," he said. "Just *look* at that snow! It's almost up to the bedroom windows at the Smiths' house." Behind him he heard a click as Lisa mechanically began to turn the volume knob on the set beside him. All of them were too old to have on-off buttons.

"It doesn't seem to work," she said.

"They're probably not plugged in," Wesley heard Kurt say. "Look behind and see if . . . no, look, there isn't even a cord."

Wesley turned from the window and stared gloomily back at his brother and sister. "Don't mess with them."

"They don't have any cords," Kurt said as he peered behind one set after the other. "Why on earth does he keep them up here?"

"Maybe the cords are curled up inside or something," Lisa suggested.

"Don't be an idiot." Kurt was now pushing behind the middle television against the back wall. "There *must* be a cord somewhere."

"I said don't mess with them."

"But they're not even plugged in."

"Well then, let's get out of here before we do some damage." Wesley was normally edgy, but he suddenly felt he had had enough of the forbidding attic. "Come on. Stop fiddling with those things."

There was again a click as Lisa turned another volume

13

knob. "Listen! It's humming!" she said.

"It can't be," contradicted Kurt. "None of them are plugged in. I've checked them all. There aren't even any plugs in the room."

Wesley and Lisa stared at the set in the far corner of the attic. It certainly was making a humming sound.

"Turn it off, Lisa, and let's go. I'm not sure we're supposed to be here. Uncle John. . . ."

"O.K. Just a minute, Wes. Look. . . ."

A tiny, intense purply green spot appeared in the center of the screen. Suddenly it spread to cover the screen with familiar horizontal lines. Kurt turned from the set he was examining and joined the other two. "It's crazy," he said. "None of them are plugged in. There's no current here."

"Turn it off, Lisa, and let's go."

Nobody moved for a moment. Then Wesley angrily stepped toward the lighted screen. Afterward he wished he'd stepped forward more quickly. He was just reaching for the volume control when computer letters began to jiggle themselves in lines across the screen. Lisa read the words aloud.

"*Look all thou wilt at the pictures and see* . . . it doesn't sound like a weather report . . . *List' to whatever they say to thee* . . . sounds like the Bible. *The pictures you see are but one, not four* . . . *And each to the others may serve as a door* . . . *Once mayest thou enter by climbing the frame* . . . *Once mayest thou enter but never again* . . . *Once, yet I pray thee to shatter the bond* . . . *And pass Through the glass To what lies beyond*. . . . I wonder what it means?"

Kurt said, "It's more like a riddle than the Bible."

Suddenly the words disappeared and began to reappear as they had done at first. Wesley's arm had dropped to his side and a look of bewilderment had replaced the worry on his face. For a few moments they stared in silence. Lisa and Kurt squatted on the floor.

"Try another channel," said Kurt.

"No, don't," said Lisa. "Let's at least wait to see what happens. It may be a decent program."

"I think it's some kind of commercial," said Wesley whose arm had for a second time dropped to his side.

But no picture came. The riddle repeated itself five times. As it began for the sixth time, Wesley said, "That does it," and impatiently turned the knob. Instantly the square of lines shriveled to an intense blob of light in the center of the screen. They watched it slowly fade to a point and then disappear. It was as though a spell had come over them. Wesley stood while Kurt and Lisa remained squatting on their haunches. Everyone felt a little dreamy. Finally Wes broke the silence. "Come on," he said. "Let's get out of here!"

"But *look!*" Lisa squealed in excitement.

All three were suddenly aware that the sets beside the one they had been watching were turned on.

"Color! It can't be. They're too old!"

"They're not moving!"

"Must be station identification."

"Or technical difficulties beyond their control."

"I can't see how they came on at all."

"Did you switch them on, Lisa?" Kurt was speaking.

"No, I never touched them."

"Weird."

"Look, I said we never should have come up here in the first place. Turn them off." Wesley sounded angry which meant he was a little scared.

"No, leave them. You never know what the program might be."

"Can you see what channels they're on?"

Kurt stared at the channel changers. "They're both on four," he said frowning.

"But there *is* no channel four."

Even Wesley was puzzled.

"It is weird. No plugs, no wires, no antennas . . . switch them off anyway."

"'They're not on, Wesley. I told you I never touched them."

"They must be." Wesley moved toward the middle set. He grasped the volume switch. A strange look came over his face. "You're right. It's off. Let's see what happens when I turn it on." He turned it on and off several times. The only sound was the click of the switch. The pictures remained as they were.

Fascinated, the children stared at the two pictures. On the center set they saw a bearded young man in the kind of clothes you see in English history books or in Robin Hood programs. His hands were manacled and held by chains to a rough stone wall behind his head. He sat on a flagstone floor with a fur cloak covering his legs. On the upper right of the picture five stone steps led up to a heavy oaken door.

"He must be a prisoner," Kurt said.

"Look at his eyes. They look right at you," Lisa said with awe in her voice. It was true. Though the man neither moved nor spoke, they all had the curious feeling that he was looking at them, looking at them as though he wanted something from them.

"It's not like a TV program," Lisa said. "I mean he's not like an actor. It's as though he's a real person."

"Stupid!" Wesley was growing more anxious. "It's just one of those pictures they put on when . . . ."

"When the set is turned off!" Kurt completed. "Listen, we can't go till we turn them off properly anyway. If we leave them like this Uncle John will know we've been here."

Lisa was looking at the next picture. It showed a room with dark, wood-paneled walls. On a heavy oak table lay a huge, leather-bound book with a brass clasp locking the pages together. A large key lay beside it, together with a strangely carved wooden box.

Something made her turn round. "The other two sets are on too," she said in bewilderment.

It was true. Both screens had come alive. Both bore motionless colored pictures. One showed a forest with a curiously shaped cottage before which a peasant lady brushed leaves from the pathway with a broom. The other showed what looked like an enormous cavern, where hundreds of horses knelt on the floor and knights in armor either lay on the floor by their sides or were draped across the saddles of the kneeling horses. Slowly Lisa began to chant:

Look all thou wilt at the pictures and see.
List' to whatever they say to thee.
The pictures you see are but one, not four,
And each to the others may serve as a door.
Once mayest thou enter by climbing the frame.
Once mayest thou enter but never again.
Once, yet I pray thee to shatter the bond
And pass
Through the glass
To what lies beyond.

"O.K." Wesley said crossly. "So you've got a super memory. What we need now is some way to turn the sets off."

"Of all the freaky things, ..." Kurt was saying. "Wes, don't you see? She means the riddle is about the pictures on the sets!"

Even Wesley forgot his uneasiness momentarily. "I'm sure there's no connection," he said. "It must be a coincidence."

"Well, there *are* four pictures," said Lisa a little defensively. "And they do look sort of connected."

"O.K. Then perhaps you should try to pass through the glass to what lies beyond."

Wesley was being his know-it-all, superior self again, Lisa thought. She turned to look at the first picture of the prisoner chained to the wall. Outside, the late winter afternoon was slowly darkening and the screens glowed brighter in the semidarkness.

"It almost looks like 3-D," she said slowly as she stared, "almost like a tiny theater stage with no glass in front."

"There's glass there all right. You'll feel it if you touch it." Kurt was finding the room interesting. He did not share Wesley's anxieties.

Dreamily Lisa got to her feet and moved over to the dungeon picture. Her fingers reached out to touch the glass screen. What happened next was the most frightening thing Kurt or Wesley had ever experienced.

They saw, or thought they saw Lisa's hand pass inside the set, followed by her arm. The only thing was that once inside, the hand and arm became tiny.

"She's kneeling on the picture frame!"

"Stop it, you idiot! Stop it and come back!"

Wesley hurled himself forward and tried to seize Lisa as she was sucked into the TV like a pile of dust into a vacuum cleaner. For a second they saw her—a tiny Lisa inside the picture, staring at the man manacled to the wall. Then one by one the pictures faded, and the two boys found themselves standing in the semidarkness, alone.

At that moment they heard the telephone ringing downstairs.

2
The Captive King

Lisa didn't *feel* as though she had been sucked into a vacuum cleaner, but she was very surprised. One moment she had been startled to find that there was indeed no glass on the front of the television. And then it had seemed that everything in the picture was swiftly growing larger and wrapping itself round her. A moment later she stood on stone flags inside a small stone-walled room. In front of her sat the man she had seen on the television set.

Lisa liked him and for a few moments they stared at each other. He didn't seem surprised though she could tell by the way he was looking at her that he could see her. His hands were purple as they hung down from the manacles above his head. The fingers were swollen and four heavy, gold rings were biting into the flesh. His matted dark hair and beard did not spoil the warm nobility of his face. His red tunic was torn and dirty, and she saw him shiver a little in spite of the fur cloak covering his legs. A belt of gold links encircled his waist while boots of soft leather with pointed toes showed beneath the cape.

"I'm Lisa," she said. "Who are you? And where is this? I've never been inside a television set before."

A smile spread like sunshine across the man's face. The pain that creased his forehead disappeared for a moment and his blue eyes shone.

"Welcome, little maiden," he said. "I am grieved that I cannot rise to show you more courtesy. Right glad am I to see you. The Shepherd said you would come to rescue me. I often doubted the lore of the books, but now it seems I would have done well to have had more faith. There is a mist at times but today it shone clear. I saw you coming. Welcome, little maiden. Would that I could offer you food and drink, but you see my limitations."

Lisa's mouth slowly opened. "Is this part of the television?" she asked again. "It's kind of exciting but I never knew it could do things like this." Then her face clouded. "But it's not television. It's real." She stepped forward, her footsteps sounding on the hard stone floor and bent again to see what it felt like. As she did so she became aware of the odor of stale sweat that hung around the man and of the cold damp of the room.

"Who *are* you?" she asked again, this time a little more anxiously.

"Who am I, little maid? You look upon Kardia, rightful king of Anthropos, unhappily now a prisoner in his own country. But where in Anthropos I know not with certainty. Indeed at times I think I may not be in Anthropos at all. You speak of visions, telly visions. Of visions I know a little, but nought of 'telly.' "

Disconcertingly it began to dawn on Lisa that she had somehow arrived in another world or another time. She pushed the thought to the back of her mind, though not before she had turned round, half expecting to look back into the attic. Only a stone wall faced her.

"Do you not see the glass, little maid?"

Lisa stared at the wall. It consisted of rough reddish stone. One small stone was round and smooth, about the size of a tennis ball.

"Look into it, little maid, while the clearness remains. It was through yon portal you came. Surely you knew that?"

As Lisa stared it seemed as though a dim, square-shaped light glowed faintly inside. Suddenly the sphere itself lit up, and across its surface two tiny figures moved. With a shock she recognized Wesley and Kurt in the attic on Grosvenor Avenue. Both of them had stopped and were staring toward her, but she could tell that neither of them saw her.

"Wesley," she cried, "look! It's *me*. I'm here."

Suddenly their hands grew very large and seemed to cover half the surface of the glass stone. Then a grayness covered it, its surface roughened and the light within it disappeared. For a moment she was stunned. It was as though the last link between the dungeon and the house on Grosvenor were suddenly cut off.

She drew a deep breath and turned to the king. "I'm not going to cry," she told herself. "It's probably only a dream, and if it is, it's going to be a nice one."

"They call it a proseo comai stone," the king was saying. "Usually we just say proseo stone, for that is shorter. Through it may come the desires of one's heart. It is said there are many such stones in the kingdom, and there are those who speak of the miracles they bring. The

Shepherd's father in ages past gave them to the realm that it might prosper. And this one brought you to me. That is indeed a miracle. But how you shall help now, I know not."

Lisa was about to say, "I don't believe in magic." But before the words came out of her mouth she realized that she would not be speaking the truth.

"Come and sit beside me, Lisa. I know not why the stone has answered my longings with a maid. Nay, do not weep. The stone has sent you to help me."

"I'm not crying," Lisa said a little indignantly, though the truth was that her lips were quivering and one tear had dropped from her right eye and plopped onto her sweater while another tear was trickling down her left cheek.

She moved toward him, for in some way his presence, even though he was chained to the wall, was comforting. She was glad she was wearing her old jeans, for the floor was damp and dirty. As she turned to sit to the right of him she saw the pile of straw on which he sat. There was room enough to squeeze beside him. Again she noticed the smell of old sweat. But instead of repelling her it gave her comfort. It is reassuring to meet a real human being when you are whisked out of your uncle's house into a dungeon.

"That's better, child. I would put my arm about you but for these chains. Use my cloak. There. You will be warmer now."

"If you're a king, why are you in a dungeon? I mean, what did you do?"

"Little one, it is not what I did, but what I failed to do that brought me to such straits. I grew careless. I let evil men deceive me. He who now calls himself king is a sorcerer. The books warn of such but I heard of his fame from afar. It was I who invited Hocoino to Anthropos."

"Hocoino? Is that the sorcerer's name?"

"Aye, Lisa. That is what they call him. And it was in an evil moment that I wrote to him and bid him come to my court. To say that I was proud, that I was bewitched, that I was young and lacked judgment might all be true. But they offer no excuse."

For a few moments they were silent.

Lisa was not sure how she should address a king in a dungeon. Ought she to call him, "your majesty"? Would "sir" do or would it have to be "sire"? She did not for a moment doubt that what he said was true, but it took a great deal of getting used to. Anthropos was evidently a country, and Kardia was its rightful king. Somebody called Hocoino, a magician, had become the king of the country, and Kardia was imprisoned. Most puzzling of all was that Kardia seemed to expect her to help him. Of course he was mistaken about that. What could a girl do to help an imprisoned king? For one thing, how could she get out? The thought was disconcerting. The peculiar stone . . . what had Kardia called it? . . . a proseo comai stone seemed to provide little help. It would be nice if she could get back through it again. But even if she did, how would she help Kardia?

Suddenly she realized she didn't want to help Kardia at all. She wanted to be back in Uncle John's house on Grosvenor. Adventures were fine when you read about them in books, but this kind of adventure was unpleasantly frightening. True, she was not chained to the wall like Kardia, but she was locked inside a cell with him.

Saying "Excuse me, sire" (it didn't sound too bad once she actually said it), she walked over to the proseo comai stone. For a moment she stared at it. Then touching it with her finger she experienced a curious, warm vibration throughout her body. In a kind of desperation she pulled a Kleenex from the pocket of her jeans and began to rub the roughened surface in an attempt to make it like glass again. In some way, she felt, it must be connected to the television set in Uncle John's attic. If magic had brought her here, then magic could perhaps get her back. Kardia had said, "There is a mist at times but today it shone clear." Perhaps if she could get it to shine clear again, there would be some way of getting back through it.

Desperately she rubbed it with the Kleenex. Once or twice she thought that perhaps the surface was beginning to get smoother. But the longer she tried, the more helpless it seemed.

"What are you doing, Lisa?"

She turned to him, conscious this time that tears were running down her cheeks and that she no longer cared whether the king saw them or not.

"I want to go home," she said. "I thought perhaps if I rubbed the stone clear I might be able to get to Uncle John's. I'm frightened. I don't know how I got here and I don't know how to get back."

The king sighed.

"Then I have done you ill, little one. For it was my longing that brought you. True, I little knew that a maid would be the answer to my longings. I thought a dozen armed warriors might be sent to rescue me. Yet you came. And I doubt not that your coming will indeed lead to my release. The stones do not always answer our longings in the way we want them to, but they never play us false."

Lisa mopped her cheeks with the ragged piece of Kleenex. She blew her nose as well as she could, but she really needed several more tissues and wished she had come prepared for an adventure if she *had* to have one.

There was something about the king's face that made her feel she was being mean and cheap in trying to get back to Uncle John's. He did not scold her in any way. His look was simply one of concern and sadness. She became more aware than ever that he must be very uncomfortable, indeed in pain.

She leaned against the wall.

"How ever *can* I help you?" she asked. "I'm locked up here like you. If I could get back through the stone I might get Wes and Kurt. Perhaps even Uncle John—or the police. But if I can't get back...."

"If you cannot for the moment return to the place you came from, perhaps you could aid me by escaping from my jail and by telling my friends where I am. My subjects are loyal. They will get word to the Princess Suneidesis, my bride-to-be. Perchance she will find some way to rescue me if she but knows where I am held."

Lisa looked at him. She certainly would like to see him freed from the horrible manacles that held his blood-engorged hands. There was something about his eyes that made her forget for a moment her own problem. Did he really have in mind some way in which she might get out of the dungeon? But where would she go if she did get out? How would she know her way about a country she had never been in?

She was about to slip back into thinking how much she would prefer to be with Kurt and Wesley when the king spoke again.

"Can you saddle a horse, little one?"

Lisa's heart leaped. "Sure, your majesty. I just love horses."

"Can you pull the straps tightly, so that the saddle stays in place?"

"Yes, your majesty." Lisa was glad for all the horse-manship she had taken at summer camps for the past three years. She loved riding. She loved horses. For a moment it seemed to her that perhaps her adventure might have a pleasant side to it.

"Hearken, little one. One hour from now my jailer will return. Three times each day he comes. My lamp," he glanced at an oil lamp on the wall opposite where Lisa was standing, "must always be well filled so that any who wish to see me may do so from the bars in the door." Lisa glanced at the heavy oak door and saw for the first time the bars that divided the small open square near its top.

"Always he brings me food, fills the lamp and takes me to a small courtyard that I may walk and ease my body."

"Your majesty, who *is* your jailer? Are there many?" Lisa's mind was filled with fantasies of brutal soldiers. Horses sounded fine, but she had little relish for meeting the king's enemies.

"My jailer is no man, but a jinn, a jinn that does the bidding of Hocoino. Fear him not, little one. He will not harm you. He does not know you are here. Only beware then that he sees you not. As to others in this place I cannot say. From the courtyard I have heard the coming and going of men and of horses. And I doubt not that there be stables. Seek them out, and when you have found them, hide there till darkness. Tell all whom you meet that I am still living and am a prisoner here."

"But where is *here*, your majesty? And how shall I know which way to go?"

"That I cannot tell with certainty. Only I know that we are in the southern forests, either of Anthropos or of the land of Playsion, a country south of Anthropos. In either case, ride north."

"Your majesty, ..." Lisa did not know how to put it.

Were the skies above Anthropos the same as those above Canada? Was there a pole star?

"Your majesty, I don't know which way north is. In my country we have a northern star called Polaris, but perhaps the stars here are different."

For a moment the king looked surprised. "Forgive me, little one. I expect you to have knowledge which you could not possibly have. In the north is the great star, Numa. No other star in the whole sky is as bright as he. He will be your guide. As for your journey and all you may meet in the course of it, I doubt not that he who sent you hither will guide your steps."

Lisa was not nearly so sure as Kardia about whether matters would be so simple. But somewhere deep in her mind she began to feel, not that she had been here before, but that she was meant to be here. Even the problem of how she would get back to Uncle John's and of what he might think if he found her missing no longer troubled her. This was not going to be a nightmare, but the best kind of dream.

Of course she knew it wasn't a dream. But just as in some of her nicest dreams she had tried hard not to wake up or if she did wake up, had tried her hardest to get back to sleep and get into the same dream again, so now, for the first time she was glad to be in Anthropos and with King Kardia, even if for the moment they were shut in a dungeon. After all, the dungeon was not a bad one. It was not filled with stenches; the walls were not slimy; there were no rats (or were there?) and there was actually a light. They could have been in pitch blackness.

She went back to sit beside the king, pulling his fur cape over her jeans as she did so, and leaning half on him and half on the rough wall behind them. The cape was lined with a soft silk. The straw pricked her ankles, but she was protected elsewhere by her heavy jeans. She even began to daydream of dashing on horseback into the capital city (after she had asked Kardia where it was) and leading an army into the south to free him.

A thought suddenly occurred to her.

"Your majesty said to wait until darkness. Isn't it dark now? It was getting dark when I came."

"No, child. It lacks an hour yet to sunrise, or so it seems to me."

"How can you tell?"

"By a feeling in my bones, child, and by the level of oil in the lamp."

Lisa looked and saw that the lamp was not made of metal but of something that looked like glass. The oil in it was getting low.

There were more questions in her mind, but she felt disinclined to talk. She let her head fall sideways against the king's chest and found herself drowsy. A moment later she was fast asleep, in spite of the cold and the discomfort.

3

"Welcome to Anthropos"

Wesley's mouth was open, and though something inside him was screaming no sound came from his lips. Steadily the telephone continued its ringing. Neither of the boys moved.

"Answer it, for Pete's sake. Answer it. I just can't leave this room," he said hoarsely to Kurt.

"No, Wes, you answer it . . . I'm . . . I wouldn't know what to say."

Wes gave a sharp cry halfway between a sob and a snort, and tumbled impetuously down the stairway to the second floor. He snatched the receiver, fumbled and dropped it, picked it up, and said "Hello?" only to hear a click and the buzz of the dial tone. Angrily he slammed it back onto the holder and tore up the stairs again.

No sooner had he reached the top than the telephone rang again. This time his "o-o-ogh" was a howl of rage.

"Hallo?" said a woman's voice, "Dis is a Missus Janofski. My husband he try to shovel da walk, an' he gotta bad pain in his chess."

Wesley could not understand. It was as though the words did not penetrate his mind. He heard his own voice saying, "Oh, I'm sorry. Can we help?" and Mrs. Janofski replying, "No, thank you. Da snowmobile shea-comin' to take him to da hospital. But I go wid him, ya? I not come around you kids today. You be O.K.?"

Wesley felt dazed, his mind churning with fear. Again he heard his voice speaking politely, filled with a concern he did not feel. "Oh, of course, we'll be all right, Mrs. Janofski. I'm terribly sorry. I do hope he's not too bad."

"He not very good, I don' tink."

"I'm sorry."

"Ya, O.K. I go an' wait da snowmobile. Bye now!"

He heard the click at the other end of the phone. The house suddenly seemed fearfully empty, cut off from everyone he knew. Uncle John would not be back till Monday or Tuesday. Mrs. Janofski would have been a comfort to have around. She was solid, motherly and re-assuring.

His legs felt weak and his mouth was dry. He turned on every light switch he could find as he made his way to the attic. As he entered the door he saw a switch outside it and turned it on.

"Oh, thanks," Kurt said as Wesley stumbled wearily through the door. "I couldn't find the light switch." He was kneeling before the screen through which Lisa had disappeared, tinkering with the controls.

"Here, let me have a go!" Wesley still felt as though he were in a nightmare. His palms were sweating and his fingers trembled. He knelt beside Kurt, nudging him aside.

"I can't get any sign of life out of it," Kurt said. "I don't think we'll get it to work whatever we do. How in the world did she put her hand through the glass?" Both of the boys instinctively touched the screen feeling for a weakness. At one point they pushed gently with both palms (it was then that Lisa from inside Kardia's dungeon saw the four large hands on the proseo stone), but the window was solid and unyielding.

"We *gotta* do something!" Wesley always felt responsible when things went wrong. Often he would criticize his brother and sister, but usually deep inside him he had the feeling that he himself was to blame. He had that feeling now. Why had he ever let them all come into the attic? Why had he not insisted they all leave instead of tinkering with the sets? Why had he sarcastically suggested that Lisa "pass through the glass"?

"Wes, I'm scared."

Wesley turned from the unresponsive set to look at his brother. As he saw the fear in Kurt's eyes he steadied himself. He mustn't panic. Whatever happened he mustn't panic.

He squatted on the floor and turned with his back to the television, then forced himself to speak and think slowly.

"We're on our own here."

Kurt said nothing.

"Mr. Janofski just had some kind of an attack and Mrs. J. is waiting for a snowmobile to take him to the hospital. She won't be coming over."

Wesley paused, but Kurt remained silent.

"Until the snowplows have cleared the streets there will be no traffic except for emergencies."

"This *is* an emergency," Kurt interrupted.

"O.K. You're right. How do you suggest we get help?"

"We could dial emergency."

"And what would we tell them?"

"We'd tell them that . . . O golly, I see what you mean. They'd think we were nuts."

"Or else that we were trying to fool them. Can you imagine what the operator would say when we said our sister had disappeared into a television set?"

"We could just say she'd disappeared."

"But what would we say when they came? Imagine a couple of people from the Fire and Rescue Department arriving and asking us where we'd last seen her. . . ."

"They'd look in the snow."

"A fat lot of good that would do."

Wesley was still trembling a little. He gripped one shaking hand with the other, hoping Kurt would not notice.

"What was it we did that started the whole thing?"

"What d'you mean?"

"Well, if we go back and retrace all our steps—you know, who did what first and then what happened and so on—we might be able to find a way of doing something."

Kurt looked doubtful.

"Anyway, that's what the police do. They sort of re-enact the crime."

"O.K. Well, first we all came into the room," Kurt said slowly. "And you went to the window and said something about the view. . . ."

Wesley stepped over to the window. The street lamps made the snow look incredibly beautiful. On the far side it had drifted high on the walls of the houses. Tree trunks seemed shorter as though a section had been taken out of them. The eerie silence was broken by the muffled sound of a snowmobile. Wesley saw, long before the machine came into view, the dancing yellow reflection of headlights flickering on the snow as the snow-mobile approached the intersection with Grosvenor. A moment later it turned slowly toward him, and he saw one man riding on it, pulling a long sleigh behind him on which there seemed to be a pile of blankets. He slowed down the machine and drove as closely as he could to the front door of the Janofskis', where he disappeared from view.

"They've come for Mr. Janofski," he told Kurt. "Guy on a snowmobile pulling a sled. We might be able to see them from the bay window of Uncle John's study."

For a moment they forgot their own dilemma and hurried to the floor below, where it was possible to see the front of the house next door. The driver of the snowmobile had disappeared into the house and with him the blankets. Kurt perched on the radiator under the window, enjoying the warmth as it penetrated his pants.

A moment later they saw a yellow oblong of light fall across the sleigh as the front door of the Janofskis' opened. It seemed strange to see no steps leading up to the door which opened directly into the deep snow. As he descended, sinking more deeply with each step, he held the stretcher higher, so that it emerged more or less level, the blankets strapped down in a crisscross fashion.

"How ever will they get him on the sledge?" Kurt asked. "He'll be up to his waist in a minute."

By now they could see Mrs. Janofski emerging from the door, bending low as she struggled to grasp her end of the stretcher.

"That's Mr. J. on the stretcher. You can see his face where the blankets are round his head," Wesley murmured. "Golly! I hope they don't slip."

"You'd think there'd be someone else to help. Usually they send two or three," commented Kurt.

"They can't. Ambulances won't be able to drive till the snow is cleared. In any case the ambulance crews are all stranded at home. People just have to stay put. The guy with the snowmobile is just a volunteer to help until the snowplows get going."

Somehow Mrs. Janofski and the snowmobile driver got to the bottom of the steps. Both were waist deep in snow, dragging and pushing the stretcher over to the sleigh. Wes was so intent on what they were doing that he found his own arms straining to lift the stretcher.

It took an age to get it strapped on the sleigh. Finally the front door closed. Mrs. Janofski bent forward to kiss her husband tenderly, then struggled to get onto the rear seat of the snowmobile. For a while it seemed as though the effort to haul herself up would be too much, but finally with the help of the man she made it. A moment later the engine sputtered to life, the headlight was switched on, and the two brothers lost sight of the machine as it turned north from Grosvenor in the direction of the Health Sciences Centre. As it did so they remembered their own problem.

"O.K. Let's get back to work." Wesley was both relieved and curious to find that a good deal of his panic had subsided. Instead a tingle of excitement and hope flowed over him as they headed again for the attic.

He positioned himself by the window.

"O.K.," he said. "Now you fiddle with the volume knob on this set on my left."

"But I was looking around for cables and things."

"We can do that later. I want you to do Lisa's movements first."

"She said this one wasn't working."

"O.K., turn it on and see." Wesley turned round to watch his brother.

"It's not working any more this time than last time. It can't if it's not plugged in," Kurt grumbled.

Wesley ignored him. "Which one did she try next? This one on the other side of me?"

Kurt thought for a moment. "No, I don't think so. I think she was fooling with *that* one in the far corner."

"Of course, by jiminy, you're right! That was the one with the riddle on it. Try it and see if it comes on again."

Kurt crossed over to the old set and turned the volume knob on. Both boys held their breath.

"I think it's humming," Kurt said.

Then to their joy first the tiny dot of light appeared at the center of the screen and then the whole screen was covered with the fine lines. With their eyes focused on the television and their bodies absolutely immobile, both boys merely gave a soft gasp as the familiar computer letters jiggled into place.

"D'you think we should let it go through several times like we did last time?" Kurt asked.

"I don't know. How many times was it? Four?"

"No, five—I think."

"It may not matter, but perhaps we'd better do it exactly as we did last time."

Wes bit his lip in impatience. The process seemed to be taking much longer this time than it had earlier. At last, as the first line began to spread itself across the screen for the sixth time, he reached forward and switched it off.

Both boys waited tensely. Suddenly the set in the other far corner flickered into life again, bearing the same color picture it had borne the first time.

"The two on either side of the window are on too," Kurt said turning around. Only the set through which Lisa had disappeared remained dead.

35

Kurt thumped firmly on the top of the set. Nothing happened. He tried again saying, "Mebbe it's just . . . y'know . . . a bit slow." But no amount of thumping, switching, coaxing had any effect. The set remained cold and dormant.

Wesley drew a deep breath. "Hold it," he said. "There must be a clue in the riddle. There was that bit that said, 'Once mayest thou enter.' Could that have something to do with it?"

Kurt thought for a minute. "You mean once someone has gone into the set, then . . . in that case we're no further ahead."

"Yes we are, though. There was another bit that said, 'The pictures you see are but one, not four, *and each to the others may serve as a door.*' Mebbe one of us could try another picture and find Lisa that way."

"Not one of us—*two* of us," said Kurt steadily. "Let's not get our forces divided if we don't have to. But in any case if you're right, it means we could choose *any* of the three. Which one should we try? Perhaps only one of them will work."

"I don't like the one with the book and key."

"Why not? It could be the key to open Lisa's cell door."

"I never thought of that."

"But on the other hand it might not. How d'you feel about the cave?"

Wes stared at it. "It looks pretty spooky. What'd we say to those guys if we woke them up? 'Please, Mr. Knight, we've lost our sister'?"

Kurt didn't laugh.

"They could be under some sort of spell."

"Look at the one with the old woman!" There was excitement in Wes's voice. "D'you remember what Lisa said? She said it looked as if there was no glass there and as though it was like a little stage in 3-D."

Kurt stared at the picture of the old woman.

"You're right. It *does* look like what she said. That could be the one we're supposed to take."

"Here, grab my hand!" Wesley's excitement was rising. "Now, let's squat close together, as close to the set as we can, with our knees on a level with the bottom of the screen. O.K. When I say *now,* push your free hand into the TV. Ready? *Now.*"

What followed for both boys was a curious sensation. When they told me about it afterward the only thing they could compare it with was coming up and breaking the surface of the water after a dive in a swimming pool. If you've ever done *that,* you'll know what they meant. The only difference was that they suddenly found their heads bursting up through the soft earth of a forest floor. Propelled sharply upward they had to steady themselves when they found they were standing side by side, still holding hands, on a pathway surrounded by tall forest trees. Wes began to mechanically brush the earth from himself. A strangely shaped cottage stood about twenty yards in front of them, and on the path before it an old lady was sweeping. Her hair was white, her skin, nut brown, and she wore a long blue dress dotted with tiny flowers.

She looked up and saw them.

It was hard to tell what she was thinking. She seemed puzzled but at the same time very interested in them. She dropped her broom, walked to where they stood, laid her hands on both of their shoulders and said in a clear, beautiful, bell-like voice, "Welcome to Anthropos."

4

Lisa Disappears

Lisa woke suddenly. For a moment she could not understand what had happened to her bedroom at Uncle John's. Then with a rush her strange adventure came to her and in the dim lamplight she turned to look at the king.

"He comes, little one." The king pointed to the steps leading up to the door. Beyond them was a space between the steps and the wall. "Hide yonder," he said. "Make neither movement nor sound, and he will not perceive you."

Lisa shivered. Her limbs were stiff, but she scrambled toward the steps in the corner and squeezed her body into the narrow space beyond them.

"When he comes," the king said, "he will not unlock the door for he passes through it. He will fill the lamp, leave me bread and water, then open the door so that he might take me to the courtyard. He will leave the door open and every other door that leads there. As soon as we are gone, leave the cell and follow us at a distance to the courtyard. Hide in the corner of the porch, so that as we return he will not see you. What you do thereafter *you* will have to decide. Only I pray, find a horse and ride north, and may the Shepherd's father be your guide. Hist! He comes."

Lisa did not know how Kardia knew that the jinn was coming. There was no sound of footsteps. The only thing she noticed was that their cell seemed to be getting darker. Then, as she looked at the heavy oak door above her it seemed as though darkness itself was pouring from the wood and rolling in a cloud down the steps, rolling and rising and moving toward Kardia. Fearful but fascinated she peered over the edge of the steps to see what was happening.

The wave of darkness had now reached Kardia. Suddenly there was the sound of clanking metal. The king's arms fell helplessly to his side and the chains and manacles swung loosely against the wall above his head. At that moment the whole cell was filled with darkness. The only things that Lisa could see were Kardia's face, floating like a disembodied head at the other end of the cell, and the flame of the lantern. Cold nausea entered her soul. Shivering uncontrollably, not only with cold but with a nameless terror, she shrank back as far as she could. The dungeon grew colder. Thoughts of death and evil filled her mind. She closed her eyes tightly and put her head between her knees, biting her lips to stop herself from screaming.

Then, even though her eyes were closed, she saw a beautiful blue light. In some inexplicable way the light comforted her and took away her terror enough that she

...she gasped at what she saw...

opened her eyes. The light shone, blue and piercing, filling her with strength. It seemed to be shining up at her from between her feet. Slowly she reached for it, the light illuminating her extended fingers. She touched it, picked it up and felt it with both hands. It was a stone the size of a pebble, attached to a delicate necklace of metal links. She gazed at it for several moments and then slipped the pendant over her head so that the stone rested on her chest.

Instantly the cell grew light again. Peering above the steps she gasped at what she saw. An enormous snake of gleaming, poisonous yellow, a snake with scales that was as slimy as ignorant people think real snakes are, was pouring oil into the bowl below the lantern wick from a single, large green hand that extended from below its mouth. Lisa could not tell how long the snake was. The twists and coils of its hideous body filled the whole cell. One coil lay perilously close to the foot of the steps where she was crouched. Another was wrapped round Kardia's waist.

In spite of the courage the stone gave her, Lisa shuddered as she saw the king. His head was held high in princely defiance. He was rubbing his bruised wrists to get the circulation going again, biting his lips with the pain. Yet his eyes showed courage and determination. Suddenly she knew that whatever happened she must not fail him. Nothing in her life had been as important as this. Whatever price Lisa had to pay, Kardia must be freed from the evil beings which had imprisoned him.

She was so absorbed with these thoughts that she forgot the blue stone she had been playing with absent-mindedly. Without thinking she drew the necklace back over her head and put it beside her. Instantly the cell was again filled with blackness and an oppressive sense of evil. The yellow snake disappeared.

"It's the pendant!" she thought to herself. "It must have some kind of magic to help you see things in the dark." She slipped it on and immediately she saw it all again—the dimly lit cell, the king held in one of the jinn's coils, and the green hand pouring the oil. A moment later the lamp was full. Promptly the vessel from which the oil was poured was thrown into the air and disappeared. The green hand shriveled like a balloon when you let the air out and disappeared inside the jinn. The jinn's coils began to move and it turned its head toward the door. Lisa curled into a ball and shrank back as far as she could into her corner. Again she closed her eyes, and again the comforting blue light penetrated her eyelids to fill her with courage.

She heard only the sound of Kardia's footsteps. At first it seemed he was being dragged across the flagged floor, but almost immediately she heard him stumble a little and then begin to walk steadily. His footsteps approached her across the dungeon floor and climbed steadily. She heard the door swing open with a creak. A moment later the king's footsteps sounded from the corridor, growing ever more faint.

Lisa drew a deep breath and slowly opened her eyes. Eagerly she looked at the stone only to see to her astonishment that it shone suspended in the air below her head even as it hung about her neck. It took her several seconds to realize what had happened. Quickly she reached for it with her fingers to notice that although she could feel her hands, she could see neither of them. In fact, to her dismay she could see only the floor, the walls and the steps. Her own body had disappeared. She could feel it. Her legs pressed against the hard floor. Her unseen hands reached out and touched the wall. But she herself had disappeared. She was invisible.

Instantly she forgot about the king's instructions and removed the chain from her neck again. To her relief she saw her blue jeans, her sneakers, her sweater and her hands. She still had a body. The stone hung from her hand, suspended from its delicate, gold chain.

Some people who have never been invisible imagine that it would be fun, but to Lisa it was terrifying. It is, in fact, unnerving when it happens to you for the first time. To wave your arm in front of your face as Lisa did and to *feel* your arm but to see nothing, makes your heart bump noisily in your invisible chest. But Lisa got used to it. She took the pendant off and put it on several times.

Eventually she pulled herself up out of her corner and stamped her left foot which had fallen asleep. Then she walked round the cell. If you have ever been invisible yourself, you will remember what it was like when you first began to walk and to run. It was tricky, wasn't it? Lisa found that if she had the pendant on and was looking at the floor, she tended to stumble because she was relying on her eyes instead of on the feel of her feet. Once she looked straight ahead and let her feet look after themselves, she managed better.

After practicing for a few minutes, Lisa suddenly remembered that she must escape. She put on the pendant and moved toward the steps, hesitating for a moment at the foot of them. Careful not to look down, she felt with her feet for each step and reached the top without difficulty.

She peered cautiously out of the door.

"Silly!" she said to herself. "No one can see me anyway."

Yet she was so used to being visible that it took quite a lot of courage to step into the middle of the corridor which ran in both directions from where she stood. She had to look at herself, or *try* to look at herself, several times to make sure she could not be seen.

"Hm, it seems to make visible things *in*visible and *in*visible things like the jinn, visible. . . . I'm sure Kardia's steps went *that* way," she said looking to the right. Boldly she walked along the corridor, passing through several unlocked doors, her sneakers making no sound. There were also many locked doors along the hallway, some with metal grills in them and others without. Light showed from none of them while the corridor itself was lit only by the stone.

Yet at the end of the corridor there was a dim gray light as though something of the outer world was penetrating. She hurried forward. Reaching the end of the corridor, she looked left and saw to her joy a long flight of stairs leading up into the early morning sunlight. Eagerly she began to scramble upward. But it was then that everything went horribly wrong.

The stairway opened onto a wide porch, and no sooner had she reached it than she saw the terrible head of the jinn, its piercing black eyes staring straight at her. "He can see me!" she thought. For a second or two (remember the stone gave her unusual courage) she tried to see if there was any way she could get past him into the courtyard, but in a flash his coils had filled the porch, blotting out the sun. Lisa turned and hurried down the steps. At the bottom she paused to look back. The jinn was only a third of the way down the steps advancing slowly at the pace of the king.

"If only I can reach the cell I can hide in the corner by the steps again and maybe it won't see me. Maybe it will think I ran on down the corridor. After all it never saw me in the cell before, so it can't expect me to go there."

She sped headlong down the corridor, and whipped round into the cell. Then turning to look back, she saw to her relief that the jinn had not reached the bottom of the steps. "Oh, *thank* you," she said, not knowing to whom she said it, and leaped into her little corner to curl up once again, the precious stone still around her neck.

She was panting, her heart was pounding and her mouth was dry. A moment later she heard the sound of Kardia's footsteps advancing along the corridor.

"It's coming," she said to herself, and began to quell her panting as well as she could. By the time the footsteps reached the cell door she was able to breathe silently with her mouth open. Slowly the footsteps sounded on the stairway next to where she crouched. As they reached the bottom they stopped. Lisa trembled but did not move. Then, dreading what she would see, she slowly looked up. Kardia was looking backward toward the jinn whose coils had begun to fill the dungeon. Then as she lifted her eyes further, she saw its head, the wicked black eyes staring maliciously down at her.

Or at least so it seemed. Her heart stood still. *Was* it staring at her? Or was it her stone? Suddenly she saw the reflection of its blue fire in the jinn's eyes and glanced down at her chest. Yes, that must be it. She covered it with her hands, but it glowed undimmed through them. Filled with fear she glanced up again only to see to her immense relief that the jinn was definitely not looking at her, nor even at her stone. Slowly its gaze shifted from her to examine every crevice and crack in the cell. Then it proceeded to march Kardia across to his place by the straw, make him sit down and raise his hands. It then manacled them once again above his head.

By now the gleaming yellow coils filled the cell. Slowly they uncoiled themselves and the head moved toward her corner. Then, without paying the least attention to her, it passed silently and ponderously out of the door which boomed shut behind it as the lock clicked back into place.

She saw that Kardia was smiling. "Well done, little maid," he was saying softly. "May the Shepherd guard you and may the Shepherd's father direct your steps. Bless you for your courage, little Lisa."

Lisa's heart sank as she heard the words. She knew she had failed him. Slowly she got to her feet and walked toward him.

"I'm very, very sorry, your majesty," she said. "But I was too slow. I just got to the porch when the jinn blocked my way."

A look of amazement spread across the king's face. "Lisa, my child, where are you?" he cried.

"I'm right here, your majesty . . . oh, I forgot," and she pulled the pendant from round her neck.

Then the king's jaw dropped and his eyes opened wide. For a full minute the king and the Canadian girl stared at each other, neither knowing what to say.

The king was the first to speak. "Child," he said, "I knew not that you possessed magical powers. Why did you not tell me? What are your powers? You can appear not only through the stone but appear and disappear at will. I perceive that you may be of greater value to the kingdom of Anthropos than I had realized."

"Your majesty," replied Lisa, dropping onto the straw beside the king, "I don't have any powers. I found this pendant between my feet when you sent me to the corner by the stairs. I could see it shining even when my eyes were closed. I didn't know it was magic. I put it on and suddenly I could see the jinn."

"The jinn? But the jinn is mere darkness, deceit and

terror. It has no bodily form."

"No, your majesty, the jinn is a snake, a horrid, yellow snake. I saw it when I put the stone round my neck. What I didn't know was that the stone made me invisible. It was only when you left the cell that I discovered that."

"Lisa, I pray you to let me see the stone."

Lisa held it out to the king who looked at it as well as he could from his painful position. His eyes widened as he stared at it.

"Child, do you know what this stone is? I cannot be certain, but I think it is the Mashal Stone. If it is, then it has power to bring hidden things to light and make honest things invisible to natural sight. The Mashal Stone is spoken of in the books. For eight hundred years it has been missing from the kingdom—no one knowing where it was. The Evil Lord of the Castle Authentio stole it from my forebears. Though he was overthrown, it was never seen again."

"Why does it take my fear away?" asked Lisa.

"It has many strange properties. It makes evil men blind and good men to see. It is said to shine brightest when great perils threaten Anthropos and to all but disappear when no danger threatens. The Shepherd used Mashal to confound his enemies. Some say it is alive itself, often acting on its own will. Many are the tales told of wonders wrought by Mashal."

"Then it must belong to you," said Lisa, a little sadly. She had begun to enjoy the pendant and had almost hoped it was hers to keep.

The king looked at it and then at Lisa. "Truly it belongs to the Shepherd, and he gave it not to me but to Anthropos. It helped to keep us humble and to walk in true ways. It belongs to no man or woman but now to the whole realm. And it tells me something else. It tells me we may be in the Castle Authentio, for thither was the stone last seen.... And if that be so, we are but twenty leagues south of Nephesh, the capital."

He paused and thought for several minutes. Lisa felt he must be falling asleep, but a moment later he spoke, frowning and uneasy.

"Child, it may be that with the Mashal Stone we may both escape. So far the jinn knows not that you are here."

"I think he might, your majesty. I was sure he saw me at least twice."

"No, my child, he could not have seen you or you would not still be alive."

"But the stone! It shone so brightly that I could see its reflection in his eyes."

"No, Lisa. He is incapable of seeing the stone. Evil eyes cannot see the Mashal Stone. Hearken, here is what we must do. You shall wear it when next the jinn comes hither. You shall follow us from the cell, keeping as near me as is possible. At the porch the jinn will let me go, that I may walk freely beyond it. From within the porch you shall hand me the stone. When I disappear, he will not likely notice you but will search for me. Hide quickly beneath the bench on the porch. It is too small to hide a man so he will not look there. First he will search the courtyard and then the porch, but almost at once he will speed down the stairs to my cell. Then we must run to the gate of the courtyard. I shall lift you to the top of it and then climb after. We shall need horses—all the horses in the stables, if we can free them. May the Shepherd then direct our steps.

"And now, have you eaten? See, here is bread and water. Would that it were better fare. The jinn gave me no time to eat today."

Lisa looked at the straw on the other side of Kardia,

and saw a pewter plate with a few crusts on it. Beside it was an earthen pitcher of a dull red color, filled to the brim with water. She did not feel very hungry, but was thirsty.

"Your majesty ate nothing?"

"No, Lisa. It must have forgotten. My jailer cares little about my comfort."

"I'm so sorry. You must be hungry and thirsty. Here, let me help you eat."

"No, Lisa. It is best that I not eat. In fact, it is also best that you not eat."

Lisa looked a little surprised.

"If the jinn finds the bread and water gone, he might suspect something is awry. A chained man cannot feed himself."

For some reason this made her angry; angry that his hands should be manacled above his head and that he was so helpless. She also felt a tenderness rising up in her and longed more than ever to help him. She found she bitterly hated the jinn and burned with indignation at the magician who had imprisoned Kardia. In her mind she again saw herself as noble and fell in love with a story she was making up in her mind about herself and Kardia. Perhaps he would ask her to marry him when she was a little older. Then she would be a queen and their children would be princes and princesses....

"But if we each take a little water," Kardia interrupted her thoughts, "and allowed most of it to remain, he will not notice, and we shall gain some relief."

She lifted the pitcher of water to his lips. A little flowed down his beard and spilled on his tunic. Then she drank. The water was cold and delicious, unlike the water from the faucet at Uncle John's which always tasted of chlorine.

"I thank thee, little maid. Now put on the Mashal Stone and rest for a little while."

She remembered Kardia's cape and picking it up from beside him, spread it over both of them, curling into an invisible ball and resting her invisible head on his lap. She had not realized how tired she was and was asleep in a moment. But it was not of marriage or princes and princesses that she dreamed. Down endless dark corridors a monstrous, yellow snake pursued her as she grasped at a blue light which seemed always a little beyond her reach.

5

What They Saw in the Pool

Anthropos?

Both boys looked up into the lady's blue eyes which shone with wisdom and kindness. Neither of them knew what to say. Where was Anthropos?

"My name is Chocma," the lady said, dropping her hands to her side and looking at them gravely.

"I'm Wesley," Wesley said offering his hand, "and this is my brother Kurt."

The lady hesitated a moment, staring at his outstretched hand as though she did not know what to do with it.

Wesley, embarrassed, was about to remove it when she reached forward with one of her own, held his fingers lightly between hers and made a curtsy—a surprisingly graceful curtsy for someone as white haired and wrinkled as she. She did the same to Kurt as he offered his hand.

"I am glad you have come," she said, smiling now, "though I expected none so young."

"Please, where *is* Anthropos?" Wesley asked her. "We really don't know where we are."

"Anthropos is a country, south of the Great Sea, bordered on all sides by the realm of Playsion," she said quietly. "And where do both of you come from?"

"From Winnipeg, Canada," Kurt said eagerly. "I've never heard of Anthropos. Where is it? Is it one of those new African countries and are most of the people here black?"

The smile left Chocma's face. "Anthropos is not of your world nor yet of your age. I have heard naught of Winnipeg—but there are many worlds I know not."

Wesley trembled.

"We're looking for our sister. Her name is Lisa. She disappeared into a television set. We're awfully worried about her. She just disappeared and then the picture went dead. We really would be grateful if you could help us find her."

Chocma searched their faces as if she were trying to understand them.

Wesley continued. "There was this picture of a sort of dungeon and a man with his hands chained to the wall above his head. . . ."

"Could you describe the man?" Chocma interrupted.

"He was—oh, sort of not really old."

"About twenty-five?"

"Yes, I think so, and he wore a red thing, a sort of shirt with a belt. There was a fur cloak over his legs."

"Was he bearded?"

"Yes, ma'am. And when Lisa went up to the set she disappeared inside it. We could see her for a moment inside the set, looking at the man. Then it all disappeared."

"I understand not all that you say, but I think, I think
..." and her words trailed into silence.

"Will she be all right? Can we get her back? We're
terribly worried about her."

Chocma turned, inviting them to follow her. As they
walked together toward the cottage she said slowly, "She
will be safe. Yes, she will be safe. But where she is I know
not. You have come, and she too has come, to a world
unknown to your own world. A different kind of world.
'Tis likely she is in Anthropos. She may be with the king
for we are certain he is imprisoned. But safe—yes, all
whom Gaal invites here are safe."

"I don't understand," Wesley said, filled with dread of
an adventure which seemed to be getting deeper and
more complicated by the minute. "You mean we can't get
her back? We thought we could find her by coming here,
at least by going into the television set."

"I am sure you will find her," Chocma said, "though it
may take a long time. You and she were sent here to restore Kardia, king of Anthropos, to his rightful throne.
It is my belief that your sister is now with Kardia."

"But nobody sent us here. We just came," Kurt ob-
jected. Chocma smiled and looked at him.

"You knew of Anthropos and knew how to get here?
And you possess the necessary magic to travel between
ages and worlds?"

"No, but. . . ."

"Then rest assured, my lord Kurt, that whether you
know 'tis so or not, you were *drawn* here and drawn here
for a purpose."

Wesley's bewilderment grew. "Please stop!" he said. "I
mean, let's stop walking." They paused and faced one
another. "You don't know exactly where she is. You also
don't know how long it will take to find her, but you *do*

know we were drawn here. Who drew us? You?"

Chocma hesitated.

"It could be so. I longed for the king to be restored. Anthropos is full of evil and suffering. Our people starve because of a long drought. In my longing I cried to Gaal, the Shepherd. And he has answered my call. But the power that translated you from your world to ours was the power of Gaal."

"Gaal?"

"Gaal, the Shepherd, Son of the High Emperor."

"Of Anthropos?"

"Of all worlds, all ages, all universes, all that was, that is and that shall be."

"Will we get to see this Gaal?" Kurt asked.

"Perhaps."

"And," Wesley was more worried than ever, "how will we get back?"

"Gaal will send you back."

"When?"

"When the time has come."

"Oh, no! What if Uncle John comes back and finds we're gone? Mum and dad told him to make sure. . . . Oh, laws. . . . It'll be in the Tribune and the Free Press. I can just see the headlines. 'Three Children Lost in Blizzard. Police Have No Clues'!"

For a moment there was silence. Wesley was twisting his fingers and staring into space. His hands were cold and sweating. As you probably realize by now, he took matters more seriously than his brother and tended to look on the dark side.

He felt two hands being laid on his shoulders. Looking up, his eyes met Chocma's, and he was surprised to see how blue they were and how they made her wrinkled face light up. They reminded him of the Caribbean Sea, of beaches and palm trees and of feeling the hot sun on his skin.

"Don't be afraid, my lord Wesley. You can trust Gaal to see that all shall be well."

Strength flowed from her eyes to his. Slowly his muscles relaxed, his heart stopped beating so loudly and his panic began to subside. He stared back at Chocma, sighed softly and said, "Thank you. I'm O.K. now."

They resumed their walk. Neither of the boys had paid much attention to the cottage, so absorbed had they been with such strange events. Now as they stared they saw that it wasn't a cottage at all, but a large flat piece of board, like a billboard, with a cottage painted on it—a painted piece of scenery with a path leading up to the door.

The door was the only real thing about it. It was small with a brass knob which looked as though it was meant to be used. Solemnly Chocma opened the door. Through it they could see a forest glade, filled with grass and flowers, and surrounded by forest trees.

She turned, smilingly to them. "Be not alarmed at what shall happen," she said. "Only follow me."

Then she bowed her head (for the doorway was low) and stepped through it. As she did so she disappeared. For a split second they could see the back part of her moving forward—then nothing at all, nothing except the sunlit grass and flowers.

Kurt and Wesley looked at each other.

"She said to follow her," Kurt said.

"But she's not there," Wesley replied.

"I guess she meant to step through the door...."

"Sure. Go right ahead!"

It was not the first time Wesley regretted the words as soon as they were out of his mouth, for with a grin Kurt ducked his head and darted through the low doorway into nothingness. Wesley was appalled. He was alone in an unknown world, staring through the doorway of a painted piece of scenery into what looked like a real forest glade.

Cautiously he went to the side of the billboard and peered round it into the glade. The glade was still there. It looked real enough. Stepping past the board, he saw that it was exactly what it seemed, a board held up by a framework at the back. It looked very unmagical. "Mirrors," he thought, "they do that kind of trick with mirrors." Yet behind the wooden screen there was no sign of a mirror. He stepped farther into the glade but could see only flowers, grass and forest trees all around. There was no sign of Kurt or Chocma. Bewildered, he walked to the door from the glade side and stared at the pathway beyond it; completing his circuit, he walked right round to the forest side again. Cautiously he approached the doorway and pushed his hand through it. But when it disappeared he pulled it back, relieved to find it still existed. Then taking a deep breath he ducked his head low and stepped through the doorway.

For a fraction of a second he could still see the forest glade while at the same time he saw another scene that he could not understand. It was like looking at a double exposure or a fade-out on TV. Then the glade disappeared and he found himself standing on the flagged entrance hall of a castle. Chocma and Kurt were watching him from a broad flight of stairs facing him and Kurt was saying, "Cowardy-custard!"

Wesley stood open-mouthed.

"There are realities beyond those your eyes see," Chocma said to him. "Welcome to the House of Wisdom."

"Is this where you live?" asked Wesley in astonishment.

"This is my home, and it is here that I teach."

Bewildered, excited and shaking his head Wesley found himself joining Chocma and Kurt. He heard himself repeating, "Oh, wow! . . . Oh, wow!" Though his fears were beginning to diminish, his astonishment was boundless. With a resounding boom a door behind him closed. Swinging round, Wesley saw not a small, rough door but an oak one, tall and wide, with black iron hinges. Had it remained open they would have seen the forest pathway through the opening. Kurt's eyes sparkled with glee. Wesley remained wide-eyed.

The stairway led them to an antechamber with a wide fireplace at one end of it, beside which sat three dwarfs all wearing green hats, leather jerkins and garments that looked like coarsely woven, russet brown tights tucked into boots with long pointed toes. Shorter than both the boys but deep-chested and immensely strong, they stood up as Chocma and the boys approached them. Their hands were disproportionately large. Long beards, one of them iron gray and two of them black, hung below weather-beaten faces.

"Good morning, my lady." Gunruth, the leader of the three, removed a long-stemmed pipe from his mouth as all three bowed to her.

"Good morning, Gunruth. Here are two to help us, come from worlds afar through a proseo stone. Let me present their young lordships Wesley and Kurt to Gunruth and his sons, Bilith and Bolgin."

The three bowed again and taking a cue from them, Wesley and Kurt bowed (a little awkwardly).

Gunruth had his eyes on the floor. Uneasily he said, "My lady, we had hoped for. . . ."

"I know what we hoped for, but here we have two

whom Gaal sent. He does not make mistakes."

"No, my lady."

"Already their sister, the lady Lisa, has penetrated the dungeon where his majesty is chained."

Gunruth's eyes opened wide. "Then his majesty. . . ."

"His majesty an hour ago was alive, imprisoned and with the lady Lisa. More than this we do not know."

Chocma and the two brothers left the dwarfs talking animatedly among themselves. They came into the most stunning room the boys had ever seen. Immense as a Gothic cathedral, its walls rose dizzyingly to a ceiling far above them supported by the delicately entwined branches of six trees, three on each side of the hall. Six mammoth trunks grew through the stone floor while a seventh formed part of the far end of the hall. Inside its base a throne had been carved.

Colored light, mostly of a pale blue, poured through windows along the side walls. It was a room that made you want to walk very quietly and that gave you the feeling that you ought to whisper.

"This is the Hall of Wisdom," Chocma said, her clear voice echoing against the stone walls. "It is here that I teach those who will learn. These are fewer of late for the land favors magic to wisdom."

She led them the full length of the hall to a low doorway beside the throne in the foot of the seventh tree. They went into a large, circular room where windows looked out on another room with a pool beyond which was a rough wooden table set with food. To reach the table, chairs and food they would have to cross the pool.

As he stared into it, Wesley couldn't tell how deep the pool was. Steps leading down from the doorway spiraled around its sides to what seemed an unfathomable depth. Other steps spiraled upward, crisscrossing the down-

The Hall of Wisdom

ward steps and leading out of the pool on the far side. (It sounds strange I know, but both boys insist that it was so.) Chocma began to descend the steps saying, "This is called the Pool of Truth. 'Tis called so because it reveals true things and because it gives us the true form we should possess here in Anthropos. It also has powers to heal ills caused by deception—if we but let it."

They watched her, fascinated, and held their breath. As she descended into the water, the skirts of her long dress ballooned up. She pressed them down and a moment later was waist deep, then up to her armpits and then her neck. A moment later all they could see of her was her floating, white hair. The broken surface of the water reflected a thousand dancing fragments of the windows above. Of Chocma they could see nothing.

"Why doesn't she float?"

"Mebbe she can't swim."

"Don't be an idiot. She seemed to know what she was doing."

"I wonder if it's cold."

"I don't know. Kurt, how long can she stay down?"

They both stared into the water.

"Kurt, look—her hair."

"But it's a gold color."

A head broke the surface on the far side of the pool, a beautiful head with golden hair flowing down. As she mounted the steps both boys gasped to see the slim straight figure of a Chocma who was now wearing a blue gown of silk and blue slippers. Around her neck were flowers and flowers crowned her head. Not a drop of water clung to her as she stepped out fresh and dry on the far side of the pool.

"Are you Chocma?" Kurt was always the bolder of the two boys.

"Yes, my lord Kurt, I am Chocma. This is the true form I am meant to possess in Anthropos." The voice was Chocma's.

"Wow, you look stunning!"

"I perceive you pay me a compliment, my lord."

"How old are you?"

"I have no age. I always was."

The boys did not understand, and I suppose most of us would have been puzzled too. Chocma's face at first looked young and beautiful. It bore no wrinkles, and her eyes shone violet. Yet there was that in her face which suggested agelessness, a solemnity and an air of power which made you realize she was no girl.

Eagerly Kurt stepped into the water down the stairway and more hesitantly Wesley followed. To neither did the water feel like water, and it certainly was not a bit like wading from a beach into the cold sea. All they experienced was a tingling on their skin. Kurt held his nose when his head dipped below the water, and he found to his astonishment that he could go on walking downward without floating. His body felt no different than when it was in the air. In fact he felt as though he was in air, so much so that he took his hand from his nose and began to breathe.

"Well, I'll be jiggered," he said, quoting one of Uncle John's favorite sayings.

He turned to speak to Wesley, but Wesley was nowhere to be seen. I cannot explain why this was so, for both boys vowed to me that they entered the water almost together. At least Wesley swears that he followed right behind Kurt, but he also says that once his head was under the surface he could see nothing of Kurt. Since both gave me similar stories, I suppose I'll have to believe them. But like you I have no explanation for it.

Kurt says when he got to the bottom of the pool after two and a half turns round the spiral, he found himself facing a mirror. He was startled to see a reflection of himself wearing a blue, woolen tunic edged with gold around the neck and lower edge, a leather belt and thonged leather sandals. As he looked down he discovered that this was indeed how he was dressed. "This is better than Disneyland," he breathed. What happened next was yet more startling.

As he stared at the mirror his image dissolved in swirls of mist which cleared to reveal a red-headed, red-bearded dwarf. There seemed to be no glass separating the two, as though the mirror had become an open door. Kurt was about to speak when behind the dwarf a second figure appeared, an old man with an extremely handsome smiling face. He was wearing a black robe. Kurt was enormously attracted to the man yet frightened of the immense power and the hint of cruelty and ruthlessness in the cold eyes and mouth. A voice seemed to speak from the mirror itself though the lips of neither the dwarf nor the figure behind him moved. "Beware the deception of these that thou lookest upon."

Almost at once everything vanished—mirror, dwarf and black-robed figure. Kurt found himself facing the steps that curved upward and, shaking his head in wonder, began to climb them.

Wesley's experience was similar but not quite the same. He was astonished, as Kurt had been, to see no sign of his brother ahead of him. He was also astonished to see no stairs spiraling up.

"Where on earth has he disappeared to?" he thought. "And where are those other steps that wound upward?"

Like Kurt he quickly sensed that he was not floating as he would have done in water but was in air, a magic kind of air that made his skin tingle. Wesley says he *thinks* he went about five and a half circuits before he reached the bottom though he can't be sure. But like Kurt, he was startled to see himself facing a mirror and wearing a blue tunic and sandals instead of sweat shirt, jeans and tennis shoes. Wesley also watched his mirror image dissolve. But he faced a sword-carrying man wearing a white garment from whose face shone kindness and truth. Neither the man nor Wesley moved. After a moment the man's deep voice sounded, "When you are perplexed, feeling torn and not knowing which way to go, follow me. I will take care of the consequences."

The man and mirror vanished and like Kurt, Wesley faced the ascending spiral of steps. He broke the surface to see Kurt beside Chocma.

"Where in the world did you disappear to?" he asked.

"Where did *you* disappear to?" Kurt retorted. "I never saw a sign of you till your head came up just now."

Eagerly, constantly interrupting each other, they exchanged stories. Chocma listened gravely. "Come now and eat," she said. "You can talk more later. But you will be wise to pay heed to the words that were spoken to you. Fix them in your memories and call them to mind when you see the persons you saw in the mirror."

"You mean we're really going to meet them?" Kurt asked.

"The mirror never lies."

They sat down to eat a meal of oat cakes and fresh milk, surprised to find how hungry they were, and plied Chocma with questions. "The other pictures we saw in the television," Kurt asked, "what do they mean? I mean the cave with the knights. What is that?"

"It is called the Cave of Qava. There the most valiant knights of Anthropos lie in enchanted sleep, waiting for someone to open the door of the cave and break their enchantment."

Kurt wanted to know more and asked how many there were, how the door could be opened, how long the knights had been there, who put them there and a score of other matters. As she talked Chocma told them many tales including the stories of the book, the key and the box.

"The key is the key to the Cave of Qava," she said. "The book contains the history and laws of Anthropos—words of power, the reading of which can break every evil spell. The box contains a golden orb before which the gates of Nephesh, capital city of Anthropos, will always burst open."

For a moment there was silence. The boys had finished eating.

"Just one thing puzzles me," Wesley said. "Where are we? I know you said we are in Anthropos, and I know you said this is the House of Wisdom. But this whole building, where is it? We could see nothing of it until we came inside."

"Look out of the window," Chocma said pointing to a bulging bay window close to the pool. They did so and saw the forest glade.

"I can just see part of the path you were sweeping when we arrived," said Wesley. "How come we couldn't see this building?"

"True wisdom cannot be seen from outside, only from within," she said slowly.

As the boys continued to stare, the forest glade melted, and to their astonishment they saw gray seas around them. Enormous waves crashed against the walls.

Even as they watched, the sea also disappeared, and they saw in succession a bare and dusty desert, a dense jungle, and a city busy with traffic and crowded with tall buildings. Finally both boys caught their breath as they stared out at a brilliant star-sprinkled blackness. They looked down on stars below them and at moons and planets all round as well as above them.

"Where *are* we?" Wesley asked again.

"True wisdom remains unchanged through time and space," Chocma stated. "There is nowhere it cannot be found. It is the same in all worlds, all ages, all universes."

"And is there only one way to enter?"

"Usually, yes," Chocma replied, "but in extreme danger some have entered through the windows." The boys remembered her words when later on Lisa burst through one of the hall windows on a flying horse. But that is getting ahead of the story.

Once more they saw the forest glade, but with a change. Hoof beats sounded. In the glade four riderless horses, flecked with foam and sweat stood breathing heavily. Twenty or thirty dwarfs poured out of the House of Wisdom to surround them.

What happened next took them all by surprise. So suddenly that no one saw how it happened, the king appeared on one of the horses and a cry of surprise broke from many throats. The reins of the horses lay in his hand. He looked up and waved toward the window.

"The man in the dungeon!" cried Kurt.

"His majesty!" said Chocma softly.

"But where is Lisa?" was the question that fell from Wesley's troubled lips.

6

When Lisa
Got Left Behind

Lisa's dreams changed. Someone was burying her and earth was crushing her limbs. Demons were sticking hot needles into her face. With a start she woke, horrified to find the cell filled with the gleaming yellow coils of the jinn. Straw where her head lay was pricking her face and she could feel the terrible weight of one of the jinn's coils resting on her legs. For a few seconds she was bewildered and frightened. Then she remembered. It could not see her. She was invisible.

Kardia was standing, alternately biting at a crust of bread and rubbing his wrists and hands. She could see the marks of the manacles on his wrists. After a few moments, with great difficulty he bent down (a coil of the jinn was round his waist), lifted the earthen jar to his lips and drank deeply. He sighed and his face spoke of pain. Beyond him she could see by twisting her head that the jinn's green hand was pouring oil into the lamp from a vessel. Curiously, she felt no fear, but *that,* as she was later to discover, had something to do with the Mashal Stone she was wearing.

"I wonder whether he'll throw it into the air and make it vanish again," she thought to herself. She watched carefully. Sure enough, the green hand flung the vessel ceilingward, but this time it seemed to burst like a bubble and be no more. Meanwhile the hand, crumpling like a deflated balloon, shriveled disgustingly into the jinn's neck (if any part of the long creature could be called a neck). Then little by little all the coils were set in motion, one of them to Lisa's horror slithering its weighty way across her legs.

The coil round the king moved horizontally to the foot of the steps and Kardia walked slowly, wrapped in its embrace. By the time he reached the foot of the stairs the jinn's head was level with the door. As Lisa watched it, the door burst open in the same way it had done the first time. Slowly the king began to mount the steps. Lisa thought he seemed weary. A moment later the last coil of the jinn passed across her. With a shudder at his sliminess she sprang to her feet. This time she must make no mistakes. She would not let Kardia down again. This time they were going to escape.

"Kardia's left his cape," she murmured, seeing it in a heap on the straw. "I wonder if he forgot it. But maybe the jinn would be suspicious if he had taken it."

She stooped, picked it up and pulled it round her shoulders. It was heavy and looked as though it would be too long for her, but before she had a chance to see it, it vanished. She could feel the weight of it on her shoulders just as she could feel her own body, but she found she was staring through it and through herself at the floor. It made her a little giddy again to be able to bend down and look through herself, but catching her breath and hitching the cape up as well as she could by feel, she walked quickly across the floor and up the stairs.

The cape grew heavier with every step, pressing down on her uncomfortably. She tripped once on the steps, then pushed her way past the door. How far had they gone? Whatever happened she must not fail again.

She was relieved to see that the jinn, which had now coiled itself completely round the king, was only a few steps ahead of her. As noiselessly as she could she caught up with them. Slowly they walked down the long corridor, lit by the blue light of the Mashal Stone. Softly, scarcely daring to breathe, Lisa tiptoed behind the tip of the jinn's tail. Soon they had reached the foot of the stairs. As quietly as she could she crept up the long stairway after them but found it impossible to keep up with them, getting farther and farther behind.

By the time they reached the top of the long flight of stairs to the porch, Lisa's legs felt weak from the weight of the cape, and she was breathing heavily. She paused for a minute to rest, sitting on the bench looking at Kardia and the jinn in the courtyard. The noonday sun made her squint.

As soon as she recovered her breath she glanced round. Tall buildings framed a grassy lawn on three sides, while a wall with battlements connected the buildings on the fourth side. The courtyard was smaller than she had anticipated. The grass was brown. Cracks could be seen in the earth.

Near the middle of the wall, two turrets stood like sentinels on each side of a large iron gate. Beyond was a grassy space, and beyond that what Lisa took to be the main castle walls. The jinn was settling himself comfortably around a waterless fountain in the center of the courtyard. No one else was in sight. An uncanny stillness made her do all she could to breathe silently.

Kardia was strolling toward the porch. As he reached it he turned his back to her and she removed the pendant and dropped it into the palm of the hand he extended backward. Instantly she felt darkness and fear settling over her.

"Very good, little maid," Kardia murmured. "Now while I am still visible, keep behind me until I am near the bench. Then get beneath it and stay there till the jinn has passed."

He backed slowly toward the bench, and Lisa, covered by his movements, crept beneath it.

"Your majesty, I have your cape," she whispered.

"Leave it, child. It is of no consequence. Are you hidden?"

"Yes, your majesty."

"Now, remember, I shall wait at the gate on this side. Stand there and I will lift you so you may gain the top. May the Shepherd give us both strength."

With the cape still round her, Lisa watched his back as he took the pendant to slip it over his head. Then there was nothing, nothing but the dry, brown grass and the courtyard. Yet it all seemed darker. A dense blackness covered the fountain where the yellow coils were no longer visible.

"Be of good courage, little maid," she heard the king say, his voice sounding as though he were some distance away.

She felt hot and prickly beneath the bench. Beads of sweat began to trickle down her face and neck. Now that the stone was gone, her courage seemed to have gone with it.

For a while, nothing happened. Then the darkness began to change its shape, growing till it filled the courtyard and blotted out the sun. She could still see, but things lost their colors. The grass turned from brown to gray and the stonework, black. Blackness entered her brain and with it a sense of death and of danger. A rotten smell filled her nostrils, and she struggled not to breathe the foulness. Slowly the darkness deepened till it filled the whole porch. She could see nothing. Then, as quickly as it came, it passed and she watched it—a wave of blackness passing down the long staircase.

"Now's my chance," she thought, her heart pounding in her chest.

She scrambled to her feet leaving the cloak under the bench. Yet as she looked back at it, the softness of the dark brown fur and red of the silk lining looked so very desirable that she snatched it up, folded it into a large, clumsy bundle, and ran as hard as she could toward the gate.

As she ran, she could feel the cape unwrapping itself and slipping from her grasp. One corner of it was flapping against her left knee. She tried as she ran to hitch it up higher, but a moment later she caught her foot in it, tripped and fell hard onto the grassy lawn.

"Leave it!" Kardia's voice rang out. "Leave it, child! Let it be!"

She struggled to her feet, still obstinately clinging to the cape, but a piercing pain in her left ankle caused her to fall again. Once again she struggled to rise. She found she could put no weight on her left foot and hopped and hobbled blindly forward, dragging the cape behind her.

The sound of Kardia's running feet came toward her from the gate. A moment later she felt herself being lifted in his invisible arms and smelled the same comforting smell of his sweat as he ran toward the gate.

Why did the gate seem so far away? Why was it growing dark again? Why was it black? Why was she being pulled in two directions at once? She heard Kardia's yell of rage. She felt her body rising upward and his cries going farther away. Where was she? For a while she was conscious only of terrible pain and blackness all round. Dizzy and confused, she heard the slam of a heavy door, found herself sitting on straw, and as the darkness lifted saw she was in Kardia's cell again. But neither of Kardia nor of the jinn was there any sign. The only other occupant of the cell was a bright yellow cat which sat quietly licking its fur two or three yards away from her.

It took her some time to realize what had happened. She could not believe, yet slowly she realized she had to believe, that the jinn had captured *her* not Kardia. Where was he? Was he still in the castle? Where was the jinn? How would she get out? Would the king come back?

Her ankle throbbed painfully and she began to cry softly. Thoughts of Uncle John and the house on Grosvenor filled her with longing. What about Kurt and Wesley? Surely they could do something to get to her. Perhaps the proseo stone would provide a way of escape. After all, Kardia doubtless had escaped by now. Her mission was probably accomplished.

Normally she would have turned to the cat for comfort. It never occurred to her to wonder where it came from. The only thought in her mind was to get out of the dungeon. Somehow she got to her feet and half hopped, half limped to where she had last seen the proseo stone. Still crying, and half blinded by her tears, she groped to feel for the small, round stone. But she could neither see nor feel it. Sobbing, half from pain and half from hopelessness, she continued to search along the wall. Perhaps it was farther to the left....

She was not sure how long she had been peering and groping when a voice said, "You won't find it, you know. Once you've come through it you can never get back again. I thought you, being a witch, would know that."

Lisa swung round. The cell was empty. Only the yellow cat, its back to Lisa, sat in the middle of the cell licking its left paw and rubbing it around its left ear the way cats do.

"Who are you?" she asked to no one she could see.

"I am the jinn of course. My name is Ebed Ruach. I am the slave of whoever has the power to command me." Was the *cat* talking? Lisa could hardly believe her ears. That strange yellow color—where had she seen it before?

"You ... you were a great snake last time I saw you," she said breathlessly.

The cat whipped round and spat.

"You seem to have more powers than I thought, witch," it hissed. "I was covered in darkness. What are your powers? What do you know? Are you greater than my master, Hocoino? I warn you, if you try to control me and you lack the power, I shall destroy you as I destroyed many before you."

Lisa stared wonderingly at the little animal. For a moment she forgot her painful ankle at the weird turn of events.

"I don't know what you are talking about," she replied. "First of all, I'm not a witch. I'm a girl and I came through the television. I don't have any power and I know nothing about magic." She was about to explain about the Mashal Stone, but something checked her. Plainly the jinn was the enemy. One gave nothing away to the enemy.

For the first time in her life Lisa saw a cat smile. "No,

my dear, of course you have no powers. Doubtless there is some simpler explanation of the way you spirited the king from under my nose. You came through the proseo stone. Doubtless that too was an accident...."

"It *was!*" protested Lisa.

"...and now you wish me to believe that you are nothing more than a little girl, not a witch who travels between worlds, whose spells can make a king disappear from beneath the midday sun. Your story is very convincing."

Lisa disliked the cat, but inwardly she was also pleased. It was pleasant to be regarded as someone possessing magical powers. She limped across the room, avoiding the cat which slowly turned round as she passed it, and sat down on the straw, pulling Kardia's cape around her.

She stared at the jinn, and the jinn stared back.

"The cape, now," it almost purred, "the cape too has no magical properties, am I correct?"

Lisa thought a moment. Did the cat not realize the cloak was Kardia's? Did it think it was a magic cape? If she said it wasn't, then the jinn would almost certainly mistrust her and try to take it from her. On the other hand, to say it had magical powers would be to lie. Ought she to lie? Though if the jinn *believed* she was lying, ironically he would leave her with it. It would only take it from her if it believed the cape had magic powers. She longed to keep the cape. It reminded her of Kardia and made her feel safer. Suddenly she had an idea.

"If I were you, Ebed Ruach," she said, trying to sound stern, "I would not either touch the cape, or speak of it without great reverence."

For a moment the hair stood up on the back of the cat's neck. Then it settled down again. Lisa's words had had an effect.

Slowly it came to Lisa that the jinn was unsure of itself with her. Obviously it thought she had powers. Perhaps that was why it had not ventured to manacle her hands, as it had manacled Kardia's. Yet it was not sure how great her powers were. If it thought her powers were very great, it would probably do her bidding. If not (Lisa tried to puzzle the matter out), if not, it was not really clear what the jinn would do.

Of one thing she was certain. If she was to tell the truth, half the time the jinn would believe she was lying. The more she insisted she was just a girl, the more it would believe she was a witch.

She smiled as sweetly as she could. "You really are mistaken, you know. I'm not a witch at all. And as for other worlds, I'm not even sure what world I'm in now."

Again the jinn-cat turned and smiled. "Then how did you know about my snake form? Not even my master knows that. And how did you pass through the goblin guard to enter the castle, unless from another world you really did come? And how did you spirit away the king?"

Lisa thought furiously, but the more she thought the less she could think of some way of dealing with the jinn. Perhaps (she shuddered at the thought) she could coax it in its cat form to go to sleep and then kill it. She had always loved cats. So everything inside her was revolted by the thought. How could she kill a cat? Yet when she remembered the gleaming yellow snake and terrible darkness, her heart hardened.

"Come," she invited. "Sit on the cloak with me and let me stroke you."

The jinn hissed. "Do you think I am so easily deceived?"

"There's no magic in it. It's just a fur cape."

"Then why did you warn me not to touch it?"

77

Lisa bit her lip in frustration. For a few moments neither of them spoke.

Suddenly the jinn said, "My master is very powerful. He pays well. He has often mentioned his need of more witches. Perhaps we could come to some arrangement."

Lisa's mind was racing. "I don't imagine your master will be very pleased with you now that you have let the king escape."

"Nor would he be pleased to know you were the one who contrived his escape," the jinn countered. "But it is possible that between us we might allay his wrath and benefit both our positions."

There was an even longer silence. Lisa's ankle was throbbing less but it was still painful. She was also, in spite of the bewildering turn of events, still sleepy. Remember, she had had only four hours of sleep. It was still really nighttime in her own world.

"I want to sleep for a while," she said. "We can talk later." But what would the jinn do if she slept? "Come and lie with me as I sleep," she invited it, only to be greeted by yet another hiss. But the hiss told her something. So long as the cloak was around her she would be safe.

Wearily she wrapped the cloak about her and curled up on the straw, shifting her position so that she could keep her eyes on the yellow cat. For half an hour as her eyelids drooped, opened and dropped again, she watched it. But it never stirred a muscle. Presently she found she could no longer keep her eyes open. The last thing she remembered was a yellow cat staring at her with unblinking eyes.

7

The Riderless Horses

The invisible Kardia had almost reached the gate when the green hand of the jinn appeared from nowhere, swiftly snatched Lisa and lifted her cleanly out of his arms. For a fraction of a second he was too surprised to react. Then swinging round he saw the great yellow snake and one of Lisa's legs (the good one) hanging down from the hand. He leaped up and seized it. Instantly he was whisked six feet above the ground and with a shout of rage realized he was helpless to free her. Indeed, he might do her injury. As the monster writhed toward the stairway Kardia let go of Lisa's leg and tumbled onto the grass. Unable to control his rage and calling, "Lisa, Lisa," he pummeled his fists on the unfeeling yellow sides of the jinn as it swept past him. As the tip of the twitching tail came level with his chest it swung him an accidental blow, knocking him, winded, onto the ground.

For a few moments on hands and knees he fought for his breath, vomited a little, then began to breathe more normally. "I must not act rashly," he told himself. "If by the goodness of Gaal I am free, I must use my freedom wisely."

He sat on the grass, still invisible, thinking for several minutes.

"I must see what has befallen the maid," he said. "Then, if this is Authentio, I shall ride, with or without her to the house of the wise woman which would be but an hour's ride from here. It may be that even with dwarf help we can surprise them and seize the castle before any man expects us. Surely the wise woman will know how to deal with the jinn."

He rose slowly to his feet, crept down the stairway and made his way cautiously by the blue light of the Mashal Stone to his cell door. Beyond it he could hear faintly but clearly the conversation between Lisa and the yellow cat. As he listened, a smile spread across his face.

"The maid has wisdom beyond her years," he thought. "She has wits to match the evil one. She will be safe for a while."

Quickly he retraced his steps, crossed the inner courtyard and climbed the gate into the outer. No sooner had he done so than he saw two things: first that sentries were posted along the outer walls and beside the drawbridge, and second that the castle was swarming with goblins. The goblins were of every form and size, some like grotesque pigs, foxes and underfed dogs, others more human in shape, with large soft heads and staring eyes. The latter, unaffected by the fire, carried burning darts in their belts.

"It is the Mashal Stone," Kardia muttered to himself. "By night they might take forms like this, but never by day. There are hundreds of them! What of the woods beyond?"

Silently he ran toward the main gate. Three men, one of whom was the captain of the guard, were playing cards. A bottle of wine was being passed among them as they argued about the game. They slurred their words and were clumsy in their movements. "Drunk," Kardia thought. Making his way into the tower beside the gate he climbed the staircase that led up to the wall. You may remember that castle walls are wide, permitting soldiers to move on top of them. A sentry was slowly walking toward him. Kardia leaned on the battlements to let him pass and glanced at the countryside beyond the wall.

There could be no doubt of it. The castle was the old Castle Authentio. A steep slope cleared of trees and bushes led down to the woods. From the drawbridge below him an unpaved road also wound down to the woods. Everywhere, down the slope and among the trees, ugly forms of the goblins could be seen, the two-legged ones occasionally fighting among themselves or kicking and abusing the four-legged ones. Kardia's frown deepened as he saw their numbers.

"We must come by night," he said slowly to himself. "By day they would never be seen."

He made his way from the wall down to where the card game was being played. The portcullis was up, the drawbridge down and the men too drowsy to act quickly. He hurried into the stables, where he found a dozen horses, some lying, some standing. Selecting the two he thought to be the best, he unhooked saddles from the wall and dropped them onto the ground.

He was not sure how they would react to his being invisible. Cautiously he removed the Mashal Stone and approached the large dapple-gray mare he had selected to ride himself. Patting her gently he found her only too willing to be befriended. Continuing to pat her he put on and took off the pendant, appearing and disappearing several times. At first she snorted and shied away, but as he continued to talk to her and as she learned that the voice and the smell of him remained even though the sight of him did not, she seemed reassured. He repeated the process with a young roan stallion. Then he saddled and bridled both the horses and quietly led them onto the grass of the outer keep. No one seemed to be aware of what was happening.

As quickly as he could, he mounted the mare, took both bridles in his hands, slapped and spurred the mare and galloped with both horses toward the drawbridge. As he whisked past the three drinking men, he saw a look of bemused wonder cross their faces at the sight of two saddled but riderless horses thundering across the drawbridge and galloping rapidly along the road to the woods. Glancing back, he saw they had risen to their feet, the captain still with the bottle of wine in his hand, staring agog at the two horses. Even the goblins turned to stare in wonder.

"That will give me a fair start. Their fuddled wits will hardly lead them to the truth, I'll warrant. I wonder how long it will take them to set out in pursuit," he muttered.

With the wind in his face, the clean smell of open air was like wine to Kardia. Suddenly he found himself laughing aloud at his freedom. The horses too seemed glad of the gallop and made headlong for the forest below.

Once in its cool, dappled shade Kardia slowed their pace to a steady canter. A plan was forming in his mind. "Pursuit there will be," he thought slowly, "but if perchance only two or three are sent to catch the horses, then

I may gain four or five horses instead of two. The Mashal Stone gives me the advantage." Thirty minutes later he came to a narrow stone bridge across a river. Before crossing it he led the horses into the water and let them drink a bit.

It was only a little beyond noon. The woods were strangely quiet with only an occasional birdcall. Kardia noted with a worried look the dryness of the ground, the burned look of weeds and the absence of flowers. Even the trees seemed to be dying. Only those by the river remained green, and the level of the river was low. Two sounds greeted his ears—the rush and gurgle of the river (now bordered by cracked, dried mud) and the occasional buzzing of a fly. One was delightful and the other was unpleasant, but a reminder of his freedom nonetheless.

A moment later he looked up, startled. The sound of the river had drowned out other sounds. Quickly reining the mare he rode her into cover of the bushes beside the river, leaving the roan to drink. He could hear them clearly now . . . the sound of two? . . . three? . . . no, two galloping horsemen coming toward the bridge from the direction of the castle.

Then there were shouts and cries and two men. The captain of the guard and his lieutenant drew rein at the river bank not three yards from where Kardia and the mare were hidden. To Kardia's relief the mare made no sound.

"I like it not," said the lieutenant. " 'Tis witchcraft. He is saddled and the bit is still between his teeth." The lieutenant looked scared. "I like it not," he repeated. "There is an air of mystery here. It reeks of evil."

"I care neither for evil nor witchcraft," retorted the captain. "Take him and let us be on our way after the mare."

Cautiously the lieutenant led his horse into the water. Now if you know anything about horses, you will know that the lieutenant's horse would be more interested in water than obeying its master. Moreover, the lieutenant was in no hurry to put his hand to the bridle of the roan. The roan raised its head, whinnied and went on drinking.

The captain's eyes were on them. "Quick now," he said, "and let us be on our way." His own horse snorted and made as though it wanted water too. Quietly Kardia rode up to the left side of the captain's horse. Perhaps the sound of the water covered his movements, or perhaps the wine in the captain's head and his preoccupation with the horses in the river distracted his attention. Whatever the cause, he neither heard nor saw the mare until it was beside him. As he reached for her bridle, he felt a tug at his side and was startled to find that his sword was rising out of its scabbard. He grabbed for the hilt, missed it and cut his hand badly on the rising blade. For a moment he stared stupidly at his hand from which red blood was spurting. He never saw the sword, wielded by an invisible arm, slice cleanly through the air to the back of his neck. A second later his head toppled from his body and rolled into the river. Slowly his body slid sideways from the saddle and thudded to the ground.

When the lieutenant looked up he saw several things all at once—the headless body of his superior beside his horse, the dapple-gray mare and a sword which floated through the air above her. As the horse and sword came into the river toward him, he screamed in terror, leaped from his horse and splashed downstream. When he told the story afterward he swore to everyone that the last he heard was the diabolical laughter of an evil demon.

But the laughter was Kardia's. Not that Kardia enjoyed killing or frightening people, but the look on the man's face had affected him the same way as the sight of a fat man slipping on a banana skin might affect you. You *know* you shouldn't laugh, yet you can't help it; and the more you try to make a straight face, the more helplessly you laugh.

But as he stared at the body of the captain he shook his head in sorrow. "I will bury you later, my friend," he said. "Four years ago you swore fealty to me as long as you had life. The oath was soon forgotten."

Then he dismounted, removed the man's sword belt and dagger, and put them on himself. He cleaned the sword carefully, replacing it in its scabbard which was now on his left side. Next he collected all four horses, mounted the mare and rode over the bridge with them all, a fierce song of triumph rising to drown the sadness in his heart.

8

A Council of War

The Hall of Wisdom, which was also called the Hall of the Seven Pillars or sometimes Chakam, was filled with dwarfs and wolves who had gathered from all the neighboring areas as the news of Kardia's escape had spread. The dwarfs occupied the right side (if you were looking at them from the throne). On the left the wolves, not looking at all fierce, were sitting and panting with their tongues hanging out. Here and there a few older ones were lying down. The rest had their ears cocked and seemed very interested in what was going on.

Chocma was seated at the foot of the seventh pillar with Kardia standing to one side. He had bathed himself in the Pool of Truth and was resplendent in purple and gold robes. His hair and beard were no longer matted. His face looked rested, his eyes alert and the thin circlet of gold that rested upon his head looked as though it

The Council of War

belonged there. Kurt and Wesley, very excited to see such a strange crowd in so awesome a room, sat immediately in front of him on the steps leading to the throne where Chocma sat.

A mixture of growlings, whisperings, grunts and throat clearings echoed throughout the hall. Gunruth, Bilith and Bolgin sat cross-legged facing the boys, while behind them were several hundred of their clan. Dwarfs of every variety were present—red-headed, black-haired and blond. Some argued fiercely with one another; others remained silent and still.

The king knelt on one knee as he whispered to the boys, "Gunruth is the chief of yonder group," indicating a cluster of three hundred dwarfs all dressed like their leader. "Gunruth is in the prime of his life—one hundred sixty-eight years old, if it mistake me not."

"A hundred sixty-*eight!*" Kurt exclaimed. "How long do dwarfs live?"

"Some of the *Matmon,* as we call them, live as long as three or four hundred years. They used to live longer. They work in the mines from forty years of age to three hundred. But only male dwarfs of between fifty and two hundred fifty are permitted to fight in battle. Gunruth is a great Matmon warrior. With the short sword you see at his side he once slew two giants in single-handed combat. His renown among the Matmon is great."

"Giants?" Wesley asked. "Are there giants in Anthropos?"

"No," replied Kardia. "But a few still exist in Playsion, our neighbor on our eastern, southern and western borders."

"There must be hundreds of dwarfs ... I mean, Matmon here," murmured Kurt.

"Over two thousand," Kardia said. "Yonder more of

them are seated—Vilkung, Bereth, and Lechesh and their followers. Those are they who dress in blue and have black beards. Then there is Borglun with his sons Borab, Norab and Dorab, and all their clan. They too dress in blue, but you will notice that their hair and beards are reddish brown. They came here centuries ago from the mines in Playsion."

"Who are the really red-haired dwarfs at the back?" Wesley asked.

"I know them little," replied Kardia uneasily. "Their leaders are Inkleth and Habesh, the twin sons of Inklesh. Fierce is their wrath. 'Tis said they kill first and think after. Some speak of goblin blood in them. I fear we may need to discipline them well. The clan by the second pillar on the right . . ."

"The blond ones?"

" . . . they of the straw-colored hair are the clan of Vorklund, Visgoth and Behrens. They are children of the far north who settled here five centuries ago. They love song and feasting. They sing their tales round a winter's fire at night. In war they are mighty, in metalwork most expert of all, and they alone among dwarfs have learned to sail the high seas, traveling to distant lands few others have seen."

"What are all the dogs doing here?"

"Dogs?"

"Yes, all those dogs on the left there. There seem to be more dogs than dwarfs."

"Ah, you mean the wolves, the *Koach* as we call them."

"Wolves?" Kurt swung round to look at Kardia's face.

"Aye, boy. Wolves. They are good creatures. I think of them almost as my subjects. Chocma is fluent in their tongue and many of the dwarfs likewise speak it. They are valiant fighters, fearless of men or goblins."

"But why are they here? I thought this was a council of war."

"And right valuable is the counsel of the Koach. They are our allies, as well as our servants. Many a battle has turned on their words of wisdom. Garfong here," Kardia pointed to a huge white wolf at the foot of the stairs, "has sent out his scouts, his twin brother Whitefur and the swift runners Leanshanks and Lightening. Soon they will bring us word on how things lie at Authentio and in the woods around."

"I thought wolves were always . . . well, *bad*," Wesley said hesitantly.

Kardia smiled.

"So also do ignorant people think. So indeed thought Hocoino. But he was soon to learn how loyal the Koach are to Anthropos. The wolves are our strength. We should be in chaos were our Koach to turn against us. But Gaal has given us the wolves to serve us. There are but three thousand of them here in Chakam, but all the Koach throughout Anthropos number hundreds of thousands. Garfong is the leader of this pack. He is a powerful prince among his people."

Wesley looked down at the huge white creature lying three or four feet from him and found himself staring into the dark pools of the creature's eyes. Words like *noble, valiant, wise* passed through his mind as he looked at Garfong, prince among the Koach, brother of Whitefur, and lord of the two scouts, Leanshanks and Lightening. Were the eyes telling him something? He saw warmth as well as nobility in them as they looked deeply into his own.

A silence began to settle over the assembly. Grunts, groans, coughs, murmurs subsided into stillness. The wolves pointed their ears toward Chocma. The boys heard the rustle of her dress as she leaned forward from her throne to speak.

"Welcome, dear friends of Anthropos, loyal subjects of Kardia and servants of Gaal," she said, her voice ringing among the tall pillars that towered over the heads of dwarfs and wolves. "Welcome to your followers, noble Gunruth, Bilith and Bolgin; welcome to Vilkung and his mighty clan; welcome to you, dear Borglun, and to your sons Borab, Norab and Dorab, and to your great host of brave followers; even to you Inkleth and Habesh, of whom we have heard much, welcome most heartily to the Chakam and to our council." A low growl came from the throats of a few of the wolves at that point, but Chocma waited till they died down and proceeded as though she had not heard them. "Welcome finally most noble Vork-lund, Visgoth, Behrens and your people. Welcome, all Matmon, to Chakam."

At this point Gunruth rose to his feet, climbed the steps to the throne and stood beside Chocma on the other side from which Kardia stood. Chocma continued.

"Welcome likewise to all the Koach. Welcome, most princely Garfong. . . ."

As she spoke, Gunruth the dwarf began to utter a series of short, sharp barks, interspersed with an occasional howl. The wolves were obviously listening intently.

"Can't they understand ordinary speech?" Kurt whispered to Kardia. "Dogs can."

"Many of the Koach can and some speak it," replied the king soberly. "But it is courteous to address them in their own speech."

"But I thought you said Chocma could speak their language. Why does she use Gunruth to interpret for her?"

"It would be discourteous to you, your brother and to

me if Chocma were to speak in counsel in a tongue we understand not."

Something of the solemnity of the occasion began to fill the boys with awe.

Chocma, with Gunruth as interpreter, continued. "You all know the evil that has come upon Anthropos. For three years drought has plagued the land. Famine threatens to kill us all. Kardia, your rightful lord, has until this day been held prisoner in the dungeons of Authentio, guarded by an evil jinn, but was rescued at noon by the lady Lisa, the sister of my guests the lord Kurt and the lord Wesley." Kurt and Wesley blushed. Kurt looked at his fingernails intently and Wesley stared at the floor. They felt both embarrassed and proud, embarrassed at the attention they received and proud at the mention of Lisa. (They had talked long and hard about her with Kardia before the council had begun.)

"You also know that the throne has been usurped by the evil sorcerer, Hocoino. Let us never underestimate his power for it is great, nor his wisdom for he understands many of the deep and dark things. Let us likewise not underestimate his evil for it is bottomless."

Roars of approval, barks and applause interrupted Chocma, and she and Gunruth paused until it subsided.

"But it has always been in the darkest hours of Anthropos that Gaal has visited the realm. He alone can restore Kardia to the throne. He alone can bring the rain we so desperately need. There is word that he may already be in Anthropos."

The whole assembly was now still, silent, waiting to hear what she would say.

"It is the will of Gaal that Kardia be restored to his throne, that Hocoino be destroyed, and that freedom and peace return to Anthropos again. We are met tonight to consider the first steps by which the restoration be accomplished. With this in mind, your lord, King Kardia, will speak to you."

Once more the excited barking, applause and yells of approval broke out and continued for several minutes as Kardia held up his hand for silence.

"Dear friends," as he spoke, Gunruth continued the interpretation in wolf speech, "I thank you most heartily for your welcome and for your loyalty. No king ever had better subjects than I. In bringing Hocoino to Anthropos I failed you. No doubt the famine we suffer is because of this. Many of you warned me of his treachery, yet I ignored your warnings. And now, in my humiliation, you have stood by me." His voice faltered for a moment, and Wesley felt embarrassed, wondering if Kardia was going to weep. But he continued.

"I shall not rest until I have put right the evil I brought upon you all. Many problems face us. I know you are brave enough to march at once to the capital, but this would be folly. We need more of you Koach, more of you Matmon. We need the enchanted knights. Above all we need the help of Gaal."

A low murmur ran through the hall again, echoing slowly into silence.

"But I have a debt of honor that I must repay before this night is past. The lady Lisa who rescued me sits at this very hour in the dungeons of Authentio. She is but a child, yet she came from another world at the bidding of Gaal to rescue me. Her courage and wisdom are great, but I fear for her life if she stays there long. Before we fight Hocoino, I must set the lady Lisa free. Who will come with me this night to rescue her?"

"I will!" shouted Wesley and Kurt, simultaneously jumping to their feet. But their shouts were drowned by roars that filled the hall. Every dwarf was on his feet. The wolves were now standing, their tails stiff behind them, their heads lifted high, howling with one accord. The hubbub was indescribable. Gradually it developed into a rhythmic chant, "Long live Kardia, long live Kardia. . . ." Kardia, his face alight with a glad smile, was waving his arms for silence. Eventually he succeeded in quieting them all. One by one they sat down. But the atmosphere remained charged. The prospect of action had filled everyone with excitement and new hope.

As the noise subsided, three wolves, their leader white like Garfong, had entered the back of the hall and were making their way down the center between the dwarfs and wolves. They reached the steps leading up to the throne as the hush finally settled over the assembly. Whitefur, Leanshanks and Lightening had returned from their mission.

With a combination of both growls and barks Whitefur addressed himself to Kardia. Gunruth quickly interpreted.

"Authentio is in a state of readiness," he said. "Goblins have taken up positions behind every bush on the northern slope of the hill leading to the castle. They seem aware that trouble may be about. Their numbers were too many to count. Of men there seem to be few. Thirty or more are concentrated along the northern wall, but none could be seen on the west or east and none on the southern wall. They seem to lack leadership. The portcullis is down and the drawbridge is up. It seems they expect an attack."

"And it seems," Kardia answered, "that they expect it from the north. Let us then give them exactly what they expect!"

Gunruth looked sharply at Kardia.

"Who among you would enjoy a goblin hunt?" Kardia cried.

Once again the wolves jumped up, their eager howls echoing through the hall.

"Then you shall have what you want. Good Whitefur, lead your brother's pack slowly to the border of the forest at the foot of the northern slope of Authentio. Let no wolf be seen until the signal of a single howl from Garfong is given. And when the signal is given let a howl ring out from all, such as the woods have never heard. Let no wolf venture within twenty yards of the castle walls. Beware of the boiling oil poured over the battlements. But leap in and destroy every goblin you may find.

"The goblins will escape by any means they can into the forest. Those of the Matmon who wish may await them there. The remainder of the Matmon should send messengers to all their dwarfish kin to assemble here seven nights from tonight. It is from here that we shall march against Nephesh."

From his place on the floor of the hall, Inkleth, his matted hair and beard a flaming red, rose to his feet. As he looked at Inkleth, Kurt's heart skipped a beat. It was the dwarf in the mirror. "We have been accused before now of having goblin blood in our veins. Be that as it may, we are no friends of goblins. If it please my lord Kardia, our clan would wish to wait in ambush in the forest to fall upon the fleeing goblins. Only we pray that the lady Chocma ride with us and that she read aloud from the Book of Wisdom. For it is well known that while even at night the goblin people become shadows that are hard to see, the reading of the Book of Wisdom causes them to be seen clearly. Let the lady Chocma ride with us and let her read aloud from the Book of Wisdom. Let the lady Chocma read the Book, and my people will rid Anthropos of every goblin in the region of Authentio."

A murmur of approval rumbled over the rest of the dwarfs. Wesley turned to the king. "But your majesty, how will this all help Lisa?"

"Never fear, my lord Wesley," he replied smiling. "The assault on the northern slope will accomplish more than ridding Anthropos of tens of thousands of goblins. It will divert the attention of the few men in the castle. Who knows, it may draw the jinn itself into action. And while the tumult is at its height the two of you will scale with me the southern wall of Authentio to set the lady Lisa free."

Turning to Garfong he said, "No one knows the paths of the southern forests as you, good Garfong. Lead us if you will by the most expeditious route to the southern side of Authentio. And do you, good Gunruth and Bolgin, come with us on horseback bringing your dwarfish ropes and ladders so that we may set the lady free. With the stone on the pendant we shall have little problem in outwitting the jinn."

Then to the assembly as a whole he cried, "Down with the vile Hocoino!"

"Down with Hocoino," roared the dwarfs mid the howling of the wolves.

"All hail to Gaal!"

"All hail to Gaal!"

Then the bell-like voice of Chocma sounded, "Salvation to his majesty, King Kardia!"

"Salvation to King Kardia!" the echo roared back.

Then dwarfs and wolves scrambled to their feet and the Hall of Wisdom began to empty.

9

Scaling the Walls of Authentio

They made a curious procession, shifting from shadow to moonlight—a loping white wolf gliding like a ghost and three cantering horses following. Kardia, armed with shield, helmet and sword, was mounted on the first horse. Wesley and Kurt rode bareback on the second, marveling at a skill they had never learned but which seemed easy in Anthropos. Behind them bringing up the rear were Gunruth and Bolgin, coils of rope almost covering their squat bodies.

The muffled sounds of the horses' hoofs could be heard easily above the soft sounds of the sluggish river beside them, whose flow was almost inaudible. Whenever they emerged from the shadow of the trees the treacherous moon painted them brightly with her silver fingers as they followed the river bank. So though they might be far from their goblin enemies, they kept to the shadows as much as they could. It was only later that Wesley and Kurt learned the reason for this.

"We have to make a wide circuit by following the River Rure," Kardia had explained to the boys two hours before, having already consulted with Garfong. "It brings us at length to the Ford of the Dragon, one league south of Authentio. We cross the river there and proceed north through the woods to reach the southern slope below the castle."

They were now fairly close to the ford. The river to the right of them glittered black and silver under the moon between wide banks of dried mud and sand. A stiff breeze shushed the boughs of the trees, sometimes drowning out hoof beats and the soft wash of the river. An endless chorus of frogs croaked tunelessly against the gentle orchestra of wind and water. It was a night that could intoxicate you with the magic of moonlight, woodland and fresh breezes.

But Wesley was too worried to be enchanted.

"Isn't this *great!*" Kurt said, suppressed excitement making his voice shake a little.

For a moment Wesley did not reply. His mind was picturing the scaling of a castle wall, and he felt the same hollow feeling he had experienced before singing a solo in the music festival the year before. But this time it felt worse.

"It may be great, but it's also dangerous," he said eventually.

"Oh, *Wes.* Kardia is with us. Nothing bad is going to happen. It'll be a piece of cake. We'll just sneak up the back wall and get Lisa out before anyone knows what's happening."

"I hope so."

"Come on, Wes, you're not chicken, are you?"

Such a question would normally have stung Wesley into an angry reply, but at that moment he was too worried to react that way.

"I can't chicken out, even if I want to. There's Lisa to consider. But somehow I have a feeling that it's all going to go wrong."

"It can't go wrong, Wes. The goblins and a few soldiers will never be able to stand up to the wolves and the dwarfs. And Chocma has some kind of magic in a book. It'll be a walkover."

Wesley was silent again for a few seconds. Kurt was probably right but the unhappiness only grew deeper inside him.

"It's not the goblins I'm worried about," he said eventually. "Things have gone wrong from the start. We've no business being here. We had no business going into the room in the attic. The battle may go fine, I don't know, but it's Lisa I'm worried about. It's my fault she's in trouble. There's some weird thing called a jinn imprisoning her. I used to like fairy stories when I was a kid but this stuff—it's evil and cruel. What could Kardia do against the jinn when *he* was in its power? What's happening to Lisa now? How do we know she's even alive?"

"Don't *say* that, Wes!" Kurt sounded frightened himself.

"Well, do we know?"

"Sure she's alive. We're going to rescue her, Wes. We're going to climb the wall. Kardia says the door can be kicked in. It's solid, but it'll give way eventually. He'll wear the pendant. The jinn won't be able to see him."

"It couldn't see him last time. And last time Kardia couldn't rescue her even when they weren't in a cell."

Wesley's logic was irrefutable. What new thing could

Kardia do now that he had not done earlier that day?

"At least he has his sword, Wes."

"Can swords kill jinns? Maybe they can. But from what Kardia said, the thing is enormous. Boa constrictors are nothing compared with this monster."

"Listen, Wes. Kardia isn't a fool. He knows what he's facing. If he didn't think there was a good chance of rescuing Lisa, d'you think he'd bother to make the attempt?"

"Yes, I do."

"You do?"

"Yes. I think Kardia's the kind of person who would always risk his life for someone else. Especially if he felt he owed the person something. But he's made mistakes before. And bravery isn't enough—not when you're facing something like this jinn thing."

Kurt's high spirits began to sink slowly toward his feet. Somehow the night changed. Whereas before the soft beauty of moonlight dancing on the water delighted him, now he grew uneasy about shadows, black and menacing between the trees. What terrors might the night not hold? At first their expedition had been the wildest kind of fun. There had been, to be sure, just a tinge of fear, but only enough to add salt to the adventure. Now he began to feel small, foolish and threatened. Yet there was no turning back. Garfong loped steadily ahead of them. Kardia, his shield slung over his back, was looking ahead for the first sign of the Ford of the Dragon. Their own horse cantered steadily, and, skilled as bareback riders or no, both boys began to feel a soreness in the parts of their anatomy unaccustomed to riding. Behind them the two Matmon, the dwarfs, were following. Both boys had the same panicky sensation you get on a roller coaster when you are reaching the top of the first long slope and you know you can't get off. Yet somewhere deep within them they didn't want to quit. Danger or no, success or failure, they knew they wanted to go forward.

They were now heading west, somewhere to the south of Authentio. Soon they would cross the river that still lay to their right.

"There it is!" Kardia shouted suddenly. "It lies beyond yonder great oak where the river grows wider and where the boulders break its surface. We shall have no difficulty crossing for the river has never been so low."

Garfong did not alter his step but trotted steadily forward. Both boys' hearts began to beat a little faster. Behind them Gunruth and Bolgin never shifted their positions as though they had not heard. Two minutes later they drew rein at the ford.

The river was certainly broader and shallower where they had paused, running over pebbles and among a few boulders. In most places it seemed only a few inches deep. A cart track from the south opened into the ford from the southern forest, and on the far bank they could dimly make out that it pursued its way northward.

"What road is that?" Kurt asked as the three horses stood reined on the bank.

"It passes by the east side of Authentio," Kardia told them. "It is at this point that we shall most be in need of the guidance of our good friend Garfong for we must approach the castle not by the road but through the forest." The two Matmon had dismounted and surprisingly were staring skyward. Garfong too, sitting on his haunches, had his head tipped back and was searching the skies. Kardia slipped from his saddle. The boys clumsily followed suit. They were standing beneath the huge boughs of the great oak tree. All three horses, in the shadow of one of its boughs began drinking the river water while beyond the tree in the moonlight the Matmon and Garfong continued to stare toward the stars.

"What are they looking for?" Kurt asked.

"They hear sounds like the cries of the night warriors. The Qadar may be abroad. The Qadar hunt in the night doing the bidding of Hocoino's master, flying the heavens over the length and breadth of Anthropos. While we were on the river bank we took a certain amount of risk. Crossing the ford we must be more cautious for their eyes are keen and their rage is terrible."

Wesley shuddered. He had no idea who or what the Qadar were, but the sound of their name struck fear into his heart.

Suddenly a low growl swelled from Garfong's throat. At the same instant Gunruth, one hand on Bolgin's shoulder, pointed upward. A second later Garfong had leaped under the shadow of the oak while the two dwarfs and Kardia rushed to seize the horses' bridles and drag them from the water into the bushes beneath the oak.

"Lie down!" hissed Gunruth.

Kardia and Bolgin were busy dragging the horses farther into the bushes.

"Still. Be still. Not a move!" Gunruth hissed again. All of them froze. Wesley and Kurt lay on their faces by the trunk of the oak. Kardia and Bolgin held the horses' bridles in the depths of the bushes. Garfong stood on all fours, his white hair bristling, while Gunruth on one knee stared white-faced at the sky through a gap in the branches.

The boys could now hear the piercing cries of the Qadar, cries that grew rapidly louder as they approached. Kurt lifted his face from the earth and stared ahead at the moonlight on the water. Blackness had almost blotted out the river. Then in one shocking instant the whole river boiled black while with a terrifying shriek that could have been heard for miles around, a great mass hurtled over their heads. The boughs of the forest trees bent and creaked before a rush of wind like a tornado stripping leaves from their branches. The river continued to boil and foam. Kurt felt as though his tunic was being torn from his back. The screams of the horses were drowned in the rush of the wind and the terrifying shriek above them.

Yet in a moment the night warrior was gone. Boughs unbent, moonlight danced on the river. All noise subsided. They heard Kardia's voice saying, "Steady, girl. Steady," as he quieted the horses.

"Was that one of them? Did it see us?" Wesley asked shakily as he rose to his knees.

"I doubt it saw us, my lord," Gunruth replied. "If it had seen us we wouldn't be here."

"Then why did it come so low?"

"Who knows?" Gunruth said. "Who can explain the doings of the Qadar?"

"Will there be more?" Kurt was kneeling too and his voice was as shaky as his brother's.

Gunruth rose and stood between them. Placing his arms around their shoulders he pulled them roughly onto his great chest.

"Fear not, my little lords," he said. "Gaal is far greater than the Qadar. To us they seem the scourge of the night skies. But to him they are nothing and less than nothing; and they say Gaal is back in Anthropos."

Kardia had succeeded in quieting the horses. He returned with Bolgin to join the group.

"Hist," he said. "We dare not go into the moonlight and watch. But we have ears and we may listen."

All of them strained their ears. They could hear the

soft murmur of the river and the soft sighing of the leaves. But they could also hear the shrieks of the Qadar continuing far in the sky above them.

"We must have patience," Kardia said. "They will not stay forever."

He pulled his shield from his back and laid it on the ground, opened a leather pouch of food and offered it to the boys and to the dwarfs. It contained rolls of pastry and meat. Wes shook his head. His mouth was dry and the sight of the meat pies sickened him. The rest helped themselves and munched steadily. Kardia poured wine from a leather bottle into a small silver goblet that was also in the pouch.

"Here, my lord Wesley, drink to control the cold that plagues you."

Wesley was shivering though the night was warm. He reached for the goblet and tipped it cautiously toward his lips. The taste was harsh and strong so that he coughed and spluttered.

"Drink, my lord. Drink deeply," Kardia insisted.

Wesley forced the wine down his throat. He felt a glow of warmth in his chest as he handed the goblet back to Kardia. Slowly his fears subsided as he watched the others munch their food and pass the goblet among themselves. Garfong wolfed his pie in one swallow, then went to the river bank to drink. Little by little the shrill cries of the Qadar grew fainter. Garfong returned from the river and lay at Wesley's feet, looking into his eyes. Impulsively Wesley reached forward and fondled the great shaggy head. To his surprise low rumblings in Garfong's throat formed themselves into human language.

"Gaal is great," the wolf seemed to be saying. "Gaal is greater than the jinn. Gaal is greater than Hocoino. To Gaal all power is given. We are the servants of Gaal."

Wesley could not believe his ears. "You can actually speak," he said.

The wolf continued as though he never heard. "It matters little what happens at Authentio. Gaal will rescue your sister if Kardia should fail. Do not fear, my lord Wesley. Gaal is the ruler of life and death."

Long and deep the two looked into each other's eyes. Suddenly Wesley wrapped his arms round the great creature's neck, burying his face in the rough white fur. "Thank you, Garfong," he said. "I'm still scared and I know nothing about Gaal but thanks anyway. I guess I've got a lot to learn."

Kardia was in quiet conversation with the Matmon.

Turning to the boys he said, "There are now no sounds of the Qadar. For the last five minutes I have heard nothing. You, good Garfong, scan the skies. If all is clear you and I shall cross first. The rest of you stay mounted under the oak. Once we are safely across, and if there is still neither sign nor sound of the Qadar, the lords Wesley and Kurt must follow. Gunruth and Bolgin will not move till the lords Wesley and Kurt have crossed, and then, if still there is no sign of the Qadar, you may cross. But cross in haste. The night skies have eyes."

Six pairs of eyes, two human, two dwarfish and two equine, watched anxiously as Garfong and Kardia splashed across the shallow, moonlit water. Tension mounted the farther they got from the shore.

"They're almost halfway across," Kurt said breathlessly. Unconsciously he had raised his arms, palms facing Kardia as though he were pushing them across the river. "Oh, hurry. Do *hurry,*" he muttered.

"The Qadar will not come back for an hour or more," Bolgin said cheerfully. "With the speed of wind they circle the whole country like sentries of the skies. They travel faster than lightning strikes and are leagues to the west of us at the moment."

"They have been known to turn back when they are suspicious," said Gunruth cautiously. "They can climb to greater heights than our eyes can see, watching the land from the high regions. We shall do well to take care."

With the aid of Gunruth and Bolgin both boys clambered awkwardly onto the bare back of the great black horse they had been riding. Wesley clung to its thick mane and Kurt grasped Wesley's waist.

"They've made it," Wesley said shakily as Kardia and Garfong disappeared into the trees on the far bank. The boys felt exposed as they started across the gurgling water. Every step took them farther from shelter. Kurt craned his neck and listened carefully. But there was no sound except that of the river. Only as they approached the northern bank were they startled by the hoot of a night owl. Five minutes later the whole party was reunited under the trees beside the beaten earth roadway.

The part of the journey that followed was the most difficult. Garfong plunged into the bushes following a path that to humans and dwarfs was invisible. Undergrowth was too thick for them to ride so that the horses had to be led. Kardia, warning the others to keep well behind him, hacked at the foliage and tendrils with his sword, muttering as he did so, " 'Tis ill use of a good weapon." Nevertheless it made their passage easier. Not that their progress was rapid. Both boys' legs were scratched. Kurt's tunic was torn. How the dwarfs managed, they never knew. After an hour or so they were sweating and panting, their legs feeling rubbery and weak. Yet they were forced to march onward, their pace never slackening.

"How much farther?" Kurt asked. It seemed an age since they had left the river.

"Hist. Make no sound," Kardia spoke softly. "Very soon now we shall break cover at the southern slope below the castle. Let us proceed with caution."

Five minutes later, as Kardia predicted, they saw through the trees the moonlit slope of a grass-covered hill and, as they reached the edge of the clearing, perceived the steep walls and turrets of Authentio Castle at its crown.

"Wow!" whispered Kurt. "Are we going to climb *that?*"

For several minutes they stared from the shelter of the trees. Kardia stood stroking his beard, his eyes scanning the battlements. There was no sign of movement. A dreamy silence seemed to wrap an enchanted castle.

"Can they really have left the southern wall unguarded?" he breathed softly.

"I see neither shadow nor sign of man," Gunruth returned.

"Then we will test them and give our signal to our forces in the north," Kardia said. "Good Garfong, howl as never before."

Slowly Garfong raised his head to the sky. An eerie sound broke from his throat into the night. It echoed hollowly against the castle walls and filled the night air for a mile around. Still there was neither movement nor sound from the southern wall of the castle. But seconds later from the north came the faint sounds of answering wolf calls and the distant shouts of Matmon. Wesley felt his heart beating.

"They heard us!" Bolgin said joyfully.

"They begin the attack!" Gunruth's eyes were shining.

"Any fighting men they have in the castle should be drawn to the north wall," said Kardia, "But I fear they may post a sentry on the wall ahead of us. And there is no cover on the slope."

From somewhere in the castle a trumpet sounded. Still there was no movement on the southern walls. Sounds of shouting, of the baying of wolves and of the shrill screams of goblins could be heard in the distance.

Gunruth turned to Kardia. "Sire," he said, "we shall not know whether the wall is guarded unless we approach it. Your majesty's life is too precious, and your majesty's body too big a target to risk. Let Bolgin and your servant climb the slope first. Should a trumpet sound or arrows be shot, the worst that could happen is for my son or me to be wounded. But if naught befalls us your majesty and their lordships can follow us."

Kardia hesitated.

"Very well," he said at length. "If by the time you are halfway up the slope there is no sign of your being seen, we shall tie the horses here and follow you. But have a care. Be not reckless in your approach."

He turned to the two boys. "It pleases me little to expose children to danger."

"We're not children!" Kurt protested.

Kardia looked grave. "Already by my carelessness I have placed your sister's life in dire peril. I would never forgive myself if aught were to happen to the two of you."

"Your majesty, I must come with you," Wesley said earnestly. It's my fault too that Lisa's in trouble. I *must* help. Please don't try to stop me. I couldn't bear to be left behind."

Kardia looked from one to the other wondering how to respond.

"But who will guard the horses? Who knows but that the real peril may lie not in the castle but in these woods where roving bands of goblins would gladly rob us of them. They fear humans and would never attack the two of you. They likewise fear wolves, and Garfong is well known to them. Who will guard the horses for me?"

For a moment nobody spoke. Then Kurt said the bravest and most unselfish thing he'd ever said in his life. "Let Wes go with you, your majesty. I know the way he feels. I'll stay here with Garfong and watch the horses for you."

Still Kardia hesitated.

"*Please,* your majesty," Wesley said not very far from tears in spite of his age.

"Very well then. So be it." He unhitched a bow from his saddle and strung it. Then fitting an arrow carefully in the string he said to the Matmon, "Go then while I watch the battlements. And ill may it fare with any archer that shows his head and shoots at either of you from the walls."

Quickly the two dwarfs began to climb the slope. They spaced themselves carefully about ten yards apart and moved in a zigzag fashion. Ropes and climbing tackle were around their bodies and short swords at their side. Their heads were protected with light metal helmets. But they moved with swift agility. Kardia's eyes remained fixed on the battlements, and he continued to grip the great bow in his left hand.

"Can you tie up the horses?" he asked quietly, still staring at the battlements.

"Yes, sir!" Kurt said eagerly.

"Wait then. If there is no sign of movement when our dwarfish friends are halfway up the slope, your brother and I will set out. Then tie the horses. Till that time hold their bridles."

All of them watched as the dwarfs climbed. Still there

was no sign of their having been seen. Kardia laid down his bow and replaced the arrow in the quiver beside his saddle. His shield was still upon his back so he swung it round to carry it in the hand with which he had held the bow.

"Now!" he said to Wesley. "Let us be on our way."

Wesley never knew afterward how he had kept up with Kardia. For a man who had been months in a dungeon the king seemed incredibly fit. Wesley's legs were already rubbery, but before long he was blinded by sweat and gulping great drafts of air as he followed in the wake of his energetic leader. He longed to stop and rest but knew he dare not. His throat was parched, red dots danced before his eyes and his chest was on fire. He glanced upward only to see an appalling distance still to cover. Once he stumbled and fell, and Kardia hearing him turned swiftly and pulled him to his feet. Somehow he doggedly put one leaden leg after another. The distance between himself and Kardia was slowly increasing, but the king showed no signs of flagging. By the time Wesley reached the foot of the towering stone wall and flung himself exhausted on the ground Kardia had been there for almost half a minute.

There was no moat on the south wall of the castle, the steepness of the slope being considered defense enough. Only on the north and east sides was there water to contend with.

Gunruth and Bolgin had already unraveled and laid out their equipment. In low tones they and Kardia were discussing the best point at which to scale the wall. Wesley sat up to watch them.

"Stand clear!" Kardia said sternly. Quickly pulling Wesley to his feet, Kardia stumbled with Wesley and Bolgin about twenty yards from where Gunruth stood with a piece of metal shaped like a small anchor, to which a long piece of thin rope was attached.

"He has the strength of five men," Kardia murmured as Gunruth skillfully whirled the great iron hook around his head at ever greater speeds. Suddenly he released it to soar toward the top of the wall. For a second they heard the ring of metal on stone but almost at once the iron fell back down. Gunruth repeated the operation several times. The rope, though thin, was heavy so that an enormous impetus was needed to hurl it over the wall. On the fifth attempt, however, the iron did not return. They watched as Gunruth tugged repeatedly at the rope, testing it with his weight. It held firm.

Instantly Bolgin, the smallest and lightest of them, ran forward to clamber up the rope. Once at the top he looked cautiously to either side. Then he disappeared from their view. A moment later he began to pull the rope upward. As he did so, a woven silk ladder attached to the end of the rope began to slowly snake up the wall.

Instantly Kardia ran forward to climb. "My lord Wesley, follow the moment I am halfway up. Look not downward. Test each step before placing your foot upon it. Never take hand and foot from the ladder at the same time. Hasten not, but climb slowly. 'Tis better to reach the top at snail's pace than to hasten and fall to your death."

Kardia himself climbed like an agile monkey and all too soon Wesley's sweating palms were applied to the rope ladder. He had no fear of the first part, having the same love of climbing that most boys have. But as out of the corner of his eye he began to catch sight of the long stretch of wall and to feel somewhere inside him that the ground must now be far below, he took a deep breath. "Don't look down," he told himself. "Look at the ladder.

Test each step. That's what Kardia said. Never take a foot and a hand off at the same time."

The climb took longer than he thought it would, but at length he saw above him the faces of Kardia and Bolgin and their arms reaching down to him. Only as he came level with them and as they grasped his armpits did he permit himself to look at the horrible drop below. Dizziness and nausea swept over him for a moment, but he was hauled too quickly over the parapet for the feeling to affect him. Two minutes later Gunruth had joined them, and all four crouched staring at the few soldiers (perhaps thirty or more) on the north wall, separated from them by the two courtyards.

Now that they were on the top of the wall, the sounds of the battle to the north of the castle could be heard more plainly. The baying and barking of the wolves and the screams of the goblins mingled in a dreadful chorus. The soldiers' attention was fixed on what was taking place in the woods to the north.

"Gaal grant that the Qadar return not," muttered Kardia. "But we must be about our own business. There are but two stairways down from these walls. One leads from the tower above the drawbridge, the other to the inner courtyard. If I mistake not the nearer one descends but a few paces from where we are now."

Crouching, they followed Kardia. Sure enough about ten yards to the east of where they had climbed the wall, a stairway led them from the inner side of the wall to the inner courtyard. They ran across the grassy space to the entrance of the dungeon stairway. To their joy the door was open.

Kardia stationed Gunruth and Bolgin on either side of the entrance. "Let no man follow us," he told them. "Should they of the castle discover us, use your swords and cry out to me. My lord Wesley, follow me to the foot of the stairs but no farther. The rest, I alone must do."

Wesley hoped that Kardia could not hear the beating of his heart as they crept down the stone staircase. The darkness was overcome by a strange blue light that shone from the beautiful stone hanging from the pendant Kardia held in his fingers. At the bottom of the stairs Kardia paused. "Stay here, my lord," he said to Wesley. "Pray to Gaal if you can. Farewell."

The last thing Wesley saw of Kardia was his smiling face as he slipped the pendant with the blue stone over his head. Then there was no one with him. Only the quiet light remained. Kardia's chuckle startled him, but with a surge of joy he realized that the stone *did* work. At least Kardia would be invisible.

Pray to Gaal? Pray to the Shepherd? Who *was* the Shepherd? Slowly the blue light passed along the corridor until it paused opposite the door of Lisa's dungeon. Then came the sound of Kardia's heavy shoulder as his invisible body was flung against the door. A few seconds later the blow was repeated.

Pray to Gaal? Wesley had never been taught to pray to anyone. "Let him break it down," he breathed, not knowing to whom he said it.

A third pounding was accompanied by a cracking sound. Wesley held his breath. Then came a flash of brilliant light, the sound of splintering wood, a brief burst of flame and smoke from the doorway. Then silence.

As the smoke cleared Wesley saw that the faint blue light still illuminated the open doorway. Pieces of the shattered door lay in the corridor. Wesley stumbled in the darkness toward the opening to the cell.

"Kardia," he called, "Kardia, *Kardia!* Lisa, are you there? Lisa! Lisa!"

10

Wishes Don't Wash

Wrapped in Kardia's cloak, Lisa lay quietly, conscious only that she felt warm and sleepy. She opened her eyes and stared at the stone walls of the cell wondering where she had seen them before. Then out of the corner of her eye she caught sight of the yellow cat licking its paws. Once more the memories of her strange adventures and of her curious conversation with the jinn came back to her.

She had no idea what hour of day or night it might be. She let minutes slip by, neither moving nor speaking but quietly closing her eyes and snuggling under the warm cape, trying not to think about her unhappy predicament. But the anxious thoughts kept pushing themselves insistently into her mind.

"Does it really think I'm a great witch?" she thought. "Suppose it discovers I'm not?"

She remembered both the appalling blackness and the huge yellow serpent. How many more things could the jinn turn itself into? It was hard to believe the cat, the darkness and the great serpent were all one. How had she dared to think she could fool so formidable a foe? What would she do if the jinn took her to see its evil master? The more Lisa thought the more troubled and fearful she grew.

As her fears grew larger and darker, a new thought began to take shape in her mind. Supposing Kardia did not come back to rescue her? Supposing he couldn't? Supposing he didn't even care?

A few hours before it had been so easy to trust him, but now that she was alone, locked in the same cell that had held him so long, she no longer felt sure of anything. As her fear grew, so did her resentment. Why was she the one who got into trouble? Why hadn't Kurt or Wesley gone into the television?

You and I know that Lisa had only herself to blame for her predicament. Her own curiosity had led her to put her hand into the television. Wesley had done his best to stop her from doing so. And as for her fall and her capture, she could only blame her obstinacy in hanging onto the cloak when she should have let it go. Kardia had told her to leave it. By her stubbornness she had lost precious seconds in which she could have been rescued.

But when you are frightened it is hard to see things as they are, and you or I might have felt bitter or angry too if we had been in Lisa's shoes. She vaguely remembered Kardia's talk about the Shepherd. From the way Kardia spoke, it sounded as though Gaal, as he called him, was powerful and that he was on Kardia's side. Yet if he was powerful, why had he not kept Kardia out of the evil clutches of the sorcerer? Who was he, anyway? Perhaps he didn't even exist. Perhaps it was all a fairy story. And in any case how would the Shepherd (just supposing he *did* exist) know anything about her own plight?

The more she thought about matters the more hopeless they seemed. The more hopeless matters seemed the more frightened Lisa grew. And the more frightened she grew, the more angry she felt toward her brothers, toward her Uncle John, toward Kardia and toward the Shepherd (if he existed). Perhaps if she had not been so frightened and so angry, she would have realized that it is better to trust good people than wicked ones and people you know rather than people you've never met. But Lisa lost all her common sense because of a shaking that grew steadily inside her.

At last in desperation she resolved that she might just perhaps be able to fool the sorcerer in the same way she had fooled the jinn. Perhaps the sorcerer would think she knew more powerful spells than he did. After all, the jinn hadn't needed much persuading. All she had done was tell the truth. She had not even tried to deceive him . . . except about the cloak. Perhaps if she just stuck to her story, the sorcerer would believe what the jinn believed. And if he didn't she would *join* the sorcerer. She would offer to help him. She would fight against Kardia, and even against her brothers and Uncle John. Serve them right!

"I hope he makes them say they're sorry," she muttered to herself.

She opened her eyes and saw that the yellow cat was now staring at her.

"I trust you slept well," it said quietly.

"Very well, thank you." Lisa hoped her voice didn't sound too shaky. She sat up and pushed her hair out of her eyes. Her limbs felt stiff and a little sore, but her ankle was a lot less painful. She wondered whether she would be able to walk on it. Cautiously she tried to waggle her foot and was surprised at how little pain there was.

The cat continued to talk. "I hope you do not expect that his former majesty King Kardia will feel any gratitude to you for his escape," it began slowly. Lisa made no reply. She was not sure what to say. "He has never been noted for gratitude, and he is not likely to be grateful to a would-be kidnapper. He is in any case totally without friends or influence. His only hope will be to flee from Anthropos as quickly as he can. For what purpose did you plan to use him?"

"Use him?" The words slipped out of Lisa's mouth before she could stop them. *Use* him? What did the cat mean?

"Yes, *use* him," it continued. "I wish you would not continue to play this silly game of 'Let's Pretend.' Obviously you were trying to kidnap him, and nobody kidnaps a king for nothing. Did you wish to hold him for ransom? Why did you come here to get him out of his cell?"

Lisa's head whirled. So the jinn thought she had been trying to *kidnap* Kardia instead of rescue him. The cat seemed to expect her to reply, but once again she was not sure what she should say.

"Perhaps you keep a collection of kings? Do you turn them into puppets and play with them?"

"It's none of your business."

Lisa decided that the less she told the jinn the more he would make up himself. She sat up, hugging the fur cloak around her.

"I'm hungry," she said surlily.

At once a flash of light filled the room and a silver tray appeared on the floor before her. On it was a plate of steaming fish, a bowl of oatmeal, a bowl of honey, a crystal jug of creamy milk, a small loaf of brown bread, and crystal glasses and silverware. Lisa's eyes widened.

"I have no doubt," said the jinn, "that you could have provided yourself with better fare, but if you keep pretending to possess no magic powers, you will have to make do with what I can offer."

Lisa said nothing. Her mouth was watering at the smell of the food, and she reached forward for the spoon. Normally she would not have looked at the oatmeal. As for fish she usually avoided it because she hated fish bones. But fish, bread and oatmeal all awoke a craving within her. She poured milk and honey on the oatmeal and eagerly tasted a spoonful. Within fifteen minutes everything was devoured—oatmeal, bread, honey (her fingers were sticky) and fish. But Lisa was puzzled. It wasn't just that she felt she could eat more. It was as though the food had done nothing at all to take her appetite away. She was, if anything, more hungry than she had been to start with.

"I'm still hungry," she said to the cat.

"Of course," it replied.

"What d'you mean, 'of course'? Usually I feel full when I finish eating."

"Ah yes, but then you normally eat *real* food."

"*Real* food? You mean it wasn't real food that I was eating just now? It certainly tasted like it."

"No, I'm afraid we can't produce real food with *our* magic. Perhaps you can with yours. Our enemy Gaal the Shepherd specializes in real food. Our skills lie in creating the smells, the sight and the taste of food. If we want real food, we have to get it from the fields which are controlled for the moment by his magic. If you want real food I'll have to go and bring it to you. And I'm only allowed to bring dry crusts to prisoners."

Even a dry crust would have been better than nothing, but Lisa had forgotten her hunger momentarily in the startling nature of her discovery.

"Can you make crêpe suzettes? And angel food cake? Or ice cream sundaes? Or chocolate candy?"

Another flash almost blinded her. The first tray vanished and in its place stood a second tray bearing a plate of flaming crêpe suzettes (Lisa had only had them once in her life), a large angel food cake, two ice cream sundaes and a large box of chocolates.

The jinn looked interested. "I have never seen such food before," it said thoughtfully. "You must come from a distant world."

"If you didn't know what I was wishing for, then how could you make them come?"

"That is easy, my dear. I only need to listen to your

wishes and change them into illusions. The illusions came out of *your* mind, not out of mine."

"Illusions? What are illusions?"

"As if you didn't know! Illusions are things that look, taste and smell like your wishes but don't really exist. What you see in front of you isn't real. It's just your own wishes taking a physical shape."

"You mean those are not *real* ice cream sundaes or *real* chocolate candy?"

"Exactly. But you can enjoy them just as much as if they were."

Lisa took a deep breath and began to eat. It was, as the jinn had said, delicious to taste. Yet the more she ate, the hungrier she grew. Before long she was greedily stuffing handfuls of chocolate candies into her mouth, almost choking herself in the process. But when they were gone and the tray was empty she found she craved more. She was about to ask for more when the jinn said, "Perhaps you care to bathe yourself and change your clothing."

Lisa certainly felt dirty and sticky. She was by nature a clean and tidy person, and as the jinn spoke she realized that a bath and a change of clothing were even more appealing than more ice cream and candy. As she raised her head she saw for the first time that the door of her cell had been replaced by soft blue curtains.

"Your bathroom and dressing room lie beyond," the cat said, seeing the direction she was looking.

Lisa rose to her feet cautiously, testing her ankle for pain. It was still stiff, but she found she could put her weight on it. Limping just a little she made her way up the steps and peered between the curtains. What she saw made her gasp with surprise. Instead of the dark corridor was a beautiful modern bathroom, sparklingly clean with mirrors, piles of fluffy towels, beautifully colored soap and a tiled shower with a glass door. What surprised her most was to see her mother's best evening gown draped over a chair and her mother's high-heeled silver slippers beside it.

Lisa lost no time throwing off the clothes she had slept in and getting into the shower. There was shampoo, a hair rinse and a huge pink cake of soap with a lovely smell. The water was hot—and she stayed under it as long as she wanted letting the jets of water push comfortingly into her skin.

The towels were enormous, and she wrapped herself in a pink one as big as a blanket. There was steam on the mirror so she couldn't see herself properly until she rubbed it with another towel. Then she stared at her face in bewilderment.

A dirty mark, probably from when she had fallen on the lawn outside, streaked across her forehead. Carefully she washed her face again in the sink and then dried it. But as she stared in the mirror the mark was unchanged. She also noticed, as the mirror cleared itself of steam, that there were brown chocolate stains round her mouth. She could feel too that her hands were sticky from the honey.

"I must scrub myself with a face cloth," she murmured in bewilderment. "The water here must be hard or something." But though she scrubbed and rinsed, and scrubbed and rinsed again, the stains on her face and stickiness on her fingers remained.

"If it's not real food, it certainly makes you really dirty," she said in frustration. "Maybe it's the soap that's no good."

She dressed in the silky underwear that was laid out and put on her mother's evening gown which to her great surprise fit her perfectly. The silver slippers were also the right size, but she wobbled uncertainly when she tried to walk, and her ankle began to ache again. Determinedly she strutted into the cell and made her way carefully down the steps. Turning to look back, she saw the curtains and the bathroom had disappeared and only the heavy oak door remained.

"Did you enjoy your shower?" the cat asked.

"It was very nice in a way . . . but I'm still dirty. Is there something wrong with the soap and water?"

"They were not real soap and water, you know."

"Not real?"

"No, real cleaning can only be carried out by Gaal. For our part we're not prejudiced about the thing Gaal's people call dirt. Really there's no such thing as dirt."

Lisa stamped her foot and was instantly sorry because it hurt. "Don't be silly," she said. "What are the marks on my face if they're not dirt?"

"They're marks on your face, I suppose. You'll get used to them after a while. In some ways they make you look prettier."

"And what about the stickiness on my hands? You can't pretend I'll enjoy *that!*"

"No, but you'll find it useful. If you want to steal something, for example, all you need do is place your hand on the thing you want and it will stick to your fingers. You won't even have to close your fist."

Lisa was too surprised to say anything for a moment. She felt angry, very unhappy, but still curious.

"Where did the bathroom go?"

"Well, it's not a *real* bathroom, you know."

"But I had a shower, and the water was lovely and hot, and the soap lathered beautifully and had a lovely scent."

"Of course. That's all a part of our magic. My master can make *wish* soap, soap that smells and lathers but never washes, and water that feels as though it is wet but can neither rinse nor quench thirst."

An unpleasant thought occurred to Lisa. "Then what about the clothes I'm wearing? Are they . . . ?"

"They're *wish* clothes. They're no more real than the food you thought you ate or the shower you thought you took."

Lisa ran her fingers over the silky cloth of the dress. It certainly felt real. She looked down at the front of her then twisted her head and shoulders both ways to see as far as she could behind herself. Quickly she put her hands behind her back to feel that everything was there. Certainly she seemed to be dressed with real clothes.

"You're just fooling me," she said. "There are no such things as wish clothes. How is it different from a real dress?"

"It looks the same, it smells the same and it feels the same, but it will never keep the cold out."

It was then that Lisa realized that she was cold in the damp cell. The effects of the warm shower had quickly worn off and she had begun to shiver. She reached down to pick up Kardia's fur cloak and pulled it round her shoulders.

"I wanted you to look your best when you meet my master, Hocoino," the jinn said. "He should arrive here very soon now."

Lisa felt uncomfortable standing up in high-heeled slippers so she sank down cautiously onto the straw. As she did so she had the distinct impression that the floor was vibrating. A moment later she had no doubt.

"The floor . . ." she said.

"My master is coming," the cat replied.

The trembling grew stronger and the room began to darken. Suddenly it seemed that the whole room was tipping backward and backward as though it were spinning on a wheel. Lisa had no breath to cry or scream. The darkness was intense. Suddenly she saw a vertical line of brilliant purple light in front of her, and as the line appeared the shaking and spinning ceased. Slowly the line of light broadened until it became a wide opening in the wall of the cell. Then through the light came the most frightening figure Lisa had ever seen. The light behind him disappeared, and she found herself face to face with Hocoino.

He must have stood eight feet tall and was extremely thin, draped in black velvet which fell from his hood to his feet. Gold braid down the length of it made the robe look rich. But it was his face that frightened Lisa. It was the face of a corpse—smooth, gray and dead. A straight line of scarlet gashed the face where a mouth should have been. His eyes burned with black fire. Thin eyebrows curved in a contemptuous arch above them.

Lisa licked her lips. "I too have powers," she said, suddenly feeling as though she really were a witch from a distant world. Her heart churned but she no longer cared what happened. "It was I who came from afar by magic. It was I who set Kardia free from this fool of a jinn. I could help you, Hocoino. Do you wish me to bring Kardia back? Perhaps we could make some sort of deal."

Hocoino stared at her for a long minute. Then he turned to the cat. "The girl is right. You *are* a fool," he said quietly. "This is not a witch. It is a child, a rather stupid child. Why did you fail to warn the guards when Kardia disappeared so they might prevent his escape?"

The yellow cat's fur stood out stiff and its eyes were wide and black. "He was no more!" it hissed. "You are wrong. She is a great witch. For all I know she may have him still in her pockets!"

Hocoino reached forward and picked up the cat by the skin of its neck. As Lisa watched in horror he took it by the neck with both of his strong white hands and gave a sharp twist. There was a crack, and the cat hung limp for a moment. Her skin shivered as she watched it turn from a dead cat into a small yellow serpent that rapidly shrank until it was no larger than a thick piece of wire. With deft movements the sorcerer twisted it into a ring and slipped it on his thumb. A moment later a small golden serpent in the form of a ring stared with dead eyes at Lisa. In a way, she had grown fond of the jinn—at least in its cat form. She felt depressed and frightened by the cold, ruthless cruelty the sorcerer displayed.

Again he stared at her with no change in his expression, toying with the serpent ring. Then he turned his attention to the cell door. Again there was a flash and the sound of splintering wood. Once again the cell began to spin dizzily backward. Lisa heard running footsteps and the voice of her brother Wesley crying, "Kardia! Kardia! Kardia! Lisa, are you there? Lisa! Lisa!"

II

The Knighting
of Nocham

Wesley could see nothing when he reached the cell doorway. The faint blue light in the corridor served only to illuminate a fog of smoke. Feeling his way carefully he walked down the steps to the floor and began groping his way along one wall.

"Lisa! Are you here, Lisa? *Lisa!*" Only the hollow sound of his own voice could be heard. With a sinking heart Wesley fought against what his mind told him: the cell was empty. Slowly he worked his way round the second wall to the third.

It was then that his feet kicked against a pile of straw while one of his hands touched a heavy chain hanging down from the wall. "This must be where Kardia was chained," he thought. Feverishly he groped among the straw. Almost immediately his hands encountered something soft and warm.

"Lisa!" he cried again as with both hands he eagerly felt the shape of the soft, warm thing. But again his heart sank. It was Kardia's cloak still warm from Lisa's body. Of Lisa there was no sign.

"A light," he said to himself. "A light is what I need." Only then did it occur to him to wonder what had happened to Kardia. Had Kardia gone too? Desperately he groped his way back to the steps leading to the cell door. But the light? Now that the smoke was dispersing and his eyes had grown accustomed to the blackness of the cell, the blue light in the passage shone brightly. And if the light was there, then Kardia must be there too, for the light came from Kardia's pendant.

He stumbled quickly up the steps.

"Kardia?" he said. "Kardia! Are you there? Can you hear me?"

There was no answer.

The blue light came from a brilliant shining point on the floor. Wesley knelt down and groped with his fingers around it. To his joy he found himself touching the Mashal Stone.

"Golly, I hope he's all right. If I can get the pendant off, I'll be able to see him." Slowly he worked it off and Kardia's body immediately appeared. Turning the blue light toward him, Wesley saw that the king lay awkwardly on his back against the wall of the passageway. As he stared at him, wondering what to do, Kardia's eyes opened. For a moment he stared uncertainly at Wesley.

"My lord Wesley," he said slowly. "What of the maid, Lisa?"

"I think she's gone, your majesty. Perhaps if I could use the Mashal Stone, I could see better."

He returned to the cell door. By now the smoke was gone. Blue light from the stone lit every corner of the cell. It was empty except for Kardia's cloak. Wesley went inside, picked it up and returned both the pendant and the cloak to the king.

"No, your majesty, there's nobody there. This is your cloak, I think. We saw it on the television."

Kardia slowly reached for it but remained lying down. " 'Tis still warm with the warmth of her body," he murmured. "Gaal alone knows what has happened."

He struggled to a sitting position and began to move each of his limbs in turn. "I know not what took place," he said softly, "but in the mercy of Gaal there seems to be little the matter with me." Slowly he stood upright and handed the cloak to Wesley.

"Wrap it about yourself, my lord," he said. He placed both his hands on Wesley's shoulders. "It grieves me much and it must grieve you more. But the maid will come to no harm. She was brought here by Gaal. Fear not. Follow me. For the moment there is naught more we can do for the lady. In the meantime a battle is being fought."

Within two or three minutes Kardia, Wesley, Gunruth and Bolgin were climbing the stairway leading from the inner courtyard to the south wall. Once again the sounds of battle greeted their ears. Carefully concealing themselves, they watched the soldiers on the northern wall, all of whom had their backs toward the four. But they were doing little beyond shooting an occasional arrow.

"I think that their leader is the rogue of a lieutenant who leapt into the river yesterday," Kardia said. "We could rid the castle of its sorry crew though some might still have a little loyalty left in them. It would pain me to kill all of them without cause. Gunruth and Bolgin, go round the west side of the wall. Conceal yourselves at the northwest corner, and should any man flee, attack him.

Take advantage of their height. Slash with your swords at their legs and hold your shields high. My lord Wesley, follow me. Once the dwarfs are in position I shall put on the Mashal Stone. Remain hidden at the northeast corner until I wave my sword up high. Then reveal yourself and cry out. Once they see you, conceal yourself again. There be but five men on this side of the tower of the gateway, and they will run toward you." He smiled as he spoke. But in Wesley's face there was no answering smile. He hardly heard what Kardia said. All he could think of was Lisa.

Quickly the two dwarfs left them, making for the west side of the castle walls. Kardia, followed mechanically by Wesley, hurried in the opposite direction. "We shall arrive at our positions about the same time," Kardia said.

Events were happening too quickly for Wesley to collect his thoughts and feelings. Perhaps it was better so. In some ways it deadened the pain he felt. As in a dream he followed a pace behind Kardia until they reached the northeast corner round which Kardia peered.

"It is as I thought," he said. "There be but five men on the near side. If we work quickly we can dispatch them before any of them on the far side know what has happened. My lord Wesley, be valiant! Once the five are killed your task will be to bar the door leading down to the gateway. Do you see the opening on this side?" Wesley stared and saw in the moonlight a partly closed, arched doorway leading into the tower under which the portcullis lay. "There is but one stairway leading down from the wall to the guard rooms and the drawbridge. Gaal must indeed be with us for if my eyes mistake me not the key has been left in the lock." Wesley stared, but he could not tell whether Kardia was right or wrong.

Kardia grinned reassuringly and laid his hand on Wesley's shoulder. "Fear nothing, my little lord," he said. "All will be well. And make no move till you see my sword raised high. Once the men on this side are dispatched then run and lock the door, guarding the key." His sword was in his scabbard. He slipped on the Mashal Stone; and Kardia, his sword and scabbard all disappeared from view.

"Your majesty . . . I can't see your sword!"

Wesley heard a chuckle behind him. "When I lift it *so*," Kardia's voice said as in the air his uplifted sword appeared, "you will see it. But when I sheath it *so*," and the sword plunged downward into its invisible scabbard, "then none but Gaal can see it. Fare thee well, my lord!"

There was silence. Wesley felt rather than heard or saw that he was alone. He stared at the five men, the nearest of whom was but fifteen yards away. None of them seemed very alert. Their bows were leaning against

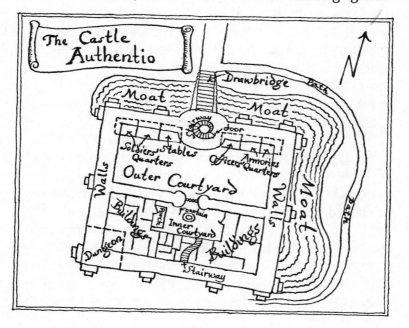

The Castle Authentio

the wall. Only one had a sword and scabbard. They were idle spectators of the battle down below.

Wesley knelt down and continued to peer round the corner. For several seconds nothing happened. Then to his surprise the bow of the nearest archer began to move slowly behind him. A moment later it soared up into the air and downward over the wall. The man never moved. Evidently he failed to see it. Then, one by one every other bow was carefully removed from the wall. All four bows were dropped over the inner side of the wall into the courtyard.

Then he saw what he was waiting to see, a sword floating high in the air, the tip pointing skyward. With his heart beating suffocatingly he stepped out from cover and stood facing the five men.

He opened his mouth and tried to say, "Hi, there," but no sound came. He tried again and this time the words came out thin and squeaky, but the sound was too faint. The men continued to stare over the wall, ignoring him. In desperation Wesley stamped his foot and yelled with all his lung power, "Hey, you dumb idiots— *look at me.*" This time three of the men turned. Three mouths opened silently. The man nearest him reached for his bow and twisted round bewildered at not finding it. Then with a shout of rage he ran toward Wesley.

Wesley's legs refused to function. Horrified he stared at the distorted face of the running soldier, aware that by now the other four were following. His mind told him he should be running too, but his feet seemed bolted to the floor. The first man was so near that Wesley could see his teeth and his large staring eyes. Then without warning the man's legs flew backward into the air behind him and he fell with a heavy thud two yards in front of where Wesley stood.

After that things happened so quickly it was hard to remember the order of events. Two more men tumbled sprawling over the first, a fourth was suddenly jerked up onto the parapet, then fell screaming over the wall. The last man hesitated for a second as a flying sword sliced neatly through his neck.

"To the door! Lock the door, my lord!" Kardia's voice rang out. The cry startled Wesley from his frozen fear. And in a moment his fear was turned to bitter, angry exultation. The three men in front of him were scrambling to their feet, but instead of running away from them Wesley darted nimbly past and ran as hard as he could to the door of the stairway. What happened behind him he never knew. The heavy door creaked into place with a hollow boom. For a second it seemed as though the enormous iron key would not work, but with a click it finally did. For good measure Wesley swung a huge oak beam into a heavy iron socket barring the door from the outside. Then he tucked the key into the belt of his tunic. As he turned to look behind him he saw four men sprawled on their backs, two of them headless. To his surprise he felt no horror, only a joy (of which he afterward felt ashamed) that a blow had been struck against Lisa's captors.

But there was no time to think. He heard the sound of Kardia's running footsteps going past him and a moment later the king's voice called out from the west side of the north wall, where most of the soldiers had stationed themselves.

"I am Kardia, rightful lord of Anthropos," he said. "To those who surrender and acknowledge my sovereignty I will show mercy. Those who resist me shall forfeit their lives. It is vain for you to hope to escape. My plans are laid. But I prefer to show you mercy."

Wesley crept round the tower to see what was happening. Twenty-five men had swung with their backs to the outer parapet, staring bewildered toward where they thought they had heard Kardia's voice. One of the men, the lieutenant, was standing on the parapet itself above the heads of the rest.

"It's a trick," he said, "Heed not the voice. Hocoino has sent word that the former king of Anthropos has been recaptured. Hocoino is lord of Anthropos."

Still the men looked bewildered.

Kardia's voice called out again. "For those words, sir lieutenant, I shall hurl you from the battlements, and your followers shall see whether I am in chains or not."

For a moment no one moved. All were staring at the lieutenant. Then suddenly his feet were knocked from under him and with a scream of terror he disappeared from view over the castle wall.

"Does anyone else doubt that Kardia, king of Anthropos, is free?" Kardia cried. "There is mercy for those who repent and death for those who would escape. Make your choice. But make it quickly for my time is precious."

Two men at the west end of the north wall began to creep quietly round the corner to the west wall. Nobody saw them, but a second later there were yells of pain. Both men lay on the ground. Two small shadows swung axes above their heads, and the men were silenced. The shadows disappeared.

Still nobody moved or spoke until three men nearest the tower above the gate slowly began to move around it as though they were making for the stairway. Wesley hurried back away from them and crouched in the shadow of the parapet. The rest of the soldiers remained rooted to the spot. One of the three hesitated, his back against the tower wall. The others disappeared from the view of the soldiers and into Wesley's line of vision. He watched them struggle with the beam, then try the door.

"It's locked," one said, thrusting his shoulder against it. It was the last thing he did. A second later his own head and that of his companion fell to the ground. Kardia's invisible hands picked the heads up one at a time, then sent them hurtling along the broad surface of the wall like a gruesome pair of footballs. The rest of the soldiers stared in paralyzed fascination at the grim spectacle. Again Wesley crept round the tower, carefully avoiding the bodies of the soldiers. As he peered round he saw that not another man moved.

"Are you now willing to accept the sovereignty of your rightful lord and king?" the invisible Kardia called out again. "All of you deserve to die for your treachery to the crown. Yet I am still of a mind to show mercy."

The sergeant at arms, an older man with a gray beard, stepped forward. "Sir, if you are indeed our sovereign lord, show yourself to your servants. So many dark and magical things have come to pass in the kingdom since you—if it be indeed you—were dethroned. Be not impatient with your servants, but show yourself."

Instantly Kardia stood before them, his sword still drawn in his hand. A gasp from twenty throats could be heard. At the western end of the wall Gunruth and Bolgin stood watching. One by one the soldiers dropped to their knees.

"Let those who would serve me come and swear loyalty over my naked sword," he said sternly.

Wesley had never seen anything so moving as what followed. The sergeant was the first to stand and looking Kardia in the eye said, "My liege, I will not swear an oath because I fear your sword. You speak rightly that your servants deserve to die. Yet would I serve you because you are my rightful king. I shall kneel before you. Sever my head from my shoulders if you will, for I am ashamed. But if you let me live, know, O king, that I will love and serve you forever." And so saying he strode forward and knelt at the king's feet. There was a long pause.

All the time the sergeant was speaking Wesley had crept to stand behind Kardia. As the sergeant moved to kneel before Kardia, something caused Wesley to look into the king's face. He was not surprised to see tears running down Kardia's cheeks and into his beard so gripped was he himself by what was happening.

The sergeant bent his head.

"What is your name?" the king asked.

"My name is Nocham, if it please your majesty."

"Do you swear to follow me to death, Nocham?"

"Aye, your majesty, for the sake of Gaal will I serve you to the death."

Kardia smiled through his tears. He placed his sword lightly over the shoulders of the kneeling sergeant. It was still bloody and blood dripped on the sergeant's back. In a resounding voice Kardia cried out, "I accept your oath of fealty. Rise, *Sir* Nocham."

Bewildered, the man looked up into the king's face. The turn of events had been so rapid that he could scarcely grasp what was happening. With mock severity Kardia said, "To your feet, sir knight! It ill befits a gentleman of your dignity to respond so tardily to my commands."

The soldiers by now were smiling and as the new knight rose to his feet a sudden roar broke out from them. "Long live Kardia! Long live the king!"

Then one by one, all of them without exception came and knelt before him.

12

The Rout of the Goblins

For the first time Kardia, the dwarfs and Wesley had time to look over the wall at the battle below. At first Wesley was confused by what he saw. The hillside was a sea of moving creatures beneath what looked like a fireworks display. There were shouts, screams and howls. Hardly a square yard of the hillside was bare.

Then as he stared he noticed that the creatures on his left were all Matmon, most of them the red-haired followers of Inkleth and Habesh. Stretching down the hill three or four deep they were wielding axes and swords or shooting arrows into a mass of goblins who occupied the center of the hill.

Then on his right he noticed the Koach, the wolves. Never in his life had he seen so many of them. They were a moving sea of darting bodies under the moonlight. As he watched them closely he saw that each time a wolf darted forward to seize a goblin, the goblin shriveled like a balloon which the wolf would shake and drop to the ground. Strain his eyes as he might, Wesley could not see what happened next. It almost seemed as though each deflated goblin sank through the earth. But he could not be sure. The moon could have been playing tricks on his eyes.

Something else he saw made his heart sink. What looked like fireworks were actually flaming darts flung by goblins into the ranks of the Koach and the Matmon. The dwarfs seemed able to catch them on their shields. But many Koach fell howling with pain.

As he went on looking he saw that the two lines of Matmon on his left and of Koach on his right formed a V shape, the point of which was at the bottom of the hill. The nearer ends of both arms of the V were but fifty yards from the castle walls so that the goblins were being driven toward the castle in a triangle, which would soon reach the north wall of the castle.

Kardia turned to Nocham. "Wesley, give me the key and unbar the door. Good Sir Nocham, take with you the lord Wesley and one of your best men and go to the foot of the hill on the south side of the castle. There you shall find horses with the lord Kurt and the Koach king, Garfong. Instruct Garfong to proceed to the foot of the north hill and to bring with him as quickly as he may three hundred Koach into the courtyard of the castle. Bid him do so quickly and unobtrusively. By the time you return, the drawbridge will be down to receive you."

"Very good, sire. Ho there, Chazak!" Sir Nocham cried. "Come quickly! Lead on, my lord Wesley!"

Wesley turned from the scene below and ran round the battlements to the south wall. Finding the silk ladder and peering over the wall at the immense depth below, a wave of dizziness swept over him. But as he glanced over his shoulder again he saw Sir Nocham and Chazak looking at him expectantly. There was no turning back.

"Look not downward," the words sounded through his brain, "Never take hand and foot from the ladder at the same time. Hasten not, but climb slowly."

Look not downward. He already had, and as he saw the appalling drop, the earth below seemed to sway sickeningly as though he were on the top mast of a sailing ship in a storm at sea. Sir Nocham and Chazak were still staring at him. His lips were pale in the moonlight and for a few seconds he pressed them together. Then he said the words that were drumming through his brain.

"Look not downward. Never take hand and foot from the ladder at the same time. Hasten not, but descend slowly."

"Aye, aye, my lord," replied Sir Nocham gravely. It occurred to Wesley afterward that the instructions may have been unnecessary. But he had given them so he himself would have an extra moment to pull himself together.

Carefully, *not* looking down, he clambered across the parapet on his stomach, feet first with his back toward the terrible void. Then he wriggled backward over the edge gripping the sides of the silk ladder and hoping the two men could not tell how panicky he felt.

"Perhaps you could follow me, Sir Nocham, when I give a call to say I am halfway down." The words came out of his mouth breathlessly.

Then before he had time to change his mind, gripping the top rung desperately, he slithered down a little and groped with both feet for a rung of the ladder. For a moment they scrabbled against the stone, feeling nothing. He skinned a knee but he did not feel it until much later.

Then to his relief, first one foot and then the other found a soft silk rung. The descent had begun. By the time he was halfway down the breeze was drying his sweat and he had regained his composure.

A second fear gripped him once he reached the ground and began to wait for his companions. He heard, or thought he heard, the thin, high shrieks of the Qadar, but his eyes searched the skies vainly for any sign of them. "Must be my imagination," he murmured uneasily.

Once all three had gained the foot of the wall they scrambled down the slope, stumbling, falling, rolling, leaping, until they reached the treeline where a white wolf leaped on Wesley, knocking him down and licking his face.

"Garfong, you old rogue!" Wesley wrapped his arms round the huge creature. "How good to see you!" Then more soberly, "Thanks for saying what you did about Gaal and Lisa. Though we didn't find her, what you said was a real help." Then he paused and looked carefully into the eyes of the wolf. "I was sure I heard the sounds of the Qadar a moment ago."

"I have watched and listened well. There is no sign of them, my lord."

"You are sure?"

"Quite sure, my lord."

Wesley drew an anxious breath. "I guess we're safe for the moment then."

Kurt ran to join them. "Lisa? Did you get Lisa?"

Wesley shook his head. "She was gone when we got there. But Kurt, I think it's going to be all right. Don't ask me how I know. I just *know*."

"Boy, that's a change of tune for you! Who are these men, Wes?"

Wes sprang to his feet. "Oh, I'm so sorry. Sir Nocham, Chazak, this is my brother, Kurt." They shook hands. "And this," said Wesley, kneeling to wrap his arm again round Garfong's neck, "is the most powerful Koach king in Anthropos."

The two men stared at the magnificent creature. Almost at once, Sir Nocham began to speak in the tongue that by this time the boys could recognize as wolf speech. Garfong listened carefully, his ears pricked forward. A low growl rumbled deep inside him. A moment later he was loping westward along the treeline.

Sir Nocham turned to the boys. "My lords, the hill behind us is steep. It will be better to lead the horses up diagonally to the southeast corner of the castle wall. We must have a care lest they break their ankles. There is a pathway which begins but a short distance to the east of us that follows the eastern wall where we may ride round the outer edge of the moat below the north wall. We must hasten if we are to reach the drawbridge before the goblins are driven in."

The horses were untied. Only two of them were saddled, Kardia's dapple-gray mare and the horse the dwarfs had ridden. Kurt seized the bridle of their own horse. "Perhaps you could lead the way, Sir Nocham," Wesley said, marveling at the way he seemed to be taking command after his panic on the wall. "Take the mare if you will. She is his majesty's horse. The roan was the one the dwarfs rode. It might be better for Chazak to ride him."

Sir Nocham opened his eyes wide, then burst into laughter. The two boys stared at him. Chazak laughed with him until the boys began to laugh too, though neither of them was sure what they were laughing at. All the time the two men were staring at the mare.

"Hey, what's tickling you guys?" Kurt asked between his snickers.

"His majesty's horse, is it? *Now* I understand it! Oh 'twas a merry sight to watch them galloping across the drawbridge with bits between their teeth, galloping in madness down into the forest!" Sir Nocham laughed again. "The captain, for 'twas his horse, was nigh out of his wits. What did he do but seize that jackass of a lieutenant (Gaal rest his soul) and set off in pursuit! *Now* I know what happened. 'Twas his majesty playing his invisible games and stealing the best horses in the stables from under their noses. Ho! Ho! Ho!" And he slapped his thighs as tears of merriment ran down his cheeks.

It took a minute or two for him to recover. "You must pardon the merriment, my lord," he said to Wesley. "Let us be on our way."

They found the path and led the horses up the long, steep slope. It took more time than Wesley had thought. The path was steep so that sometimes they had to drag the nervous horses. When at last they reached the top, they found themselves as Sir Nocham had predicted at the southeast corner of the wall.

Here the path broadened and all four mounted, the boys doing so with some difficulty, both sitting bareback on the third horse. Sir Nocham led them at a canter below the east wall. Ahead of them the shouts of the fighting grew steadily louder. As they approached the northern corner, more and more of the battle came into view. At the corner of the north wall they reined their horses and stared at the scene below.

Trapped inside the V below the castle, the goblins still struggled in vain to break through the Matmon line on the west and Koach line on the east. But there were changes. Fewer arcs of fire soared from the goblins who seemed to have sensed that the castle behind them might not be a refuge but a trap. The point of the V at the lower end of the slope had begun to open. By a huge effort wolves and dwarfs pulled it together again, but only for a few seconds. Then the pressure of ten thousand goblins drove it open. For a moment it looked as though the goblins might burst through the gap to disappear into the woods.

Then below the opening of the V at the forest edge a burst of blue fire rose like a dome above a tiny figure on horseback. It was Chocma, Chocma calmly reading from the pages of an open book. At least they guessed that was what she must be doing. The distance was too great to see or hear clearly.

The terrified screams of the goblins now drowned the baying of the wolves and the shouts of the Matmon. It was as if the tide that had been going out had suddenly turned and was coming in. With desperate haste the goblins began to scramble up toward the castle gates. Many were trampled underfoot and disappeared into the earth. The lines of the wolves and the dwarfs closed in.

"Quick, my lords, ere it be too late," Sir Nocham cried. "Gallop for the drawbridge before the goblins reach it."

Suddenly Chazak drew his horse alongside the boys. Two swords were in his hand, the hilts toward them. "Take them, my lords," he said. "I brought them lest we encounter the powers of darkness. They are of logos-tempered metal which no goblin can resist. Take them! I have one in my own scabbard!" Then before they knew what was happening they were galloping hard for the drawbridge, sixty yards away.

Sir Nocham was ahead of the brothers while Chazak was even with them on the side nearest the moat. They were still thirty yards away when they saw that the first of

the goblins had begun to pour across the drawbridge. "On, my lords. On! Do not stop!" Sir Nocham cried. "Ride into the midst of them! Hew them down!"

The hubbub was indescribable. Suddenly they were surrounded by goblins, trampling on goblins. Next they were on the drawbridge urging their horses through the press of them, slashing awkwardly with their swords at some who tried to mount the horses to pull them down.

Out of the corner of his eye Wesley saw Chazak's roan perilously near the edge of the drawbridge. Suddenly it reared, whinnied, missed its footing and fell with its rider into the moat below. But there was no hope of stopping. Carried by a river of screaming goblins, they were swept beneath the portcullis and into the outer courtyard before they had time to think.

A flaming dart grazed Kurt's right shoulder causing him intense pain. There seemed at first no way they could extricate themselves from the goblins. From every side the evil creatures were trying to swarm up the sides of the horse. Both boys had to swing their swords constantly. Their movements grew steadily clumsier. Kurt wept half from anger and half from pain.

Then Wesley, noticing that the crowd was less dense at the periphery of the courtyard, turned the horse to escape the mob of goblins. Once he reached the back of the courtyard, he raced the horse back and forth along the turf. It was harder for the goblins to gain a hold when they were galloping, and for the time being they could let their heavy swords hang down. A moment later, Sir Nocham joined them.

Kardia's voice called from above them. "Stand well to the rear of the courtyard! Keep back!"

Suddenly from the eastern side of the courtyard came the howls of the Koach. "Where the dickens did *they* come from?" Wes asked in wonder.

" 'Tis Garfong and his followers," Sir Nocham said.

"But how did they get in here before us?" Kurt asked between his gasps for breath and of pain.

"They have the speed of wind," Sir Nocham answered.

Pandemonium broke out anew among the goblins. Careless of all that awaited them, more were pouring through the main archway into the courtyard. None of them now took any notice of the two horses for the terror of the wolves left room for nothing else in their minds. Arrows from the eastern wall flew over the heads of the Koach to bury themselves in the screaming mass that scrambled toward the western wall. A second volley followed, then a third. From the east of the courtyard the Koach snapped at their heels, leaped on their backs driving them steadily against the western wall. More goblins poured through the archway until it seemed that there must be several thousand of them crowding toward the southwest corner of the courtyard.

At that moment Chocma appeared in the gateway, dismounted slowly carrying her book and harp, and disappeared into the tower beside the gate. She reappeared by the inner parapets of the north wall and began to read once again. Screams of goblins, snarls of the Koach, shouts of men and the Matmon all combined to make a deafening tumult of sound. Both the boys' and Sir Nocham's horses were pressed back against the gateway of the inner courtyard. Yet above the tumult the bell-like voice of Chocma rang clearly. And as she read from the book blue light surrounded her in an expanding bubble. It grew wider and taller until the courtyard was alight with blue fire under a dome that arched hundreds of feet above them protecting them from the prying eyes of the Qadar who were sweeping the southern skies for the second time that night.

All sound and movement subsided as the words continued. The Koach ceased to snap and growl. Men and Matmon grew silent. The screams of the goblins were heard no more. Slowly they began to shrink—smaller ever smaller. Before long Wesley saw that like liquid they were sinking into the earth.

"Where are they going?" he whispered to Sir Nocham.

"They go to the Halls of Deepest Darkness to await the judgment of Gaal."

Still Chocma read until not a goblin remained. Then the Matmon and the Koach shook themselves as though they were waking from a dream and moved into the center of the courtyard. Sir Nocham smiled and pointed to the gateway where Chazak, dripping wet and leading a shivering roan, came in among them.

Chocma closed the book and picked up her harp.

Under the dome of blue light, from the throats of men and dwarfs, and even from the throats of wolves there rose a strangely harmonious song such as Kurt and Wesley had not heard before. It gave them the feeling of snowcapped mountains, of surf on the seashore, of being tucked warmly into bed by their mother, of kindness and courtesy, of sacrifice, joy and pain. Marveling they listened. And as they listened they slid drowsily from their horse to sit on the ground. By the time the music died away and the dome of blue light began to fall, they were nodding sleepily. Long before it reached the ground, Kurt and Wesley, lying full length, were fast asleep on the dry, burnt grass, their aching muscles forgotten and unfelt.

13

Lisa Gives Up

Whirling backward into blackness, Lisa lost all sense of where she was and what was happening. A roaring filled her ears.

She could feel that her body had left the floor and she groped with her arms and kicked with her legs to grasp at something—anything. Yet all around her there was nothing, nothing but empty blackness and a noise of rolling thunder.

Then the same line of brilliant purple appeared in front of her as a feeling of firm ground pressed under her feet. The line widened to an opening. She staggered toward it uncertainly. For a moment all was dazzling light and then, she had no idea how it happened, she found herself in a great and gloomy hall surrounded by tall glass windows. Had it been daytime she would have delighted to see the multicolored glass. But because it was night, the hall was lit only by three smoking lamps suspended from the ceiling above. Long shadows and dim recesses fell back from tall pillars. Ten yards ahead, Hocoino was striding away from her across the hall.

"I wish he weren't so horrible," she thought. "I wish he'd come back and be kind."

As she spoke it seemed as though Hocoino split in two. She saw two Hocoinos identical in all respects, both robed in black velvet, both eight feet tall, both with faces of death, thin lips of scarlet, burning eyes and eyebrows arched in scorn. Both stopped and turned to face her. For a second they stood side by side, like identical twins. Then one swung on his heel and continued on his way. The second came toward her, as terrible in appearance as ever.

Yet he spoke gently to her. "You wanted me to stay with you?"

"Oh, yes. Please. I'm frightened. Where am I? And what happened to you? Are there two of you?"

"Two of us?"

"Yes, you sort of split in two. Are you both Hocoino?"

"No, my dear. I am but your wish."

"Then you *are* Hocoino!"

"No, I'm just your wish *about* Hocoino. The real Hocoino is over there. He'll come back when the time arrives to sacrifice you. Till then you may have whatever you wish."

Lisa's head was spinning. Too much had happened in the last few moments for her to grasp what was going on. "But if you're not Hocoino, who are you?"

"I am your wish."

"You mean you're not *real?*"

"Wishes are real. I am as real as your wish is. You wished me to be kind, so I will be kind. What would you like me to do for you?"

Lisa stared at him. He looked frightening and grue-some. "I wish you looked like my Uncle John. I'd feel better if you did."

No sooner had the words left her mouth than the second Hocoino vanished and her Uncle John appeared, warm, tweed-suited, bespectacled and with rumpled hair, opening his arms to receive her.

She flung herself at him. "Uncle John, Uncle John. Oh, I'm so glad you came!"

The rough scratch of his tweed jacket against her cheek, the bear hug of his strong arms about her made her feel that her troubles were over. Uncle John! Dear Uncle John. Now everything would be all right again. No more jinns, no more sorcerers, no more dungeons or stupid kings. Uncle John would make everything right.

She felt her hair being caressed tenderly. "Take me home, Uncle John. Take me out of this horrid place. I'm so sorry we went in the attic upstairs. We didn't mean any harm."

Uncle John said nothing. He tilted her head up to look into her eyes. "It must have been a horrid experience for you."

"It was. Oh, it was! But now you can take me home." She stared at his face but he said nothing. "You *can* take me home, can't you?"

"Take you home? Where is home?"

"Where is home? Why, in your house on Grosvenor."

"Grosvenor?" Uncle John looked puzzled. Angrily Lisa tried to shake him.

"Don't make fun of me. I can't bear it. Take me back home."

Uncle John stared tenderly down at her just as he had done so many times in her life. "Lisa, I have no home. I'm not your real Uncle John. I'm just the wish you asked for. You mustn't think I came from that other world you speak of. I was just born minutes ago, and as soon as you finish with me I shall evaporate again."

Lisa's eyes widened. Then she flung herself headlong at his feet, beating her fists upon the floor in a storm of weeping. "It's not true! It's not true! It can't be true! You *are* Uncle John. You've *got* to be Uncle John."

The figure that looked so like Uncle John waited until she had calmed down. Eventually Lisa sat on the floor and looked up at him. Occasionally a sob almost like a hiccup shook her frame.

"Do you remember the food the jinn brought you?"

"Yes."

"Was it *real* food?"

"It *tasted* real."

"Did it satisfy your hunger?"

"No."

"Listen, Lisa. I cannot satisfy your heart like your real Uncle John either. I too am only a wish. I'm your wish for Uncle John."

Lisa gazed at him for several minutes. "But you're *exactly* the same as he is."

"I *look* exactly the same."

"You *talk* the same. You *feel* the same."

"But I'm only a wish."

"But you're *solid*."

"Oh, we wishes can be solid enough. It's just that we can never bring happiness."

Lisa began to cry again. "It's horrid, it's simply horrid. Part of me wants to hug you and part of me wishes I'd never seen you."

"You have only to wish me to go away."

Through her tears she stared into his face.

"How can I wish you would go away? I *love* you."

"Not really. You love your Uncle John. I'm only your wish. And if you stay here you can wish for whatever you want. Gaal is the only source of real things."

Lisa drew a deep breath. It was very hard to say it, perhaps the hardest thing she had ever said, but she made herself say it. "If you're not my real Uncle John, I . . . I wish you'd go away."

Instantly she was alone. All around her was the empty hall with its three dim lights, its pillars and its dark shadows. Lisa's head began to throb. Rage shook her limbs while fear twisted her stomach. She did not know with whom she was most angry. She was angry with Uncle John for not coming to her rescue. She blamed Wesley for the troubles she had brought on her own head. But it was against Kardia that she eventually expressed herself.

"Kardia left me! He ran away and left me to the jinn. He shouldn't have done that! I hate him! Why can't I go home? Uncle John—my real Uncle John—where are you?"

She stood up. A wild idea came into her head that if only she were to shout loudly enough her uncle might hear. So she screamed with all the force in her young body. "Uncle John! Uncle John! I'm *here*, Uncle John! Uncle John, can you hear me? Listen to me! I'm lost and I don't know how to get back! Come through the television and get me! *Please!*"

The darkness mocked her with echoes as she continued to shout until her voice grew hoarse and her words were choked with sobs. She called for her mother and father in the Middle East, standing now on one foot, now on the other and clenching and unclenching her fists. Her face was swollen and distorted.

"Your words will be lost among the stars. They cannot

be heard by those you call."

Lisa started. She had no idea where Hocoino had come from. He looked down at her with no expression on his pallid face.

"I want to go home."

"The uncle you call does not want you. He sent you here."

"I don't believe you!"

"Yet I speak truly. You have also a brother who hates you and who tricked you into coming."

"Well, *that's* not true. Wes told me to leave the TV sets alone."

"Quite so. In the cunning of his heart he knew you would defy him, and he also knew the secrets of your uncle's magic mirrors. You did not come here by the power of Gaal but because your uncle is a magician."

"He's not a magician and he doesn't have any magic mirrors." Lisa knew, of course, that Hocoino referred to the TV sets. He ignored her and continued.

"Your brother wanted to be rid of you," he insisted coldly. "His desire to leave the room of the magic mirrors was a pretense."

Lisa's mouth was dry. She saw nothing of malice in Hocoino's eyes. Even though she believed only half of what he told her, her mind already full of resentment switched automatically to her quarrels with Wesley. Indeed as she thought about it she could only remember their quarrels and Wesley's nagging, know-it-all manner. Uncle John? Of course he wouldn't come! Whatever made her hope he would? Hadn't he always said no when she wanted anything badly? Bitterness crept over her.

"If you really want to go back to them I could try to send you." Hocoino's voice was expressionless. Lisa looked at him.

"Will you? Please?" Bitter or no, she wanted to go home.

"I shall need your cooperation."

"What d'you want me to do?"

"You might not like it."

"I'll do anything, sir. Just send me back home."

"Then repeat after me: I hate my brother Wesley, and I swear by the Lord of Darkness that I will have revenge."

Lisa opened her mouth but no words came. At that moment she felt as though she really did hate Wesley, but she found she couldn't say it.

"I can only help if you cooperate."

She drew a deep breath. "I hate my brother Wesley, . . ." she began softly.

"Louder, please!"

"I hate. . . ."

"Still louder!"

Lisa began to shout. "*I hate my brother Wesley, and I swear by the Lord of Darkness that I will have revenge!*

"That'll teach him!" she said to herself. "That'll show him!" For a second she almost felt happy.

"Now Lisa, I want you to say: I hate my Uncle John, and I swear to disobey him forever."

This time there was no hesitation. Lisa found herself shouting exultantly, "*I hate my Uncle John, and I swear to disobey him forever!*"

Hocoino was gone. She was alone once more with her thoughts as the echoes of her shouts reverberated round the building. But she no longer wept. I cannot say she felt happy, but she did feel sort of fierce and proud as though she was better than people like Kardia, Wesley and Uncle John. She sat down on the stone floor to await whatever was to happen. "They'll be sorry when I get back. And they'll be surprised. Just wait till I tell them. . . ."

"I hate my brother Wesley," a girl's voice rang through the darkness. Lisa jumped once more. Who was mocking her? She didn't recognize the voice. Or did she? It sounded like. . . . Where had she heard it before? Slowly the unpleasant suspicion forced itself on her. It was like her own voice. It *was* her own voice, echoing loudly from the pillars and the alcoves of the hall.

"I hate . . . I hate . . . I hate . . . I hate . . . Wesley . . . Wesley . . . Wesley . . . Wesley . . ."

At first she thought her voice sounded powerful. The words rolled majestically round the building.

"Lord of Darkness . . . of Darkness . . . of Darkness . . . revenge . . . revenge . . ."

She shivered ecstatically. Had she really sounded like that? Maybe she could become a movie star!

But the echoes refused to die and the more they bounced from the walls, the less enchanted Lisa grew. She grew weary of her voice. Words that at first sounded noble began to sound silly and mean. Before long she wished she could turn the echoes off. Her proud feelings leaked from her like air from a balloon when the string is not tied tightly enough.

She cringed as the echoes continued and began to stop her ears. Suddenly she knew, without being told, that she was neither grand nor powerful and not at all majestic.

"I wish they'd shut up!" she muttered aloud.

At once the echoes died into silence. The wish-magic had acted again. But it could not keep the echoing voice out of her mind where it continued to mock her with her own silliness. Yet the more she hated her silliness, the more deeply she clung to her resentments.

Fear began to haunt her again. "I've really done it now," she said to herself. It was as though she had slammed a door and all her friends were on the other side. "And it's all their fault," she said quietly. "They can open the door if they want. But I'm not going to. When I get back home, they're going to have to apologize."

She had never in her life felt so alone. When would Hocoino come back? How would he send her home? Doubts plagued her. *Could* Hocoino send her home?

She would not at first let herself think what she knew in her heart to be true. "Of course he wouldn't fool me. Why should he?" Yet the suspicion refused to go away. She pictured his corpselike face and was sorry she had trusted him. How could anyone trust a face like that? Just as the echoes of her voice refused to die away, so the face of Hocoino continued to haunt her. His thin red lips now seemed cruel. She remembered, too, the ruthlessness of his hands as they had broken the cat's neck.

An hour passed, then another, and yet another. All her tumultuous feelings left her one by one. The cold, the darkness and the stillness seeped into her bones.

She made a pathetic figure squatting crosslegged on the stone floor, dwarfed by the size of the building. Her head was slumped on her chest and her hands rested idly in her lap. You might have thought, if you had seen her, that she had been turned into stone. She looked as though she had been left behind and forgotten.

And this was what she was thinking about—being abandoned. She felt that Uncle John had forsaken her, that Wesley and Kurt had forsaken her, that Kardia had forsaken her. She felt the same emptiness she had once experienced when all her friends ran away from her at a berry-picking party, and she had been lost in the woods. Even her fear of Hocoino and of what might happen to her seemed nothing to this quiet despair. She had no hunger, no thirst, no wish to laugh or cry.

Her head bowed lower still. If you had asked her how

she felt at that moment she would have said, "I don't have any feelings." A little while before she had longed to get back home, but now things seemed too hopeless for her to care.

Then slowly she became aware of how stiff and chilled she was. With a sigh she struggled to her feet. And as she did so she once more saw the figure of the sorcerer striding across the hall toward her. He was followed by three strange creatures with large bulbous heads, frail little bodies and long arms and fingers. Since Lisa had never seen a goblin before, she did not recognize what they were.

For a moment she wondered whether to turn and run, but a moment's thought convinced her of the futility of doing so. Besides she no longer cared what happened to her. She felt no fear of Hocoino as he strode toward her, the little goblins running to keep pace with him. Nothing mattered anymore.

The sorcerer walked straight to where she was. He neither spoke to her nor looked at her. "Take her to the high altar," he said to the goblins. "Chain her with chains. Then leave her. Ebed Ruach will guard her. At midnight she will be offered to the Lord of Darkness."

Lisa scarcely heard him. It was as though she was dreaming. One of the goblins gripped her arm with his cold hand and mechanically she let him lead her. Ebed Ruach? Where had she heard the name before? Then out of the corner of her eye she saw Hocoino uncoiling the gold serpent ring from his finger. As he dropped it to the floor the yellow cat landed softly on its feet. Tail in the air, it led the dreary procession toward a tall archway at the western end of the hall. Hocoino turned on his heel and left them.

Neither the cat nor the goblins made a sound as they

walked. Only the silly clicking of Lisa's mother's silver slippers echoed hollowly on the flagged pavement. The hall reminded Lisa of an enormous church with all the pews taken out. As she stared at the altar she recognized there was something wrong. It was as though the church ended, ended in a huge archway. The altar itself was outside under the moon. And what an altar! The nearer they drew the more massive it seemed. Though Lisa did not know it, the altar stood at the center of what once had been an evil city whose buildings had been razed in ancient times by its enemies. Only the stones, the altar and the ancient temple remained. Hocoino had restored the old walls. Beyond it was a vast semicircle of white stones formed by groups of three—two massive uprights connected by a headstone. Dully she realized that the semicircle was similar to pictures of Stonehenge from ancient Britain.

Soon the cool night air was about them and they were walking across the grassy turf between the building and the altar. Only then did Lisa realize how vast the distances were. She kicked off the silly slippers and walked barefoot. Her ankle was almost better but it was easier without shoes. The yellow cat still led the way, one goblin holding her arm and the other two behind her.

The area around the tall white stones seemed huge. It was surrounded in turn by an ancient wall of stone. When she glanced back to see the building they had emerged from, she perceived two things at once. First, the building, whatever it was, was dwarfed by the immense area surrounded by the stones and the wall, and second, instead of being a mere semicircle, the stones formed a complete circle. It enclosed the building and the huge mound they were now ascending to the foot of the altar.

The altar itself had a broad base and tall sides of rough white stone with carvings of every variety—of satyrs, serpents, dragons and of animals and beings that Lisa had never seen before. Some of them could not be clearly seen because of the moonlight and because the stone was weathered. There was strange writing. There were pictures of battles, of chariots, of swords, of demons, of flames, of grotesque distorted faces. There were moons and suns, stars and planets, symbols that looked like zodiac signs and signs she could make nothing of. Somehow she knew that they were unbelievably ancient and must belong to ages long forgotten. As though she was in a daze, she felt the cold stone of steps beneath her feet and followed the yellow cat up to the top where there was the foul odor of things long dead.

"Lie down on your back," Ebed Ruach said to her. Mechanically she did so, staring up at the full moon which was almost directly above her. One by one her wrists and ankles were enclosed in iron manacles and chained to rings on the corners of the altar. The stone beneath her back was rough, cold and slimy with the blood of recent sacrifices. She was shivering uncontrollably. But nothing seemed to matter.

"You may go, now," she heard the cat say to the goblins. "I, Ebed Ruach, will guard the little witch."

A few moments passed in silence. Then the cat spoke again. "My master is rarely wrong. But this time he has made a mistake. I know you have powers. I do not know why you have not chosen to use them. But I must warn you that when the moon sinks to touch the top of the thirteenth stone, Hocoino's knife will divide your body into four quarters. You are to be a sacrifice to the Lord of Deepest Darkness, the master and ruler of us all."

Lisa heard the words but they were only so many

sounds. They didn't seem to be related to her. She no longer cared what the cat did or said. Perhaps if she had known of the battle miles to the south where Kardia, Chocma, Kurt, Wesley, Gunruth, Bolgin, Garfong, wolves, goblins and dwarfs were at that very moment fighting the Battle of Authentio, she might have felt different. As it was she had no feelings at all—except of cold stone and the filth that seemed to be eating into her very heart. She knew she had been foolish to suppose she could trust a wizard. But she no longer cared. She no longer cared about anything.

Ebed Ruach's voice went on. "Since I cannot trust you, I must use the only power available. I must wrap you in my darkness."

Slowly the moon darkened. Twisting her head to either side Lisa could no longer see the ring of stones. A moment later the same dreadful darkness she had known in the dungeon was all around and within her. There was no moon, no sky—nothing but cold and blackness. She was not even sure whether she still had a body or whether her body itself had dissolved in the blackness.

"Am I dead?" The thought hung in her mind like a slowly twisting mobile.

"Am I dead? Perhaps I am. But it doesn't seem to matter. Perhaps that's what it's like to be dead—nothing matters." Her thoughts drifted past one another in the blackness. "Wishes are no good. . . . nothing is real. . . . nothing is real. . . . perhaps *I'm* not real. . . . perhaps there is no *me*. . . . someone said the only real things came from Gaal? . . . Gaal. . . . is Gaal real? . . . what does it matter? . . ."

Somewhere within her came the faintest feeling that something (she was not sure what) did matter. It was like a tiny spark in the deadness of her body and mind. "Gaal ... Gaal ... where had she heard the name? ... The Shepherd ... even the witches said Gaal made real things."

How many hours had she been lying like this? Or was it days? Or months? Or years? How had she gotten here? Struggle as she might she could be certain of nothing now, nothing but the name of Gaal. Slowly from her throat a sound came, "Gaal, Gaal." And then several moments later, "Gaal, give me something real."

There was a change. The feeling inside her, the very faint feeling that something *did* matter grew slightly stronger. And with it came a trembling little hope.

"Gaal, Gaal," she said again. "I don't know you. Can you help me? Will you?"

With a rush all the blackness and hopelessness returned, the numbing cold and the feeling that she wasn't there at all, that she didn't exist, that nothing existed. But by now her lips were working on their own. "Gaal, where are you? Who are you?" She could hear herself saying the words almost as though she were listening to someone else.

Blue. Blue light. Where was it coming from? She opened her eyes and saw far, far above her in the blackness a tiny white thing at the top of a long shaft of the same kind of blue light that had shone from the Mashal Stone. The white thing was fluttering down toward her, and as it came the light grew more beautiful, more intense. Warm tears, the first warm things she had felt, flowed down the sides of her face and into her ears.

Suddenly the sky was clear again, the moon still shining. Great yellow coils of the monstrous serpent, Ebed Ruach, were coiling themselves round her. But the blue light shone brighter than the moon and the fluttering white thing continued to descend like a pigeon.

The serpent's head reared high above her as if to strike at the pigeon and swallow it. But instead the serpent itself began to shrink in size. Quickly it released her and slithered from her range of vision.

The pigeon was now circling ten feet above her head. One by one the manacles fell from her and she sat up, stiff and cold. On the slab beside her she caught a glimpse of something gold. It was the serpent ring, Ebed Ruach, now a piece of metal. Quickly she knocked it off the edge and heard it tinkling and falling down the steps of the altar.

All round her the blue light shone. The white pigeon alighted at her feet. Then it fluttered round the top of the steps as if inviting her to follow. As she stood on the altar to do so she saw what she had not seen before. Beyond the ring of stones and the old wall on a slope that fell downward to a river, there were more buildings in the moonlight. Below them a city lay. But she had hardly time to notice. The white pigeon was fluttering ahead, and as quickly as she could, she followed, down the steps, across the turf toward the dark building. How tired she was, and how cold! But while before she didn't care at all what happened, now she didn't care how tired or cold she was. All she wanted to do was follow the white pigeon and stay in the sphere of soft blue light around it.

Into the dark hallway they went where the smoky lamps burned on. But now a blue radiance lit the hall. Now hopping, now fluttering, the pigeon led her to a huge central pillar. And there it stopped, staring intently at it. Lisa stared too. It was certainly an immense pillar, at least twenty feet wide at its base. Why had they stopped? As she watched she saw the blue light shrinking and growing more intense. Suddenly it shone brilliant and clear on a carved, stone rose, one rose among a bunch of carved, stone roses.

Hardly knowing why she did so, Lisa grasped the rose in her hand. Immediately a section of the stone pillar swung out leaving a great opening that revealed a flight of steps winding into the ground.

She turned to look at the pigeon. But it was gone. The blue light had disappeared. Yet in the winding stairway below her the same blue light was glowing.

Under the circumstances she did the only thing she could do. Carefully placing one foot after another she began to descend. But no sooner had she started than the door in the pillar closed with a hollow boom behind her.

14

The Bridge across the Chasm

It seemed to Lisa that the staircase would never end. Downward, ever downward she went, imagining that she must be getting near the center of whatever world she was in. Although she did not know it, she had begun her descent from the crown of a fairly high hill.

Being broad, the steps were easy to follow. Here and there lights buried in the rock lent soft blue radiance to the stairway. Her legs began to get decidedly wobbly, but she did not hesitate. The farther she descended the more alive she felt. The hollow bang of the door in the pillar had not seemed to shut her in, but to shut *out* all the horrible things of the past hours. It had shut out jinns and dungeons, sorcerers, goblins and altars. And though she was sorry the white pigeon had not come with her, she felt freer than she had for many hours.

Of one thing she was sure—the blue light was something good. She had been terribly mistaken not to trust Kardia. It had been the blue light of the Mashal Stone that had shown her the way things really are. She remembered with feelings of shame and regret the strange courage that had flooded her heart when she found the pendant in Kardia's cell. There had been blue light around the pigeon and blue light showing her the secret handle in the stone pillar. Even now she was surrounded by this same blue light. In spite of her tiredness, hunger, cold and weakness, a little song began to bubble up in her heart.

Blue light is true light,
Conquering even the blackness of night,
Tum-te-tum, tum-te-tum, tum-te-tum-tee
Da-dee-da, da-dee-da, da-dee-da-dee.

She hummed and sang gaily in time to her feet on the steps, forgetting about the length of the journey down to the bottom, concentrating on how she would get words of the last two lines to work out.

Blue light is true light,
Conquering even the blackness of night,
Lighting my footsteps from up on the wall
Tum-te-tum, tum-tum, tee-tum-tum, tum-tall.

She stopped singing and frowned. "What rhymes with *wall*? Tall? Ball? Fall? Call?" There was no end of words that could rhyme, but none of them satisfied her. Then with a heartbeat there came the word she had cried out on the altar. *Gaal.*

Blue light is true light,
Conquering even the blackness of night,
Lighting my footsteps from up on the wall
Leading me, leading me onwards to Gaal.

She stopped and her heart beat loudly. "I'm not sure I want to meet Gaal." For the first time in hours she felt the stickiness of her fingers. She remembered the stains on her face. Suddenly her mother's evening dress felt ridiculous. What on earth would Gaal think of her if she did meet him?

Slowly she renewed her descent. The song was no longer fun, and she tried to put it out of her mind. But the more she tried, the harder she found it. Endlessly it sang through her brain, keeping time with her footsteps the farther she descended.

Blue light is true light,
Conquering even the blackness of night,
Lighting my footsteps from up on the wall
Leading me, leading me onwards to Gaal.

At last she reached the bottom of the stairway to face two passages, one on the right lit with the same blue light that had accompanied her down the stairway and the other turning left. She hesitated.

"You take the left-hand passage now," a voice said from her left. "I have been sent to guide you from this point on."

As she peered into the dim red light she could see the silhouette of a bent old lady leaning on a cane.

"Come, my dear. Don't be frightened."

First by blue
Then by red.
Eat my food
And then to bed.

Lisa stood stock still, trying to see the lady's face. "I can't see properly. Who are you?"

"I am the guide of the tunnels, my dear. Here, let me take your arm and show you the way."

Still the rhyme was running through Lisa's mind. Almost without thinking she repeated it out loud.

Blue light is true light,

Conquering even the blackness of night,
Lighting my footsteps from up on the wall
Leading me, leading me onwards to Gaal.

No sooner had the words left her lips than the blue light around her flared up, penetrating even the left-hand passage. In a flash she saw that what she had taken for an old lady was in fact a huge and ugly spider. Behind the spider a web filled all the passage. But as the blue light faded again only an old lady's silhouette could be seen.

Lisa caught her breath and ran as hard as she could down the right-hand passage. Once she looked over her shoulder, but seeing no one following she slowed to a walk. Finally she stopped, leaned against the wall and stared long in the direction she had come. "It was the blue light that first showed me that Ebed Ruach was a yellow serpent," she said to herself. "I guess my rhyme is right. Blue light *is* true light."

The stone passageway along which she walked had damp, rocky walls and proceeded straight ahead for a couple hundred yards where it divided again, one part curving to the right and the other to the left. "I wish I could find somewhere to sit down and eat," she thought. As she reached the division she saw that the left-hand passage was lit with a bright purple light similar to the light she had seen in the cell when Hocoino appeared.

She paused at the junction and stared down the left-hand passage.

"Blue light is true light," she repeated to herself. Yet she felt a strange curiosity to know what lay down this second left-hand passage. Certainly it looked brighter than the one she was already pursuing. The walls were lined with colored jewellike stones. Moreover, a smell of baking bread assailed her nostrils reminding her how very hungry she was. Warm air brushed the skin of her hands and face as she approached the entrance of the purple tunnel.

"It can't do any harm to go a *little* way along the tunnel just to find out what it's like," she said to herself. "After all I can always turn back if I don't like it." She could only see about ten yards of the passage for it made an abrupt turn to the left ten yards from where she stood.

"Blue light is true light." The words repeated themselves mechanically in her mind, but they did not seem important anymore. The brighter light, the pretty stones, the warm air and above all the smell of baking bread slowly drew her into the left-hand tunnel.

"I'll just go as far as the corner," she told herself. "That can't possibly do any harm. At least I'll be able to see what lies round the corner. Perhaps I can even get something to eat."

Slowly she walked along the short passage. Something inside her protested that she was walking into danger, but she ignored the warning signals. "I won't actually go round the corner," she told herself. "I'll just *peep* round and see what there is to see."

What she saw surprised her very much. She found herself looking into the prettiest little cave which looked for all the world like the inside of a kitchen. There was a carpet on the floor, a table with a snowy white tablecloth, a loaf of steaming fresh bread and a wooden chair.

It was too much for Lisa. "Surely nothing can go wrong now," she said. "I'll just eat some of the bread before going back along the proper tunnel."

Quickly she entered the cave, sat down on the chair and reached for the loaf. The crust was crisp. She breathed deeply the warm, fresh smell of bread. It never occurred to her to question where the bread had come from or who had put it there.

She picked up the knife, smiled to herself and began to cut the loaf. Immediately the cave was plunged into darkness, and the loaf and the knife in her hands dissolved into thin air. She sprang to her feet and tried to find her way out of the cave. She groped for the table in front of her only to find there was no table. She felt for the chair behind her, but it too was gone.

"The walls," she said, "if only I can find the walls I shall feel my way out." With her hands stretched out she walked toward the right-hand wall. Two steps—no wall. Four steps—still no wall. "I must be going the wrong way," she thought to herself as she changed direction. But nowhere, however far she walked in whatever direction could she find any wall to touch. Her hands and legs were shaking. What had happened to the small cave? Suddenly, in the dark, she had found herself in a vast area of nothingness. Again and again she told herself, "There *must* be walls. I'll just keep walking in one direction."

Of course you will say she was walking in circles—and you may be right—but if so, they were very big circles, much bigger than the little cave she had been in. She was hopelessly lost and in the dark.

"It's not my fault," she said anxiously to herself. "How could I have known what would happen? It's not fair. I only went a tiny little way from the blue passage. Gaal (whoever he is) must be real *mean*."

She sat down in a blackness which extended endlessly in all directions. Her first angry outburst had passed. A more realistic grasp of her folly began to dawn on her mind. "I ought never to have left it for a second," she said biting her lip to keep back her tears. "If ever I get back to it again I'll never, *never* leave it. But how will I get back?" How had she gotten away from the darkness before? Was it when she called on Gaal? But would Gaal answer her this time? Perhaps he would be angry about her willful folly. After all, she had called him mean a few minutes before. But she had no choice.

"Gaal," she breathed softly, "I still don't know you. I've been stupid again. Please help me."

For a few moments nothing happened. Then far above her the thin blue pathway of light shone and with it came the fluttering white pigeon. As it reached her again, it fluttered and hopped ahead of her so that the two of them walked forward in a bubble of blue light. Relief and gratitude filled Lisa's body and limbs. "Oh, *thank you,* Gaal," she said. "Little bird, did Gaal send you?" But the pigeon said nothing. It only hopped and fluttered in front of her.

The walk seemed a surprisingly long one.

"Surely we must be at the junction of the two tunnels by now," Lisa said half to the pigeon and half to herself. Yet on and on they went for almost half an hour until Lisa perceived somewhere ahead of them the same blue light that surrounded the pigeon.

A few moments later she stood once again where the tunnel with the blue light divided from the shorter one with the purple light. The pigeon had vanished, but nothing else had changed. The same warm air came from the left-hand tunnel and with it the same smell of fresh bread.

But this time the smell of bread horrified her. Her flesh crawled with fear. She never did find out what had gone wrong but vowed to herself as she set out determinedly that never again would she be lured away from the tunnel with the blue light.

If she had been hungry, cold and tired when she set

out, she was even more so now. In addition her bare feet were blistered and sore. Yet she was glad to be once again in the tunnel with the blue light. In fact she began to hurry along it. But in her mind the question kept hammering itself, "How much farther will I have to go? Does it go forever?" Once she breathed again, "Gaal, (there must *be* a Gaal), please make it end fast." Then to her dismay she saw ahead of her yet a third division in the tunnel.

"Well, at least I'll know which one *not* to take this time," she said. "I don't care what smells there are or how pretty the tunnel is. If it doesn't have *blue* light I won't follow it.

But her resolve was badly shaken when she reached the division. To be sure the tunnel that veered left had green light with no other attraction. It was the blue tunnel that frightened her. She could see that soon a chasm opened up, and that to cross it she would have to walk along a narrow roughhewn log about as long as Grosvenor Avenue was wide.

There was no point in pursuing the other tunnel. She knew by now that it would lead her falsely. But the chasm? She crept to the edge of it and peered down cautiously. It glowed with a soft red light. She saw that it was deep but did not dare lean forward to see *how* deep.

Stepping back she knelt, then lay down flat and inched her way forward until her head was over the edge. What she saw made her sick with fear. She could not see the bottom. The sheer walls of the chasm seemed to stretch down endlessly. As she stared at the vast drop beneath her she began to feel not only sick but dizzy. Tremblingly she pulled herself back and stood up again, well back from the chasm's mouth. How was she to get across?

In the distance, on the other side of the chasm, she saw that someone was walking toward her. Whoever it was walked with a swinging stride, vigorous and strong. As he (she was sure it must be a he) drew closer, she could see that he wore a simple white robe and that his hair and beard were also white. This puzzled her, for he walked with the vigor of someone young and strong. His back was straight and his shoulders broad. A sword in a scabbard hung from a gold belt around his waist. "Perhaps he's very blond," she thought to herself. "It's hard to tell in this light. But in any case, maybe he can help me over that awful log." The man was soon approaching the far end of the chasm. When he got there he stood and smiled at her. His hair *was* white and his beard too. But his brown eyes were young. And so was his face. Or was it?

Afterward when she tried to describe his face, she could never do so. It was young yet it was old, very, very old. It was merry yet it spoke of untold sorrows. It was kind yet it was stern; tender yet incredibly tough; gentle yet as strong as steel. As she stared at him across the chasm she felt both terribly glad to see him and terribly afraid. She was so afraid in fact that for the moment she forgot her terror of the chasm.

"Lisa, you must cross the bridge."

His voice was warm and deep. He was not scolding her, just stating a fact. Yet she knew he was also giving her an order.

"Who are you?" She already knew but she had to ask.

"I am the Shepherd, Gaal."

"You don't look like a shepherd. Where's your shepherd's crook? Where are your sheep?"

"Anthropos is one of my sheep."

"But Anthropos is a country."

"Countries are my sheep but so are you . . . if you want to be."

...she saw that someone was walking toward her...

If she wanted to be?

A rush of feeling rose from the soles of her tired, sore feet to the crown of her head. Oh, *how* she wanted him to be her Shepherd! Somehow he was more comforting than ten Uncle Johns all rolled into one. Tired, hungry, weary and a little frightened too, she longed to belong to the man on the other side of the chasm.

But instantly she was aware of two things. Could he see how dirty she was? How sticky? How ugly? Did he really know that she had once said there was no Shepherd? Did he know she had been ready to side with the magician and to betray Kardia? The second thing that frightened her was the chasm. He made no attempt to cross it, but stood on the far side waiting for her.

"Do you want me to be your Shepherd, Lisa?"

She hung her head. "Yes."

"You don't sound very happy with the idea."

"I'm scared. You might not want me if you knew. . . ."

"If I knew about your sticky hands? And your smudgy face? If I knew you had said I didn't exist? If I knew you wanted to join Hocoino and said you hated your Uncle John? I know all these things, Lisa, yet I would still like you to be my sheep. The question is, Do you want *me* to be your Shepherd?"

Lisa's head was still bent. "Will I have to cross the chasm?"

"Yes."

"I'm scared to."

"I know. But I won't let you fall."

"The log may not be steady."

"I put it there myself. It's as steady as the rock on both sides of the chasm."

Lisa looked again at the wood and saw something she had not noticed before. On the far side there was a bar, resting in a slot in the rock. The rough bridge was a T shape, with the crosspiece at the T at the far end.

"I'm scared. I really am scared. You don't know what it's like. . . ."

"I *do* know. I know the terror in your heart. But I will never let you fall."

Lisa was trembling. Somehow she knew that behind her lay everything in her past, not only the ugly and shameful things that had happened in Anthropos, but all that she was and had been.

"What if you're not real? What if you're only another of my wishes like Hocoino or Uncle John?"

"In that case I won't be able to help you. If you stumble on the log you will fall. But I am real and I will not let you fall."

"How can I *know* whether you can help me or not, whether you're real or merely my wish?"

"Only by crossing the chasm."

"And if I fall?" She could scarcely say the words so fiercely did her heart beat.

"I will reach out and catch you."

Lisa remembered a game she had played as a child, a game which you may have played yourself, of falling backward, trusting the person behind you to catch you. But this was far, far worse.

She hated to say she didn't see how he could. "But the gap is much wider than your arms."

"Is it?"

"It sure looks like it."

"Lisa, look at me!"

Lisa lifted her head and looked at his amazing face. He held her eyes in his.

"Lisa, do you think I would let you fall?"

She gazed at him steadily. As she did so something was

born in her that had never been there before. Suddenly she knew how groundless, indeed how silly her fears had been.

"No. You wouldn't let me fall. You wouldn't *ever* let me fall."

"Then keep looking at me and walk forward. That's right! Now a little to the left. Good. Now put your right foot forward." She felt wood under her foot, solid wood, but she kept her eyes on Gaal. "Keep looking at me, Lisa. Walk toward me. That's right. Keep on walking."

Never for a moment did she take her eyes from Gaal's face—never, that is, until she was about two feet from him. Then it occurred to her that she must be just about across the bridge. The temptation to look down to see became too great.

Instantly she realized her mistake. Endlessly below the thin bridge a vast gulf fell downward. With a scream she swayed dizzily and knew that nothing could prevent her from plunging into it. Wildly she waved her arms in an effort to maintain her balance. One foot slipped and she found herself falling sideways.

Strong hands gripped her arms. Strong arms lifted her clear of the rough wood. Suddenly she was pressed against Gaal's soft white robe and found his arms around her, holding her close. She shut her eyes tightly, felt him lift her and walk several paces away from the chasm.

Then he set her down, still holding her closely.

"It is never good to look down."

"No, Gaal."

"But you are safe now."

"Yes, Gaal."

Still she buried her face in his robe and clung to him. There was a perfume about him, something like the smell of freshly sharpened cedarwood pencils which she found infinitely comforting.

"Am I safe now?"

"Perfectly safe."

"Is it near the end of the tunnel?"

"Almost."

"Can I open my eyes?"

"If you want to. But look up, don't look down."

What she saw when she looked up she never forgot as long as she lived. The same strong face was smiling down at her as though she were the only person in the world. Tears spilled from his brown eyes and ran down his cheeks like a spring shower in the sunshine.

15
A Second Council of War

The Hall of Wisdom had grown bigger. Wesley and Kurt knew it the moment they took their seats on the left of Chocma's throne and saw the greater numbers of Matmon and Koach that filled it. They could see that the pillars were taller, the walls farther apart, the windows bigger and the ceiling higher.

"It was full *last* time we were here," Wesley said to Chocma, "but there are far more dwarfs and wolves here than before. It's as though the hall is a balloon being blown up."

Chocma chuckled. "So that is what you think, is it?" she asked. "You actually think the hall has grown. In fact, it has not. It is your ability to see that has grown. You could not see its real size before. Even now I suspect you do not really see how big it is. It is so big that the whole of Anthropos—in fact the whole world and a good many more worlds beside—could reside inside the Hall of Wisdom."

What she said still made no sense to Wesley. Like Kurt he was still puzzled how an invisible castle (you would hardly call it a cottage) could be so big on the inside. "Wisdom looks small from the outside yet is infinitely large inside," Chocma had said. Wesley shrugged his shoulders and gave up on the problem of how it happened. He had seen with his own eyes that the cottage was a billboard. He had also seen with his own eyes that it was simply enormous on the inside.

But there were other remarkable properties of Chocma's cottage. Three days had passed since the Battle of Authentio. The dead had been buried, the wounded treated and the fighters rested and fed. What had amazed Kurt and Wesley just as much as the inside size of the hall was the infinite quantity and variety of food with which Chocma could feed and refresh an army. If you remember that everywhere else in Anthropos drought, famine and starvation devastated the lives of the people, you will realize what a remarkable place the cottage was. Both boys were delighted by the healing power of the Pool of Truth. Kurt's shoulder, agonizing after it had been pierced by the goblin's flaming dart, had been cleaned and healed after another tingling and painful dip.

Silence descended on the gathering as Kardia rose from his seat at Chocma's right. He looked at them all in a new way. There was pride in his eyes and joy on his face.

"My very dear friends and my loyal subjects," he said, "I thank you all for your part in the victory that was granted us at Authentio. Any goblins remaining in Anthropos are few indeed. You all fought with valor and courage. More important our victory confirms the rumor that Gaal is indeed somewhere in Anthropos."

Both Matmon and the Koach were looking expectantly at him. The newly enlisted soldiers gazed at him from immediately below the platform. Sir Nocham's face shone with happiness. Kurt, seeing the multicolored sunlight shining diagonally down between the seven pillars upon the multitude, drew a deep breath at the wonder of it all.

Our greatest danger," Kardia continued, "will be in the flush of our victory. Do not suppose that the rest of Anthropos will fall into our hands as easily as Authentio. The army opposing us is greater by far than we who are gathered here."

A low murmuring spread throughout the ranks of the Matmon. The fiery Inkleth leaped up and waved his arms. "Your majesty, we care not how great the force may be! We are not afraid. No one can withstand us. Let us advance at once to destroy them."

There were howls from the wolves and shouts from the ranks of the Matmon. Kurt's heart beat furiously.

"Be quiet! Sit down! Don't interrupt!" several Matmon called out.

Inkleth was still standing, his flaming hair lit by sunlight. He would have gone on speaking but the king addressed him directly.

"I have no question about the courage of my Matmon, least of all of you, Inkleth, having witnessed your valor on the hill below Authentio. But there we faced only goblins and a handful of men. To retake this land we face not only a whole army of men but the great man-eating ghouls with their long fangs and their red, hairy bodies; we shall have to fight seven-headed ogres stronger than any beings known; we shall face flame-throwing furies and be assaulted by flying harpies. We shall also be pursued and harried by the giant bloodhounds whose height is as the height of horses and who tear and devour whatever stands in their path. Moreover, who knows whether the Qadar might not also assault us? For centuries none of these creatures have been known in our kingdom. But now they are coming from the deep places of the earth and from distant lands to seize this kingdom for the Lord of Deepest Darkness."

Inkleth sat down and for a few more seconds murmurings and growls could be heard again. Kardia continued.

"Among the men who have sworn allegiance to Hocoino are some who fight fiercely and well. She whom I fear most is a woman, the Lady Sheriruth. I have word that she is followed by five thousand archers, all mercenaries from afar, whose poison-tipped arrows cause the wounded to spend the rest of their lives in a sleep filled with dreams of desire till they waste away consumed by their own dreams."

There was now complete silence. All of them had watched the slow deaths of dwarfs, wolves or humans wasting to skeletons, their eyes staring wide and their lips fixed in a smile so enchanted by their dreams that they would not wake even when they could. Solemnity swept over the Matmon like the shadow of a cloud across a field.

"Sir Gregorio Gaavah has likewise under his command seven hundred knights who have sworn to die rather than bow their necks or their knees to any being."

All of them knew, too, of the contemptuous defiance of Sir Gregorio, a knight who scorned High Emperor, man and beast. "Who is Gaal?" he had once asked. "If he exists, which I doubt, I will make *him* bow the knee to *me*." It was rumored that Sir Gregorio Gaavah had sworn allegiance to the Lord of Deepest Darkness. Personally I doubt the truth of the rumor. What I *do* know is that long ago he had urged Kardia to renounce his allegiance to Gaal and to Gaal's father, the High Emperor. He had been the first to defect from Kardia and to vow to fight him to the death.

"And if 'twere not enough to fight against ghouls, ogres, harpies, dream arrows and the followers of Sir Gregorio, we shall face Sir Percy Pachad, who likewise commands two thousand spearmen whose spear wounds drive man, Matmon or beast out of their wits so that they flee, believing all hell pursues them, tortured by terror till they drop dead."

To Wesley it sounded ghastly. If Lisa were in the hands of such horrifying people, what chance did they have of seeing her again? His heart sank lower and lower as he listened to Kardia. Once again his it's-all-my-fault feeling began to trouble him. The colored sunlight from the windows seemed to grow darker as Kardia went on speaking.

"My dear followers, I would have no right to call on you to face such formidable foes. But my kingdom belongs to Gaal, and these are not only my foes but foes of Gaal. Whether therefore we live or die we must fight them. But we shall not sell our lives cheaply. The question is not *whether* we should assault such enemies, but *when, where* and *how*."

For a few moments pandemonium broke loose. I happen to know that Kardia already talked things over with Chocma so that he had a pretty good idea what kind of battle plan to follow. In any case most of the suggestions were silly and came from the younger folk among the Koach and the Matmon.

At first you couldn't hear what anyone was saying because everyone was talking, or shouting, at once. Kardia had to raise his hands and yell (Wesley thought he had never heard such a loud voice), and even then he could not get people to speak one at a time. You know what it's like when a lot of people are all bursting to tell about the most brilliant idea in the world even though all their ideas are different.

Finally a sort of chanting took on among the younger dwarfs which drowned out all the other noises. "*Tun*nel, *tun*nel. *Let's* dig a *tun*nel. *Tun*nel, *tun*nel. *Let's* dig a *tun*nel." They kept it up so long that it got on Wesley's nerves. Eventually Kardia got them quieted down.

"Very well," he said, "if we are to dig a tunnel I presume that you mean we must dig one under the walls of the city. The best defended and most strategic area is the Ancient City, Bamah, in the northwest. It is there that Hocoino has rebuilt the ancient temple and strengthened the walls. What is your will about where the tunnel should start?"

Once again everybody had a different idea. Digging and mining, as you have probably been told already, is something the Matmon know all about. They had suggested a tunnel originally because digging tunnels was one of the things they did best. Give a dwarf a pick and some rock and he'll start hacking away in no time. But the Matmon usually dig for metals, especially gold, so they don't give much thought about *where* they dig just so long as there's something to dig *for*. Naturally most of them (remember the younger ones did most of the talking) thought of places where gold or diamonds or something of the sort could be mined. Someone even suggested that if the tunnel were dug through the right kind of rock they could all make themselves rich as well as winning the war.

Kardia listened for a while then held up his hand for

silence. "How many of you know of the Qadar?"

The silence grew ominous. Everyone feared the terrible night warriors. Wesley and Kurt, remembering the boiling blackness of the river and the terrible rush of wind and the unearthly scream, felt the hair on the back of their necks begin to stand up. Kardia went on.

"Daily they grow in numbers and in boldness. How long do you suppose it would take them to find out where you were digging and what your purpose was? To construct a tunnel, a good, wide tunnel that could take horses and their riders, indeed a whole army, would call for the work of hundreds of the Matmon. Would such a beginning escape the eyes of the high-flying night warriors? And do you suppose that they would leave us to dig in peace? Remember, Hocoino doubtless knows already of the Battle of Authentio."

For a moment nobody replied for the answer was obvious to them all. Then Gunruth stood up, his eyes grave and a worried frown wrinkling his brow. "May it please your majesty," he began, "even the eyes of the Qadar rarely pierce the leaves of a forest. The borders of the Forest of Blackness lie two and a half leagues from the walls of the Ancient City of Bamah." He remained standing and Kardia turned to look at Chocma.

"We have word that the elm trees are beginning to wake," she said. "So far they are drowsy and are unlikely to consume a moving being. But we do not know when or whether they will waken more fully. The longer our victory over Hocoino delays, the more awake the evil trees will become."

"My people know the danger of the elm trees, your majesty," returned Gunruth. "It is also known that the ash trees likewise show signs of movement but that oaks sleep more profoundly than ever. Yet we have a treaty with the Duin people who would keep watch over the trees for us. They are nimble and have magical power over the trees so that their value to our cause is great."

"You speak and think well, my good Gunruth," the king replied. "Tell me then how long would it take, working day and night with changing shifts of your people, the Matmon, to dig from the borders of the Forest of Blackness and to emerge inside the walls of Bamah?"

Gunruth wrinkled his forehead even more, and there was another hush in the hall. "It would take between three and four months," he replied finally.

A low murmur ran over the assembly.

"Already we face superior forces," Kardia replied evenly, "and every day they receive reinforcement from the realms of darkness. The ghouls grow in numbers and strength. It is rumored that a group of giant bloodhounds are ravaging their way toward the capital from far in the west. The growth in the numbers of Qadar is the most fearful matter of all. Hardly a night passes but one or two more fly across our borders, arriving from the distant Halls of Deepest Darkness. In three months' time the forces against us will be insuperable." He paused for a moment and then turned to Chocma. "My lady," he said bowing gravely to her, "all of us would deem it a favor if you would impart to us some of that wisdom for which this hall is famed."

He sat down and Chocma, her voice sounding clearly to the farthest parts of the hall began to speak from her throne beneath the seventh pillar of wisdom. "If we had the help of the five hundred enchanted knights," she began, "our forces would be more even. Each of them is worth six or seven of the enemy. Their shields, like those of the Matmon are covered with aman and the swords and spears are of finest tempered logos. Again, if we had in our possession the Book of History and True Wisdom, its light could destroy even a night rider. With it I could slay many more of our more unnatural enemies than with the smaller book I now possess. If his majesty, King Kardia, had in his hands his orb, the gates of the Lower City, Nephesh, would open to him as he advanced toward it. The light from its rubies and emeralds have power to blast the gate apart. How we would invade the Ancient City, Bamah, I know not."

Inkleth again had jumped to his feet and cried out, "*If*, my lady, *if, if, if!* We do not have the five hundred enchanted knights. The key to the Cave of Qava lies in the enchanted Tower of Geburah, and your ladyship knows right well that neither man nor beast, Koach, Matmon nor any inhabitant of Anthropos can approach within a mile of the tower so powerful is the magic that guards it. Even your ladyship would be powerless to go there. Let us dig! We have picks. We have shovels. We have muscles. But books, orbs, keys and knights we have none, nor will have until our enemies are defeated!"

Chocma began speaking the moment he stopped. "We can have all these things, my good Inkleth. We can have them all and that very soon. It is true that no inhabitant of Anthropos can pierce the power of the magic that surrounds the tower. But here in the Hall of Wisdom we have with us their lordships Wesley and Kurt, neither of whom are inhabitants of Anthropos but who have come from other worlds through a proseo comai stone and have been brought here by Gaal, I doubt not, for this very purpose."

Wesley's pulse began to accelerate and Kurt drew in a quick breath. Neither of them understood exactly what was involved, but clearly a most unusual adventure was being suggested for them. Wesley hoped so because he still felt very responsible for Lisa. He wanted badly to do something to rescue her. Kurt hoped so because adventures were fun. After all, they had come through their first battle very well.

But Inkleth had not finished. No one likes to have his or her ideas turned down. So you mustn't imagine that Inkleth was wholly bad. He had certainly fought bravely at the Battle of Authentio and had been the first to volunteer his people. But Inkleth had his weaknesses, one of which nearly ruined them later on. He was also as hotheaded as his bright shock of red hair suggested.

"Pshaw! Children! What can children do? This is a battle for experienced warriors!"

Kardia interrupted him. "Inkleth, Inkleth, my respected Matmon warrior, there are things that children can do that warriors cannot. Surely you know how their lordships helped Sir Nocham in the Battle of Authentio. Have you forgotten that I was set free from a dungeon not by a warrior but by a little maid, the lady Lisa, who at this very hour is in the hands of Hocoino?"

Inkleth's face grew as red as his hair. For a moment no one was sure what he was going to do. Then he said, "Your majesty is right. I spoke in haste. But 'tis a dangerous mission we would send them on. Might I crave your majesty's permission to guide them, at least as far as I can?"

The king paused. Inkleth was impulsive and might prove unreliable. Moreover, Kardia had not recovered fully from his mistrust of Inkleth. Much hung on the success of the boys' mission. Yet it was important that he show confidence in Inkleth.

"Gladly, my good Inkleth. I willingly accept your offer of service. But beware of your hasty spirit. It can play you false."

Inkleth's face remained red, but whether from pride or from a sense of triumph it was impossible to say. As for Kurt, he bit his lip saying, "I guess the mirror was wrong."

There was a lot more discussion after this but I shall not bore you with what everyone said. They all agreed it would be best not to attack either the capital city, Nephesh, or the Ancient City, Bamah, that lay above it. Instead they would gather on the Heights of Rinnar, to the west of the two cities, with the idea that Hocoino's forces would be lured out of the cities to attack them. (Check it on the map so you can see how their plan would work.)

You see, if you are going to have a battle, you should always try to choose the place *you* want for the battle, the place that will favor you, not your enemy. And the Heights of Rinnar could be attacked only from one side. It was a beautiful spot to fight from for the enemy would have to climb up a hill to attack. From the inexhaustible food stores in the House of Wisdom, they could take enough food to last them for a month. If they could hold the attacking forces for a day or two until the enchanted knights were set free or until Chocma could use the Book of History and True Wisdom as a weapon against their more evil foes, there would be real hope of victory. An air of hope and excitement could be felt throughout the Hall of Wisdom.

"Let us to bed that we all may be refreshed," Kardia said. "At dawn chief Inkleth and my lords Wesley and Kurt will set out on their perilous journey. May the mercy of Gaal protect them. There is room for all to sleep. Let none leave the cottage for no evil eye can see us here. The cottage itself is invisible to evil eyes. At noon tomorrow we will advance north to the Heights of Rinnar."

The Koach and the Matmon rose from their places and stretched. They had been sitting or, in the case of the Koach, lying for a long time. Suddenly with a crash one of the great windows on the north side of the hall burst open and in with a draft of cool night air swept a flying horse that circled over their startled faces, bearing two women on his back.

16

The Bayith of Yayin

Throughout the rest of her life Lisa often thought about her walk with Gaal to the door leading out of the hillside to the Bayith of Yayin. As they walked hand in hand down the dimly lit corridor she grew more confused. From somewhere inside her a song of joy was rising, joy that she could hold Gaal's hand and walk with him. Yet shame threatened to strangle her song of joy. The dimness hid her burning cheeks. Never in her life had she felt so ugly, so dirty, so messy. And the farther they walked, the uglier, dirtier and messier she felt. But with every step too the song sang itself more fiercely.

She remembered how she had buried her face in Gaal's white robe and stole glances sideways at him to see whether any of the smudges had rubbed off to soil it. But as far as she could tell there were no smudges. The robe was alive with cleanness, a cleanness more like fresh mountain streams than sterile hospital sheets. Even the air around him was clean, but again it was the cleanness that reminds you of the smell after a thundershower, not of kitchen floors scrubbed with Lysol.

But the cleanness, far from giving her pleasure, only made her more aware of her messiness. Her mother's favorite evening dress seemed more ridiculous than ever. She would have felt better wearing her old jeans. With a start she remembered too the foul blood over which she had lain on the altar and which must now be covering her back. With her free hand she touched the back of her hair to discover that it was indeed slimy and sticky. She shuddered. Then staring at her hand in the dim blue light she saw it was smeared with a dark brown mess.

Yet Gaal had wrapped his strong arms round her. He had hugged her to himself. He had lifted her bodily to carry her away from the edge of the chasm. Surely some of the foulness must have soiled his sleeves; but she could see no sign of it. She stared at the hand with which he had touched her hair and shuddered.

An idea came into her head which made her heart beat with fear and shame. She felt an urge to wipe her soiled hand on the sleeve of his robe. She knew it would be wrong, like a mechanic wiping greasy hands on a customer's new suit. Yet struggle as she might she could not rid herself of the idea.

She stared in fascination at the long white sleeve above the hand that held hers. The fingers of her free hand itched to touch it, to soil it, to smear the ugly substance on her fingers over it. The idea was shocking and she fought it back, but she could not overcome it.

In horror she watched her hand rise against her bidding and move to touch the sleeve. Convulsively she seized the loose cloth and clung to it as they walked to-gether. Her hand began to burn. Then she wiped her palm as she let her hand slide down and then took it away. Palm and fingers stung with fiery pain that lasted several minutes.

But the sleeve remained purest white. As she stared at her hand it was, if not clean, a lot cleaner than it had been before. Most of the foulness had gone. Yet not a trace of it could be seen on his sleeve. He simply continued to walk ahead as though he was unaware of what she had done. Then the song in her heart burst out so loudly that she almost wondered whether he could hear it. It was a song whose beautiful words she could not understand and whose music was wild and free. And the voice that sang was like the voice of Gaal yet like her own voice too.

She stared repeatedly at her hand and at his sleeve. What had happened to the filthiness? Was Gaal a person who couldn't be dirtied? Did dirt burn away to nothing when it touched him? The more she thought, the more she marveled. Gaal was not just clean. He was cleanness itself. And the more she marveled, the more her heart sang its wild song.

By now she could see that the tunnel ended in a flat wall of rock. Gaal walked steadily toward it until they both stopped face to face with its smooth solidity. She looked up to see him staring down at her face.

"There is a door ahead of us," he said. "You must com-mand it to open in my name."

She could see no door. "In your *name?*"

"Yes, in my name."

"Will it open?"

"Of course."

She felt very silly. But after all there was only Gaal

there to see her. She looked at him again but his face was grave. Then looking back at the rock she drew a deep breath and said firmly and clearly, "Open in the name of Gaal!"

Slowly, silently and to her great astonishment a whole wall swung out to reveal a soft black sky in which a pale moon, much larger than our moon, was swimming gently toward the horizon. The door of rock in the form of a great ellipse must have been at least a yard thick, weighing thousands of tons. Yet it moved like a cat stalking soundlessly across a carpet. The doorway was wide enough for horsemen to ride through six abreast and high enough so they wouldn't need to bend down. This is in fact what Lisa saw happen a little later. But I am getting ahead of myself.

Filled with awe Lisa passed with Gaal through the opening and out onto the banks of the River Rure. Turning, she stared into the corridor behind them. Gaal was smiling. "Rocks and caverns have never been able to hold me," he said. "Why don't you command it to close?"

"Can I?"

"If you bid it to do so in my name."

She stared again at the passage and at the massive door of rock. They looked as if they would be there forever and that nothing could make them go.

"Close . . . in the name of Gaal!" she breathed softly. As silently and as smoothly as it had opened, the rock glided back into place. They found themselves staring at a grassy hillside on which no trace of rock—no crack, no smallest evidence of a tunnel—could be seen. No dream of a corridor could have been more vivid. Yet no hillside could have been more solid and earthy. The door of rock was like the ending of a story and the closing of a book.

"Mark well where you stand," Gaal said to her softly.

"You will see above us, immediately over the center of where the opening was, that there is a tree. It is the only tree on this side of the river below the walls of the ancient and evil city of Bamah. Behind us as we face the wall is the River Rure." The tree was a dead tree whose two sinister arms stretched greedily into the night sky. She was sure she would never forget it. "At this place you may command the tunnel to open in my name whenever you are doing my bidding."

Beyond the tree Lisa could see the massive walls of what Gaal had called the ancient and evil city of Bamah. To the south, on her left, she saw in the moonlight that the enormous wall turned eastward to cross the river. A massive portcullis was down, blocking any possible river traffic. Between the portcullis and the wall that went south, an immense gate filled an archway.

"Is that the gate into Bamah?" she asked.

"No, Lisa. Through that gate you could never get into Bamah. Bamah is the ancient and evil city, doomed to be destroyed. The gate does not lead into Bamah but into Nephesh, the capital city of Anthropos. The wall above us here turns westward on this side of the gate to separate Bamah from Nephesh. Very soon I intend Kardia to take his proper place in Nephesh, but Bamah I intend to destroy forever. Only a lake will remain where Bamah now stands."

"You mean there are *two* cities?"

"Yes, little one—two cities side by side, one above the other; one to the north and the other to the south; one ancient, evil, and ruined, Bamah, the other younger and cleaner, Nephesh, whose unhappy inhabitants are practically starving. Listen to them, Lisa. Listen to their cries."

For a moment Lisa heard nothing. Then, so close that

it could have been in the air above her, she heard the feeble crying of a child. She could also hear the sound of a mother crooning mournfully.

"Sleep, little one. Daddy will bring bread. Daddy will bring bread in the morning. Sleep, dearest. Don't cry. Oh, Gaal! Why must she suffer like this? How can I feed a child when there is no bread and when my breasts are dry?" And all the time the fretful crying of the child continued.

But now there were other sounds. Like the noises of an ugly orchestra slowly rising to a discordant crescendo— the cries of babies and young children, the shouts of quarreling men and women, sounds of blows and of slamming doors, pleadings, moanings, wailings, sighings —rising and falling yet ever increasing in volume and swirling in the dark air round their heads.

Lisa buried her face in Gaal's robe. "What is it?" she cried, "What is it? Please make it stop!"

Slowly the sounds abated.

"Some of them have already died, Lisa. Others still are starving." The look of pain on his face was indescribable.

"Why are they starving?"

"Because there has been no rain in Anthropos for several years."

"Is that because of Hocoino?"

"It is because of Hocoino."

"Did *he* stop the rain?"

"No, Lisa. He does not possess that sort of power."

"Then who did?"

"I did."

By now they had turned and were facing the river. Lisa could see from the wide strips of dried mud on each side of the river that there must have been much less water in it than usual.

"You did? Why?" She looked at his troubled face.

"I did it to save Anthropos from a fate much worse than starvation."

Lisa remembered the cold, deathlike face of Hocoino slashed by his thin red lips. She remembered the burning eyes of proud hate and she thought that she could understand just a little bit what Gaal meant. A country governed by Hocoino would know only terror and evil. But ruled by a Kardia who served Gaal, justice would flourish and peace would return. She shuddered and tried to forget the sounds she had heard.

"Come, Lisa." He took her hand again utterly careless of whether or not it was dirty or sticky, and began to walk toward the river to tread on the dry, cracked mud beside it and to stare over mud and water, silent and still in the moonlight. "What do you see, Lisa?"

"The river . . . and all this dry, cracked mud."

"Look ahead of you. Look closely."

Was she imagining it? A mist was rising, so faint that she could not be sure whether her eyes deceived her. Soon she was more certain. It *was* mist—mist that rose and spread outward before them, mist filled with red sunlight that glowed from inside it, mist that moved toward them and enveloped them in light, mist that blotted out the night sky until when they looked up they saw the red sky of dawn in place of black. And when they looked down they saw grass in place of mud. When they looked in front of them they watched the mist clear away to reveal a palace of marble lit with rose-colored light. The steps of the palace invited them to enter a luxurious interior where they could see jeweled, fluted columns and banners of scarlet and gold.

"Where are we?"

"We're on the muddy banks of the River Rure."

"Yes, but what is this place?"

"It is my Bayith of Yayin."

"I beg your pardon?"

"My *Bayith* of *Yayin*."

"Then we're not beside the river anymore. I can't see any dried mud and I can't see any river."

"No, little one. The river, it is true, has disappeared, but it is still here. Instead of seeing the river you see my Bayith."

"You mean the Bayith is not real?"

"It is real, Lisa, and it is everywhere."

"I don't understand. This palace, this Bayith of . . . what did you say?"

"Yayin."

"This Bayith of Yayin . . . it just rose out of the ground . . . out of a mist?"

"No, Lisa. The mist was just your eyesight clearing. My Bayith of Yayin is everywhere—even on the dried banks of a failing river. Come inside with me!"

Still holding her hand he walked over the grass toward the palace. Lisa was saying the strange name over and over in her mind. "His *Bay*ith of Ya*yin;* his *Bay*ith of Ya*yin*." As they approached the marble steps Lisa saw a large white horse with enormous feathered wings extending up and out from behind his neck. The flying horse (for that is what it was) was resting on the grass flicking his tail occasionally. Lisa stared at it fearfully as they passed in front of it. It stared back, and she could have sworn that it winked at her. She felt it was making fun of her, so she turned away, conscious again of her dirty, bedraggled appearance.

Then as she looked up she saw the most beautiful young woman she had ever seen, dressed in a simple white woolen gown with a red satin sash. Thick black tresses fell over her shoulders, tresses as black as her beautiful eyes. A slim gold circlet alight with red stones crowned her. It was then that the horror of her filthiness so filled Lisa with shame that she pulled her hand from Gaal's.

"Please, I can't go inside. Not like I am. I couldn't bear it. Please, Gaal, you must know how I feel. I'm filthy. I'm not fit for your Bayith of Yayin. I'd be ashamed to meet the lady in the entrance way. Please get me clean. I tried to wash in the bathroom by the cell, but the dirt wouldn't come off. The soap was wish soap. Is there some way I can be cleaned and dressed properly?"

"This is one reason I brought you here," she heard Gaal say. "Wash yourself in my pool." He pointed to a marble circle on their right at the foot of the stairway. In the center a column of water rose and fell with a constant splashing. Fiery light from the morning sun shone through the fountain, lending it the same rosy light she had seen in the mist. "It is called the Fountain of Dam."

"Do I need soap?"

"No, Lisa. The water itself will clean you."

Lisa looked at him in bewilderment, but he returned her stare with a smile.

"Do I take my clothes off?"

"No. Just go in as you are."

She walked to the pool and sat on its edge dangling her feet in the water. Coolness soothed their aching.

Lisa never liked getting into cold water gradually. It was always better to get it over quickly. So she pulled out her feet, stood on the edge and plunged head first toward the rosy fountain. For a moment she caught her breath with the cool shock, but almost at once she felt like swimming hard. The water seemed no different from any other water. She swam (she was a good swimmer) up to the fountain and let its tumbling waters splash down on her. Putting one hand up to feel the back of her hair, she found to her surprise that the filthy stuff that had clung to her was gone. She stared at both her hands to find they too were clean.

And in staring at her hands she noticed something else. Her mother's evening dress had had long sleeves. Her arms were still covered, but now a white gown fell from two gold clasps on her shoulder.

Bewildered, she made her way to the side of the pool and, as she left the water, was amazed to discover she was dry. Her new gown was soft and comfortable, falling down to red shoes on her feet. There was a red sash, like the lady's, around her waist, and as she lifted her hand to touch her head she felt a metal circlet around it also like the one of the lady at the top of the steps.

She looked at Gaal. "I *feel* clean. Am I? Really clean?"

"Cleaner than you have ever been in your life."

"And these clothes ... are they *wish* clothes?"

"Do they keep you warm?"

Lisa had just left the cold water yet her skin glowed with warmth. The soft wool gown wrapped her with heat in the cold morning air. "Oh, yes, Gaal. They're warm."

"That is because they are real. They are not wish clothes. They come from the domain of my father."

"What about these pretty shoes? What are they made of? They've taken all the soreness from my feet. They feel like slippers."

"They are shoes of *basar*."

"Shoes of what?"

"Of *basar*."

"And what is basar?"

"Shoes of basar never wear out. They enable the wear-er to run swiftly and surely on my errands."

"Shoes of red basar," she said softly. "And the red sash round my waist?"

"It is called the red sash of qosht. It is handwoven. Qosht is red in the daylight when it can be seen clearly, but in the darkness it shines blue, to show things as they really are."

"It shines?"

"Yes, like the lights in the passageway and like the Mashal Stone."

She thought for a moment. "So I will never need to be in the dark again."

"No, *never,* Lisa."

She felt embarrassed about her next question and blushed as she said, "I ... I have a sort of ... of crown on."

"Yes, little one, it is a crown of ..."

"Of gold?"

"No, of something much more precious than gold, of tiqvah, a metal that endures when all gold will have gone."

"Tiqvah?"

"Yes, little one. Tiqvah. To wear a crown of tiqvah is never to lose heart. With crowns of tiqvah women never despair and with helmets of tiqvah warriors fight on forever."

She removed the crown to stare at the gleaming red stones. They were just like the ones the lady on the stairway wore.

"The jewels are beautiful," she breathed softly. "What are they?"

"They are zabach stones."

She repeated the name slowly. There was something as lovely about their name as about their color. "Zabach stones, zabach stones. Where do they come from?"

"They come from living purity, crushed between rock and fire."

She stared at him, shocked and not comprehending. "And you give them to me? Are there many of these zabach stones? I don't really want to take them from you. It sounds terrible, I mean, someone being crushed between rock and fire."

"There are many, many of them. I give them to everyone who belongs to me. Even my warriors wear helmets of tiqvah set with zabach stones."

It seemed unreal. She had never felt so clean, so warm, so safe and so at peace. But there were too many things to remember—a red sash of qosht that shone blue in the dark; red shoes of basar in which she could run swiftly on Gaal's errands; a crown of tiqvah set with jewels of zabach, a crown that would never let her lose heart. It was all hard to take in. Only moments before she had been ugly, filthy, messy, sore and absurd looking. Now she felt like a princess. And it was not just a wish. It was real.

Out of the corner of her eye she saw the lady, dressed just as she was herself, walking down the steps to meet her. She was smiling and holding out her arms to Lisa. Slowly and hesitantly Lisa walked up the steps to meet her. The lady put her arms round her and held her close. They looked into each other's faces.

"So you are the lady Lisa," the deep voice of the girl said, looking down at her fondly. "You are the one who came from other worlds to rescue him whom I love more than any other."

"Who are you?" Lisa asked.

"I am Suneidesis, bride-to-be of my lord Kardia. I cannot tell you how grateful I am for all you have done for

Kardia whom I love. You set him free, and soon we shall join him."

Shame filled Lisa's heart and she looked down, still held in the arms of Suneidesis. "You don't really know what happened. It wasn't the way you think. You'd hate me if you really knew."

"But I do know." Suneidesis said quietly. "What matters is that you are delivered and have come back to us. I know you would never go back to Hocoino."

Lisa shuddered. She said nothing out loud, but in her mind she was saying, "Never, never, never, never...."

They heard Gaal's deep voice beside them. "The lady Lisa is hungry and weary. We must feed her and let her rest. A feast is waiting for us."

With a joy she had never known before, holding Gaal by one hand and Suneidesis by the other, she walked up marble steps and into the hall of jeweled pillars where a table in the shape of a half-moon had been set with three places, all on one side. There were fruits of every variety—grapes, mandarins, oranges, peaches, apples, pomegranates, pineapples, watermelons, papayas, passion fruit, guavas, figs, dates and fruits of kinds that Lisa had never seen before. There were fresh bread, wafers, cold cuts of meat, cheese of every color and shape, honey, nuts, preserves, wine and milk and so many other foods that Lisa could never remember them all afterward.

"Eat, little one," Gaal said. "Fill your stomach as well as your heart. Eat till you burst!"

"But I thought the land was starving. Can't we take them *this* food?"

"It is starving in the midst of plenty. They will not come to me for rain and food. They go to Hocoino for wishes and illusions. Therefore they starve. They could not see this food, Lisa. Their eyes are blind to it, and their tongues cannot taste it."

For a moment Lisa stared at the food and struggled with the memory of people who were starving. She could not clearly understand what Gaal was saying. But soon the food itself began to blot everything else from her mind, and she found she was eating hungrily.

Lisa's memories were vague about most of what happened during the meal. The food was delicious. She had never before tasted anything like *that* sort of breakfast. And of course the food was real. It made her feel full, slightly too full, but entirely satisfied.

One thing she did recall was looking up at the mass of flags and banners hanging from standards at the top of the columns over their heads. All of them had the same awesome design woven round lettering she had never seen before.

"What are they for?" she asked Gaal.

"They are to hang over my guests," he replied.

"And what do the letters say?"

"They say *abaha*."

"Abaha? What does that mean?"

"It means that I will never desert anyone who eats with me in my Bayith of Yayin. I will stay near them forever."

After that things grew fuzzy in her mind. Several times Lisa found her head dropping forward sleepily. She did know she felt a happy contentment. When she woke up much later that day, she had the vaguest idea that she had been carried in the arms of Gaal, her head resting on his shoulder. She also fancied—or did she dream it— that Suneidesis had tucked her between the sheets of the softest bed she had ever slept in.

17

Murder in the Palace Gardens

During the afternoon of the same day, after the most refreshing sleep she could ever remember, Lisa was sitting beside Princess Suneidesis on the steps of the Bayith of Yayin. The princess said little. To Lisa she seemed sad yet at peace. Lisa wondered who she was and what thoughts lay behind her beautiful expression.

"Your royal highness," Lisa had begun, after working out the wording carefully in her mind.

"Yes, your gracious ladyship?" Suneidesis had replied, a sudden and unexpected twinkle in her dark eyes.

Lisa tried again because she wanted to know the princess. There was no time to work out the wording. "You're teasing me!"

"Your ladyship is unusually perceptive."

"Oh, please!" Lisa suddenly fell silent. She had wanted to learn about Suneidesis' story. But perhaps it was none of her business. They were silent for a moment or two. Lisa felt half ashamed of herself and half angry. It was Suneidesis who broke the tension.

"Tell me how you came here, Lisa."

She looked curiously into Lisa's face. "Is it true that you came through a proseo stone?"

"That's what Kardia said, I mean, that's what his majesty said."

"*Kardia* will do. And if you find it easier to call me 'Sun,' I shan't mind. In fact I prefer it."

"I'm still not sure what a proseo stone *is*. Kardia said it had something to do with Gaal and with wanting Gaal to do something... bring help to Anthropos. But I didn't even know that there *was* an Anthropos, and I certainly didn't plan to help anyone."

"So you came from another world to help us. That has happened before. And Gaal seldom uses powerful people. Neither knights nor kings. 'Tis strange." She paused and seemed to be lost in thought for a minute. "What is your world like? And how did you set out?"

It took Lisa a long time to tell the story, for the princess interrupted her many times with questions. Imagine yourself trying to explain television, credit cards or supermarkets to someone in Anthropos. Lisa was never very sure that her royal highness, the Princess Suneidesis (Sun for short) got a clear picture of our own world. But in the process of trying to understand, the two grew closer and found they liked each other. Their bonds grew deeper when Lisa learned the story of Suneidesis' coming from Playsion to Anthropos.

"I've known Kardia since I was three," she told Lisa. "And we were engaged when I was six."

"When you were *six?*"

"Yes, Kardia was about fifteen at the time."

Lisa thought she remembered about other countries in our own world where similar arrangements were made. "And you love him?"

Suneidesis looked at the ground. "Yes, I love him. I love him greatly. He is all I have since my parents were murdered."

Lisa caught her breath. Suneidesis continued to look down at her feet and did not speak for several minutes. Lisa wondered once again whether she had been tactless in asking questions. At length she said, "I'm sorry, Sun. I didn't mean to hurt you."

"You have not hurt me, Lisa. I find it difficult to speak of. I am yet angry, angry at myself for being such a fool. Both Kardia's parents were dead, killed in a hunting accident not long before Hocoino came to Anthropos. That would be almost seven years ago. Then, three years ago we came here to Anthropos on a special visit. We thought that it would be a sort of holiday though we were really coming to make arrangements about our wedding, Kardia's and mine. We had no idea what Hocoino was like nor how much power he had gained."

She paused for so long that Lisa thought she had forgotten she was there. But eventually Sun continued. "Even I could tell that Anthropos was different. Kardia was different. He was worried. He talked to me little. There had been no rain that year. It was the first year of the great drought. And somehow—I do not understand the details—several of those who were close to Kardia, the Chancellor of the Exchequer, Lord Tushiyyah, and other counselors whose names I have forgotten, were accused of plotting to kill Kardia and take over the kingdom. My parents said the story was false. My father insisted they were all innocent."

"And what happened to them?"

"No one knows. There was a trial. They were condemned to life imprisonment. I cannot say whether they are dead or alive. My father said that the trial itself was a plot—Hocoino's plot—and that all the evidence was false. He had merely wanted to get rid of Kardia's true friends."

"But what happened to your parents?"

"I believe they tried to warn Kardia. My father was certain Kardia's counselors were innocent. He could not trust Hocoino. I think he was afraid of him. I know not what my father said to Kardia, but in the end we spoke heatedly together—my mother, my father, Kardia and I. My father said he would not give me in marriage so long as Hocoino was allowed to remain in Anthropos. He was sure that Hocoino was a sorcerer and that he wanted to rule not only Anthropos but Playsion and all the nearby countries. The only person who could stop him, or so my father thought, was Kardia.

"But Kardia was already helpless. He was angry with my father and . . . oh, I do not like to think on it. They shouted at each other. My mother wept. I wept." Again Suneidesis paused. Then she said, "And that was the last time I saw all three of them . . . together."

"You mean they all disappeared?"

"You could put it that way, but it was more horrible than that. We left Kardia to go to our quarters. We were all bitter with grief. I refused to say good night to my father, something I had never done in my life. It was different with my mother who came to my room. We talked and cried together. But nothing was solved. I was only sixteen, but I loved Kardia and my mother knew it. Yet what could she do?"

Again there was a pause, and again Lisa remained silent.

"Later that night as I watched from my window I saw my parents walking up and down the banks of the River Rure where it flows past the palace gardens. Suddenly I saw my father point to something that he seemed to see in the river. He climbed down the bank and then helped my mother down so that I lost them from view. I never saw them again. The next morning the vice chancellor came to tell me they had both drowned."

"Oh, how horrid!" Lisa cried. She wanted to say more but didn't know what to say.

"If only I had had a chance to make peace with my father. That was the worst thing of all." Suneidesis' voice was flat and emotionless. "Kardia never came to see me. Hocoino came. He said Kardia was too ill to come. I did not want Hocoino to talk to me because I was afraid of him, yet on he spoke. 'I do not wish to add to your highness's grief,' he said, 'but I feel it my duty to tell you that your parents took their own lives. Apparently they were distressed by your determination to marry against their will. They threw themselves in the river.' It was false— but I believed it, believed that my own parents committed suicide!

"But the monster did not stop at this. He said, 'I must also advise your royal highness that his majesty, King Kardia, has become mentally deranged. It would appear that the High Emperor and Gaal the Shepherd have withdrawn their support from Anthropos. The death of your parents plus the loss of the High Emperor's support have robbed his majesty of his reason. I have made temporary arrangements to rule the country until his majesty's mind is restored.'

"You have no idea what my feelings were. I felt it was my fault that my parents had died and my fault that Kardia had been driven out of his mind. And I was alone, terribly alone. The servants in our party returned to Playsion, sent back by Hocoino. That puzzled me too, but I had no way of stopping them. They had departed without my knowledge.

"Every night I had dreams, horrible dreams. In one dream fingers were pointing at me and voices saying, 'It is *her* fault. It is *her* fault,' and I would awake crying and trembling.

"In another dream Hocoino was making me work for money. 'If you can earn a hundred gold pieces in the next three months,' he would say, 'I could bring your parents back to life and make your lover, King Kardia, well again.'

"I think the dreams must have had some effect. I wrote long letters to Kardia to encourage him and poems to cheer him. I had an idea too that the best of physicians from far-off lands might be able to make him well. I went to ask Hocoino about it, but he said that there was a threat of famine and that the country was without money. I sold my jewels and asked Hocoino to let me work. I could embroider. I could sing and play the harp. I could paint—and my paintings were good, or so people said.

"So we made an arrangement that he would pay me to sing and play when he entertained state visitors. He also arranged to sell my embroidery and my paintings. I worked from the time I got up till the time I went to bed. Sometimes I worked on into the night by lamplight.

"I was never allowed to see Kardia and sometimes I grew so tired I wanted to give up. Yet my dreams drove me on. It seemed as though *I* was at the root of the trouble and only I could put it right. And so I became a slave, Suneidesis the slave, in bondage, trying to undo what never could be undone.

"One day a kitchen maid asked to speak with me. She

seemed fearful and begged me to tell no one what she had to say. She was betrothed to a footman who had served Kardia but who now obeyed Hocoino. She told me that both of them had been down by the river on the night my parents died, within ten yards of them. Hocoino was standing in the water and had beckoned my parents down to the river's edge. As they went to speak with him two spearmen thrust spears into my parents' backs. 'Let their bodies flow down a mile or two. See that you alone take them out of the water,' she had heard Hocoino say. 'No blood will be found on them. I have taken care of that. Give me your spears and go. And when you have found them, raise hue and cry. Tell all who come that you heard them both declare that their lives were worthless because of their wicked daughter. Then bring their bodies back to the palace.'

"Nor was that all she told me. The whole palace knew, and all had feared to tell me, that Kardia was sane and probably still alive, a prisoner in the dungeons of Authentio.

"When she left me I thought long and hard about what I ought to do. I knew of the wise Chocma and of her cottage, invisible to all evil eyes, in the Forest of the South. I determined to leave the palace that same night and find her. But I was caught.

"The rest takes little telling for you have experienced it yourself. Hocoino was spending more and more time rebuilding the walls around that center of evil power, the Ancient City. I was taken to him in the night and chained high on the ancient altar. Kardia had spoken of Gaal, and so to Gaal I cried. That is why I am here. I had become a slave to Hocoino, and Gaal has set me free." She smiled slowly and repeated, "And Gaal has set me free—just as he will set us all free."

"So Gaal and the High Emperor still wanted to help Anthropos?" Lisa asked, anxious to get the details straight.

"Yes."

"And Hocoino was just telling you lies. . . ."

For a long time they sat together without speaking. At last Suneidesis said, "I once thought I would never be happy again." She smiled a broad smile. "But I *am* happy. I am happy even now, without my parents and Kardia."

Lisa decided that there were few people she liked more than the princess of the Bayith of Yayin. In fact she liked everything that happened there. Gaal would appear and disappear but usually joined them both for meals. Lisa would sit as close to Gaal as she could and would often lay her hand on his arm—not to clean it as she had tried to do in the tunnel but just because she felt closer to him when she touched him. Occasionally he would sit her on his lap and fold her in his arms. And at those times she would want nothing ever to change, only that she could sit there forever.

The one thing that made her nervous at the palace was the white-winged horse. Ever since it had winked at her she had felt uneasy. It wasn't until two days later that she raised the matter with Suneidesis.

"Oh, *him!*" the princess laughed. "He was not making fun of you. He probably thought he was flirting with you!"

"Flirting with me? A horse?"

"Well, not exactly flirting. You see he is most vain . . . and somewhat cowardly. He thinks we dote on him, and in a way we do. You see he is so vain that he is droll and makes us all merry. Even Gaal smiles when we speak of him. He winked his eye to impress you. Why not go and meet him? He would be glad of someone else to appreciate him and all of his finer qualities."

"What's his name?"

Suneidesis began to giggle. She found it hard to speak. "I know not what ..." she began, and started to laugh again. "I know not what his *true* name is, but he has given himself the name of, oh, dear ..." and she laughed so helplessly that she ended by begging Lisa's pardon. "You shall ask him yourself," she said at last.

Half an hour before lunch Lisa did. She still felt a little nervous, especially since the creature was looking at her intently as she approached him along the grass.

"Good morning," she said timidly. "My name is Lisa."

"Good morning, Lisa, you must have been busy since you came."

"Busy?"

"Why, yes. Usually people come to see me before they do anything else at the Bayith—to ask my advice and that sort of thing. So I knew something must have held you up."

"Well, I was a little bit scared of you."

"Of course, of course. Brave men have trembled on seeing me for the first time. Ladies are usually enchanted. But then you are rather young, are you not?"

Lisa felt cross. "I may be young but I'm not afraid of horses. It's just that I've never seen a flying horse before. Can you actually fly?"

The flying horse stood on his feet, spread his huge wings, leaped into the air, flew in a wide circle round the palace, and landed to face her once again. Something about the whole performance made Lisa think of ballet, but she was not sure whether she should say so or not. It wasn't so much the gracefulness (though he certainly was graceful) but the absurd tiltings of his head, and the little aerial pirouettes that he performed.

Lisa watched her words carefully. "Thank you," she said finally. "That was very beautiful."

"Nothing, a mere nothing, I assure you. Any time. There *is* just one thing I think we ought to get straight, however. The description *flying horse* is not accurate. I let people use the term because they understand it better. But in actual fact I am not a horse, flying or otherwise."

"Yet you look like one."

"Of course."

"You mean you're really some sort of bird?"

"Dear me, no. What a silly idea. No, I am related more closely to the angels. I suppose you might call me an equine angel."

"Oh." Lisa couldn't think what else to say.

"An angel's body doesn't have to be like a human body, you know."

"I see."

216

"So though I am not offended that common people regard me as a flying horse, I prefer that people like yourself should recognize my angelic status."

"Thank you. I'll remember that."

"What did you say your name was?"

"Lisa."

"What a short name!"

"Well, there's really more to it but I like Lisa for short. What's your name?"

Did you ever see a flying horse smile? A sort of dreamy, ecstatic look came over his face. He closed his eyes and said, "My name is," and here he took a long breath, "Theophilus Gorgonzola Roquefort de Limburger V." Then he sighed a long sigh of contentment, and his eyes (to Lisa's relief) remained closed for a while.

Lisa knew a lot about cheese. She liked Cheddar and Cheshire and Crackerbarrel and Wensleydale and a whole pile of others. But she couldn't stand the *smell* of the ones in the flying horse's name.

"I chose the names myself," Theophilus said, "at least every name except Theophilus. That's the name I like the least, but Gaal insists that I keep it."

"But what made you choose names like Limburger?"

"The perfume."

"The perfume?"

"Yes, the perfume. Gaal told me about them."

"Gaal told you?"

"Haven't you noticed the perfume around him?"

"Yes, it's like freshly sharpened pencils."

"Not strong enough."

"I think it's very nice."

"Not really. I wanted something much stronger. In fact I asked Gaal to tell me some of the stronger smells from distant places. I have even asked him to *give* me

those smells but I am unable to get him to agree. He said
the names were bad enough. But I think they have a
certain dignity—Theophilus Gorgonzola Roquefort de
Limburger V."

"And what do you do, Mr. Theophilus?" (Lisa didn't
dare say the rest of the names, in case she might giggle.)

"Do? Oh, yes. I see. You mean, what do I *do?*"

"Yes, that's what I said."

"You must learn to express yourself more elegantly.
Do? What do I do now? Really I am connected with Gaal.
He needs someone sensible around him. Someone who
can think. Someone who is not merely bold (I cannot
stand silly ideas of *bravery*) but *subtle*. Someone who dis-
cerns the delicate nuances of diplomatic exchanges. So
you might say I am the power behind the throne. I give
Gaal his ideas. I advise him. I drop hints where they are
most needed in the proper quarters. I give Gaal advice
whenever I see he needs it."

Lisa's mouth had been opening wider and wider—not
because of what Theophilus was saying but because another flying horse, in fact a flying mare had quietly come
to stand beside him. And as Theophilus tossed his head
to emphasize his last statement, he too saw the mare.

Have you ever seen a dog put its tail between its legs
and slink past its master? Theophilus did it better. His
wings wrapped themselves round his head. He rolled on
to his side and curled his legs as close to his body as he
could. He looked for all the world as though he was trying to make himself invisible.

"Theophilus!" the mare said sternly. (She was Theophilus' wife.)

"I know, dear. I'm sorry, dear. I don't seem to be able
to stop doing it. I think it must be my sense of insecurity."

"Sense of insecurity, my foot. You'll have a fine sense

of insecurity when one of my foals breaks a wing trying to pirouette around the central turret of the palace. Get them down at once! And don't ever let them fly up there again!" She neighed fiercely, nipped Theophilus' shoulder and screamed, "Now off with you. Bring them down at once, I say!"

Gaal, who was watching, was obviously trying to suppress a smile. The mare looked at him pleadingly. "Can't you stop him? I bite him. I kick him. I lock him in the stable. But he can think of nothing but preening himself in front of young humans."

"Oh, dear. Yes, dear," Theophilus was saying. "I really wasn't being serious. I'll go right away, my dear. I'm sure they'll come to no harm. I'm so sorry, dear. You're absolutely right. I'm just an empty-headed fool. You see every time I open my mouth...."

He was still talking as Gaal took Lisa by the hand and drew her toward the palace for lunch. "I would invite them both to join us," he said to Lisa, "but it is more than he could take at the moment. Besides, his mare never stops nagging. However, he shall have a job to do after lunch. It is time we got Kardia and Suneidesis back together again, and you and your brothers too. I shall ask him to fly you and Suneidesis to Chocma's cottage this afternoon."

18

The Chase of the Qadar

After lunch while the sun was still high in the sky, Gaal, Suneidesis, Lisa and Theophilus were standing at the foot of the palace steps. "You must go straight there," Gaal said to them. "So long as the sun is well above the horizon the Qadar will not fly. Toward sunset they begin to venture abroad, and by the time darkness comes they are fully awake and dangerous."

Theophilus still had to do most of the talking. "Yes, Gaal. Certainly, Gaal. Of course *I* would never think of delaying, but I am glad you mentioned it for the sake of the young ladies. They need to understand the dangers and the urgency of the situation. You were very wise, Gaal, as indeed you always are, to select me to take care of them. Young people nowadays...."

But Gaal was not listening. Over his arm he carried two soft, hooded fur capes lined with white silk. "These," he

said, "are to keep you both warm in the high, cool air."
Lisa gasped as she saw her own cloak—soft and much
lighter in weight than Kardia's. She thought she had
never seen anything so lovely.

"Oh, thank you, Gaal," she said as she flung her arms
around him. She was thinking of how she had felt three
nights before on her arrival—the filthy and absurd ur-
chin, trailing along in a ridiculous evening gown. "You
made me clean inside as well as outside," she said. "I
don't understand how it works, but I've never met anyone like you before. I don't understand about living
purity being crushed between fire and rock. But, but,
. . . ." and she buried her head in his fragrant, cedar
robe again.

Theophilus cleared his throat. "As you said, Gaal,
there must be no delay. I take it that you want *me* to be
in charge of the operation since neither of the young
ladies has experience in aerial combat."

Gaal smiled. "If you do what you are told, there will be
no aerial combat. As for being in charge I want both you,
Lisa, and you, Theophilus, to obey Princess Suneidesis.
She will be in charge and you will follow her directions."

"I think you are making a mistake, Gaal, if I may say so.
If you will think about the matter for a moment, you will
realize. . . ."

"Theophilus!" Gaal's voice was stern, but his eyes were
twinkling.

"Yes, Gaal. I am sorry, Gaal. You *are* always right, I
just thought. . . ."

"It is always good to think, Theophilus, but you should
think *before* you speak rather than after."

"Yes, Gaal. I am sorry, Gaal. I. . . ."

Gaal continued to address Lisa and the princess. "In
case there should be any delay and in case the forces of

darkness attack you, I have for each of you a light shield of aman. They will deflect any spear, sword or flaming arrow. The crowns of tiqvah with the zabach stones will protect your heads, and it is well that you are still wearing your sashes of qosht. These books (he produced two small leather-bound volumes) emit strong light when they are opened. It is a light that evil powers cannot stand."

Finally he gave a letter to Suneidesis, addressed to Kardia. He urged them several times not to delay, but to make all haste to the House of Wisdom. Then he helped the girls to mount. For Lisa it was a new experience to ride a flying horse, something she had never done in her life. She sat behind Suneidesis, who held the reins in her hands, and she felt very insecure. As she looked back at Gaal, she saw to her astonishment that the palace, grass, pool and fountain had all disappeared. They were standing on the hard, cracked mud of the River Rure while on the hilltop rose the ancient walls of Bamah.

A moment later at the command of Suneidesis they rose smoothly into the air, circled slowly as they rose higher, and watched the tiny white-robed figure below them grow smaller.

Lisa would have waved but she was terrified that she might fall. So she wrapped one arm around Suneidesis' waist and held her shield in the other. Her little book was securely tucked into her sash.

Soon the city below seemed like a map. Toward the horizon the hills began to sink and to change shape while the forests farther to the south looked like a dark blanket covering the ground. Gaal disappeared from view. Around the river the quiltlike pattern of farmlands looked brown and dead. No wheat was growing.

"There is still hope of a crop if the rains come within the next week or so," Suneidesis called back. "And I am sure they will once Hocoino is overthrown."

Lisa said nothing. She was concentrating on not falling from Theophilus' back. The great slow flapping of his wings made her uneasy. She would have preferred a seat inside an aircraft with stable wings.

"It takes years before one begins to appreciate the finer points of flying," Theophilus said.

"I'm sorry, I can't hear you. The wind is blowing in my ears." Lisa shouted back.

"I said it takes *years to appreciate* the *finer points* of *flying,*" the horse repeated.

Lisa was still not sure what he said, so she replied, "We really do appreciate all you're doing and we think you're a wonderful flier."

"Have a care," said Suneidesis leaning sideways to speak into Lisa's ear. "Flattery makes him play the fool." But the warning had come too late.

"One loses altitude quickly by pulling in one's wings to the side like *this,*" Theophilus said. Lisa's stomach rose up into her head—and to somewhere above her head as they began to plummet. She would have screamed, but she didn't have any breath to scream with.

"Desist, poltroon," Suneidesis said to the horse. "We are on a mission for Gaal not in a circus. Let us have no more foolery, please."

"Very well, your royal highness. Just as you say. I am distressed you so little appreciate the skills by which your flight is made possible."

"Much more will we appreciate a safe arrival at Chocma's Cottage before sunset," the princess responded. You could tell that Suneidesis was used to taking charge.

For a while no one said anything more. The landscape slowly unfolded below them. Houses, hedges, trees and farms were made vivid by the deep shadows cast by the afternoon sun. Lisa began to feel more secure, but she grew a little stiff as one hour after another crept slowly by.

She could tell that Suneidesis was both happy and excited. Her cheeks were flushed with something greater than the wind. She was to see Kardia after three years of separation. Lisa wondered how it would feel to love someone like Kardia. She thought of the silly ideas she had of marrying him herself when they were in the cell together. But she was just as excited to observe her new friend's joy.

Both girls were lost in their thoughts for a while. Their cloaks kept them warm, Theophilus' wings flapped rhythmically, while they idly watched the landscape below. Without thinking, Suneidesis had let the reins lie loose in her hand.

Suddenly she started.

"Where are we, Theophilus? We should be almost at Chocma's by now. I have never been there, but the places below us do not look as Gaal described."

"I see you are observant, your highness. No, I am not surprised that you do not recognize any landmarks below. I decided to follow a route which would allow me to inspect certain cave openings where the Qadar are rumored to hide by day. If we spot any signs of activity we shall know what to expect."

"Theophilus! Where *are* we? What is the hill below?"

"I am not *completely* sure, your royal highness, but I would guess...."

"You mean that we are lost? You know not where we are?"

"I would not put it so strongly, your highness. We are

approximately over the Caves of Aphela. The hill below is probably the Hill of Aphela. Now if only I could locate Chosek...."

Suneidesis' eyes flashed.

"Theophilus, you are not only disobedient, you are a fool. You were told to go directly to Chocma's Cottage. In what direction lies the cottage and how long will it take us to reach it?"

She was angry with herself because she had been thinking so much about Kardia that she had failed to check on their direction and had let the reins hang loose.

"My lady, there is really no cause for alarm. If I may make a suggestion, it would be well to complete our reconnaissance now that we are here...."

"Theophilus, in what direction does Chocma's Cottage lie?"

"Well, I cannot be absolutely certain, your highness. The wind factor has to be taken into account. Our air speed and our ground speed...."

"Theophilus, do you or do you not know in which direction Chocma's Cottage lies?" As Suneidesis asked the question she saw with dismay that the sun was low on the horizon. Soon it would set.

"Your highness, if I turn approximately ninety degrees...."

Suneidesis seized the reins and tugged them to one side. Both girls stared at the sun as gradually it swung behind them. It was beginning to redden as it sank toward the horizon.

"It is my own folly," Suneidesis said half to herself, half to Lisa. "I was dreaming of Kardia instead of concentrating on our flight. It is well that Gaal gave us the shields and the books. We may need them before we finish the journey. Now fly, Theophilus, fly as fast as you can. And tell me the first landmarks you recognize."

I will say this for Theophilus that he would respond when you called on him. The sweep of his wings grew longer and the rhythm faster. You could feel him surge forward. The wind blew harder in their faces.

"If I may venture an opinion, . . ." he panted.

"You will venture nothing," Suneidesis replied. "You fly as you are bidden, and you will keep your opinions to yourself."

Lisa's heart seemed to be rising up into her throat. She was not sure what the Qadar were, but the thought of being lost or of encountering flying marauders in the dark was unbearable. Some adventures made you pleasantly excited. Lisa felt nothing now but cold fear. Suneidesis had clearly taken charge, and it was obvious from her deft movements and the look of concentration on her face that she was experienced not only in riding, but in riding flying horses.

The sun behind them was touching the horizon. Ahead the sky was deep blue, and a couple of bright stars or planets (Lisa had no means of telling which) were shining like pale jewels. Below them most of the land was in shadow with just a hilltop here and there crowned red by the setting sun.

Then as she looked over her shoulder, Lisa saw two tiny specks against the background of the sinking red sun. She screwed up her eyes in an effort to see them better. But whatever they were, they were too far away to see clearly.

As she continued to stare two things began to happen. First, she began to see several green suns whenever she blinked. (Try staring at the setting sun and blinking, and you will see what I mean.) Second, she was sure that the two black things were getting bigger. What were they?

227

There were no aircraft in Anthropos. Could they be birds? If so, they must be very large ones for they were a long way away.

She continued to stare as the sun slid down until she was sure that the creatures were winged and were flying toward them. Cold, sick fear clawed at her chest.

"Sun," she said, "there are two black things flying toward us. You can see them against the setting sun."

The princess turned her head for a moment and stared. Then she swung her shoulders forward again. "Qadar!" she said into Theophilus' ear. "Fly as you have never flown before. Lose not height. We may need all the height possible before long."

The horse's ears flattened against his head. If he had been flying hard before, he flew harder now. Foam from his mouth occasionally flew back, caught by the wind and flattened itself on Lisa's cloak or in her hair.

"Keep a good watch, Lisa! Tell me if you see them getting closer."

"It's hard to see them. They're above the sun now. It's almost gone under. But they do seem to be getting bigger. I can't be sure but it almost looks as though they're catching up with us. But they're to the left of the sun now."

"They could be trying to cut us off if they've seen us," Suneidesis said. "They can fly much faster than we can. Our only hope is to press on as fast as possible and hope either that they have not seen us or that we can soon find Chocma's cottage."

Theophilus' sides were heaving. He was taking great gulps of air and was too breathless to do anything but fly. From his flattened ears Lisa got the impression that he too was frightened.

"Oh, joy! Look ahead!" cried Suneidesis suddenly.

"See that beam of light a little to the right on the horizon? That's from Chocma's Cottage. No evil eyes can see it, but it shines out like that every minute or so. Still, it is a *long* way away."

Lisa turned to look and saw a blue pencil of light in the distance. The blueness cheered her immensely. She turned again to try to discern the night warriors. They were larger, yet harder to see against the afterglow left by the sun which was now below the horizon. And the black creatures were definitely moving not only toward them but trying to get ahead of them. As she watched them Lisa knew with strange certainty that they had been seen and were being pursued.

She glanced round again looking for the blue pencil of light and saw it flash briefly, then disappear. It seemed horribly distant.

"Sun, what *are* the Qadar?" she asked.

"They are special emissaries of the Lord of Darkness," she replied. "They range the skies at night to report changes in the landscape. They watch for movements of men or beasts. They have orders to destroy anything or anyone loyal to Gaal."

"Will they reach us?"

"I don't know."

"Sun . . . I'm scared. In spite of the crown of tiqvah, I'm still scared."

"I know. I too am afraid. But Gaal's eyes never turn from us. Keep watching the Qadar and tell me what you see. Use your shield and your book if they get close. We are not powerless, you know. They dread the light from the book."

For twenty minutes in the deepening darkness they continued their headlong flight as the light from the cottage seemed to be getting much closer. Their sashes and the zabach stones in their crowns began to glow with blue radiance.

"Sun, I can't see them anymore. The sky is too dark."

"Very well. Keep a watch out on our right side and to the front. It is their custom to attack from ahead. I shall watch the other side for if there are two, it is also common for them to attack from opposite sides at once. When you see them, tap my shoulder. Wait till they are close and open your book, aiming the light at them. Be not surprised if I have Theophilus drop suddenly."

Several more minutes passed. Both girls strained their eyes to the sides and ahead of them. Every minute brought them nearer Chocma's light.

"I think we're going to escape them," Suneidesis said softly. "In three or four minutes we'll be there."

Theophilus' speed never flagged. He was wet with perspiration, nostrils aflare, breathless but flying powerfully. Then in the dimness ahead and to the right Lisa saw a great batlike shadow with a rider robed in black, a rider shaped like a man but bigger than a man.

"One of them's coming on the right," she whispered tapping Suneidesis' shoulder.

"And another on the left," came the soft reply. "Get hold of your book."

It meant letting go of Suneidesis for now Lisa needed one hand for the book and the other for her shield. The huge batlike creature approached at incredible speed. A streak of flame came directly toward Lisa. She raised her shield, fumbled to open her book, then suddenly felt Theophilus drop like a stone below her. It was a horrible feeling, but two flaming spears had passed harmlessly above them (though she did not have time to notice them). The Qadar wheeled round to make a second attack. Suddenly Lisa felt herself pressing hard against the horse's back as he checked his downward motion.

"Lisa, I must drop my shield. I need one hand to guide Theophilus and another to use the light from the book. Keep looking back. They might come from above and behind on both sides of us. You shall have to use the shield for both of us. Tell me everything you see."

For two minutes they saw nothing but the stars and heard nothing except the rush of the wind and the terribly labored breathing of Theophilus. Lisa was now sitting by balance alone, her feet in the stirrups, her shield on her left arm and her book in her right hand.

Then the stars behind them to left and right were blotted out. The same piercing screams that had so startled Kurt and Wesley ripped the night apart. Two immense figures riding their batlike chargers and bearing flaming spears simultaneously hurled them at the girls.

Several things happened at once. Lisa instinctively raised her shield before her eyes only to have it knocked back by the force of a heavy flaming spear so that her arm struck her a blow on the face. For a second the shield seemed to be many times its usual weight. Then something flaming dropped from it into the darkness below and the shield became lighter again. At the same time Suneidesis had skillfully maneuvered Theophilus in a downward spiral. The Qadar swept scarcely five or six feet over their heads as Theophilus twisted toward the treetops. Again there was silence. Events were happening so quickly that Lisa had no time to marvel at how she had kept to the saddle.

Not more than five hundred yards ahead of them the blue pencil from Chocma's Cottage shot into the sky. In the light of it Lisa saw the two Qadar flying swiftly at them again, both wheeling round toward them from

a distance of two hundred yards. But out of the corner of her eye she saw something else. Suneidesis had slumped over the neck of Theophilus. She turned her head quickly and to her horror saw that the princess seemed to be unconscious, sliding slowly from the back of the horse.

"Sun!" she screamed. "Sun! Wake up!" Flinging the shield from her own left arm and tucking her book into her sash she seized the waist of the older girl and held it fiercely. "Make for the light, Theophilus! Make for the light and fly right into it! Never mind the Qadar! Fly for the base of the light."

The weight of Suneidesis was incredible. Lisa pressed her feet hard into the stirrups. Her right arm was aching unbearably.

"The book!" she suddenly thought. "I must use the book!"

Fumblingly she pulled it with her left hand from her

sash and opened it with her thumb. Two great black shadows were almost upon them again. As the book opened, piercing blue light shot like lightning from it into the night. Lisa turned it onto one of the shadows. To her amazement the shadow burst into flames and plunged down. She caught a glimpse of the second Qadar only feet behind them and swung the blue beam at it. Again there came the terrible scream. Flame leaped from the bat around the giant black shadow of the warrior. In desperation he leaped, arms spread wide, to seize Lisa, but as the light struck him he withered and fell, missing Theophilus' rump by a handbreadth.

Suneidesis was still sliding. Lisa dropped the book, held on to the princess with both arms and breathed, "Gaal. Oh, Gaal. *Please.*"

Seconds later they burst into a great hall of seven pillars which was filled with dwarfs and wolves. Theophilus made a last gliding circuit and landed neatly on the floor of the hall where Lisa and Suneidesis tumbled to the ground in front of Chocma's throne.

19

The Journey Begins

By dawn the following morning Wesley, Kurt and Lisa felt far from wide awake. They yawned, they shivered and their eyes felt sore. In the great hall Inkleth handed to each of them a large leather pouch and a leather water bottle. The pouch was stuffed with a two-day supply of meat, cheese and bread. Each of the children would very much have preferred two or three more hours in bed. None of them felt like talking. The problem with real adventures is that they're never comfortable. They may be thrilling to read about, but aches, cold, hunger and going without sleep as well as being scared out of your wits are all part of real-life adventures.

Lisa's muscles ached from her exertions on Theophilus' back and from some minor bruises when she fell from him. All night she had dreamed of black shadows and flaming spears.

When they had arrived the night before, there had been a tremendous sensation and a great deal of fuss. Princess Suneidesis, as it turned out, was seriously hurt. A Qadar spear had sliced cleanly through her shoulder, almost severing her arm. Because she was unconscious from shock and blood loss, there was some question whether she was still alive. Kardia had been beside himself with fear and grief. But the Pool of Truth had healed her and taken her pain and weakness away. Lisa even felt envious that Suneidesis was still snug in bed.

Wesley and Kurt had been overjoyed to see Lisa. All three talked until late in the Hall of Wisdom, questioning, interrupting one another, laughing and talking all at once as they exchanged stories. Finally Chocma had had to urge them to their quarters, or they would have had no sleep at all. Wesley could vaguely recall Kardia talking to Inkleth somewhere near them. Kardia had had a letter in his hand (the letter from Gaal), and he had seemed troubled as he talked with Inkleth.

And now Chocma, who was watching the distribution of rations, also looked troubled. She stared at Inkleth keenly, frowning. She had (no one knew why) taken on her peasant form again, standing ramrod straight with a brown wrinkled face and white hair plaited round her head.

Quietly she showed the boys how to strap the leather pouches into the belts of their tunics and helped them tighten the straps of the water bottles slung over their shoulders. Lisa's food bag had a longer strap and hung with her water bottle over her shoulder.

Once they were ready, Chocma addressed all four of them—Inkleth, Wesley, Kurt and Lisa. "Let me review your instructions. His lordship Wesley is in command of the expedition. All of you, including Inkleth, must follow his orders. There is no mention of you, Inkleth, in the letter, but his majesty, King Kardia, is grateful for your offering the expedition your expert knowledge of the land."

Inkleth's face showed no expression. You couldn't tell from looking at him whether he had any feelings about not being in command of the expedition. Wesley felt both puzzled and embarrassed—puzzled at Inkleth's calm, knowing how impulsive and quick-tempered Inkleth was, and embarrassed because Inkleth was a well-recognized chief of a large group of the Matmon and an experienced fighter. Kurt, in defiance of the warning in the mirror, was determined to make friends with Inkleth.

Chocma continued. "As you leave the cottage, Wesley, you will see a pigeon hopping and fluttering ahead of you. Follow it through the woods to a stream that is a two-hour journey from here. On the far side of the stream you will find an ancient pathway of brick and stone concealed beneath an arch of low branches. It will take you to the shores of Lake Nachash where a fishing boat is tied to a wharf. You should arrive at the lake by this evening. It will be safe to sleep in the cabin by the wharf, but *only* there. Do not set sail by night. Do not sleep anywhere but in the cabin.

"You will set sail tomorrow morning. The journey to the old keep will take the better part of a day and will involve difficult sailing on troubled waters against contrary winds. You will sail due east, until you see the Island of Geburah and the ancient keep of the ruined Castle of Geburah. As you approach the island, steer to its south side, where in the side of the cliff you will notice a wide opening. You can sail right through the opening into the rock under the keep. The opening is guarded by an iron door. Bid the door open in the name of Gaal and sail into the channel directly under the keep. Every locked door in the keep except one will open in the name of Gaal. There are three rooms above the ground floor. The treasure room lies just below the roof. You will take from it the book and the key. You will also open the wooden chest and take out the jeweled orb. Beneath the table you will find a short, light sword of tempered logos. When the pigeon rests on your shoulder, you will find you have great skill in using the sword. It is for you to use.

"But I have one very serious warning. Below the treasure room is one that on *no* account must you open. To do so will expose you to the utmost danger.

"Spend the night in the keep and do not leave its shelter. The following morning you will again be guided by the pigeon who will lead you west from the island to a point near where you embarked. Four white deer with broad antlers will carry you to the Cave of Gaal where you will spend the night. The next morning the reindeer will bear you to the battlefield. I shall be waiting for you and the book there. Kardia will need the key and the orb."

"What is the key for?" Kurt asked.

"It opens the Cave of Qava where the five hundred knights lie enchanted. No one but his majesty can use it."

"We shall arrive on the *fourth* day then." Wesley said frowning. "Pigeon-to-stream and path-to-lake: Day one. Boat-to-island: Day two. Island-to-deer and deer-to-cave: Day three. Cave-to-battlefield: Day four."

"Yes, but that should be in time. We do not anticipate an attack until the evening of the fourth day. The evil forces are less valiant by day. And if Kardia has the key by the afternoon of the fourth day, the enchanted knights will have joined us before the battle starts. But do not take any other route. And never leave shelter at night."

There were many more questions Kurt would have liked to ask, but there was an air of haste about Chocma. They could tell she was anxious to get them on their way. Indeed her parting words as she led them to the door of the cottage were, "Let nothing delay you. Unless the enchanted knights reach us on the fourth day our chances of victory will be much less."

Lisa stared in bewilderment as they left the cottage. You must remember that although she had seen its inside, she had not seen the outside before. "What happened?" she asked, bewildered by the billboard.

"We don't know. It's always that way—flat outside, big inside," Wesley said. Lisa would have liked to ask more questions, but she forgot them in the excitement of the start of their journey.

The morning air was cold. Only the first reddish streaks of dawn lit the sky ahead of them in the east. Chocma waved good-by and the children responded. Inkleth turned his back and seemed to ignore her.

"Oh, look. The pigeon!" Wesley said as he saw the bird ahead of them, head cocked to one side, watching them keenly.

"Where?"

"I don't see it."

"Look. Right ahead there, just beside that log."

"Where?"

Kurt and Lisa stared for a moment.

Then Lisa said, "I *think* I see it. Yes, it's the same one that came down the path of blue light."

"I can't see anything," said Kurt in a puzzled voice.

Inkleth said nothing for a moment. Then, in a dry voice he said, "If your lordship can follow what you *think* you see, well and good. If not, I will lead you along a more certain route."

They followed Wesley as he moved toward the pigeon which hopped and fluttered before them down the path which led from Chocma's Cottage. It led them east directly to a patch of dense, impassable undergrowth with matted thorn branches interlacing inextricably to a height of eight feet or so. Then the bird disappeared under the mass of thorny undergrowth.

Wesley stopped.

"Your lordship seems puzzled," Inkleth observed.

"Yes, the pigeon went right into the densest part of the thicket."

"Then doubtless you will be able to pass through it too." There was an edge of sarcasm in Inkleth's voice.

Wesley felt uncertain and foolish. Taking a deep breath he walked up to the undergrowth, the rest following him. The thorns were almost touching his face.

"Go ahead, my lord. The pigeon doubtless knows the way," Inkleth taunted.

"Wes, don't you think you imagined it?" Kurt asked. "After all, it's still pretty dark."

"I saw it, Wes. It did go into the thorn bushes here. I never went wrong when *I* followed it in the tunnels," Lisa urged.

"What holds you back, my lord? Was there really a bird or are you deceiving the rest of us?"

Stung by Inkleth's sarcasm, Wesley stepped right *into* the bushes. To his surprise and joy they opened before him to form a blue-lit tunnel walled and roofed by thorn bushes. Ten feet ahead of him the pigeon was waiting at a point where the tunnel seemed to end. As the others followed there were gasps of astonishment. Inkleth came last. No sooner were all four inside than the gap behind them closed. All four found themselves in a sort of long narrow room walled and roofed with rose and briar. The pigeon hopped ahead and disappeared into the front of the tunnel.

What followed can best be described as walking inside a sort of long bubble in the undergrowth which moved east just as fast as they did. They would see the pigeon provided they kept up a good pace. Whenever it got too far ahead it would wait for them to catch up. Continually the dense tangle of thorny branches parted as they approached and closed behind them once they passed.

At one point Inkleth, on whose face there was a look of anger (remember he couldn't see the pigeon), tried to lead the party. Without realizing it he got ahead of the pigeon with the result that he impaled himself in a tangle of thorny undergrowth. The rest of them had to set him free while the pigeon waited.

No one said anything, and all three children felt distinctly uncomfortable. Wesley heartily wished that Inkleth had never come. It made it difficult for the rest of them to talk freely. All of them felt embarrassed and had taken a dislike to Inkleth ... all but Kurt who was doing his best to be sociable. For the most part, however, no one talked at all. In fact Wesley and Lisa's dislike and suspicion of him was more on their minds than the astonishing way the tunnel of thorns (as they later called it) kept opening up before them.

When Lisa finally did speak, she addressed the pigeon which by now she and Wesley could see clearly. "Thank you, little bird," she said. "I know Gaal must have sent you. Thank you for leading the way and please don't leave us." Kurt glanced round at Inkleth as she was speaking, but it was impossible to read the Matmon's expression.

Daylight was steadily penetrating the branches above them so that soon they were unable to discern the blue light. By the time they had been walking an hour and a half they could even catch glimpses of sunlight breaking through the dense bushes here and there.

Presently the bushes ended. Tall trees, beeches, oaks and elms with little or no undergrowth formed a high-arched cathedral over the dry carpet of last year's leaves. The ground sloped gently down to a stream, and soon they were glad to rest beside it.

The stream was mostly a stony bed about twenty feet across through which a small trickle of water meandered among shallow pools. They decided to drink from it and not use their bottled water, and sat munching silently from their leather food wallets. Conversation was confined to neutral comments.

"This cheese tastes good."

"It's still nice and cool. Maybe it'll be warmer when the sun gets higher."

"I bet this stream would be a rushing torrent if the drought ended."

"Look at the far bank. It's going to be tough to climb."

"Say, where's the pigeon?" Wesley asked suddenly.

Both he and Lisa stood up and looked round, but the bird was nowhere to be seen.

"How come *I* never got to see it?" Kurt complained.

"Perhaps your lordship will permit me now to guide you to the lake," Inkleth said quietly. "If we follow the stream southward, we shall be able to go round the mass of undergrowth on the far bank."

It was true. None of them had been thinking of what lay beyond the stream. But the high bank was topped by the same dense, thorny undergrowth that they had encountered from the commencement of their journey.

"Do you know the way to the lake?" Kurt asked Inkleth.

"I do, my young lordship," Inkleth said with a touch of contempt in his voice.

"Chocma said there was a path of brick and stone beyond the stream," Wesley said quietly.

"Chocma says many strange things," Inkleth said.

"But it will take little enough time to find out whether the path exists or not."

Inwardly Wesley was angry, but he, like Inkleth, was determined to keep his temper under control. He had watched Inkleth fight from the castle and had secretly admired him. It embarrassed him to overrule the Matmon chief, especially when he sensed Inkleth resented him.

Slowly Wesley picked his way among the smooth, dry boulders of the stream bed. Tree roots and stones between packed earth formed the far bank. After a little effort he was able to heave himself onto the top. Immediately he was faced with dense bush. There was hardly a foot of room on top of the bank. Wesley edged himself to the right and to the left, but there was no sign of the path Chocma had spoken of.

"Can you see anything?" Lisa asked.

"No, not yet."

"I doubt your lordship will ever see anything. If the path were to exist the Matmon would know about it. I have never heard of any such path," Inkleth said evenly.

Wesley thought a little. "I'm going to work my way twenty yards or so both north and south," he said presently. "We were pretty careless coming down through the trees, and we've probably hit the wrong part of the stream."

Inkleth's explosion of anger took them all by surprise. His face flushed, his eyes opened wide and with a yell of rage he cried, "There *is* no ancient path. What do women and children know of the ways of Anthropos? You come from other worlds. Yet you presume in your conceit to imagine you know more about Anthropos than I do—I who was born and bred here!"

Wesley almost lost his balance in turning and had grasped a thorny branch that pierced his fingers painfully. "We don't think we know more about Anthropos than you do," he said, his voice quiet but shaking a little with anger (Lisa could tell because Wesley always got white around the lips when he was mad), "but we know whom we can trust. Chocma has never proven herself mistaken since we knew her." He felt like adding, "And in any case, *I'm* in charge of this expedition," but he knew that would have been childish and would have made Inkleth angrier than ever. As it was Inkleth grew yet more furious.

"You mean of course that you do *not* trust *me.* Not only am I to be humiliated, but I am to be insulted by children."

"Wes said nothing about not trusting you, Inkleth." Lisa spoke quietly. "It was hard to trust her about following the pigeon, but you must admit it worked out in a pretty amazing way. I think Wes is right. We ought at least to have a good try about following her directions. In any case they're not hers. They're Gaal's and Gaal *made* Anthropos."

"Gaal!" Inkleth's eyes flashed contempt. "A myth to keep children happy! A sop to calm the consciences of the weak. There *is* no Gaal!"

"That's what I said a few days ago," Lisa said. "But then he rescued me from Hocoino and I got to know him. He's no myth. He's real."

"Well, keep your children's fancies. I shall go to the lake my own way," Inkleth shouted and angrily stomped southward along the bank. "Come with me if you want to reach it by nightfall!"

Lisa stood still, but Kurt, determined by now, began to follow Inkleth.

"Kurt! Kurt! What are you doing?" Lisa cried.

"Oh, I'll just follow him a little way to see where he goes."

"Don't you understand? So long as we follow Gaal's instructions we're under his protection. If we don't we have no idea what may happen. This isn't a game. It's serious!"

"Oh, get serious yourself," Kurt called back irritably. "It can't do any harm to follow him a little way. After all he does know the lay of the land."

Wesley watched them go and said nothing. It was hard to resist the temptation to go after Kurt and bring him back. Yet some obscure instinct told him that the first thing he must do was to find the path.

"Lisa," he called, "why don't you walk up and down your side for a hundred yards or so. It'll be easier for you to move than it is for me. That way we might find it faster."

Lisa hurried northward. After about fifteen yards she stopped, stared and yelled, "Wes, Wes, look here!"

"What is it?"

"There's no path that I can see from here, but there are proper steppingstones crossing the stream bed and a stone stairway leading up the bank! Maybe this is it!" She began to cross the steppingstones and had already ascended the stone stairway by the time Wesley reached her. "It's here, Wes. It's here!" Excitement filled Lisa's voice. "There are stones ... and bricks ... and there's some sort of marks and carvings on them."

Wes pushed past the bushes to reach her. "By golly,

245

you're right!" he cried. ". . . And look how the bushes are open all along the pathway!" He turned to look for Kurt and Inkleth, but they were hidden from them by the bushes and by a curve in the stream bed. Wesley ran across the steppingstones back to the western bank. Kurt and Inkleth had gone surprisingly far. Wesley yelled at the top of his voice, "Kurt! We *found* it! It's right here!"

Kurt turned round. It was impossible to see the expression on his face. He shouted something back but neither Wesley nor Lisa could tell what he said. Kurt cupped his hands and called again. This time the words reached them clearly. "Race you to Lake Nachash!" he called. "Bet you we get there first!" With that he waved and ran to catch up with Inkleth.

"The stupid, little idiot!" Wesley was enraged. The frustrations of their morning walk boiled up inside him. He began to run forward. "I'll *drag* him back if I have to!"

"Wes, Wes, *stop!*" Lisa called. "You mustn't go after him. Don't you see! That's just what Hocoino would want us to do!"

Wes turned to face her across the stream bed. "You mean let him walk into danger? Let him go off with that conceited idiot, Inkleth?"

"Wes, I know how you feel. It tears me in two to think of leaving them. But I know what happens when you let some idiot lead you to disobey Gaal's instructions." (She was thinking of Theophilus and the Qadar.) "You can't *help* them, Wes. You'll only get into a mess yourself, . . ." she was crying now, "and anyway I'm going to follow the path whether you go after Kurt or not. He *won't* come back, Wes. You know how he is. He gets all the more stubborn when you get mad. He'd never admit he was wrong in front of Inkleth, and you know as well as I do that Inkleth won't come back."

Wes sat on the bank and groaned. For a few moments neither of them spoke.

"Is there a Gaal?" he asked finally. "Yes, I know you talked about him last night. But what right does *he* have to order us around this country any more than Kardia does? Who is he anyway?"

"He's the Shepherd."

"That doesn't make sense."

"He's the Son of the High Emperor."

"That doesn't mean anything to me either."

"There's something that *does* mean something to you though."

"Oh?"

"Yes—keeping your promises. You promised Chocma . . . ."

"But I'd no idea that it might mean leaving my fool brother to go off with an idiot dwarf!"

Again there was silence. Lisa was still quietly weeping. "Wes, I'm not mad and I'm not being stubborn. But whatever you do I *must* follow this path. I know it's what Gaal wants. I'm not trying to make it awkward for you, but I'm going even if I have to go on my own. Go after them if you must, but I'm going to set out now." Slowly, and still crying softly, she turned and began to follow the winding, stone pathway.

Wesley watched her disappear as her head dropped lower and lower beyond the high east bank. In all his life he had never faced so difficult a choice. Kurt was with Inkleth. So there was someone to look after him. But could Inkleth be trusted? And what about the dangers Lisa spoke about? He felt angry with Lisa too. Was he or was he not in command of the party? A fat lot of good his leadership was doing.

As he stared up at the far bank he suddenly started.

A tall and extremely old man in a long white robe stood looking down at him. A belt of gold wound round his waist. His hair and beard gleamed white in the sun. Yet *was* he old? His face was young and his brown eyes alive with power. He looked familiar. Then with a shock Wesley realized it was the man he had seen in the mirror. For a full minute they stared at each other, and as they did so two things happened to Wesley. First, a flood of longing swept through him to know the man who looked down at him. Second, he knew that all was well and that he must follow the path.

The stranger spoke no word but turned to walk in the direction in which Lisa had disappeared. Spellbound, Wesley watched him as his waist, then his shoulders, then his head were concealed by the height of the bank. He had moved with vigor and purpose.

Leaping to his feet he ran across the steppingstones and up the stone stairway fully expecting to see the stranger walking ahead. But there was no sign of him. The bushes that walled the stone pathway were too thick to pass through, but no one was there—no one, that is, but Lisa who was sitting fifty yards farther on, her head in her hands, obviously crying.

"Lisa!" The girl looked up. "Lisa! Did you see him?" She stared at him blankly as he ran to her. "The man, Lisa, the man dressed in white with the gold belt!"

Lisa looked at him curiously. "Did he have white hair and a white beard?"

"Yes."

"And a gold belt around his waist?"

"Yes."

"Were his eyes ... oh, I don't know how to describe them...."

"Like they were on fire?"

"Yes." A happy smile began to cross Lisa's face. "Then you saw him yourself!"

"Saw who?" Yet Wesley already knew the answer.

"Why, Gaal of course!"

Wesley paused. "He must be . . . he must be a terrific person to know."

"He is."

"And I guess we're supposed to go on. I'm sorry about what I said about Gaal. I know now what you meant when you talked about him last night. Even though I can't make sense of it, I know it's right to go on. I wish I could be sure Kurt would be all right. It's like abandoning him."

Lisa smiled. "I did some pretty dumb things myself— worse than dumb things in fact—yet Gaal rescued me. It was Gaal who brought us here, you know. And he's not the kind of person to let you down even if you do something stupid."

For a while they sat and said nothing. Then, hitching his food wallet and bottle into place Wesley said, "I guess there's no sense in waiting." He helped Lisa to her feet. Slowly the two resumed their way east along the ancient path of brick and stone.

It was a fascinating walk. You could feel magic in the air. Sometimes they would pass through tunnels of briar and hawthorn, much like their "bubble" early in the morning. At other times they would wander through more open woodland. Though it was early spring no primroses, no crocuses and no daffodils were to be seen. Only dry leaves and dust covered the forest floor. Even the moss that covered the path here and there was brown and dry. Sometimes they stared at the strange writing and the symbols which could dimly be made out on the stones. They continued to walk until the sun had long passed its zenith sky, and by and by they sat down under the shade of a large oak tree.

"Feel like lunch?" Wesley asked. "It must be after two."

"I feel like a drink of water."

They stretched their legs and rested their backs on the solid trunk behind them as each of them swung their leather water bottles to their mouths. Lisa looked puzzled. There was a tiny opening at the end of a short neck. The whole bag was floppy like an old-fashioned, rubber hot water bottle, except that it didn't widen out after the neck. She placed her lips around the neck and tipped the bottom of the bottle up high. A couple of drops of lukewarm water fell on her tongue but that was all. She tried sucking which was a little better, but the water came only slowly.

"These don't seem to work," she said to Wesley.

Wesley had a look of dawning recognition on his face. He grinned, tilted his head back, held the bottle upside down over his open mouth and then squeezed the leather bottle hard. A thin jet of water squirted powerfully down his left nostril. Wesley jerked his head forward, dropped the bottle, spluttered, sneezed and said, "That's what comes, *stchoo!* . . . that's what comes from reading geographic magazines."

Lisa was laughing helplessly. "Oh, I'm sorry, Wes. I don't mean to laugh. But you looked so fu-, fu-, ha, ha, ha!" and she continued to laugh till her sides ached. Wes laughed too, mostly because Lisa had the kind of laugh that was catchy.

"I saw a picture of some man in Greece or Portugal or somewhere squirting wine from a bottle like this into his mouth," he said eventually. "I suppose it takes practice, but we'll have to learn or go thirsty."

Their first few attempts got them wet and giggly. But

eventually they became quite adept at squirting the water into their mouths. Their thirst was only just beginning to be satisfied when Wesley said, "Hold it! It'll be a long walk to Lake Nachash, and Chocma didn't mention any streams or springs apart from the one we crossed. We'd better save the water till we reach there."

They tore off hunks of bread, munching it with cheese and meat that they broke and tore with their fingers. It was messy, but it tasted good. Lisa rinsed her hands and mouth with a little of the precious water while Wesley satisfied himself by wiping his mouth with the back of his hand and rubbing his hands on his tunic.

They were surprised to find how wobbly their legs felt when they got to their feet. "How far do we have to go?" Lisa asked.

"I don't know. I'm sure we should get there before sunset. But how *much* before I don't know. We must have come about fourteen miles already."

"Lucky we have no blisters," Lisa said looking at her soft red shoes. "I just hope my legs hold out. I didn't realize we'd have to come so far."

They trudged determinedly for the rest of the afternoon. Twice they saw does, one with a fawn and another with two. Lisa wanted to leave the path to see if she could touch them for they stood stock still, staring at the two children. But both of them knew they must not delay. The farther they went the stronger the wind came blowing against them.

Then without warning the trees stopped abruptly and they felt the full force of strong wind. Below them lay a smooth slope of grass, beyond which stretched a beautiful lake along which the wind topped the blue waves with streaking whitecaps. Immediately below them was a wooden jetty with a sailing boat tied to it and some kind of hut or cabin at the nearer end of it.

"We've made it!" Wesley cried. But almost instantly he remembered that Kurt and Inkleth were not with them.

"Perhaps they're already in that little hut," Lisa said, guessing his thoughts.

Both of them, aching, wobbly legs notwithstanding, began to run down the slope to the jetty. Within minutes their feet were thumping hollowly along the wooden boards of the jetty. Wesley tried the door of the wooden building which opened easily to reveal a cabin about ten feet square, with two windows, four bunks, blankets and cooking utensils.

But of Kurt and Inkleth there was no sign.

As darkness fell Lisa was able to cook oatmeal she had found in a barrel and some strange, dried herbs she found in a jar. She boiled the oatmeal in an iron pot over a stove built of stone and heated by wood. At first neither of them could think of how to light a fire until Wesley saw a metal apparatus on the wall with a rough iron wheel that rested against gray stone.

"A flint!" he cried. "I wonder. . . ." As he pressed two springy, metal arms together the iron struck bright sparks from the flint. Straw was present in the stove, and before long they had a warm fire glowing. They also lit an oil lamp which they hung in one of the windows.

Lisa broke pieces of cheese into the oatmeal, "to give it some flavor," she said, "since there isn't any salt." They were hungry and tired, and ate the strange mixture with enjoyment as they watched darkness fall. Neither of them said much. Lisa prepared a tea from the herbs. It would have tasted better with sugar, but it was better than nothing. Since there was plenty left of both the tea and the oatmeal, Lisa covered them both "for when the others arrive." The two then went out onto the jetty to wash their dishes and spoons.

Wesley inspected the boat. It was about sixteen feet long with a lateen-rig sail, ready to hoist. The rudder and tiller swung idly astern. There would be plenty of room for all four of them, and Wesley figured that if necessary one person could handle the boat pretty easily. All the children had done plenty of sailing.

"Looks much heavier and clumsier than our Laser," Wesley said.

"But I bet it won't tip so easily," his sister replied.

The sun had set in the forest on the hill behind them. Far in the east the two bright evening stars that Lisa had seen the night before glittered like diamonds on blue velvet. Her anxiety grew as she watched them. When would more Qadar be abroad in the skies again? What other ancient evils might Kurt and Inkleth be facing?

Wesley had noticed two long, wooden oars in the bottom of the boat and lifted one of them out. "Boy, this is heavy," he said. Yet as the words left his mouth an astonishing change took place. The oar grew light in his hands. Playfully he swung it around like a baseball bat.

It was only as he was playing with it that Lisa said with awe in her voice, "Wes, the pigeon's sitting on your shoulder!" Wesley paused to look. The bird looked at him calmly. A strong wind was blowing and the waves slapped constantly against the framework of the wharf. Yet the pigeon's feathers were not ruffled.

"Wesley, I can hear something," Lisa said suddenly. Wesley listened but heard only wind and water. "Yes, I'm sure," she went on. "There was a shout and it sounded like Kurt!" Both of them strained their ears, the strangely weightless oar still in Wesley's hands and the pigeon still perched on his shoulder. A second or two later the pigeon fluttered up onto his head.

"Well, of all the weird things, . . ." he began.

"Listen! Wes! Someone is running this way!"

As Wes listened there was no doubt about it. "Kurt," he yelled, "Kurt, over this way. Come toward the light!"

But there was more light than the oil lamp in the cabin window. A brightening blue was spreading from the pigeon. The running footsteps came nearer.

"If that's Kurt, he's in a whale of a hurry," Wesley murmured.

Then they saw him, running, stumbling, staggering. They both ran to meet him, but as they did so they saw only ten yards behind him a hideous giant of a creature with seven heads, reaching forward to seize him. From one of its mouths Inkleth was hanging by a leg. It was a seven-headed ogre.

Wesley could never understand what happened next. One part of him was terrified. Yet he seemed to possess a strength and speed he had never before known in his life. He leaped forward past Kurt raising the oar above his head to bring it crashing down upon the head that held Inkleth. The skull was smashed and Inkleth fell to the ground.

Then as two large hands reached out to seize Wesley, he swung the oar first one way, then the other. To his amazement he seemed to have smashed through both of them. It was as though his arms were moving by themselves for next, in a low, vicious swing, the oar swept across in front of him to crash like an axe through both of the creature's great legs.

Inkleth had managed to crawl to one side which was fortunate, for as Wesley leaped back the body and six remaining heads of the creature crashed heavily onto the ground where he had been standing.

Once again the oar seemed to be moving itself, smashing systematically one after another of the creature's heads. For a moment the ogre lay immobile. Then suddenly the whole body collapsed, turned to black fluid and disappeared into the ground.

As it did so, the blue light faded, the oar became heavy again and Wesley moved over to see what sort of state Inkleth was in. Though he did not notice at the time, the pigeon had disappeared.

"Are you hurt?"

Inkleth was sitting, shaking his head and looking dazed. He staggered uncertainly to his feet.

"I shall be well," he said dully and limped ahead of Wesley to the door of the cabin. Wesley found Kurt white and sweat-soaked, lying exhausted on one of the bunks. At first both of them refused to eat, but after some persuasion they took the oatmeal and the herb tea, appearing too exhausted to do anything but eat.

"The ogre's gone," Wesley said.

Inkleth nodded. "I saw," he said. "I saw what you did."

"We should have stuck with you," Kurt said. "I was an idiot not to."

"You were right all along." Inkleth said, but he failed to look Wesley in the eye.

The rest of their story had to wait till morning. All of them were extremely tired, especially Kurt and Inkleth. None of them took their clothes off, but all of them stumbled into their bunks, pulling blankets over themselves. The last things Wesley heard were Inkleth's snores and the slapping of waves against the jetty.

20

The Tower of Geburah

Lisa didn't know what woke her, yet she knew she had to get up. She groaned a little as she rolled out of her bunk for it seemed that her legs had never before been so sore and stiff.

The others were still sleeping. Lisa set herself to search more carefully in the cupboard in the corner where she had found the oatmeal and the herbs. She was sure that if she went through it carefully enough she would find salt and sugar. But though she found salt, rough and sandy salt, there was no sign of sugar. What she did find, which delighted her, was a large jar of honey.

Lisa was the sort of girl who liked making meals. She crept around getting water, dry grass, wood from a woodpile, setting the table (there was no tablecloth), wondering all the while to whom the cabin belonged. She felt sure it was all right to use the supplies because Chocma had told them to sleep there.

Soon she had a fire in the stove, more oatmeal (this time with salt and without cheese) and some herb tea brewing. She even tried to make toast on the top of the stove, but this was not a success. Wesley's knife was not sharp enough, the bread was crumbly, and the top of the stove too hot so that what she got was mostly burnt crumbs and untoasted bread.

Probably it was the smell of cooking that woke the others. They groaned as Lisa had done at the aches and pains they had accumulated the day before. Kurt was decidedly grumpy. His face was pale and there were dark hollows under his eyes.

"Talk about nightmares!" he said. "I've never had such horrid ones in my life. There was this creature. . . ."

"Why don't you fold your blankets neatly and wash your face and hands in the lake?" Lisa asked maternally. "In fact all of you must tidy up and wash before you get anything to eat."

"My legs hurt," Kurt complained. "I've got a head-ache. I'm not well."

"You'll feel better when you're cleaned, tidied and fed," Lisa coaxed.

"You don't really care how I feel, do you? I'm not well, I tell you. I'm too sick to go out there."

Inkleth said very little. He tested his left leg carefully before bearing weight on it and limped toward the door.

"How bad is it?" Wesley asked.

"It is but bruised," Inkleth said turning his back. He didn't seem to want to talk about his injury.

The two of them went out of the cabin, Wesley to wash (there was neither soap nor towel, but he felt better after splashing and rubbing) and Inkleth to inspect the boat. "There's a rod here, with flies and hooks," he said. "It may be my good fortune to catch a few fish for later."

"Why don't you come inside for breakfast?" Wesley asked.

"If your lordship will but bring me bread and cheese, and some of that tea your sister is making, I shall do well. Some fresh fish may come in handy."

Wesley brought what Inkleth had requested and found him casting expertly from the jetty.

"He looks as though he knows what he's doing," he told the others when he got back. "He's even got a little basket from the boat. I guess he expects to catch something."

They began to eat.

"What happened yesterday?" Wesley asked between mouthfuls of porridge.

"We walked miles and miles and miles. You guys had it easy. I want to stay here. Why don't we just fool around today?"

"Tell us about the ogre," Lisa asked.

Kurt shook his head. "It was awful, just *awful*," he said. He described how about a mile from the cottage Inkleth had turned to see the ogre running toward them. "Boy, did we ever run! You don't know what a stinking mess you got us into, Lisa, when you did that fool thing of going into the television."

Lisa and Wesley exchanged glances, glances that said, "We'd better humor him. He's not himself."

"It must have been awful," Lisa said. "I guess warfare isn't much fun."

They elicited little more from Kurt during the rest of the meal. His manner remained surly. He seemed to have forgotten his admission of his folly the night before. Neither Lisa nor Wesley had ever known him to be in such a mood.

They collected the dishes to wash in the lake while Kurt looked out of the window. "Inkleth's leg seems better," he said. "He walked right to the end of the jetty, and he wasn't limping a bit."

"Good," Wesley said. "It must have been just stiffness from bruising that's got loosened up." Yet something about Kurt's remark puzzled him.

"I wish *I* could loosen up," Kurt grumbled. "You don't seem to realize what a time we had. I'm sore all over."

"Well, all we do today is sit in the boat," Lisa said. "Come on, Kurt, fold your blankets and clean up. I'm sure you'll feel better." Kurt muttered something to himself, but he began rather slowly to do as she suggested.

The wind was rising by the time they were ready to set sail. In their leather pouches they still had some of the cheese, meat and bread they had set out with. Water bottles were filled from the lake. Inkleth had caught three large trout which he had gutted, cleaned and tossed into the bottom of the basket. Wesley, acting as skipper, positioned Inkleth, who had no experience with boats, in the prow, where he would have no need to watch out for the boom. He positioned Lisa amidships so that she could hoist the sail once they were clear of the low jetty. He continued to wonder what it was that he couldn't figure out about Inkleth but was too busy at first with sailing to let it worry him. Later it bothered him in the way a name does, a name you have on the tip of your tongue but just cannot quite remember.

He cast off the painter, thrust the boat vigorously forward from the jetty, jumped in the stern, seized the tiller and ordered Lisa to hoist away. It was obvious that they would have to beat against the wind all day, for it was driving straight down the long lake toward them. As the wind billowed the brown canvas sail, Wesley felt the boat tug. He hauled in the sheet, and they were away on the first tack tilting to port and surging forward. Kurt sat amidships opposite Lisa and trailed his hands in the water. He made no effort to switch sides.

On either side of the lake, which was about three miles wide, dark wooded hills and rocks rose steeply. It was as though they were sailing up a Norwegian fjord. The sky was clouded, and the tops of the steep hills disappeared up into the gray mist.

Wesley preferred to sail himself. For the most part he held both sheet and tiller, putting the sheet between his teeth when he needed to use both hands (when, for example, he came about and had to switch hands between tiller and sheet). The wind rose constantly. Waves pounded the boat bursting into spray and wetting Inkleth who was crouching in the bow. Lisa passed him her fur cloak to keep him warm. Wesley felt Inkleth's weight would be useful in not letting the bow rise too high out of the water for once or twice he felt the old boat reluctant to come about into the wind.

Both his arms were soon aching. There was no cleat where he could fix the sheet to keep the sail set, and he needed all his strength on the tiller. Lisa, seeing his difficulty, came over to hold the sheet for him. "I'll keep it set, not too close-hauled," she said. "We'd better not take too many risks. The whitecaps are already streaking. You hang on to the tiller and let me know when you want to come about."

Kurt moved from amidships to join Inkleth in the bow which had the result of causing an occasional wave to break over them so that they shipped water from time to time. Wesley was irritated but said nothing.

"We don't have anything to bail with, do we?" he asked Lisa, but neither of them could see anything.

"I'm cold," Kurt shouted.

"Then come farther aft and start shifting sides whenever we come about," Wesley called.

"Coming about," in case you don't sail, means changing direction. You can't sail directly into the wind, but if you have the sails set properly, you can sneak ahead at about forty-five degrees to it, especially in a strong wind. The idea is that everyone sits on the side that rides high to weight that side down. Then when you "come about," that is, when you begin to zag instead of to zig, you switch the sail from one side to the other as you change direction. Since the boat then begins to tip the other way, everyone switches sides, carefully ducking under the boom, the heavy pole that holds the bottom of the sail down.

In a way Wesley enjoyed it since it was a challenge to forge ahead against the blustering wind. But it took all his strength to hold the boat on course. Lisa's hands grew blistered hauling on the sheet. The clouds above them thickened and darkened and the mountains grew steeper. It seemed as though the lake was also getting narrower. The wind whipped the sails angrily, tugging mercilessly at the sheet. Wesley glanced apprehensively at both shores and noted to his dismay that sheer cliffs rose from them. If they were to need to make for shore, they would have to go far back down the lake. Fortunately they shipped no more water.

They must have been sailing for five hours when finally they could see the Island of Geburah ahead of them. By now both Wesley's and Lisa's arms were aching and both of their hands were blistered. Several times they had switched between tiller and sheet, each taking a turn. All four of them had eaten little, helping themselves to their food satchels as they had a chance. Inkleth had remained silent, and Kurt had continued to be surly and generally uncooperative.

As they drew closer to the island Wesley noticed something curious. Whenever they approached either shore the wind died down. The closer they got to the island, the narrower grew the zone where the wind was blowing. In fact you could see a steadily widening belt of smooth water along each shore. It was as if a giant sat on the tip of the island blowing, and as if the wind from his mouth fanned out gradually. But there was no giant. Geburah itself was the source of the wind.

What none of them knew was that part of the enchantment of the island was its power to blow wind in four directions at once. One wind blew north, another south, yet another east and fourth one west. Thus whenever you set sail from anywhere to reach the island, the wind blew hard against you while in between the winds were narrow areas where no wind blew and where you would have to row to make any headway.

Wesley must have figured it out. He decided to get close to the island and then sail across the south wind (which is much easier than you think if you don't know about sailing) and then turn into the wind when he got at the correct angle from the opening into the rock.

"Oh, look!" Lisa cried suddenly. "You can see the ruins of the castle."

"Looks a pretty miserable place," Kurt said, and as a matter of fact it did. What with the dark sky, the steep rocks and the dark gray stone of the ruins, Geburah looked uninviting.

Inkleth was growing restless. "There is a magic that keeps all inhabitants from approaching nearer than a mile to Geburah," he said. "Some say it deals in death." His face was pale.

"Maybe the magic is just these freaky winds," Wesley said. But he spoke too soon. Without any warning a curtain of fire dropped down from the clouds to the water. The children stared in awe and fear. The grayness of water and sky only emphasized the vast leaping flames that seemed now to be rising from the water itself. The waves around them danced a blood red and gray. The island had disappeared.

Two things puzzled Wesley. First, the wind was blowing as strongly as ever, yet the curtain of fire was not affected by it. The wind did not blow the flames toward them. The other thing that puzzled him was that although the vast wall of fire was not more than a hundred yards from them, he felt no heat from it.

"I'm going closer," he said.

"Don't be crazy, Wes," Kurt shouted half rising from his seat. Wesley said nothing but continued to steer toward the billowing curtain of fire.

"Wes, turn back! You'll get us all burned." Kurt was badly scared. As for Inkleth, he was pale and beads of sweat ran in little rivers down his face. And really you couldn't blame him. After all, the others had at least been told that the magic wouldn't work on them. But Inkleth had no such assurance. At one point he looked as if he were thinking of jumping overboard. But he couldn't swim. The waves, too, were fierce and the wind strong. Lisa felt sorry for him. The boat was fairly skimming along now.

"There's no heat," said Wesley. "Gaal's orders were to go to the Island of Geburah." But a moment later he changed his mind. Each of them now could feel first warmth, then heat on their faces. "Lower the sail!" Wes called to Lisa. Slowly the boat began to drift away from the flames.

"What do we do now?" Wes asked in a puzzled voice. All of them looked at Wes except for Inkleth who glanced from one face to another.

"There is just something," said Lisa.

"What?"

"It may not work but it's worth trying." She stood up as well as she could, hanging on to the mast. "Fire, go away in the name of Gaal."

What happened next shocked them so much they were speechless. It was as though someone had turned off a switch. One second there was a billowing curtain of fire a hundred feet high, and the next second, nothing— nothing, that is to say, except the whitecaps, the long dark lake and the sinister Island of Geburah. They were so shocked that no one spoke for several seconds.

"What made you do that, Lisa?" Wesley asked eventually.

"Gaal showed me how to do it with a rock door. And you remember Chocma said we could bid anything unpleasant go away in the name of Gaal."

"You mean you can just say, 'in the name of Gaal,' and anything will happen?" Kurt asked.

"No, you have to be doing something he told you to do—obeying orders."

Kurt looked troubled. "You really believe in this Gaal person, don't you?"

"I know him."

Kurt did not respond.

"Hoist the sail again, Lisa," Wesley called. "If I can get close enough to the western tip of the island we won't even need to row. We'll be able to sail right into the hole in the rock."

A moment later they were buffeting their way east again. Wesley really handled the boat very well. He managed, just as he had said, to get from the west wind to the south wind without using their oars, and in a few minutes they were racing past the black cliffs of the long south side of the island.

"There it is," Lisa said. "See where the rock juts out? Well, it's just this side of it."

All four stared and saw that the entrance to the cave-like tunnel was barred by a dense metal grill. They were getting rapidly nearer.

"I'm going to have to change course in a second or two if we're to go in," Wes said.

"Go ahead, Wes. We're under Gaal's orders."

Judging the angle as carefully as he could, Wes turned into the wind and hauled the sheet in hard. For a moment it looked as though they were going to tip, but the next moment they were buffeting toward the iron grill in a wall of rock. Lisa furled the sail to let the boat drift gently toward the center of the opening.

"Open in the name of Gaal!" Wesley shouted, and like an electronically controlled garage door, the grill raised itself out of the water and disappeared into the rock. A minute later they were in the calm water of a huge cavern lit with dull red light. The grill clanged and splashed back into place behind them. All of them were aware of the dramatic contrast. Outside battering waves and roaring wind had made them raise their voices when they spoke. Now the sounds of wind and waves could hardly be heard. The water lapped softly against the sides of the cave wakening gentle echoes in the silence. The children spoke to one another in low voices almost as though they were inside a cathedral.

"I don't like this place," Kurt said grumpily.

"Well, it's a relief after battling the winds outside," Wes replied.

...The cave like tunnel was barred...

"Where's the tunnel that goes under the old keep?" Lisa asked.

They all looked toward the far end of the cave, but there was no opening that they could see.

"There it is on the left," Lisa said pointing.

"Makes sense," Wesley said, "because we'd passed the castle when we found the cave, and a tunnel in that position should take us right back under the castle."

He pulled out the oars, passed one to Kurt and fitted his own into the rowlock. Kurt grudgingly did the same. Slowly the boat penetrated deeper into the cave. Splashing oars (Wes and Kurt were less expert with oars than with a sail) echoed whisperingly around the rocky vault. Lisa sat in the stern looking around. Inkleth, his hands gripping the bow, stared wide-eyed toward the entrance to the tunnel. He seemed afraid—a totally different dwarf from the fiery, cocky Inkleth of the Hall of Wisdom.

A moment later their boat nosed its way into the wide tunnel. "Where does the red light come from?" Lisa wondered aloud.

"From the wall, I *think*," Wesley replied.

"I hate it. It's evil," Lisa said. "There was a spider waiting for me in the tunnel with red lights underneath Hocoino's temple. And there was red light in the chasm I had to cross." She shivered.

Inkleth spoke for the first time. "This tunnel was carved out by the Matmon," he said. "Only dwarfish arms and dwarfish pickaxes could produce such smooth work."

The walls of the tunnel certainly were smooth, forming a semicircular roof above their heads. Here and there were holes, some large and round, others slitlike. Lisa pointed them out to the others.

"Part of their defenses," Inkleth said. He seemed to be recovering from his fear. "They could pour boiling oil onto any boat that penetrated the tunnel. The slits were for archers."

"I can see a landing place ahead," Lisa said, "a sort of dock."

Sure enough, the tunnel widened about fifty feet ahead. Stone posts had been carved where the boat could be tied. A few moments later they scrambled out onto the rocky platform, stretching their cramped legs as Wesley tied up the boat. In front of them was a narrow stairway curving upward into the rock.

You could tell that there was something uncanny about the stairs though none of them could put their finger on what it was. The nearest they got was something Wesley said later, "You could feel your skin just prickling with magic."

The big problem was who would go first and who would go last? Wesley and Lisa didn't want Inkleth to go first because of their lack of trust in him. Wesley was still casting about in his mind wondering what it was that was wrong with Inkleth. As he watched him limping along the rock jetty, he searched the back of his mind for what it was about the limp that bothered him.

In the end they decided that Wesley go first and that Kurt bring up the rear. Wesley wanted Lisa to go last but she said, "Oh, no, please! I get this horrible feeling of someone coming behind me!" So they decided it would be Wesley followed by Inkleth, followed by Lisa and then Kurt. Both Inkleth and Kurt said they were making a lot of fuss about nothing.

The stairs wound up in a tight spiral. There was nothing to hang on to. So they walked as near to the outside wall as possible. Inkleth held them all back. He seemed only able to step up with his good leg and then bring his bad leg to the same level as the good one. His rate of progress was only half the speed of the rest.

The stairway ended in a black wooden door. There was a rusty ring for a handle, but Wesley could not move it a fraction of an inch. He banged against the door with his shoulder, but this was difficult since he had one foot on the top step and the other on the step below which meant that he couldn't really use his weight properly.

"Kick it," Kurt suggested. But if you've ever tried to kick upward at a heavy door from a narrow spiral stair- case, you'll know how silly Kurt's suggestion was.

"Didn't Chocma say something about doors?" Lisa asked.

"Of course, what an idiot I am. Door, open in the name of Gaal!"

The rusty ring creaked and groaned as it turned the lock. Then with a crack followed by a series of squeaks and crunches, the door slowly opened and the four of them passed through into a large square room.

What made it so impressive was the stillness and the cleanness of everything. Several windows lit the room, leaded windows of ruby red with strange designs they could make nothing of. In one wall was a massive oak door leading outside. A beautiful woven carpet of a strange and intricate design covered the floor with ani- mals they could not name, stars and what looked like some kind of lettering. A heavy oak table filled the center of the room, and there were wooden chairs beside the table and scattered around the walls. The furniture was black and covered with the most intricate carvings which matched the work on the carpet. Two of the walls were covered with shelves bearing old, leather-bound volumes and scrolls of yellow vellum.

"Wow!" Kurt said. "This is some room."

Lisa went to the shelves and ran her finger along one of them and another finger along the tops of the books. She stared in amazement at her finger tips.

"There's not a speck of dust," she said. "Someone must clean here every day."

"Or else it's magic," Kurt said.

Inkleth cleared his throat. "This is the castle keep," he said. "The rest of the castle lies in ruins. But the keep was here as a tower, long before the castle was built. No one knows how long it has been here. They say that people from other worlds came here many ages ago, but what happened to them no one knows."

Of course everyone went to look at the stonework, and what Inkleth said was absolutely true. The surface of the walls was flat and smooth. Every stone was a different shape, yet each fitted the other better than the pieces of the best jigsaw puzzle you have ever made. The wall was a marvel of building skill.

"There are said to be three rooms above this," Inkleth went on, repeating what Chocma had already told them. "The one above us is similar to this. The one above that is locked and is said to contain secrets brought from other worlds. No one living knows whether it has ever been opened. Personally I think it is idle superstition. The room below the roof is the one in which your interest lies. It has the box, the key, the book and the sword for you, my lord Wesley."

Up one of the side walls ran a broad stone stairway which they followed, this time not worried about who went first or last. Though you could tell that the whole keep was very magical, much of their fear had left them.

As they neared the top of the flight of stairs they noticed two things. In the library (as they later called it) the

stairway followed the outside wall on one side and had
nothing but a handrail on the other. It was just part of
the room. Beyond the library it became an enclosed stairway, enclosed between the outer wall and the wall of the
room on the second floor. In fact the corridor was level
for about six feet with a door which obviously opened
into the room above the library. From that point the
stairway proceeded up to the third level, lit by openings
in the wall.

The door was not locked and when they pushed it
open they saw an empty room, with a bare floor of wood,
walls of the same smooth stone and windows. The only
thing of interest was a painting that hung from the walls,
and the four of them went to stare at it. It was a portrait
of an old man. You could tell both that it was a very good
painting and that the man in the picture was a remarkable character. His face was wrinkled with age, but his
eyes were alive. You felt as you stared at it that any moment he might speak. His hair was white, topped with
what looked like a velvet skullcap. Kurt's heart beat so
loudly that he was sure the others could hear it. The man
in the picture was the man he had seen in the mirror of
the Pool of Truth. It was of this man as well as of Inkleth
that he had been told to beware.

Yet something stubborn rose up within him. For rea-
sons he could not explain he felt determined to defy the
warning from the mirror. In order to disguise his excitement he said, "Mebbe he's bald under his skullcap." The
remark had an odd effect on everyone. They all felt embarrassed, as though it had been rude of Kurt to speak as
he did. There was an air of mastery about the man, as
though he could hear every word you said and was
watching you closely. It may just have been the way the
artist had painted his eyes. For as you probably know,

there are portraits of people who seem to be looking at you whenever you are in the room. But with the old man, it was uncanny. You had the distinct feeling he could read your thoughts. In fact Kurt blushed after his remark about the skullcap.

The other interesting thing about the portrait was that though the colors used were mostly dark (for instance the man wore a black gown rather like the academic gowns people wear at graduation) the picture wasn't dowdy, dull or depressing. Not just the man, but the whole picture was alive.

They stared at it, fascinated.

"I wonder why all these things are left here—you know, the furniture downstairs and this painting here," Wes murmured. "This painting must be worth a lot of money."

"It is said that nothing of the old things can be moved. Many people have tried, but the furniture is of such weight that none can lift it or even destroy it. It is said that the picture will remain here until the man returns."

"Returns? From where?" asked Lisa.

"No one knows," Inkleth said.

Wesley stared at a gold plate below the picture. It was filled with curious writing, the same sort of writing that had been woven into the carpet down below. As he stared at it a curious thing happened. The letters didn't change but Wesley could read the words, that is to say the words came in his mind in English.

No power on earth can this my portrait take.
Until the time has come for me to wake.

He read the words aloud.

"Is it really true that people have tried to take this picture away?" Kurt asked. "It's just hanging there."

"Nevertheless, the history books record that no one has done so."

Kurt stepped forward with an air of bravado and grasped the gilt frame with both his hands. The picture was certainly heavy but he could move it. Eventually, huffing, puffing, struggling and with some help from Inkleth, he freed it from where it was hanging and laid it leaning against the wall on the floor.

"I guess it was just an old superstition," Wesley said.

The rest went on staring. And as they watched, the colors on the picture began to fade.

"Put it back, Kurt. Put it back!" Lisa cried. "Something's happening!"

But Kurt never moved. Like the rest he was rooted to the spot. By this time you could hardly tell what the painting was about. A minute later the ornate frame surrounded nothing but blank canvas. You can imagine how everyone felt. It was the sort of feeling when you are somewhere you have no right to be and you do something that's going to get you in trouble.

"Now you've done it," Wesley said to Kurt angrily. Kurt was white and shaking.

"You said it was only a superstition a minute ago."

"That doesn't mean you have a right to take a picture that doesn't belong to you off the wall. Goodness knows *who* he is or what's going to happen now."

"Oh, please don't quarrel," Lisa said. "Let's put the picture back where it belongs and get out of this room. It's too spooky. Let's go upstairs and get what we have to get and leave this place."

But try as they might to lift the painting, they could not do so. It seemed riveted to wall and floor. They could not move it even a fraction of an inch. Guiltily they followed one another through the door, glancing back at the strange blank canvas. Inkleth still limped. Wesley was the one to express the thought in everybody's mind. "We're supposed to stay the night here. It looks as though the winds have died down anyway, and we could never row back before nightfall. We'll have to sleep somewhere in this spooky place. Who knows what could attack us outside after dark!"

It was a grim choice they faced. Neither Wesley nor Lisa trusted Inkleth. Kurt had seemed both edgy and hostile since their adventure of the day before. Their choice lay in disobeying instructions and rowing without the pigeon and in the darkness or spending the night in an ancient keep which was not only magical, but menacing.

21

The Treasures in the Tower

Wesley had decided he would not even look at the door to the room on the next floor. The incident with the picture had left them all shaken and more on their guard. They had the sort of feeling you have when playing in a house that is half torn down (which can be fun, especially when you know you're not supposed to be there) and have picked up a couple of electric wires and received a shock from them. Suddenly you feel different about "fun" in wrecked houses. Magic like electricity can be nasty.

Yet when they reached it not only Wesley but all three children and Inkleth stopped and stared at the door. I suppose the same magic was working which had enabled them to read the lettering below the picture because the mysterious writing covering a small brass plate on the door seemed to say something like this (though I'm sure

it would sound better in the original language):
Here in this room alone I stay.
Awake me not until the day
When war against the Emperor's Son
May well be won.

"What does it mean?" Kurt asked.

"It means we don't touch that door, and we keep clear of this room," Wesley replied.

"Unless we believe it may help Kardia," Inkleth said quietly.

"What d'you mean?" Lisa asked.

"The war against this Gaal of whom you speak may be won in these days. King Kardia could well be defeated," Inkleth said. "You all heard him say what forces are facing him. There may be someone in here who can prevent his defeat."

"You mean there may be a friend of the Emperor here?"

"There is no Emperor and there is no Gaal. The Emperor, Gaal and Kardia are all one. But whoever waits in here may aid Kardia in his hour of need."

"Hold on a minute," Wesley said. "The poem says nothing about helping either Kardia or the Emperor's Son. All it says is that whoever is in there (and it gives me the creeps to think of who or what may be behind that door) wants to be awakened when there is war against Gaal. But it doesn't say whether the Sleeper wants to help Gaal, much less Kardia, or to help their enemies. You can take it either way.
Awake me not until the day
When war against the Emperor's Son
May well be won.

"Maybe it wants to defeat Gaal when it gets a chance."

The more they discussed the matter, the more sure

Wesley and Lisa felt that the poem could mean anything.

"Anyway, Chocma told us to leave the door alone," Lisa said. "She said we weren't to go inside it."

"She may not know herself who is waiting in the room for our summons."

Lisa was stubborn. "Whether she knows or doesn't know, fooling about with this room was one of the things we were told not to do. Our job is to get the orb, the book and the key."

Inkleth's face reddened, and something of his usual short temper appeared. "What cowards, what *stupid* cowards you are! A soldier should not merely obey orders but use his wits as well. How shall we look if we fail to seize the fortune of a lifetime and help Kardia and even the mythical Gaal. Who knows what power lies in this room?"

"That's just it," Wesley said. "We don't know. It could be a devilish power of evil."

"Perhaps it is not wits you all lack but courage," Inkleth said keeping his voice low. "You are all afraid. You're afraid because of the picture."

He shrugged his shoulders. "I repeat, my lord, that the real reason you don't want to go in has nothing to do with Chocma's orders. It is simply that you are afraid."

"I'm not scared," said Kurt.

"Then open the door," Inkleth replied.

"No, don't," both Lisa and Wesley spoke simultaneously. But it was too late.

"Open in the name of Gaal!" Kurt said.

A silence descended over them all. But the door did not move.

"Open in the name of Gaal," repeated Kurt more firmly. Still the door remained closed. Inkleth tried the handle and even hurled his weight against the door. But he

might just as well have been hitting rock.

"Well, that settles it, and I hope you're both satisfied," Wesley said turning to go up the final stairway. The others followed him with the strange feeling that a presence in the room below was listening to their footsteps. As Lisa turned she could have sworn she saw Inkleth wink and Kurt grin back at him.

A narrow doorway stood at the top of the third flight of stairs. "Open in the name of Gaal!" Wesley said quietly. This time there was the sound of a lock turning and the door creaked slowly open.

It was exactly as they had seen it on the television screen. The oak table was there, the box, the book and the huge key. Under the table was the sword in its scabbard, a sword forged from iron thunderbolts.

Wesley took it by the hilt and both Kurt and Lisa wanted to touch it. "Pull it out of its scabbard and let's see it," Lisa said. But Wesley, weighed down with his sense of responsibility, and very much on edge said, "No, we can look at it later." He strapped the weapon to his belt.

All of them crowded round. They could see no speck of dust on the table. Gently Wesley tried to raise the lid of the box, but it did not move. "I guess it's locked," he said.

"Try to open it in the name of Gaal," suggested Inkleth.

Wesley shrugged. "From what Lisa says, that wouldn't work unless opening the box was part of what we're supposed to do. I'm curious, but I'm more concerned with carrying out Gaal's orders right now than with fooling around with treasures." The others said nothing but Kurt muttered to himself.

They could and did open the book. Lisa opened it and shocked them all with a blinding flash of pale blue light.

Suddenly the whole room seemed to be nothing but light. None of them could stand the intensity of it and instinctively covered their faces with their hands. Yet just before Lisa covered her eyes she could have sworn that out of the corner of her eye she had seen an enormous rat where Inkleth was standing. She groped with one hand to close the book, and for a few moments all of them were blinking and seeing bright lights and colors as their eyes got used to normal light again.

"Wow, that sure was something," Kurt said. "I wouldn't want to be around if Chocma was using that against me." Lisa turned to look at Inkleth, but he was standing and blinking like the rest. There was no sign of the rat. She decided her mind had been playing tricks on her.

They all handled the key, testing the weight of it, examining the intricate pattern.

"I think it gives off a sort of vibration," Lisa said.

Kurt and Wesley agreed. "In fact it sort of hums like a tuning fork," Wesley said. Inkleth showed no interest in it.

It seemed that there was nothing left to do, and none of them with the possible exception of Inkleth really felt like staying in the ancient stone keep. As Lisa said later, the thought of the room underneath with a waiting something or a waiting some*one* gave them the creeps. You could never be sure whether the door might open itself in the night and the thing or being come out.

They were hungry and their food supplies were meager. "We could go back tonight," Wesley said, "and sleep in the cabin. The only thing is that the pigeon was supposed to meet us here and take us to the white reindeer." Inkleth suggested they build a fire and eat outside, reminding them that he had the three trout and suggesting he could catch more fish in the passage below.

They set out to explore the castle ruins. Trooping down the stairs they felt easier in their minds once they passed the "slumberer's room." On the floor below, they stopped to stare for a minute at the picture. It was still blank. Uneasily they left it, closed the door (because it felt better that way) and trooped through the library and out of the main doors of the keep.

Castle ruins are fascinating. You can wander round grassy spaces among tumbled walls imagining exciting battles. In one grassy square surrounded by stone foundations they found old iron and brass pots half buried in the ground, some still usable. They assumed that the room may have been a kitchen or scullery. They enjoyed the feeling of nature, the wildness, the solitude and the sense of things long past, and began to feel less fearful. Before looking for firewood they scrambled onto the tops of walls, peered down through holes into tunnels and admired the clambering ivy. It was, as Lisa said, very peaceful.

But soon they had to get down to the business of preparing a fire. Inkleth went to fish below the keep. Wood was plentiful. Trees around the castle had cast off many dead and brittle branches. They argued about where the fire should be built. Lisa was adamant that it had to be in some place where she could face the keep but not be too close to it. It still made her feel spooky.

So they picked a grassy spot about fifty yards from the main door of the keep, built a fireplace of stones and filled it with dry grass, twigs and firewood. Wesley even contrived something to hang an iron pot on. It consisted of a metal bar resting on two forked pieces of wood stuck into the ground.

"Inkleth said he would bring water up, but I don't

think he had anything to bring it in," Wesley said.

"He has his water bag," Lisa replied.

"I know, but he might as well have one of these rusty iron pots. It could be washed out and filled with fresh water."

Kurt volunteered to go with the pot which surprised Wesley. "He must be getting over his meanness," he thought to himself.

Wesley took nearly half an hour to get the fire going. The tinder worked well enough, but the dry grass was curiously slow in burning. Once or twice they nearly got it going and both of them blew till they were dizzy trying to make the wood catch fire. But all they got for their pains were smarting, watering, smoke-blackened eyes.

In the end they collected more grass, stuffed it under the twigs, and this time, with puffing, fanning and general encouragement they were delighted to see yellow flames licking upward and to hear the satisfying crackle of igniting wood.

Inkleth and Kurt came back with the water, the trout and five other fish which none of them recognized but which Inkleth assured them were very good. Presently there were enough hot ashes to cook the fish while they waited for the water to boil.

It really wasn't a bad meal. If you have a good appetite it's amazing how different things taste. Stale bread, old cheese, half-dried meat with cold water made a good start. The fish were more difficult. They pulled pieces of fish out of the ashes with sticks and ate them with their fingers. It meant getting their fingers burned and not minding eating a few ashes along with the fish. Yet they tasted delicious. All of them went on eating until they had eaten all they could, leaving the uneaten fish to burn on the ashes. They wiped their sticky fingers on the dry grass or on their clothes (which was not altogether satisfactory).

It took longer than they had thought for the water to boil. Inkleth said he had some herb tea similar to the tea they had had in the cabin. He produced a metal cup from his wallet, sprinkled a few dry leaves into the cup, poured hot water on it and passed it to Kurt. If you've ever drunk hot liquid from a metal cup you will know that the first thing that happens (until you catch on) is that you burn your lips on the rim of the cup. Kurt did just that. His head jerked back. Then he tried again to sip more carefully. He pulled a face. "Ugh, it's horrid," he said. "Taste it, Wesley."

Wesley cautiously tried. The tea certainly had an unusual flavor, but Wesley liked it. It reminded him of something herbal a strange maiden aunt had insisted he drink "to make his kidneys work properly." He drank the whole cup. Lisa drank another. "It's actually sweet," she said. "I think it's better than the stuff we had at the cabin. Try it again, Kurt. I'm sure you'll like it when you get used to it."

But Kurt shook his head firmly. He drank from his water bottle while Inkleth poured more hot water into his cup. Neither Wesley nor Lisa could remember afterward whether or not he had put any of the herbs into it before drinking himself.

By sunset each of them knew in his or her heart that they would have to go into the keep for the night. No one said anything because everyone wanted to put the matter off as long as they could, and I can't blame them. Kurt and Lisa were especially troubled. In the end it was Lisa who asked, "Where shall we sleep?"

"There are couches in the treasure room," Wesley said. "Why don't we take one each?"

Lisa hesitated. "I have a spooky feeling about the room underneath," she said. "Suppose he wakes up and starts coming upstairs? I know it's silly, but I just feel that way."

"But he could equally well come downstairs. What difference does it make whether we sleep below him or above him?"

"At least we can run outside or even down to the boat if we're on the ground floor. But if we were upstairs we'd have no place to go but the roof."

Inkleth was smiling, a little contemptuously, Lisa thought. Wesley shrugged. "It's all the same to me," he said. "O.K. Let's make it the library. Some of those chairs look pretty comfortable, and there are plenty of cushions around." He yawned. "It's been quite a day," he said. "Beating against the wind this morning made me pretty tired. I think I'll get an early night."

"O.K., but let's stick together," Lisa said. "Let's all sleep in the library and close the door at the top of the stairs."

An hour later Lisa and Wesley were soundly asleep on the library floor. Kurt was staring wide awake at the ceiling. Inkleth was snoring.

22
The Tower Destroyed

At three that morning Kurt felt his shoulder being shaken. Inkleth's voice was in his ear, "Time to go, my lord Kurt." Kurt shook his head groggily, found himself curled in one of the library chairs, stretched, yawned and got to his feet.

"What about the others?" he asked.

"They won't wake up—not after the herbs I gave them," Inkleth replied.

Kurt began to follow him across to the stairway. "Why didn't you open the door yesterday?" he asked.

"I doubt whether your brother and sister would really understand how wise and just the Sleeper is," he answered. "They have both been thoroughly fooled by Kardia."

"And are you sure the Sleeper will make me a real magician?"

"If you follow his instructions, my lord." He smiled. "We acted our parts well yesterday, did we not?"

"I got scared when I used the name of Gaal. I thought it really might open."

"I was not sure myself, my lord, for the word of Gaal is powerful. But the magic that seals the Sleeper's door is of another kind."

By this time they were climbing up the second flight of stairs. "Are you sure Gaal isn't who he says he is? Lisa just adores him."

"The Gaal delusion deceives many people. It makes them insane. The word *Gaal* is a spell which undoubtedly produces powerful effects. Someone has invoked the name to produce the present drought."

"And are you sure we can overcome such power?"

"Yes, my lord."

"And me, what will happen to me?"

"You will become one of the leading magicians in Anthropos. You will have powers you cannot conceive of now."

"There's just one thing I don't understand," Kurt said. "Why did you fight so hard against the goblins?"

"Hocoino said they would be a small price to pay for gaining Kardia's confidence. In any case we have always hated them."

Kurt's heart was beating hard. "Are you sure Wes and Lisa won't get hurt?"

"Does that really matter, my lord?"

"Well, I'd prefer them not to be harmed. Just sent back to our own world."

"It will be as you say, my lord."

"And I won't have to go to school?"

"Of course not, my lord. You will study only magic."

By now they were standing outside the Sleeper's door.

In the darkness Kurt felt his flesh creep. His heart was beating so loudly that he was sure Inkleth could hear it.

"Now, my lord, command the door to open."

Kurt's throat was dry and his voice both cracked and shaky. "Open," he said, "in the name of all the powers of darkness."

For a moment nothing happened. One part of Kurt was disappointed but another part was relieved. Then, as silent as night the door swung open. A flood of red light spilled out onto the stairway. Inside the room he could see curtains, luxurious furnishings, and in the center a throne on which sat a man, the sight of whom made Kurt gasp in amazement and shake with fear. It was the white-haired, black-robed man in the picture.

"Come in, my friends. Come celebrate with me my return to life and power," came a deep, warm voice. The Sleeper was speaking, and the two stepped inside to face him. He extended a jeweled hand first to Inkleth, who knelt, kissed it, and then to Kurt, who did the same. "I've done it now," the thought flashed through Kurt's mind. "I guess there will be no turning back after this."

"My body may sleep, but my mind does not. I know you both, and I drew you here. Inkleth, your Matmon will be the most powerful group in Anthropos. Kurt, your powers as a magician will be unsurpassed."

"Who are you, sir? We call you the Sleeper," Kurt asked shakily.

"It is as good a name as any. But my true name is Shagah."

"Is it you who rules the dark regions?"

"No, my son. I am but his majesty's ambassador-in-chief and am come to rescue Hocoino in his hour of need. Many centuries I have waited here for this opportunity. And now my hour has come."

Kurt stared at the man's face. From among his pale wrinkles shone strangely beautiful, glittering eyes. They glittered like icicles. His smile was warm, his voice gentle, but his eyes were intensely cold. Kurt found he couldn't look at them for long without dropping his own.

"It was you, was it not, my son, Kurt, who took down my picture and commenced my liberation?"

"Well, Inkleth told me to. . . ."

"And you had courage enough to obey."

"Yes, sir."

"Then I owe you many thanks. And in gratitude to you I want not only to make of you a great magician but to let you play a key role in the war that is about to be fought."

Kurt's heart continued to beat. Now he would show Lisa and Wesley! In his mind he pictured their admiration and envy. He would be able to say to them, "See, I understood what the real truth was right from the start." They would look up to him and be grateful to him. He could go back to their own world with a power that. . . .

"My son, are you willing to serve us?"

"Yes, sir."

"Then swear, my young lord, in the name of all the legions of darkness that you will do as I say."

"I solemnly swear, sir, in the name of, er, in the name of. . . ."

"All the legions of darkness."

"Of all the legions of darkness to do as you say. But, sir?"

"Yes, my son."

"Wes and Lisa won't get hurt? I know they're stuffy and square but. . . ."

"My son, your brother and sister will be protected for your sake."

"Now, Kurt, let us test your new powers. Do you see the cat in the chair on your left?" For the first time Kurt noticed a black cat curled on the chair beside Shagah. "I want you to bid its body to disappear, in my name, but leave its tail behind."

"You're not joking, are you, sir?"

"I never joke, Kurt." There was a hard edge to his voice. Kurt took a deep breath.

"Cat, disappear in the name of Shagah but leave your tail behind." Instantly the cat was just not there. Only a disembodied tail, twitching and waving remained on the chair. It gave Kurt the creeps.

"Now, Kurt, do you know what your part is to be?"

"No, sir. Inkleth didn't say," Kurt said, continuing to stare at the tail, fascinated by its twitching and waving. It was like a black, furry snake.

"You are to destroy this tower at the hour when the moon is right overhead."

"Tonight, sir?"

"Yes, tonight."

"Destroy the whole tower, sir?"

"Well, you may leave intact the ground floor so as to save your brother and sister."

"But why do you want me to destroy the tower?"

"Simply to bury the orb and the book and the key. If Kardia lacks these things, he can never win in the battle that is to come."

"Then why don't you simply take them yourself, sir? I mean, I don't mind destroying the tower—it would be great to watch it fall down—but...."

"Kurt, such is the power of the name of Gaal that we are not able to remove the king's chief treasures. We have captured them, but so long as they remain in the keep we cannot use them. But if the tower collapses, it will take hours and possibly days to find them in the ruins. By that time Kardia will be no more. True rule will have been established in the kingdom."

Kurt paused, trying to piece the startling information together. Destroy a tower! Ensure Kardia's defeat! Yet somehow he liked Kardia and both Wesley and Lisa seemed to really believe in Gaal. He pushed his thoughts aside. To be a real magician—that was the thing! To have the power to destroy buildings and to change history! Finally he said, "So what am I to do, sir?"

"When the moon is directly overhead, you are to mark a triangle in the grass with three stones. Be sure to do so well away from falling masonry. Step inside the triangle and then bid the tower fall in my name and those of the powers of darkness leaving intact the ground floor. That is all. Now come closer to me that I may give you the power you need." Shagah laid his hands on Kurt's head. A strange vibration passed from Shagah's delicate hands to Kurt's head and then to all his body. Seconds later, when the hands were removed and the vibration ceased, he knew he was a changed boy. He felt a much greater urge to destroy, to destroy anything, buildings, people, animals—anything. "There is just one thing, Kurt."

"Yes, sir."

"If you do not use the power within you to destroy the tower, it will turn and destroy you. Your body will be blown into a million pieces. Power is dangerous when it is not used properly."

In an instant the room was empty. The red light, the Sleeper, Inkleth, the throne, the twitching tail, furnishings, chairs—everything was gone. Gone without a sound. Kurt found himself alone in a bare room with stone walls and a wooden floor. Moonlight poured palely through two of the windows.

Moonlight. Had he been dreaming? Moonlight. If he didn't do what he was told within an hour after the moon reached its zenith, he might be blown to pieces. He crept downstairs to the library. Lisa and Wesley were sleeping peacefully, Wesley stretched out on the floor with a cushion for a pillow and Lisa curled in a deep armchair.

He made a lot of noise opening the main door, but neither his brother nor his sister moved. Outside the air was crisp and cold. He walked quickly to a point about a hundred yards from the keep and dragged three heavy stones to form a triangle.

He stared up at the moon. It was pretty high. It didn't go right overhead very often. How could he know when the time had come? It was cold outside, and he found himself shivering, partly from cold, partly from fear.

Doubts began to plague him. Suppose the library also collapsed? What would happen to him if he were left alone on the island? Would they come back to pick him up? What if Wesley and Lisa were injured or even killed when the tower fell? He no longer had Inkleth or Shagah to rely on.

He hurried uneasily back to the library. "Wes," he said shaking his brother violently by the shoulder. "Wes, wake up! The tower's going to fall down!"

"Shnot time yet," Wesley mumbled. "Leave me alone."

"Wes, it's important! Wake up, Wes! We gotta get out of here."

"Wassamatter with you? Go back to sleep!"

Kurt tugged the cushion from under Wesley's head. Inkleth's drug seemed pretty effective. "Hey, whadja doing?" Wesley sat up.

"Wes, we gotta get out of here! The tower's going to fall down!"

"Don't be crazy."

"Wes, it *is*. You've gotta get outside!"

Wes stood up. "Boy, do I feel weird," he said. "I'm all dizzy."

"It's a drug, Wesley, the drug Inkleth gave you."

"Huh?"

"For crying out loud get a move on, Wes! Get outside! It's urgent!"

Wesley staggered slowly to the door, shook his head again and stepped out into the cold air.

Lisa was worse. No matter what he did to her she merely mumbled. In the end he got his arms under her armpits and pulled her through the door letting her heels drag on the ground. Panting with exertion he dumped her near the triangle of stones.

Wesley was lying down on the grass halfway between the triangle and the tower. Savagely Kurt kicked him. "Hey, what's that for?"

Kurt was ready to cry with rage and anxiety. "Get up, you idiot! The tower's going to fall down any minute now!"

Wes sat up and stared at his brother in bewilderment. "What in the name of sense has got into you?" He sounded a little more wide awake.

"Don't ask questions, Wes. Just do as I say. Get back there where Lisa is."

Something in Kurt's voice woke Wesley thoroughly, and he did as he was told. Kurt glanced at the moon. Was it high enough? Did he have time to get blankets and rugs from the library to keep them warm? In desperation he ran back, grabbed anything he could and returned to his brother and sister.

Lisa was now awake and sitting up. Both were silent. A red streak of dawn became apparent in the east. The moon was overhead. It lit the keep in a ghostly fashion.

He stepped inside his triangle. Would it work? Was the moon right? He found his legs were shaking and his mouth dry. "In the name of Shagah and of all the legions of darkness I bid the keep to be destroyed—all except the library."

A flash of red light burst from his chest. With a loud crack it shot in a broad ragged sheet to hit the keep. Then slowly and gracefully a split seemed to tear the keep into two vertical halves, ripping it apart from top to bottom. Each half curved gently outward, crumbling as it fell. Then came the roar of pounding and crashing granite stones. A dense cloud of dust rose over them.

Wesley and Lisa had sprung to their feet. No one moved or spoke. As the dust died down, they could all see that the library had been destroyed as well. Wesley and Lisa would have been killed had they been left inside.

Two contradictory feelings arose in Kurt's mind. One was of fierce pride at his dramatic power. The other was a feeling that he didn't want to speak with or to look at either Lisa or Wesley. "I hope they realize how grateful they should be," he thought to himself as he began to move mechanically toward the pile of rubble.

23

Theophilus to the Rescue

Lisa and Wesley were certainly wider awake than they had ever been in their lives. As Wesley saw Kurt slouch away from them he ran forward, gripped his brother fiercely by the shoulder and swung him round to face them. Lisa quietly joined them.

For a moment no one said a word. If it had been daylight you would have seen that Wesley was white with rage. Kurt looked at the ground, rubbing one foot over the other. Then in a voice that was low but shaking with anger, Wesley said, "I think you owe us an explanation. What in the name of sense are you playing at?"

Kurt looked up. "I'm not playing at anything. I'm a magician. I blasted the keep to pieces. I could do the same to you if I wanted. I have the power inside me to do it."

Lisa said quietly, "Could you put the keep together

again, Mr. Magician?"

Kurt looked nonplused for a moment. Then he shrugged. "Why should I?"

"Because if you don't, how are we going to find the things we were sent here for?"

Kurt smirked. "That's the whole point. We're not going to be able to. That's why I did it."

"You mean you wanted to sabotage the whole operation?" Wesley was incredulous. "But why?"

"Why? Because if you dumb cluts are stupid enough to buy all the nonsense about Kardia getting his kingdom back—tough! Kardia was an incompetent king. He gave the Matmon a raw deal. He didn't know how to govern. He doesn't deserve to govern. As for the mythical Gaal, all *he* seems capable of doing is putting in mysterious appearances here and there. I'm not even sure whether he exists."

Wesley's anger was giving way to bewilderment. "What's come over you, Kurt? Since when did you become an expert in the history and politics of Anthropos? Why all this big magician stuff? You used to be easygoing and fun to be with, but now...."

Lisa interrupted. "What are we going to do now? I'm cold. We have no food. We have no way of getting down to the boat. How do we get off the island?"

Kurt looked puzzled for a moment. "Well, I imagine some arrangements will be made for me, but as for you two...."

"We can stay here and starve?"

"Well, if this Gaal you talk about is so powerful...." (Kurt was angry and sarcastic because he had begun to realize how selfish he must appear.)

Wesley sat down on the dewy grass. "When did you start thinking this way?"

"Oh, I talked to Inkleth. He knows a lot about Anthropos. He opened my eyes, I can tell you."

"He also nearly had you killed by a seven-headed ogre!"

"Oh, *that*. I didn't realize it at the time, but that was put on for your benefit. Inkleth said he was sorry he forgot to warn me. Inkleth's limp, you know, was all put on. It even had *me* fooled until I saw that he was not limping on the wharf."

It was then that it dawned on Wesley what had puzzled him about Inkleth's limp. Kurt himself had said while they were still in the cabin that Inkleth had stopped limping, but other thoughts were going through his mind: the vivid memory of his encounter with the monster, the smashed legs, the battered heads.

"So I killed an ogre who was just play-acting?"

"I must say you did a good job. I didn't know you were that strong, Wes. Mind you, you don't have the kind of power I have."

"I don't have any power at all, Kurt. The pigeon came on to me and the oar just did things by itself. I'm no magician, and I don't believe you are."

"Oh, don't you? How about the keep? You must admit that took more power than killing a seven-headed ogre."

Wes looked up at his brother. "Kurt, just do one, single thing more. Anything will do—a little thing like causing the stones that block the tunnel to clear away for us or . . . providing us with some food. I don't care what you do. You are a magician. Show us some magic. Blowing up the keep was pretty impressive, I admit, but it could be just a flash in the pan."

Kurt had the uncomfortable feeling that he was getting cornered. "I don't propose to perform just to convince you."

"The truth is you can't. You aren't a magician at all."

"Oh, yes, I am!"

"Then prove it."

"I've proved it already."

"Kurt, you're only fooling yourself."

"Oh, no, I'm not; what's more, I'm going to become a great magician. The Sleeper promised me."

"The Sleeper? You mean...."

"I wakened him."

"How?"

"I bade the door open in the name of all the powers of darkness."

Wesley was stunned. "You mean you've joined the other side?"

"Yes."

Lisa had gone back to where they had been sitting and picked up her cape and the couple of blankets Kurt had dragged out of the library. Dawn was now clearly breaking. In the gray light they could see more clearly the mound of rubble that had half an hour before been a solid tower.

"You're both shivering. Wrap these round you." Gratefully they did so.

"Kurt, how do you know you can trust people like Inkleth and the Sleeper?"

"Why shouldn't I?"

"Well, it seems to me that Inkleth's a pretty treacherous sort of character. He made out as though he was loyal to Kardia...."

"Kardia's a fool."

"But that's beside the point. If Inkleth deceived Kardia, how d'you know he wasn't just making use of *you?*"

"In what way?"

"Why to get him here to the island."

"Well, I can trust the Sleeper anyhow. He gave me real power."

"Did he?"

"You *saw*. Look at the rubble."

Wesley was quiet for a moment. "I seem to remember you saying something like, 'except for the library.' What was that supposed to mean?"

"It meant . . . I . . . I guess something went wrong."

There was another pause.

"Kurt, why did you drag Lisa and me *out* of the library?"

"Because . . . I don't know . . . just in case. . . ."

"You see, you don't really trust the Sleeper. If you had trusted him, Lisa and I would be dead by now. You've joined a side in which you can trust nobody. Thanks incidentally for saving our lives." There was a touch of bitterness in Wesley's voice.

Something was crawling toward them over the grass. Lisa saw it first. "It looks like an animal of some kind. It's coming toward us."

They all stared in the gray half light. Wesley began to walk toward it. It seemed to advance slowly and with difficulty.

"Be careful, Wes," Lisa said. "We don't know what kind of animals there are here."

Wes was only twenty yards from the creature. "It's Inkleth!" he cried, suddenly breaking into a run. "It's Inkleth and he's hurt—pretty badly I'd say."

Quickly they ran to him. He was crawling on hands and knees. Blood was matted on the side of his head and in his beard. The leg he used to limp on was being dragged. Carefully he lay down, tried to roll on one side to face them and groaned.

"Inkleth, what happened? What's the matter?"

The words came faintly but clearly. "I served my purpose for them, so they got rid of me—or tried to."

Kurt seemed agitated. He squatted down by Inkleth. "But what happened? You disappeared. Everything disappeared. Where did you go to? How did you get back?"

Inkleth was breathing with difficulty. There were long pauses between his sentences.

"We disappeared, but we did not leave. . . . We were made invisible as long as you were in the room. It was done to deceive you. . . . Only Shagah left the tower. He said good-by most courteously. . . . He said he was sorry he could no longer use me but that my death would be quick and painless. 'Your little pupil, lord Kurt, will see to that. I hope he enjoys his one fling at playing with magic!' I was bound by magic in a chair, able only to await the time when you would destroy the keep. . . . I tried to shout out, but no voice came. Then you said the words. I remember naught what happened after that. . . . When I came to my senses I found myself mostly in the open. My legs were trapped. One of them is broken. But I struggled free. . . . Then I heard your voices. . . ."

Wesley whistled. "Well, this is a fine kettle of fish. Four of us stranded. One of us injured. Two of us hopeless dopes. And Kardia in need of the treasures by tomorrow evening."

Lisa, always practical, knelt down beside Inkleth. "Let's help Inkleth. Was there any water left in the pot?"

In the gathering daylight they formed a rough stretcher for Inkleth from two branches and a blanket. Lisa, remembering her Red Cross classes, bathed his head, washing away the dried blood. The cut in it did not seem too serious. His lower right leg was obviously broken and they tried to set it in crude splints. Lisa tore another of the blankets into strips. Inkleth screamed as they tried to pull his leg straight. He begged to be given some of his herbs in water. "It helps pain and it will put me to sleep. I gave it to you last night to keep you quiet while Kurt and I did our work," he said. Lisa served it to him herself from a spoon, and in a while he seemed more relaxed and in less pain.

They next held a council of war—without Inkleth. Kurt seemed pretty depressed and took little part. Even Lisa felt hopeless. "I've lost interest in the treasures. I suppose we ought to make some effort to find them."

"Not much hope of doing so. It would take days to sort through that rubble. And even if we find them, how do we get off the island? And what do we eat?"

"Wes, when I was on the altar, I didn't even know whether there was a Shepherd or not. But I called out to him. . . . Let's hold hands. . . ." Kurt pulled his away, but Wesley and Lisa joined hands as Lisa said, "Can you hear us, Gaal? We've made a mess of things. We need your help. We need your help to find the book, the orb and the key. And we need to get off the island."

Nothing happened, but they both felt better. The first red sunlight began to cast long shadows on the grass. Then, fluttering over the ruins toward them came the pigeon Lisa had so learned to love. It settled on the grass near them, cocked its head on one side and began to hop and flutter in the direction of the ruined keep. "I guess it wants us to follow."

Wesley and Lisa followed the bird, fascinated and curious. Kurt followed at a distance, miserable and humiliated. "Your little pupil." The words repeated themselves mockingly in his brain. "His one fling at playing magic." He felt bitter, angry, sick.

Meanwhile his brother and sister were clambering up

the pile of rocky rubble to where the pigeon seemed to be pecking at something. They stared at it bewildered. "I do believe it's telling us to start looking here," Wes said. But the stones were huge. The pigeon hopped on Wesley's head.

Slowly, he lifted one huge rock after another. To his astonishment they were not nearly so heavy as he would have thought. He called over to Kurt for assistance. Kurt came and struggled to lift stones half the size Wesley was handling, but though he gasped and heaved, he had to be content to move quite small stones. "It's the pigeon again. I can see it this time," he said with bitterness. He turned his back to Wesley and squatted on his haunches, holding his head between his hands.

The sun was rising steadily. It was warm work. Lisa, who did what she could, and Wesley soon were sweating freely and were both hungry and thirsty. "We ought to move Inkleth into the shade," Lisa said.

"I'm thirsty. Is there any water left?" Kurt had spoken for the first time.

Wesley said, "Let's call a halt, have a drink and move Inkleth into the shadow."

As they moved away, the pigeon hopped back into the hole Wesley was making. Kurt stared at it balefully. What or who was it? Could it be trusted?

Inkleth was sleeping. As they moved him they were careful not to waken him. The water was far from plentiful, but Wesley portioned it out from Inkleth's cup. It tasted good. Each of them wanted more, but they all knew they must make it last. Kurt came to watch them sullenly.

They had only been back on the rubble a few minutes, the pigeon once again on Wesley's head, when Kurt excitedly said, "Look—that's the corner of the box!" And so it was. Feverishly he struggled to heave stones until his muscles ached, and soon he and Wesley dragged it over the stones to the grass. With the last jerk it fell apart and from it rolled a gold ball, bigger than your fist, encrusted with diamonds, rubies, emeralds and other gems, and crowned with a gold cross.

"Wow! Just *look* at it!"

Wesley lifted it carefully. It was heavy, glittering brilliantly in the midmorning sun. For several minutes they feasted their eyes on it. Then Wesley put it inside his leather food pouch (now emptied of crumbs) and laid it carefully on the turf beside the rubble.

It took another three hours, Lisa and Kurt doing what they could and Wesley doing the major work to get the book. Once again the pigeon told them where to start looking, but the labor, the sweating, the aching, the thirst and the hunger even with the pigeon's help were almost

unbearable. One thing I will say about Kurt is that he worked as hard as any of them. And when they found the book they were overjoyed to see it had received very little damage. There were scratches and tears on its leather cover, but its back was unbroken, and by some miracle it remained closed.

Once again they stopped for their meager drink. Inkleth slept on in the shade. Lisa said, "I don't think I can do anymore. I feel weak and *awfully* tired."

Wesley nodded. He felt exhausted himself, and he knew Kurt did. Finally in midafternoon, guided by the pigeon, they dragged themselves to a third spot on the rubble where to their joy they could immediately see the key in a crevice between two stones. It cost only a bit of effort and some skinned knuckles to retrieve it.

The book, the orb, the key. They had all three! But they were hungry, exhausted, scratched, bruised and pretty filthy. As they squatted together in a circle, Lisa said, "Look! Here comes Theophilus."

The flying horse did an aerial pirouette and a graceful landing. Nobody noticed that the pigeon had disappeared.

Theophilus cocked his head on one side. "You know, I *told* Gaal it was stupid of him to send you children on a mission like this. If I had been in charge, the whole operation would have been accomplished in minutes."

Lisa smiled in spite of her tiredness. "You don't change, Theophilus. How would you have got through the enchantment?"

"Pooh, enchantment! Childish superstitions. A being of my intelligence doesn't pay heed to superstition. Now let me tell you in detail how I would have carried out this operation. I conceived, in fact, a most brilliant plan which I'm sure you could find instructive in the future."

"For goodness sake, shut him up," growled Kurt.

Lisa laughed. It was a relief to do so after all the tensions of the day. She even began to play on the horse's vanity. "It is *present* abilities we need right now, Theophilus. We know how very clever you are, but we all need to get to the shore. And we have an injured dwarf here. Is there any way you can get him to where he can be attended to?"

"Can I? Of course, I can. I can. . . ."

"But he's on a stretcher. Supposing you dropped the stretcher when you were flying? Suppose it fell off your back?"

"*Me*? Drop a stretcher? My dear young lady, to whom do you think you are speaking? Can *you* balance a book on your head? Because if you, child and inexperienced as you are (clumsy, too, no doubt), can do *that*, how much better do you suppose that *I*. . . ."

"Of course, Theophilus, I was forgetting how exceedingly talented, wise and generous you are." Lisa's face was straight. "You must forgive us. You see, we don't meet equine angels every day. Would you mind coming over and letting us place him on your back?"

"Most certainly. Always ready to serve. However humble the task, however far beneath my status and calling. Humility, as I'm sure you realize, is one of my principal virtues. My character is as sweet smelling as my name."

Carefully they adjusted the stretcher on Theophilus' back. Inkleth was wide awake and in pain. They explained to him what was to happen. He looked frightened but nodded. A moment later, the horse's wings spread wide and Theophilus rose gently and gracefully from the ground. As he did so he called back to the children, "Oh, the leather pouch I left is for you children. I forgot to mention it when I came. So many important matters on my mind. . . ."

They had scarcely noticed the pouch. When they opened it they gave a shout of joy. Fruit, cheeses, fresh bread, butter, fruit drinks, rhubarb pie, meat pies—even plates, cutlery and a tablecloth. Eagerly they set to, and by the time Theophilus returned, they were stretched out on the grass, slumbering contentedly in the late afternoon sun.

24

Through the Forest of Blackness

The children did not need the pigeon to guide them to their rendezvous. Theophilus knew where to take them. ("Of *course,* I know! There is nothing about which Gaal does not consult me. I told him that I thought his idea was not bad, considering.") And he was quite certain he could manage the three of them. ("You probably fail to appreciate the *enormous* power in my wings.") Lisa didn't bother to remind him of the much greater power and speed of the Qadar. She was growing rather fond of Theophilus, for as she said, "You can't take him seriously, and he's too much of an idiot to get mad at."

Even before they landed, while they were still approaching the northwest shore of the lake, they saw two things. One was a group of four beautiful white reindeer with enormous antlers. The other was that Gaal was there, a little way off in the trees and deep in conversation with Inkleth who seemed to be perfectly well.

"Are you sure it's not his brother?" Wesley asked.

"No, Wes." Kurt was shaking his head wonderingly. "It's Inkleth. I'd know him anywhere."

"Well, in that case he got better pretty fast."

"Gaal can do things like that," Lisa said. She was remembering all the dirt, the hunger and the discomfort with which she came to him as they emerged from the tunnel beneath Bamah and Nephesh, and of the fountain of the Bayith of Yayin. Fondly she touched her white robe.

A moment later they had landed on a grassy bank near the reindeer who all turned their heads to watch them with large brown eyes, much larger eyes than reindeer have in our world. In fact if it were not for their size and antlers, you would have mistaken them for overgrown fawns. They wiggled their ears, twitched their noses and moved slowly toward the children. Wesley and Lisa ran forward and Kurt followed more slowly.

"Aren't they darlings?" Lisa said, throwing her arms round one of them who seemed as though he welcomed it. Wesley stroked the nose of the deer nearest him.

Kurt seemed uncomfortable. "The things that I said about Gaal," he said, "I knew when I said them that they weren't true. Please don't say anything to him."

"He probably knows already," Lisa replied. "He's like that. He knows even what you're thinking."

"Look, you guys, last time I said you were both right— I mean, in the cabin—I didn't really mean it. I wasn't sure what I meant. I was still scared about the ogre. Anyway I've been thinking. I was real mean about the keep and Inkleth and so on. I was a fool, an absolute conceited fool. Seeing the mess Inkleth was in just sickened me. I know you guys will think I'm a heel. I can't expect you to like me anymore...."

Wes swung round. "Kurt, it wasn't *you* that did all those things. You're just not like that."

"That's just the trouble, Wes. Deep down I *am* like that. I wanted to be the big magician, and I didn't care even if it meant hurting you guys. I nearly left you in the library. Gosh, when I think about that...."

"Well, you didn't. You pulled us out. I still think you just weren't thinking straight."

"That's for sure; but I'm still to blame, Wes. What d'you think he's talking to Inkleth about?"

"He's probably helping him straighten *his* thinking out," Lisa said.

"I've got a sick feeling he'll probably want to talk to me. See, they're coming this way now. Inkleth looks pretty happy. What on earth shall I say if he talks to me? Wes, I'm scared. I'm real scared. I called on the powers of darkness."

Kurt never told anybody what went on between Gaal and himself. His face was as white as chalk and his hands were shaking when Gaal beckoned to him. They spent a long time together. Sometimes they sat and sometimes they walked. All that the rest of them knew was that when Kurt came back, he was no longer afraid. You could see he'd been crying, yet you could sense that he was at peace with himself. It was months and months before he ever said anything about Shagah and the keep.

Inkleth too was a changed dwarf. He bowed to Wes and Lisa and said seriously, "My lord and my lady, I have been shameless in my deceit. I pretended to be things I was not. I have discovered to my shame that not only am I a knave, I am also a fool. Whether you can now trust me or not I cannot say. But I have sworn my fealty to Gaal, who to my amazement accepts me as though I were a king, yet I know from his eyes that he has read the deepest, darkest secrets of my heart."

Lisa left the deer and put her arms round (as you can see she was a hugging kind of person) Inkleth whose face again became as red as his hair. "We've all done wrong things, Inkleth. At least *I* have. I was just as much a fool and just as much a knave as you. Let's forget the past."

Inkleth hung his head. He simply said, "Thank you, my lady and my lord. You are more than generous."

Wes said, "Now we must think about getting the treasures to Kardia."

Inkleth looked up then. "Matters are far more grave than you suppose. By the delay we have seriously jeopardized the war. My own followers will by now have deserted Kardia. But in other ways, ways I do not fully understand, the cause for Kardia and Gaal seems well nigh lost."

"Why?"

"Because of what your brother and I did on the Island of Geburah. We released a powerful sorcerer—far more formidable and powerful than Hocoino—and we delayed the arrival of the magic treasures. The battle will probably begin tomorrow night on the Heights of Rinnar. We could have been there by then if only we had not been delayed by our folly and our rebellion."

"But couldn't Gaal just send us there by magic right away? Or couldn't Theophilus take us?"

"I do not fully understand, my lord. It seems his magic does not work like that. He said, 'When I gave you the chance to serve me I also took the risk that you would betray me. There are some rules that can never be broken. Mistakes and betrayals follow my own laws.' He also said, 'You would never grow strong if I always made it easy for you.' "

"You mean he put the power to mess up the whole operation into our hands? That we could actually wreck the war?"

"That is how it seems, my lord."

"And he won't change it?"

"It seems he *cannot* change it, my lord."

"Why ever not? It seems like a simple thing to do."

"Because to do so would be to betray all that his kingdom stands for. It has something to do with truth, my lord."

"I don't understand."

"Nor do I, my lord. What I do understand is that he did give me that power and that the damage I did to his cause was real damage."

"Was he mad at you?" Lisa asked quietly.

"Yes, my lady."

"Yet you don't seem upset at all."

"My lady, his love is greater than his anger and there is peace between us. He has conquered my heart with his love. From henceforth I am his slave."

They both stared at Inkleth. His eyes were shining. He looked defiant and happy at the same time. Lisa said, "I know how you feel, Inkleth. He had the same effect on me."

By now Gaal and Kurt were approaching the three of them. Kurt would glance up at Gaal from time to time, a smile on his tear-stained face.

Gaal sat down on the grass and they followed his example. The later afternoon sun shone on his gold belt. "Kardia and his forces will be in grave peril by tomorrow night," he said. "If they should survive the night and if you should reach them before tomorrow night is over, then matters can change.

"But you must begin this very hour to travel through

the Forest of Blackness. When night falls, its enchantment will fill you with a yearning to sleep. Do not sleep. Do not dismount from the reindeer. The elms are beginning to wake at night, and they have power to kill. The treasures you carry can also be sensed at a great distance by the forces of darkness. They may detect you and try to stop you. As you follow the path I shall point out, you will arrive presently at a great mound where there are no trees. There you will find a cave of mine where you may rest.

"The path continues beyond the mound, and will bring you to the edge of the forest, from where you will be able to see the battlefield."

Wesley, forever worried asked, "Will the war be won, Gaal? Will Kardia be victorious? Will Hocoino be defeated?"

"Why do you ask me these questions?" Gaal was smiling.

"Well, if the war isn't going to be won, there's really no point in our trying to get these things to Kardia and Chocma. It will be wasted effort."

Gaal's face was grave. Wesley knew that either he had said something wrong or else that what he was saying didn't sound convincing enough. And as so often happens when people are not sure of themselves, he started to talk all the faster. The more he talked, the more he felt he was getting into a deeper mess. "It's not that we're —that I'm afraid of danger, though in a way, I am. But it's just the waste—you know what I mean, the wasted *effort*. I mean, supposing we get killed or eaten by some of those dreadful elm trees you talk about and the war is lost anyway. . . ." The feeling that what he was saying was getting him nowhere got worse.

"Is it ever a waste of time to fight evil?"

"I don't know, Gaal. Yes, I do, though. Why fight evil if evil's going to win anyway? Gosh, I know that sounds horrible. . . ."

Gaal said nothing, which increased Wesley's discomfort still more.

"I suppose you want me to say that it's always worthwhile to fight evil even if you know you're going to lose. But that doesn't make sense. Yet you want me to say it does."

"You seem to know a lot about what I am thinking. What I really wonder is whether you trust me or not."

"Trust you?"

"Yes, you seem to suspect that I do wrong to send you on a dangerous mission like this."

"It sounds awful when you put it that way."

"And I think for the moment that you're going to have to trust me even though I don't tell you all that's going to happen."

"But Gaal, of course we trust you."

"You mean you believe I know what I'm doing?"

It would have been insulting to say no, so Wesley uncomfortably said, "Yes, I suppose so—I mean—*yes.*"

"Do you think I don't care about you? Am I, perhaps, not a shepherd after all?"

As Wesley looked into Gaal's eyes he knew deep down inside himself that Gaal *did* care. What's more, he suddenly knew that Gaal knew what he was doing. He also knew that his questions had been pretty insulting to Gaal. He felt small and cheap.

"Then do as I bid you. The dangers are real so beware of all I told you. It is not for you to see into the future, only to live in the present moment. And that involves being able to trust me."

I don't imagine you have ridden on white reindeer.

You might have ridden red deer, and if you have, you will know that you get a very bumpy, jerky ride because they are forever leaping over bushes. Another problem is that they don't bother to think about what happens to you. For instance if they go *under* something they only consider whether they can get themselves and their antlers underneath. They don't seem to realize that you stick up over their antlers. This means that you are forever being hit by branches of trees, or even being swept right off their backs. Personally I only ride deer when I absolutely have to.

But the white reindeer were different. They were trained to run smoothly as well as swiftly, and the path they were to take through the forest was clear of branches. It was in fact another of those ancient stone pathways where the strange writing was carved on the stones.

By early evening they set out. Their food bags and water bags had been replenished. Gaal had waved good-by to them. Inkleth had the book strapped to his back. Wesley wore his sword and managed to carry the orb in his food bag too. Lisa carried another of the little books of light that Gaal gave her in her red sash where the key to the cave was too. Only Kurt carried nothing. Everyone except Lisa was hanging on to the antlers and concentrating on not falling off as they made their mad dash. Lisa was the only one to turn and wave good-by. As she saw the figure of Gaal still waving she had the curious impression that they were not actually leaving him. "I hope that's how it is," she thought to herself, "because I *do* want to see him again."

They rode till sunset without stopping. A great forest of elms, oaks, ash, firs, spruces and maple trees surrounded them for miles. In places they could not see much beyond the trees and bushes. In other places the undergrowth disappeared so that they could see for a long distance between the trees. Once or twice as the darkness began to gather Wesley thought he saw shadowy forms flitting from tree to tree keeping pace with them. Lisa saw them too, or *thought* she did. But neither said anything to the other because they didn't want to frighten anyone else. Occasionally high, high over their heads came faint sounds that reminded all three children of the Qadar.

Whether there *were* flitting shadows or faraway Qadar shrieks, nobody could be sure. And as I said, no one mentioned anything to anyone else. But all of them agreed that they should not pause for a rest but should push on until they reached the clearing with the cave. There was a general feeling of anxiety. The reindeer seemed to share it for the speed never slackened.

As the darkness gathered, the children and Inkleth began to relax. Really their anxiety should have been increasing. The darker it grew the more danger there was from dark powers. But the enchantment of the forest was deceptively soothing.

"Oh, what a lovely ride!" Kurt said after a while. "It's just like a dream."

"I don't feel a bit hungry," Lisa said.

"My lady and my lords, I feel sure there will be no danger," Inkleth replied. "Our fears were in vain."

"I'm not so sure," said Wesley. As usual he was being a worrywart. "Gaal said that there was a danger that we might fall asleep, or get off the reindeer. There was something about the elm trees...." He wrinkled his brow and shook his head in an effort to remember.

By the time they had traveled for another hour, the moon was riding in the sky above them, flitting through the branches of the trees to keep pace with them.

"Is it far?" Kurt asked of no one in particular.

"I know not, my lord," Inkleth replied. "We travel by secret ways that are unknown to me."

"I could use a pillow right now," Lisa said dreamily, leaning forward and trying to pillow her head in one arm while she held on to the antlers with the other. But it was very uncomfortable and she gave up.

Kurt said, "My eyes keep closing. I'm going to fall off if I don't look out."

"That would wake you up in a hurry," Wesley replied grimly.

But Wesley himself was getting confused. He remembered his father saying, "Never go on driving when you feel sleepy. Pull off to the side of the road and take a nap. It's much safer." Well, he felt sleepy now. But there was some reason, some special reason why they shouldn't stop. But what was it? What had Gaal actually said? He could remember something about not getting off the deer. That much he could be sure of. Perhaps if they stopped and took a nap on the backs of the deer it would be all right. In a car you didn't get out; you just put your head on the steering wheel or stretched out on the seat. That was it. They were not to get off the reindeer.

"O.K. Time for a halt!" Wesley called out. "We'll take a brief nap and go on again. But nobody must get off the back of their reindeer."

"Oh, *good*," said Kurt. "I was just going to beg you to stop."

"Your lordship is very kind," Inkleth said. "We Matmon require more sleep than you humans."

They pulled back on the horns of the deer and stopped. Lisa was looking puzzled. "There's something wrong," she said. "But I can't think what it is."

"It's just that we must stay on the reindeer and not get off," Wesley said.

"I don't think so. It was something else. Somehow I'm not thinking clearly."

Puzzled, Lisa leaned forward and cradled her head on both arms. She found that it was reasonably comfortable now that the reindeer had stopped moving. Wesley did the same. In less than a minute they were asleep.

They never saw Kurt slide off his mount, stretch, rub his eyes and sleepily curl up among the roots of a huge oak tree on the left side of the path. Nor did they see the two young elm saplings on either side of the oak lean over toward Kurt reaching to cover him with their greedy arms and fingers.

Inkleth too dismounted and staggered sleepily toward a giant elm on the opposite side of the path. He did not lie but sat at its foot and rested by leaning back against the trunk. Then slowly, so slowly that you could hardly see what was happening, his body began to sink into the elm as though the tree were made of soft plastic. Little by little the trunk began to fold itself round him.

The moon slid lower in the sky. All four of them slept on.

25

The Hole Where Time Is No More

Unknown to each other, Wesley and Lisa each dreamed the same dream. Gaal was standing in the pathway ahead of them, crying with a voice that echoed through all the forest, "Wake up! Wake up! The danger is upon you! Wake up at once or you are lost!"

Startled they sat bolt upright and opened their eyes. But Gaal was not there. They saw only the moonlight making strange patterns on the pathway as it filtered through the trees. Both of them were wide awake, just as you tend to be when a dream startles you.

"We did what he told us not to do. We slept!" cried Wesley.

"Where are Inkleth and Kurt?" Lisa asked. And well she might. Neither of them was mounted on his reindeer. There was light from the moon, but it was hard to say what was real and what wasn't, what was shadow and what was space.

Wesley stared at the tangle of branches and twigs covering the bottom of the oak tree on their left. Could it be? He rubbed his eyes. Kurt's foot was sticking out from beneath them. A sense of horror strangled him.

"Kurt!" he yelled hoarsely, leaping from the reindeer's back. "Kurt, wake up, you idiot. You're trapped!"

Kurt's foot never moved. Was he dead? Wesley tore at the branches of the slender trees covering his brother, but they stuck fast to the roots of the oak. His fingers were scratched as he scrabbled and tugged frantically. One fingernail tore off but he scarcely felt it. Seeing the trunks of the elm saplings he tugged at one of them in desperation.

The oak tree above them began to shake and tremble. From somewhere inside it a deep, rumbling voice seemed to say, "Use your sword, boy! Use your sword!"

Startled, Lisa and Wesley looked up. Were they imagining it? Was the tree a person? High upon the gnarled trunk there seemed to be a sleepy face staring down at them, and arms and fingers spreading wide above it. Again there was the deep rumbling, "Use your sword, boy! Use your sword! Never trust an elm!"

Wesley snatched his sword out of its scabbard. He must be careful not to hurt Kurt. He began to hack at the thin branches and twigs of the two leaning elms. As they parted there came a strange scream of pain, a high, thin, inhuman scream which set the children's teeth on edge. But Wesley hacked on.

Before long the saplings began to spring apart still giving out their piercing, thin, inhuman wailing. First Kurt's legs and finally his body and head were uncovered. The screaming ceased. There was a last rumble from the oak tree. "Goooooood. Now I can re-e-st." Then silence.

Was Kurt dead?

Suddenly he sat bolt upright, his eyes open wide. "What happened?"

Lisa knelt beside him, hugging him and crying, "They nearly got you, the two trees. They nearly killed you. We let ourselves fall asleep. They had you fastened to the ground." He leaped to his feet fully awake and trembling.

"Where's Inkleth?"

The three peered into the deceptive shadows.

"Examine all the trees round where we are!" Wesley ordered. Everywhere patterns of moonlight and shadow bewildered them. You could have imagined anything. Then, pointing to the opposite side of the path Lisa said, "Oo-oh, look!"

The trunk of the elm where Inkleth had sat down to sleep now seemed to have a deep cleft about an inch wide stretching up from its base. Inkleth's legs were in plain view, but his body, his head and his arms all seemed to be inside the cleft in the tree trunk.

Frantically Wesley hacked at it with his sword. But he could make no impression. He hacked till he panted and sweated and until his arms ached with tiredness. Finally he looked at the other two. "I can't make a dent. What shall we do? We can't just leave him here."

"Did the oak tree really speak?" Lisa asked, looking at him.

"It sounded like it."

"I'm going to try to wake him."

She ran to where Kurt had been and battered with her fists on the trunk. "Oak tree! Oak tree! Wake up! Wake up!" A low rumble, a sort of mixture of an old man snoring deeply or else clearing his throat, made the tree vibrate.

"Hrumph, hrumph, hrumph."

Lisa had not stopped crying since Kurt's rescue and now she was crying properly. "Wake up. Oh, please, *please*, wake up! The big elm has got Inkleth in its grip!" She looked up above her sobbing. Was it really a face? Did it have one eye open and the other closed?

There was another deep rumble. The words came very slowly, as though with a great effort. "Book—book —book. Light—light—light." Then the rumbling died away to silence.

Her book! The little book Gaal gave her! With trembling fingers she snatched it, now glowing blue in the darkness, from her red sash and hurried across the path. In her haste she dropped it and for a moment could not see where it was. Then she snatched it and as she opened it a thin shaft of piercing blue light hit the trunk of the elm.

Lisa ran the light up and down the crack into which Inkleth had disappeared. For a few seconds nothing happened. "Oh, please! Oh, please, *please!*" she sobbed. The light flickered because of the trembling in her hands.

Then there came a loud creaking sound, far worse than the noisiest creaking floorboards. The split opened a fraction. Then more and louder creaks. The reindeer shuffled restlessly. Kurt put his fingers in his ears and Wesley plunged both hands into the gap as the split steadily widened. At last came a sound which I can't really describe. Lisa told me it was something like a screaming creak. And however much I questioned she could never find another way of describing it. But with the scream-creak the elm tree unfolded and Inkleth was tipped roughly forward and pitched onto his face.

No one moved. Inkleth lay perfectly still. Lisa was still

crying and Kurt and Wesley were frozen stiff with fear. "I d-don't w-want to t-t-touch him," sobbed Lisa. "I th-think he's d-dead! Oh dear! What shall we do?"

Wesley never knew how he got the words out, but in a thin, tight voice he said, "Try shining your light on him."

Lisa did. No movement. Then twitches. Then suddenly Inkleth leapt to his feet yelling, "Who is it! What? What? Where am I?"

The shock was so great and Inkleth sounded so funny that the three burst into laughter, Lisa's mingled with sobs.

"I don't see what your lordships are laughing about," Inkleth said still puzzled. "Let us mount and be on our way." Then thoughtfully he added as he struggled onto the back of his reindeer, "I had a horrible nightmare. I dreamed that the elm tree was eating me alive."

"It was," laughed Kurt. He was still laughing because he was shaky and nervous. "It was—and Lisa rescued you." Inkleth stared at them, horror on his face.

All of them struggled to get into position on their reindeer. Not another word was spoken. They pressed forward on the antlers and began to bound along the forest pathway, their hearts beating and their bodies shaking with shock.

For an hour or more all that could be heard was the gentle thrumming of the reindeer and the sound of the leaves rustling in the wind. The moon, now much higher in the sky, continued to keep pace with them, gliding serenely over branches and leaves. But there were more frightening things to cope with. Lisa was now sure that there were creatures deeper in the woods, darting from tree to tree on either side of them. They seemed to be closing in on the four of them. She would strain her eyes trying to get a proper look so she could tell what they were, but try as she might she could never see clearly.

"I don't think I'm just imagining it, but there are some creatures I can't see well, closing in on us through the trees," she said eventually.

"I noticed them too," said Wesley. "Perhaps they are some of the dark forces that are attracted by the things we are carrying."

"Wood spites and forest frights," Inkleth told them. "They are drawn by what you carry just as bees are drawn to nectar. Do not fear them, my lady. There is nothing that so scares them as a good song well sung."

"A song? What kind of song?"

Inkleth seemed to be thinking. A moment later he broke out in a beautiful tenor voice.

Wood spites and forest frights
Only safe on moonlit nights,
Drawn like moths to lamps and lights,
  Shoo! Shoo! Shoo!

Drawn by treasures of the king,
Spites on foot and frights on wing,
Hearken to the song I sing,
  Shoo! Shoo! Shoo!

Drawn by orb and book and key,
Hiding yet behind each tree,
Not afraid of you are we.
  Shoo! Shoo! SHOO!

It had a merry tune, and it made you cheerful just to listen to it. All three children kept staring sideways as they rode, peering between the trees.

"I can't see anything," Kurt said.

"I *think* I can still see them, but they're farther off," Lisa replied.

"Why don't you teach us the song?" Wesley asked.

Soon they were all singing it, yelling at the top of their voices each time they got to the last line, "Shoo! Shoo! SHOO!" And each time they sang it they saw less and less of flitting shadows until finally they were sure that they were entirely alone in the woods. Even so they kept on singing because the song made them feel so good.

At last they emerged from the forest to find themselves at the foot of a grassy mound rising in front of them under the open sky. For a moment they stopped and stared. "The path goes almost to the top," Wesley said. "I imagine if we follow it we shall get to the cave Gaal talked about."

"Good!" exclaimed Kurt. "I for one am glad to be out of that horrible forest."

Far above them the faint cries of the Qadar could be heard. While they had been singing they had not noticed the sound. But in the silence at the foot of the mound they heard the distant shrieks that filled their hearts with fear.

"They can't have seen us yet," Wesley said thoughtfully, "or they would have come down and attacked us by now."

"That is so, my lord. They are drawn by the treasures. They smell them from afar."

"Will we be safe if we can get to the cave?" Lisa asked.

"There's no place else to go," Kurt said.

"What if they see us on our way to the cave?"

"We can't stay in the forest. You know what can happen there!"

"O.K.," Wesley said, "let's ride in single file as far as we can, following the path to the cave. You first, Lisa, then Inkleth, then Kurt. I'll bring up the rear."

They arranged their reindeer in order.

"Ready?" asked Wesley. "Now *go!*"

And go they did, traveling like wind along the path that coiled up the mound. A minute later Lisa cried, "It's there! The cave! It's *there!*" Sure enough the path passed by the small black entrance to a cave. One after another they dismounted and led the reindeer with them through the low entrance. It was pitch black inside, but for the moment their thoughts were on the Qadar. Wesley remained in the entrance of the cave.

"Can you hear them, Wes?"

"Yes."

"Have they seen us?"

"I don't know. I can't see them and they still sound far away. They may be coming nearer, but I can't be sure."

The others felt their way fumblingly around the cavern. Inkleth drew a candle from his food bag and lit it with a tinder to reveal a large cave with a dry, sandy floor. He stuck the candle on a rocky ledge, filling the cave with a feeble, flickering yellow.

At the far end was a mound of straw where they could sleep, and beyond the straw, stone steps leading to an opening in the ceiling through which the night sky could dimly be seen.

"They're coming nearer," Wesley said.

"They are sure to find us," Inkleth said. "The treasures will draw them like flies to rotten fruit." But even as the words left his lips there came a rumbling from the entrance of the cave and then a solid crash. The mouth of the cave had disappeared. For a moment no one said a word.

Inkleth was the first to break the silence. There was awe in his voice. "This is indeed the Cave of Gaal. I tremble, yet with wonder not with fear. We are not trapped. We are safe. This is the cave where they murdered him. This is the cave where he slew Death itself. The old stories are true after all."

"We can't be trapped," Kurt said, "because there's a hole at the top of the steps."

"Then the Qadar will still be drawn to us," Wesley said.

"Not so, my lord," Inkleth said. "As for the hole I would not advise you to approach it. Whither it leads, I know not. But they say it is *the hole where time is no more.*"

The children stared at him. No one asked him what he meant. *Where time is no more.* Kurt felt excited, Wesley anxious, Lisa awed yet curious. Something of the magic of the cave began to make them tingle. Murder? Death? Safety? The end of time? The slaughter of Death?

They hardly noticed that Inkleth had dreamily settled himself on the straw to sleep. "I don't care what magic there is in the hole," Kurt said. "It obviously opens onto the hillside above the cave entrance. I'm going to look-see." He scrambled across the straw and climbed the stone stairs followed by his brother and sister.

"Do be careful!" Wesley said. Kurt stuck his head out of the hole and hoisted himself up with a jerk and a twist to sit on its rim.

"Be careful!" Wesley's voice sounded distant.

Kurt didn't think of it until afterward, but it was at that very moment that all their voices changed as though they came not just from three feet away in the cave but across a vast stretch of time. (He could never quite explain what he meant by this and looked puzzled when I asked him about it later. "I dunno. That's just the way it sounded," he said.)

He could neither see nor hear the Qadar. The stars shining down on him from a sky of black velvet were bigger than he had ever seen them in Anthropos, and there was no moon. For a moment he stared bewildered at the sky and at the empty hillside.

"Can you see Qadar? What are they doing?" This time it was Lisa who called to him, and once again the voice seemed "to come from a different century," as Kurt put it.

"Your voice sounds weird. No. No Qadar. They've gone completely. I can't see any of them. Everything's quiet too. The sky's full of enormous stars. Beautiful. There's no moon either."

"What's wrong with your own voice? You sound like you're a long way off."

Kurt stared down at the three shadowy faces looking up at him only a yard from his feet. "Search me! Your voices sound funny too—like we're talking over a radio or something." For a moment or two they continued to talk—half intrigued, half frightened by the strange distortion in their voices.

"It's like there's a glass screen between us and we're talking by telephone," Wesley said. "It's . . . it's uncanny."

"Well, there isn't a glass wall!" Lisa pushed forward. "Shove over!" she said to Kurt jerking herself up to sit beside him.

Immediately she noticed several things at once. First, the sound of Kurt's voice did not change. He said, "Here, let me make a bit more room!" And then the sky. Kurt had said there was no moon, but there was. As for stars, she could hardly see any. She was just about to say so when she moved her head slightly. Instantly the shrieks of the Qadar filled her ears and the sight of their winged descent sent a stab of pain into her chest.

"Oh, Kurt. Quick, look!" She moved closer to him and pointed. Yet as she moved, the moon and the Qadar vanished in a flash. Brilliant stars stared like unwinking jewels and shone down on her as they did on Kurt.

"Look where?" Still his voice sounded far off.

"The Qadar. They were all there a second ago."

"You must have imagined it. Where?"

Lisa pointed. In the direction of her finger a bright blue star was rising above the horizon. Then as she leaned forward it vanished and the rest of the stars with it while Qadar shrieks filled her ears again.

"Kurt, Kurt, whatever is happening? They're back again. Look. Can't you see them? They come whenever the stars go out and the moon comes back."

Kurt stared at her. "There *is* no moon." He looked up again and spread his arms wide. "There's nothing but stars, beautiful stars all over the sky. There's no sign of the Qadar." His strange, distant voice was bewildered. "What's happening to us, Lisa?"

Lisa angrily grabbed his head between her hands, twisted it round to where she could see the Qadar and pulled his head in front of her.

"O-o-oh! What in the world . . . ?" he cried, and his voice for a moment was normal. Then, "Look, quit twisting my head. I can see all right!" and he pulled his head from her grasp and sat upright again. For a moment he had seen what Lisa saw and heard what Lisa heard, but the moment he resumed his normal position the sky was wiped clean of moon and Qadar and studded with jeweled stars again.

"Lisa, come nearer to me! That's right—as close as you can!" As Lisa obeyed she saw the sky as Kurt saw it. The silence and the stars made them feel a little dreamy so that they had no wish to move or even to think.

Wesley's voice sounded centuries beneath their feet. "Hey! What's going on?"

Lisa's reply made no sense. "We don't know. But it's very nice."

They heard the sound of Wesley forcing his own way up through the hole. As he did so and jerked himself into place, the most startling thing of all happened. Wesley was bathed in sunlight. There was no sign of a source of light apart from the stars, yet it looked as though the full sun shone on him. Both of them blinked as they stared.

"You never told me it was daylight! And where's the forest gone? There's nothing but little clumps of trees here and there." He stared at them with a frown. "I can hardly see you. You look like a couple of shadows blotting out the sun."

All three stared at one another, sitting around the rim of the hole above the cave. Wesley's body was sharp with brightness but his voice was distant. "Inkleth said something about 'the hole where time ends. . . .'" For several seconds nobody moved. Then Wesley said, "Perhaps we *are* in different centuries. Let's all keep edging very slowly, inch by inch round the hole. It seems that different things happen according to our position!"

"I'm scared." Lisa looked it.

"Well, let's do it. Come on! We can always drop back into the cave."

What happened next would take too long to tell in detail. In any case all three saw things they had no words to describe. There was an island that floated in a dark and silent sea, an island from which stairways reached into the clouds. Cherubs and demons hurried between the clouds and the island. And it seemed, though they could not have told you how, that the island was Anthropos. But quick as light the scenes would shift as they moved their positions. Lisa screamed at one point. "They're killing him! They're murdering him!"

"Murdering who?"

"Murdering Gaal!"

But in a moment the vision had gone. Sometimes the hill would swarm with armies and the air be filled with the clash of metal, the screams of horses and shouts of men. Or the Qadar would swoop around them shrieking. Suns would whirl across the sky. Darkness would succeed light with bewildering rapidity. A comet soared red and fierce across the sky lighting the black forest with blood. Once Wesley thought he saw a boy like an old picture of Uncle John running in desperation toward the cave. Blizzards would swirl icily around them or heat burn them.

Finally Lisa cried, "I'm going down. I can't stand it!"

The other two stumbled after her and the silence of the cave fell round them like a warm, soft blanket. For a moment they stared at one another. Then without a word they crawled beside the sleeping Inkleth on the straw and fell into a dreamless sleep.

The Battle of the Heights

The night was still and silent. A silverblue moon bathed the Heights of Rinnar and the great forest at its feet. No sound broke the quiet. No movement disturbed it. Serene and majestic, the great rock kept watch over sleeping trees for miles around.

Resting in shallow trenches in a long uneven line above the northeast slope, lay the Koach. So still did they lie, they might have been carved out of stone. Not an ear twitched. Not a head moved.

Far on their right the Matmon crouched behind earth ramparts, their bows in their left hands, their arrows in their quivers. They too waited silently, scarcely daring to breathe, straining their ears for the least sound from the forests below. But the only sound they heard was the beating of their own hearts.

Only Kardia could be seen above the ramparts, a pale,

equestrian statue carved in gray rock to dominate the heights. Frozen in stillness he peered toward the foot of the hill, watching for any movement. But he saw none. Only the twitching of the horse's tail told you that man and horse were living beings.

Sir Nocham and his archers stood in trenches in front of Kardia, moving gently from time to time to shift their weight from one foot to another. Like the dwarfs they strained their ears for sounds from below them.

Down among the shadows of the forest a silence almost equal to that above was broken by stealthy rustles of movement, the occasional crack of a dry twig or the stomp of a horse's hoof. Facing the Matmon trenches, hundreds of horsemen, Sir Gregorio's knights, waited among the trees for the order to attack. To the north of them archers by the thousands knelt behind the trees. Their palms were wet with perspiration for they were as terrified of the danger that waited for them up on the heights as they were of the tall, yellow-haired woman mounted on a great horse in their rear. The spearmen of Sir Percy, long spears in hand, stood waiting beside the archers.

Everywhere on the branches above their heads harpies and furies waited sleepily. They knew no fear. Birds with human heads and long streaming hair, the harpies smiled their cruel smiles, thinking of the joy they would have in snatching humans, dwarfs or wolves, carrying them far up into the night sky to let them drop and be dashed to pieces on the rocks below. Behind and to the north of the archers were ghouls, huge and hairy ogres, red-bodied and seven-headed, and the low-growling, giant bloodhounds, their great tongues dripping from their mouths.

The forest was crawling, vermin-ridden with evil, not

that the forest cared. Elm trees by the hundreds of thousands shifted their roots in anticipation, wishing they were awake enough to scale the heights themselves.

None of the soft sounds and movements in the forest could be detected by the waiting army on the heights. All they could see was smooth slope below them and an ocean of moonlit treetops, beautiful, eerie and frightening. Many of the Matmon wished that the battle would hurry up and start. To wait while the slow minutes crawled by was torture.

As the cold blue moon rose higher in the sky, some of them began to wonder whether there would be a battle at all. Perhaps their enemy had thought better of it and gone. Yet common sense told them it could not be so, for in the daylight they had been able to see horsemen, knights, archers and spearmen.

Without warning arrows arched like a flock of birds toward the Matmon trenches. The battle had started; the stillness was ended. With shrieks, with shouts and with trumpet blasts, the woods below disgorged their hordes which rushed up the hillside again and again. For a while it seemed they could not succeed in reaching the crest of the heights. But as the enemy forces regrouped, to surge up repeatedly, each time to face fewer and weaker defenders, Kardia could see that his defenses would not hold out.

And so it proved.

He never forgot the nightmare that followed. Suddenly the heights were swarming with seven-headed ogres, with bloodhounds the size of elephants, with galloping horses and armored knights. Harpies and furies dived between clouds of arrows to seize dwarfs and wolves, the harpies carrying them high in the sky to let them fall to their deaths on the rocks below.

There was no order to the battle. The Heights of Rinnar looked like the tossing waters of a river in flood. Shrieks mingled with groans, trumpet blasts with cries of despair or of triumph. Everywhere men, dwarfs, horses and evil ones stumbled over the dead and wounded.

Yet even as Kardia began to despair, a blue light spread softly over the heights. Chocma, wounded at the outset of the battle, had recovered enough to sit on her horse and read from her book. The umbrella of blue light began to rise. Her clear voice began to sound above the shouts and the groans. Dwarfs dropped their weapons and the strange song began to surge with new power from their throats.

It was the turn of the battle. With cries of dismay their enemies tumbled in panic toward the forests below.

The blue radiance grew in intensity, curving like a great tent above their heads just as it had in the Battle of Authentio. Its brilliance was nothing like that which shone from the book of Geburah. But it was enough. The longer Chocma read, the wider the radiance spread. Ghouls and ogres caught in its light disintegrated and passed into the ground. Others, seeing it, continued to scramble madly down the hill. Harpies and furies, screaming their rage, hovered above it for a brief while. Then gradually the noise of war diminished. Only when the last of the evil ones had left the heights did Chocma cease to read. She had done all she could, and her wounds had weakened her terribly. She slid sideways on her saddle against Kardia and lost consciousness. Carefully he dismounted and lay her on the ground.

Dawn was breaking in the east. Yet the war was far from over. Even as quietness fell on the heights they began to hear the faint screams of the Qadar in the skies far above. As they looked up they saw them. There were not just ten nor even a hundred. Hundreds and hundreds of them circled above them, their wings tinged blood-red from the earliest rays of the sun.

Hours later, after the sun had stolen over the sky and was setting again, Kardia stood wearily on the battlements, watching down below him the reorganization of his enemies' forces. His mind went over all that had happened since dawn.

The awe-inspiring sight of hundreds of high-circling Qadar, their underbellies luridly caught by the rising sun, had chilled their bodies with fear. Every face had turned to watch them. What were they about to do?

But they had done nothing. After circling in the light of the rising sun, they streamed across the sky in a long line to disappear in the direction of the Caves of Aphela. As the last of them vanished toward the south, Matmon, Koach and men shook themselves and turned wearily to the task of undoing the awful damage of the night.

All day they took turns sleeping and working. You see, there's more to a battle than fighting. You have to bury the dead. You have to get all the wounded together, see how badly they are wounded and do what you can to fix them up. Suneidesis looked after this part, helped by the Matmon women. By midday they had organized an emergency hospital well back behind the ramparts.

Kardia had wept as he saw dead Koach and Matmon lying in a trench which formed a mass grave. But people die in wars. And having begun the war, Kardia knew that cost what it may, he must fight to the finish.

One big worry had been Chocma. What was going to happen to her? Would she recover from her wounds? But Chocma was tough. Wounded or not she had no intention of resting. Despite the fact that she was weakened, it made an enormous difference to have her around. You see, Matmon who had been wounded with the dream arrows were sitting in the hospital, grinning vacantly into space. Without help they would dream on smilingly until they starved. So Chocma, weary and weak as she was, had been busy all day opening her book and reading to them.

You would have enjoyed watching the effect on them. First they would look puzzled. Then their eyes would clear and they would stare at Chocma as though they hated her. Then their faces would relax. Some would smile with a new kind of smile and thank her. Others would weep and tell her they were sorry. But all of them after ten minutes would be up and walking. The emergency hospital was a fantastic place to get better in.

There is something else you must remember if you are to run a war properly. You must find out what your enemies are doing. If you can guess their plans beforehand it's much easier to frustrate them. That is why as the sun was setting Kardia was again watching from the ramparts. He didn't possess binoculars, but his eyes were keen and he saw that the Lady Sheriruth and her archers had all shifted over to his left. Evidently they were going to concentrate on the Koach or at least on the trenches where they *thought* the Koach would be. "But," thought Kardia, "they will probably not start to shoot until there is moonlight." The archers had also constructed screens of interwoven branches, sort of mobile defenses they could hide behind as they moved up the hill. If they *could* move up the hill!

"So far, so good," Kardia thought. He could also see the spearmen preparing to attack on his right. Archers from the left; spearmen from the right. But where were the knights? Had they abandoned the battle? As a matter of fact (though Kardia did not know it), they had.

And what of the ghouls, the ogres, the harpies and the furies? Most terrible of all, how could they cope with the Qadar? Kardia tried to put the thought of the Qadar out of his mind. Deep in his heart he knew that if the book, the key and the jeweled orb did not arrive and if the Qadar swept down upon them, then all hope was lost.

Where *could* the children be? Was there any hope they would arrive in time?

Kardia took a breath deep into his lungs. Firmly he refused to let himself think about losing. Gaal's forces *must* win—for the sake of Anthropos, for the sake of Gaal. Yet without Gaal how could they?

You will remember that Kardia still had the Mashal Stone which as well as making you invisible enabled you to see things like goblins and ogres, even in the daylight. He slipped it over his head. A dwarf who had been watching him was startled to see him disappear and choked on a meat pie he was eating. But Kardia never saw him. He was too busy staring down the hill in search of ghouls and ogres. He stared long and hard, a frown creasing his forehead. But of ghouls, ogres, bloodhounds, harpies and furies, there was not a sign.

Something was wrong. The evil ones could not have abandoned the fight. They ought to have been in their places, ready to attack. Kardia continued to frown his invisible frown; then, as he thought more, an invisible look of worry began to line his invisible face. Could they? Was it possible . . . ?

With fear rising in his heart he ran to the western side of the heights where cliffs fell four hundred feet below him to form an impassable barrier. Impassable? But not to ogres. Or ghouls. Or harpies. Or furies.

He slowed as he approached the precipice, then peered cautiously over the edge. Dismay and anger began to make his legs tremble and his fists clench fiercely. They were there by the thousands. In fact their numbers had increased. Kardia stared at the multitude below. Why had he not thought of it before? They were trapped. They would be attacked from both sides—archers and spearmen advancing up the eastern slopes of the heights where only the trenches and ramparts defended them while the evil ones scaled the precipice to attack from his rear.

"Hocoino," Kardia thought to himself. "It's Hocoino's thinking. I should have known that only he could get so motley and stupid a multitude to act like an organized army."

Kardia's mind as well as his body was racing as he removed the pendant and hurried for a last quick council of war. Suneidesis was there, and so were Chocma, Sir Nocham, Gunruth, Garfong and Whitefur. Quickly Kardia told them what he had seen.

"If it be our hap to lose tonight's battle," he told them quietly facing the dread possibility at last, "we lose the whole war. The Qadar are almost certain to attack sometime tonight, and we must be ready for them. Listen to me. We will leave the ramparts on the northeast unguarded and empty." Kardia continued to outline his plans. "Good Garfong, lead the Koach in silence around and attack the spearmen from the rear the moment they start to advance. Fear not their spears, but attack them fiercely and suddenly."

You could tell that Garfong was delighted. He leaped to his four feet, gave a penetrating call to all the Koach and left the council. For the next two hours with excited howls and yelps they planned their role in that night's

battle. The council meanwhile continued.

"Lady Chocma, is it possible for you to hold the evil ones at bay from the rear?"

"That I know not," Chocma replied thoughtfully. "The book I carry has limited powers. It is but part of the full book of Gaal's laws and our history. I could prevent many from climbing, but should they once gain a foothold on the heights.... Moreover, we know not from whence the furies and harpies will attack. Give me Sir Nocham and plenty of archers, your majesty, and I will do what I can."

Chocma could read aloud from her book to erect the dome of blue light above her, killing everything evil that lay within range of her voice. The Book of Wisdom would be very effective.

But while Chocma's ringing voice was normally very powerful, she could not in her weakened state make it heard for a mile in either direction, and the precipice was two miles long. Reading aloud she could certainly keep herself safe, but ghouls and ogres would have plenty of room to clamber onto the heights on either side of the dome.

Chocma and Sir Nocham left to go to their positions above the western precipice. Only Kardia, Whitefur, Gunruth and Suneidesis were left. "Do you know the ancient pathways, good Whitefur?" Kardia asked.

"Aye, your majesty. There is one leading here from the south to ascend a pathway cut in the precipice."

"Then the four that went to Geburah will need someone to guide them through the evil ones."

"I will go to seek them, your majesty."

"Can you pass through the evil ones undetected?"

"Yes, your majesty."

"Then take this," the king said, offering him the Mashal Stone. "Give it to the lady Lisa, and bid her above all things to bring the book and to read it. Ten words from the book could win us the battle."

He glanced fondly at Suneidesis. "Can you still work with compassion and skill throughout the night?"

"Most gladly, your majesty." They looked long at each other, but nothing more was said.

Sunset found Kardia on the battlements, still thinking of the day's events and of what the night might bring. He had positioned his troops with care. Matmon lined the trenches on his left flank ready to fire at Lady Sheri-ruth's archers when the moon came up. Koach under Garfong were grouped behind rocks on the extreme south end of the heights, ready to slip downhill once darkness was complete. Chocma and Sir Nocham's men would watch for the evil ones from the midpoint of the precipice at the rear of the heights. Suneidesis and the

Matmon women continued to care for the wounded and prepared to receive more.

Soon the sky overhead was dark. Only in the west a red glow remained. However much Kardia strained his eyes, he could see no movements below. Each passing minute the sky grew darker until darkness was almost complete. Only to the south could a few stars be seen. Gunruth stood beside the king. Having positioned his men, Sir Nocham returned to Kardia.

"Can you see whether our Koach are leaving yet?" the king asked. All three strained their eyes. The still-ness unnerved them. If you can see what's going on you can put up with a lot. But if it is dark you can only *imagine*.

"I cannot tell whether they are there or whether they have gone," Gunruth replied. A moment later he touched Kardia's elbow. "Look downhill at the slope, your majesty!" Kardia stared but could see nothing. "Where?"

Gunruth pointed, "There, your majesty. Near the foot of the hill, to your majesty's right."

Kardia and Sir Nocham stared intently. "I may be imagining it," Kardia said, "but I believe there is move-ment. The spearmen must be beginning their ascent."

One by one the minutes continued to pass. Sometimes each of the three thought he saw movement, but no one could be sure. Silence reigned.

Suddenly their sharp ears detected the sound of dis-placed rock rolling down the hill to their right. "They are advancing," Kardia said. "Would to Gaal there were more light!"

Minutes passed. At times they were almost certain that they could see stealthy movements low down on the hill. Once or twice they heard the sounds of stealthy foot-steps. Kardia, Nocham and Gunruth were each so straining their eyes and ears that they were startled by a sudden outburst of sound. Wolf howls, snarls and human screams broke out below them, with shouts, sounds of scuffling and a general pandemonium.

"By Numa, the night star—I *wish* I could see what was happening," Kardia complained testily.

Suddenly a black shadow hurtled over the ramparts with a howl and rushed on, heading for the cliffs behind them. Then came another and another.

"The spears have wounded some of the Koach," he breathed.

"What will happen to them?"

"They will run until they die. Many will leap from the cliffs. The spear wounds have made them mad."

More howling Koach leaped over the ramparts while the pandemonium below continued. "The Koach will still do better in the dark," Gunruth observed. "Humans have little sense of smell." The hullabaloo below grew louder every minute. The three waited and watched.

From time to time more panicking Koach leaped over the battlements. The struggle had continued for more than half an hour. Suddenly they heard the clear bugle call of Sir Percy Pachad. It was sounding the retreat.

"Have Garfong call the Koach back," Kardia told Gunruth, who left immediately.

A moment later there was a second bugle call from the ramparts. Gradually the hubbub below died down. After several minutes the stealthy forms of the Koach began to be seen around the ramparts. Garfong approached the king, his mouth bloodstained.

"Your majesty, your plan worked superbly." Wolves in Anthropos wag their tails when they are happy and Garfong's tail was wagging. His tongue hung out and he was panting. Behind him the numbers of Koach swelled.

"Casualties?" Kardia asked.

"Far fewer than we thought," Garfong replied. Gunruth translated.

"And the enemy?"

"Their numbers are enormously reduced. They left many dead behind, but we did not have time to count. Less than half of them took part in the retreat."

The clouds seemed to have dispersed. Slowly the moon began to rise. Then a cry rang out from behind them. Swinging round they saw the blue light shine out from where Chocma was standing, and over the whole length of the semicircular cliffs that dropped behind them on the western and southwestern side of the heights, they could dimly perceive the massive shapes of ghouls, ogres and the swooping furies and harpies.

As he saw their number it was clear to Kardia that Chocma, even with the help of Sir Nocham's men, could not prevent them from attacking his forces from the rear.

"Garfong!"

"Your majesty?"

"Organize the Koach into bands of twenty, and go to the aid of the lady Chocma."

The Koach had already received instructions as to the bands they were to form, but it took several minutes for the counterattack to get under way. Meanwhile Chocma was being swept back by the pressure of ogres and ghouls. A small umbrella of blue light protected her and Sir Nocham's men from the furies and the harpies. More and more of the creatures were swarming over the cliff across the heights behind Kardia's army of Matmon. Before long there were hundreds, and then thousands. The moon shone down on fearful hordes.

The Koach, better organized than they had been the

previous night, were all over the heights, worrying, attacking and killing. But furies and harpies were now descending on Matmon trenches raising one after another of the dwarfs skyward and dashing them down in the valley below.

Sir Nocham touched Kardia on the shoulder and pointed down the hill to where Lady Sheriruth's archers had been. At first Kardia could not understand what was happening. In the moonlight long objects like segments of wall were advancing up the hill. "They must be the screens to cover the archers," Sir Nocham said.

They were being attacked from both sides. The confusion was such that it was impossible to say what was happening. Everywhere ghouls and ogres were harried by bands of wolves. Harpies were diving, their long hair streaming in the moonlight, to clutch Matmon or Koach in their claws. The archers were closing in from the hillside. Kardia could see that their position was extremely serious.

He called out to the Matmon, "Direct your fire to the hill below! Leave the evil ones to Chocma and the Koach."

"It fares ill with us," Sir Nocham said.

Kardia did not reply. He was watching the efforts of Chocma. Her light was failing. She seemed hardly able to stay in her saddle. The umbrella of light above her had disappeared. Her shoulder had been pierced by a diving fury. A hail of arrows from the hill below buried itself in the ramparts.

"Keep under cover until they are closer!" Kardia called to the Matmon. Then under his breath, "May Gaal help us."

Then with blinding suddenness the whole of the heights were lit by a brilliant blue. It was just as if someone had switched on floodlights over a football field. A young girl's voice rang across the plateau as if carried by a thousand loud-speakers. Everywhere ghouls and ogres shriveled to liquid and sank into the earth and the rocks. Harpies and furies withered and dropped like rain. Then, streaking across the heights came a white wolf and two white reindeer, the second one carrying Wesley on its back.

27

The Last Leg of the Journey

The early morning sun shot long shadows over brown grass. Below the cave a forest stretched out like a blue green ocean streaked with white mist. Lisa sat staring through the mouth of the cave shivering with cold and wondering how to explain the strange events of the night before. At least the cave mouth was open again. She shook her head. She thought she could smell food cooking, but thinking she was imagining it she lay down and closed her eyes.

"Good morning!" The voice was strong and cheerful. Lisa sat up with a gasp of astonishment. Standing in the middle of the cave was Gaal. She woke the others, who scrambled to their feet with laughing welcome.

Gaal too was laughing. "Come on. Who's going to eat breakfast? Will it be ladies first?"

Lisa moved toward him, and as she did so she suddenly felt his arms around her and smelled the scent of cedarwood again. It was the tunnel all over again. She was cold and was comforted by the warmth of his body.

"Oh, Gaal. I'm so glad! You really are *here!* We were so scared in the forest."

"Yes, little one, but even there I was watching you."

They scrambled one after another out of the cave into the cool morning sunshine where the white reindeer were grazing quietly, no longer on dry brown grass but on green grass around a spring they had not noticed the night before, a spring pouring from the rock beside the cave opening.

Don't ask me where Gaal got the breakfast. He had a fire with an iron pot of water boiling. He had river trout frying in butter, fresh bread, milk, honey, cream and a pot of hot oatmeal. There were even wooden bowls and spoons for all of them. The sight and the smell of it set their mouths watering and their stomachs growling, and in no time they sat around the fire enjoying themselves thoroughly. Each stole secret glances at Gaal to make sure he was really there.

It was the best sort of fire. You could feel its heat on your hands and face in the cool air, yet the smoke got in nobody's eyes. Normally Wesley would have been fussy about eating trout in a bowl that had not had the oatmeal washed out, and in any case wooden spoons were not the best implements for getting the bones out of trout. But not even Wesley cared.

None of them had realized how much Gaal had meant to them. Their excitement, instead of dying, grew all the greater as the meal went on. As they sat with full stomachs sipping hot herb tea from wooden cups they kept stealing glances at him until he began to tease them about it.

Lisa sighed with contentment. The dew had almost disappeared from the grass, and the warmth of the sun, the feeling of a full stomach and above all the presence of Gaal filled her with contentment. She saw Gaal looking at her.

"It would be nice to stay here forever, wouldn't it?"

"Oh, yes, Gaal."

"But I'm afraid there's still a war on."

The war? The events of the morning had driven it out of their minds.

"You, Wesley must be prepared to lead Kardia's army." Wesley's jaw dropped. Gaal couldn't be serious. But his face was perfectly serious.

"*Me?* But I've never even *seen* a war, Gaal!"

"Do you remember what happened when you attacked the seven-headed ogre?"

"Why, yes, Gaal, but. . . ."

"In the same way the sword in your scabbard will come alive in your hand. You will not need to think what to do. With my pigeon on your shoulder you will take to war as though you were a veteran."

Wesley was too confused to reply.

"Can you all see the hills to the west?" Blue hills rose in the distance. They nodded. "Beyond them are the Heights of Rinnar. The reindeer will get you there by nightfall *if you do not pause but run like the wind all day*. You, Lisa, are to go with Kardia to the cave where the enchanted knights lie sleeping and then guide him through the tunnel to Bamah. I want them first to burn the temple and push down the big circle of stones. Tell them that it is far more important to destroy the old city than to attack their enemies directly."

Inkleth's head was hanging down and he looked uncomfortable. "I don't know whether I can find my troops

in time for the battle. I may have made us late. I am
ashamed of what I have done."

"Look into the fire," Gaal said. Have you ever looked
for pictures in the dancing flames and hot embers? This
time the children saw a real picture. The heart of the
fire seemed far, far away. A huge oak tree seemed to
shelter hundreds of tiny dwarfs.

"The Oak of Quashash!" Inkleth cried. "Is that them?
If it is I could have them in the battle by dawn tomorrow."

"You can if you do not tarry," said Gaal.

Only Kurt remained silent. Apparently he was to play
no part in the battle. Wesley could lead an army; Lisa
would conduct Kardia to the enchanted knights; even
Inkleth would bring reinforcements from the Matmon.
But as for Kurt....

"Kurt," Gaal was speaking, "Kurt, you will come with
me. We have our own plans to make."

A smile spread over the boy's troubled face. So there
was something he could do, and he could be with Gaal!

During the day they had to eat and drink as they rode.
Inkleth, Lisa and Wesley knew very well how dangerous
it would be to dismount. From time to time they stole
glances at the trees beside them, looking for faces.

The path was dusty. By noon they were tired, but still
they pressed on. They had made too many mistakes in
the past, and could afford to make no more. Unless they
continued to ride steadily west they would not reach their
destination by nightfall.

"I've never *seen* so much forest," Lisa said panting.

"How can we be sure we're on the right track?" Wesley
worried.

"There is only one path, my lord."

"But it seems endless. We just go on and on and on. Nothing ever changes."

"We must reach the River Nachash soon," Inkleth said.

The path was straight as a ruler and paved with the curious stones they were now familiar with. Lisa turned round to look back and was puzzled by what she saw.

"We haven't turned a corner, have we, Wes?"

"No. Why?"

Lisa did not answer, but turned around again.

"I can only see about ten yards of the path behind us. It just disappears into the trees."

Wesley turned to look. It was weird. Ten yards behind them the path seemed to end. Inkleth stared too. Then even as they watched a large elm slowly waded through the ground to take up its position eight yards behind them on the path. Its movements were no different from yours when you wade in water. Lisa's heart was pounding. Its branches gently reached forward like arms toward them.

"Quick, before they close in on us," she cried.

All three of them turned and rode harder than ever along the dusty path.

"It's clear up ahead," Wesley said.

"I wonder if they're gaining on us. I don't want to look behind."

"No, my lady," Inkleth answered. "If anything we are leaving them behind."

"This is ghastly. Trees coming after you in the forest. And those trees last night. Wes, I'm scared!"

"The only thing we can do is ride."

"I hope the reindeer don't get tired."

"I'll be glad when we're out of this."

The reindeer showed no sign of slackening their pace.

Had it not been for the heat, the dust and the frightening movement of the trees, it would have been fun. But all three were afraid.

"I see the river ahead, my lord," Inkleth said suddenly. "The sunlight glances from it."

To their intense relief they saw he was right. In a few seconds the last two hundred yards were left behind, and they burst from the trees and rushed across the caked mud on the wide bank and only stopped when they reached the smooth, shallow water that had once been a wide river. Here the reindeer drank.

Lisa looked back. "The path has disappeared altogether," she said.

They stared at the wood from which they had emerged. There was no sign of where they had left it. A solid wall of elm trunks lined the river bank like huge soldiers. You got the feeling that they were all looking at you, yet as Lisa said afterward, you couldn't be sure of eyes or faces. But from time to time you did see one or the other of them shift its position slightly.

"Let's get *out* of this place," Wesley said. "Can they cross the river?"

"No," Inkleth replied. "They can hate us all they want, but they can't get a step nearer."

"I'm glad trees in our world don't move around."

"How do you know they do not?" Inkleth asked. "Our trees are asleep most of the time. It is only when there is magic around that they begin to wake up."

They turned to look at the forest before them, but again they drew back. A solid phalanx of elm trees barred their way. There was no sign of a path on either side of the river.

Lisa said, "I don't believe the trees are more powerful than Gaal. They're trying to scare us."

"So what do we do?" Wesley asked. "Walk up to them and say, '*boo*'?"

"We could try my book."

Nobody said anything. They looked up and down the river as far as they could, but everywhere they were barred. What Lisa did next took a lot of courage. She took her reindeer as close to the trees as she dared. (She had a horrible feeling that the branches might reach down and seize her.) Then she pulled her little book from her sash and in a squeaky voice began to read. At times it seemed as though some of the trees moved ever so slightly.

"My lady, the *big* book," Inkleth cried excitedly slinging it round from his back and joining her. "Here," he said, thrusting the great volume toward her. "Read this."

Her fingers tingled as she opened the book. Her eyes were dazzled with the shining blue of the pages. At first she could not make sense of the words, but then somehow she could. It felt as though her whole body was growing bigger, cleaner, stronger. Then in a voice that echoed through miles of forest, great rolling phrases poured out of her young throat. No one could remember afterward what she had said, but the effects were dramatic.

Elm trees began to push back against one another just as policemen push a crowd back. Before their very eyes a wide road opened up, paved with the old stones.

Lisa wanted to go on reading. Never in her life had she felt such power surging through her. "Wow! What a book!" she said. "Here, grab it back, Inkleth, or I'll not be able to stop reading!" Her face was shining and she was trembling with joy.

They urged the reindeer on again, and from that point had no difficulties with elms, but rode till the late afternoon.

Wesley and Lisa were weary of their journey long before they emerged from the woods. Inkleth left them to rejoin his followers shortly before the late afternoon sun cast long shadows on the ground. As the shadows lengthened Lisa began to look worried.

"Wes, I don't think we're going to make it."

"We've got to make it."

"If we're tired, the reindeer must be more tired still."

"They don't show it." It was true. Not for a second had their speed abated. Forest trees flashed by them dizzily.

"Those cliffs we keep glimpsing must be the Rinnar Heights," Wesley said.

"But they don't seem to be getting any nearer."

"Oh, come on now! Of course they are. Is the big book heavy?"

"Not really, Wes. Inkleth strapped it to me so that it rests on the reindeer's back."

"Good."

For a while they continued in silence. The trees were thinning and the sun was setting.

"There's something white on the path ahead of us, Lisa. It's moving this way I think."

"Where?"

"Right ahead, about three hundred yards away."

"You're right, Wes." Lisa's heart skipped a beat. "Friend or foe?"

"We'll soon find out." Wesley put his hand to his sword. Still they swept on without slackening their pace.

"It's a wolf, Wes!"

"Whitefur or Garfong, I'm sure it's one of them."

They slowed to a halt, and Whitefur addressed them in human speech without any greeting. "Things go ill on the Heights of Rinnar. We fear the evil ones may attack us by climbing the cliffs at the rear. Moreover, Qadar numbering hundreds are now in Anthropos. Unless you arrive soon, the war may be over."

"How far away are we?" Wes asked.

"At the speed you were traveling we could reach them in two to three hours. But if the ghouls and the ogres attack from the rear it might take longer."

"You have the Mashal Stone." Lisa noticed it at Whitefur's feet. He had dropped it from his mouth when he addressed them.

"I bring it for you, my lady. If you wear it, you can follow the ancient pathway to the top of the heights. His lordship and I may have to follow a more roundabout route. But for now we may stay together."

"Let's be on our way, then," Wes said impatiently.

No further word was spoken. Whitefur loped ahead of them in the gathering darkness. The reindeer maintained their steady speed. Before long it was so dark that Whitefur acted as a sort of pilot, a white shadow leading the way through the blackness.

Wesley, Whitefur and Lisa stared at the army of ogres and ghouls that scrambled up the cliffs in front of them. It looked for all the world as though the whole sweep of the cliffs was a crawling mass of giant insects. A path cut in the rock connecting the ancient pathway with the heights was crossed and recrossed by the creatures.

"I'll have to go on foot," Lisa said. "Otherwise, they'll see the reindeer. I can put on the pendant and carry the book tucked inside my sash. It'll be heavy, but I'm sure I can make it."

She didn't *feel* sure. It was just that she had no alternative if the battle was to be won. But the thought of moving, even invisibly, among the horde of revolting beings made her shudder. She clambered down from her reindeer.

"Here, help me get this tome inside my sash. I can support its weight with my hands."

Wesley did so. "Sure it's not too heavy for you?"

"It's heavy but I can manage."

Wesley shook his head. "I hate to let you do it. You're taking the biggest risk. Yet I suppose it's more important that you get through than I. You can wear the pendant, read the book, and you have the key to give to Kardia."

"I'm not taking much risk, Wes. I shall be invisible. How will you both manage?"

"My lord, there is a longer way that circles the base of the cliffs and approaches his majesty's right flank from the side. If her ladyship walks the ancient pathway, we should arrive about the same time. Let us lead her ladyship's reindeer."

Lisa slipped the pendant about her neck and cradled one corner of the book in her hands. Neither she nor the book was visible. They just vanished.

"Wow!" Wes was startled. "Are you still there?"

"Yes, I'm here, but I'm going now. One good thing about this stone is that it makes you feel braver. Chocma says it's because it helps you see things like they really are. Bye, Wes! Bye, Whitefur!"

They never heard her leave, but they did see a faint blue light moving steadily along the path.

28

Freeing the Enchanted Knights

Things were happening too suddenly for Kardia. One moment they had seemed on the point of disaster and the next at the portals of victory.

Across the brightly lit Heights of Rinnar, Wesley and the two reindeer came panting to him. Wesley talked breathlessly, trying to say something Kardia could not understand. "You must leave here, your majesty! Gaal says you are not to stay but to release the enchanted knights and lead them to Bamah!"

"The enchanted knights? The enchanted knights are sealed in a cave! Do you then have the key to Qava? Do you have the words to dissolve the enchantment?

"Moreover we are still under attack. The archers of Lady Sheriruth are even now ascending the hill and must be stopped. Her poisoned arrows will fill the Matmon with dreams that lead to death. How can I leave now?"

He waved his arms in frustration. Then staring at Wesley he said, "And why Bamah?"

"Gaal asked me to tell your majesty that the battle would be won or lost not here but in Bamah. The temple must be burned and the stone circle pulled down. May it please your majesty, Gaal bade me to stay here and lead your army. I know it makes no sense, but that's what he said!"

As they had been speaking Chocma had appeared beside them, her book closed, her face a gray pallor. She was about to slide from her saddle. For the moment, Wesley's confusing instructions were forgotten as he and Kardia together jumped to prevent her from falling. Carefully they laid her on the ground.

Kardia turned to Sir Nocham. "Send a runner and bid the Princess Suneidesis use some of the water we brought from the House of Wisdom as well as bandages to bind her wound!"

The sound that had filled the air, the sound of the girl's voice, and the blue dome of light began to fade. Moments later there was only moonlight. But order had replaced confusion. The Koach were reassembling, waiting for more orders. Suneidesis returned with two Matmon women and pulled back the robe covering Chocma's wound.

"Pour the water in. Do not worry that you waste it!" Suneidesis' voice trembled with anxiety.

Garfong trotted into the circle unaware of the tension, greeted Whitefur, then leaped delightedly at Wesley's shoulders. And Lisa suddenly appeared looking weary, weighed down with the great book.

"Your majesty," she said, repeating Wesley's instructions, "you are to take me to the Cave of Qava, and Gaal bids you lead the enchanted knights into Bamah to burn the temple and to pull down the ancient stones of the circle."

Kardia looked at her steadily for a moment. He glanced at the princess binding Chocma's wound and saw the color return to Chocma's cheeks. He shook his head as he looked back at Wesley who was now sitting with his arm round Garfong's neck, and then stared unbelievingly at two white reindeer and at the exhausted Lisa, a heavy iron key in her sash and a huge book in her young arms. He stared too at the army of Koach, which five minutes before had been overwhelmed with ghouls, ogres, furies and harpies. Striding to the ramparts he saw that the archers on the eastern slopes had not advanced their screens, but seemed, at least for the moment, to be immobilized. As he turned back to face the group, Suneidesis was helping Chocma to her feet. With amazement he watched her leap effortlessly into her saddle. Chocma's eyes sparkled; her bearing, in spite of her white hair and peasant dress, was noble and beautiful.

"Your majesty," she said, "there are more ghouls and ogres. The light which scared them away will not hold them for long. But if I may ride to the edge of the cliff I can destroy them while they climb. I heard what Lisa told you. Do not question the orders of Gaal, but follow the maid. Take her first to Qava which is but a few minutes from here. Let her lead you from thence into Bamah for I perceive she knows the secret of the tunnel. So far there have been no signs of the Qadar. The battle here will soon be over. The final struggle will be in Bamah around the high altar. But there may be little time to lose."

Kardia shook his head, dazed by the turn of events. Wesley and Lisa climbed onto the backs of their reindeer. A pigeon had settled on Wesley's shoulder. Slowly Kardia mounted his dapple-gray mare.

"Can you be sure to overcome the archers of Lady Sheriruth?" he asked Wesley uncertainly.

Wesley hesitated. He did not feel sure at all. But he said, "That is what Gaal told me. He said my arm and sword would do everything for me." The pigeon rested calmly on his head, and Kardia, looking at it marveled, but felt reassured.

"And you, Chocma, is your strength restored?"

"It is, your majesty."

"And you are sure you can defeat the evil ones?"

"With my book and the help of the Koach, yes! If we go now to the western cliffs, we may prevent any more of them from establishing a foot on the heights. But we must return promptly. Is it your majesty's will that we do so?" Kardia nodded. Chocma turned to the Koach leader, "Come, my good Garfong. Let your followers form a line along the whole cliff top. By now the ghouls may already be climbing again. And you, your majesty, take from the maid her heavy volume and her key. Delay not to reach the Cave of Qava! May Gaal guide and protect us all."

Kardia looked at the weary Lisa on her reindeer and reached down for the book and said, "Are you willing to help me and to help Anthropos again?"

Lisa smiled. "Yes, your majesty. But may I give the Mashal Stone to Wesley?" The king nodded and she passed it to her brother. She continued, "Besides, I have met Gaal. I know he makes no mistakes. I know he will not let us down. There is nothing he wouldn't do to help us."

Kardia drew a deep breath. "Let us be on our way."

A moment later, mounted on reindeer and mare, Kardia and Lisa were galloping to the northern end of the heights to the Cave of Qava. Meanwhile Chocma and the

Koach had fanned out to cover the wide semicircle of the western cliffs. The rout of the dark horde had begun. Wesley, with Sir Nocham and Gunruth, stared at the screens that still concealed the archers of the Lady Sheriruth on the eastern slopes below them.

"I must go down alone," Wesley said suddenly.

"My lord, to do so would be suicide." Sir Nocham's voice was anxious.

"I don't care. I've got to go. Gaal told me I wouldn't always know why I was doing what, and I don't understand any more than you do, Sir Nocham. The only thing I know is that I *have* to. And I do have this Mashal Stone. I might as well put it on. I have a feeling I have to kill this Lady Sheriruth person. I've never killed anyone in my life except for an ogre, and I'm not sure I like it."

Gunruth, Sir Nocham and Wesley stared at one another. Wes, like Kardia, then drew in a deep breath and said, "There's no point waiting; I guess I might as well go at once." He put the chain bearing the Mashal Stone around his neck. Gunruth and Sir Nocham found themselves staring at a white reindeer with a pigeon seated on nothing in the air above it. A sword appeared from nowhere, grasped by an invisible hand. The reindeer turned to face the ramparts and in one great leap sailed over them, the sword and pigeon curving smoothly through the air above it.

Lady Sheriruth, a woman seven feet tall with a haggard face, a vest of chain mail, and no helmet on her yellow hair, sat on horseback well behind the archers. She had bidden them hold their fire. Seeing the strange sight of the reindeer with a sword and a pigeon above it, she was too surprised to issue any order.

For Wesley the ride was dreamlike. Riding bumpily down the hill, he knew as he approached it that he would leap over the center screen, and as he reached it, this was exactly what happened. Reindeer and Wesley soared above the heads of a line of archers. Below and ahead of him he saw (remember the stone showed things as they really are) not a tall yellow-headed woman on the horse but a yellow, seven-headed serpent. In that moment he knew that the serpent's fangs were the source of the poison in the dream arrows.

"She is a witch," he muttered, "or else a demon." This reassured him. He felt better at the prospect of killing a seven-headed serpent rather than a flesh and blood woman. But there was hardly time to think, so rapidly was he approaching her. His sword arm raised itself and sliced through two serpent heads as he swept by. Then as the deer circled back he saw that the horse and five remaining heads were rushing straight at him.

He had no idea what was going to happen. For a moment it looked as though they would collide, but the reindeer swerved to the left a second before they met, then swung its great horns to rip open the belly of the horse. The encounter checked their momentum so that Wesley was almost unseated. Yet without any thought his sword arm swept up, and he was shocked to see it slicing through three serpent heads whose fangs were within inches of the reindeer's back.

The reindeer shook itself free. The horse sank onto its knees. With one more sweep of Wesley's sword arm the last two serpent heads were lopped off. Slowly horse, serpent heads and the vague shape of a huge woman sank like black oil onto the ground to disappear into it, leaving the earth charred and smoking.

Archers were running down the hill toward him, but he did not move. "Are they coming for me?" he asked himself strangely unconcerned. But the line broke long before it reached him, the fleeing archers giving him a wide berth.

The reindeer was breathing hard, and for several minutes Wesley sat and pondered the strange adventure he was having. Slowly he made his way back up to the ramparts. As he did so he saw two things. From around the northern limits of the heights poured a stream of the grotesque figures—fleeing ghouls and ogres. Chocma and the Koach had driven them to flight. The evil ones as well as the archers were running away.

Hurrying to the ramparts he called, "Sir Nocham! Gunruth! Call the Matmon, the Koach and your men. We must pursue! The archers we can capture, but the evil ones we must destroy!"

"Here lies the entrance to the tunnel that leads to Qava," Kardia said as he drew rein. Dim red light glowed in the tunnel facing them.

"It is an evil place," Lisa said quietly.

"Why do you say this?" Kardia asked, glancing curiously at her.

"Because of the red light. Would your majesty hand me the book?"

Kardia passed it down to her. Carefully she rested it on the back of her reindeer, opened it and began to read. Rolling syllables boomed along the tunnel from her young throat. Red light was overwhelmed by clear blue. Lisa advanced, reading as she went, filling the tunnel with sound and light that swept dimness away as the sun chases shadows. The tunnel was short. After a hundred yards it stopped and they confronted solid rock in which a hole, not unlike a keyhole, could be seen.

Kardia felt the key vibrate in his fingers. Uncannily it began to pull his hand toward the hole in the rock. A

···Lisa saw before them the cavern···

moment later came a flash and a roar. As smoke cleared Lisa saw before them the cavern they had seen on the television screen in the attic on Grosvenor. A rocky roof rose far above them, beneath which a flat floor extended to a width of at least a hundred yards and back as far as their eyes could see. Here and there long chains stretched from one side of the cavern to the other, holding the horses down on the floor. Knights by the hundreds, their swords at their sides, their lances on the ground, either lay across their horses, or slept by their sides. The same dim red light they had seen in the corridor filled all the cave. The silence could be felt. They stared for several minutes awed by the space and the stillness.

"How shall this enchantment be broken?" Kardia asked in a whisper.

Again Lisa opened the book and Kardia shielded his eyes for the brightness was as fierce as it had been on the day when Lisa first discovered the book in the upper room of the Tower of Geburah. Yet curiously it no longer seemed to affect Lisa. At first it sent long shadows from the horses, the chains and the knights, but as Lisa read, it seemed as though the light went *through* chains, men and horses alike till the cavern was ablaze with blue light and echoed with words from the book.

Then came the crash of falling chains, the sound of horses struggling to their feet. Men rubbed their eyes with mailed fists (don't ever try it yourself, it's painful) and slowly stood upright and stared at the two figures at the entrance of the cave. As Lisa stopped reading, the blue light softened and a murmur of conversation slowly swelled till the cavern was full of the sounds of living men and horses. Kardia's eyes were alight with joy.

"Knights of the king's highest order," rang his powerful voice, "welcome back to life! Welcome from the bonds of enchantment."

Lisa shivered with excitement.

From all sides came shouts, " 'Tis the king! 'Tis Kardia. 'Tis the voice of his majesty."

"Hearken to me!" Kardia's voice filled the enormous place. "You have slept for three years. But now deliverance is come! Hocoino's doom is near! I call on every one of you to follow me for the final victory!"

A roar greeted his words blending gradually into the chant, "Long live the king! Long live the king!" Kardia raised his hand. The knights farther back could hardly see him so that the shouting died out in a sort of wave, going farther and farther back until silence came again. "Let the captains now approach me." Six knights advanced from various parts of the cavern. To Lisa's surprise several other men appeared. Instead of armor they wore fur-trimmed robes of velvet and silk, blue, purple and red. These were the faithful courtiers and counselors banished when Kardia had fallen.

The enchantment of Qava had been broken forever.

29

The Burning of Bamah

The company of knights thundered down the northern slope of the Heights of Rinnar. Ahead of them two standard-bearers flew the colors of Kardia and of Gaal, a golden shepherd and creamy white sheep on a background of blue silk. Kardia and Lisa (Lisa on her reindeer) followed the standard-bearers while immediately following them were the courtiers in velvets and silks. Finally came the knights. The small army headed due north. After rounding the Rinnar Hill they headed east and were soon under the northern walls of the Ancient City of Bamah. Some of the knights were carrying the chains that had bound them to the floor of the cavern.

"Can you find the entrance to the passage?" Kardia asked.

"Yes, your majesty. It lies under a dead, forked tree, on this side of the river, just north of the gates to Nephesh."

"And how will you open the door of the passage?"

"In the name of Gaal, your majesty."

"Can knights on horseback ride through it?"

Lisa thought for a moment. She wondered about the narrow log crossing the chasm of red light.

"It is wide enough in most parts," she replied cautiously, "and the steps that ascend to the temple are broad and shallow." She felt uneasy about mentioning the log or the chasm and said nothing more.

Very soon she saw the dead tree as they turned southward between the Rure and the walls of Bamah. Its arms still eerily reached up at the moon. The company of knights drew rein behind them.

Lisa stared at the bank below the forked tree. In the moonlight there was no suggestion of any opening. She began to wonder whether she had dreamed it all. She felt a thousand eyes boring holes in the back of her head and glanced at Kardia who was watching her keenly. The two standard-bearers had moved their horses to one side, and they too were looking inquiringly at her. Behind them came the sounds of horses restlessly moving and the occasional clink of heavy chains.

Lisa drew in a deep breath. Then, her voice shaking a little, she said simply, "Open! Open in the name of Gaal!"

For a moment nothing happened, until silently, imperceptibly, a vast segment of the hill opened, revealing a broad, blue-lit tunnel stretching into the hillside. Gasps broke from the throats of the knights.

"Forward!" Kardia called, "Forward for Gaal and for Anthropos!"

As they thundered along the blue-lit tunnel Lisa discovered that her fears had been unfounded. With every step she expected to see the chasm and the narrow log impede their progress. The farther they penetrated the more puzzled she grew. "It can't have just disappeared," she said to herself. But it had. So had the side tunnels.

The rocky walls echoed with hoof beats and the murmurs of excited voices. Wonderingly the knights stared at the soft blue lights and at the ease with which six abreast they could ride at a full gallop along the tunnel.

In minutes they reached the foot of the broad, winding steps. Here they proceeded with greater caution, now riding two abreast as they clattered upward. At the top Kardia again turned to Lisa.

"The book, your majesty," she said. "The door has to be lit with blue."

Kardia passed her the great tome which she rested on the back of the reindeer and opened. She had no need to read. It was as though the open book was alive. It shot a beam of blue onto the stone door. Inside the Great Hall the pillar was set in motion. Two at a time the knights passed through the opening until they were all assembled under the smoking yellow lamps. Behind them, the door remained open.

Kardia had recovered from his bewilderment and was again king and leader. Turning to the commander of companies he said, "Take thirty knights and burn down this temple!"

"Yes, sire. Does your majesty have any suggestions as to how the fire should be started?"

Kardia stared into the dim reaches of the building. "We need more light," he said, turning to Lisa.

Again Lisa opened the book, and this time she read aloud. Once more she was overwhelmed by the excitement of powerful words vibrating through her young body as blue light filled the temple. Soon they could see that lining its walls below the leaded windows, were shelf-lined alcoves heavy with books. At the rear of the temple was a low altar with stone jars beside it.

"A library of black sorcery and jars of oil and incense, I doubt not." Kardia was smiling. "They will provide material for an excellent fire." He stared at the ceiling. Like the shelves, the beams and roof were made of wood. The stone jars by the small altar as Kardia soon confirmed were filled with oil. Lisa stopped reading and the light died down. Once the incendiary party got to work Kardia beckoned the rest of the knights to follow him through the great opening leading outside. Emerging into the moonlight he drew rein and faced them.

"Gaal the Shepherd has bidden us pull down the stone circle that surrounds us. We have chains. We have horses. Let us then move in companies to the periphery of this evil place. Let every man remove his armor and place weapons and armor under the walls of Bamah. Then let us use our horses and chains to drag the cursed stones to the ground."

The knights dispersed in companies to follow his orders. But Lisa stopped and stared wonderingly at the great altar where so recently she had been chained in blackness. Thoughts of the jinn, of her hopelessness, of the way she had called on Gaal and of the many things that followed filled her mind. Lost in her thoughts she slowly approached it. Around her, far away at the perimeter of the great circle, men had already harnessed their horses to pull down the stones. She stopped at the foot of the altar. As she stared at it she found herself breathing, "Thank you, Gaal. Oh, *thank* you!"

She was about to turn away when a glitter caught her eye on a ledge at the foot of the altar. Leaning forward she was startled to see the gold ring that was Ebed Ruach. Marveling she picked it up and stared at the glittering little eyes in the serpent head. Could it see her? Was it conscious? She shuddered, wondering what to do.

Because the book resting on the back of the reindeer was heavy, it fell open as she held the ring in her right hand. A blue light flared up to illuminate the glittering thing in her fingers. She watched in fascination as it dissolved in a wisp of smoke and vanished. Ebed Ruach was no more.

Lisa closed the book to move in the direction of Nephesh, listening to the thuds of distant stones, surprised to see that nearly half of them were down. The knights were working fast. A lurid light flickered across the ground in front of her. When she turned her head to look at the temple, she saw billows of flame flowing majestically up the inner walls and bursting through the windows. The men who had started the fire were approaching her, turning back from time to time to stare at the holocaust they had begun.

Led by Wesley, Sir Nocham and Gunruth, the Koach and the Matmon together with Chocma and Suneidesis poured down the eastern hillside from the heights, pursuing archers, ogres and ghouls. Their speed was limited to that of the Matmon which was only the speed of a fast human walk. Yet Wesley felt it would be unkind to go ahead without them.

"Your lordship, with the Koach and the lady Chocma, we could overtake them and destroy the evil ones at least," Sir Nocham said.

"And expose ourselves to the archers?" Wesley asked. "We need the Matmon with us to meet archery with archery. Moreover, Lady Sheriruth's archers may have been under a spell. At one time they must have belonged to Kardia. Perhaps they can belong to him again."

"But in the meantime, my lord, the distance between

us increases every minute."

Wesley did not reply for a moment. When he did, it was to ask Sir Nocham, "What are those big things ahead?" He pointed north to three rocky projections rising like giant teeth fifty or sixty feet high.

"Those are the Lesser Rocks, my lord."

"I cannot make out clearly the evil ones or the archers, but could they make some sort of stand there?" Wesley did not know the pigeon rode still upon his shoulder. A military wisdom which was entirely alien to him filled his mind.

"It could well be, my lord."

"In that case, it might be better for the Matmon with shields to advance cautiously and for us to have the Koach run in a wide arc to attack them from behind."

"It is well said, my lord."

Sir Nocham drew rein while the rest came to a halt behind him. Orders were given to Koach and Matmon leaders. Gunruth obviously liked the idea.

Garfong as the senior Koach led the wolves in a wide circle, ascending the Rinnar Hill in order to reach a point from which they could descend behind the Lesser Rocks.

Then, more slowly, Wesley led the Matmon north toward the Lesser Rocks, drawing to a halt just out of the range of arrows. There was no sign of archers, ghouls or ogres.

He turned to Chocma, Suneidesis, Gunruth and Sir Nocham. "I can run over to the rocks in less than a minute," he said, "and see where they are and how they are disposed."

"Are you mad, my lord?"

"Not mad, Sir Nocham. I have the Mashal Stone."

He slipped on the pendant, dismounted, and ran invisibly and silently toward the rocks, slowing as he got near and directing himself toward the first and most westerly rock. Cautiously he slowed to a walk and passed between the first and the second rock which lay a little farther back.

The ground was uneven and boulder-strewn. Archers were standing and lying, arrows on string, both among the boulders and in the shelter of the first rock. Dimly between the second rock and the third and largest one he could see the flitting shadows of ogres and ghouls.

The pigeon was still on his shoulder. Wesley's mind went back to the way Kardia had behaved at the Castle of Authentio. His heart beat faster. What had worked in Authentio might work now. In a clear voice he called, "Archers of Anthropos, I am the lord Wesley from worlds afar. You cannot see me though you may see the pigeon of Gaal on my shoulder. The so-called Lady Sheriruth is dead. Her power over you is gone. I call on you in the names of Gaal and of Kardia to yield to your rightful lords. Those who submit will be granted free pardon. Those who do not will be put to death."

Cries of astonishment greeted his words. Men who had been lying down rose to their feet as though wind was blowing over still water sweeping a sudden storm of waves.

"You think," Wesley continued, "that you have laid an ambush for us. You are not the ambushers, but the ambushed. We are now in position to attack you from all sides." A wolf howl from the hillside confirmed his words. "I shall return to the Matmon. Hold counsel among yourselves. If you decide to return to your true king, advance toward us with your hands raised. Should you not come very soon, we shall advance and destroy you along with the ogres and ghouls."

He turned to go, hearing as he did so that an excited

discussion had broken out behind him. He felt good about his challenge, even though he had been partly bluffing. It was true that the wolves would sweep down from the west, but the archers were not completely surrounded. However, what Wesley did not know was that Inkleth and his followers, armed and eager for battle, were at that moment marching and were little more than a mile north of the Lesser Rocks.

He told the others what he had done. Quietly they waited. Minutes passed.

"I do not see them coming," Suneidesis said softly. But she spoke too soon. As the words left her mouth they saw first a score, then a hundred, then more than a thousand men begin to move toward them, their hands raised above their heads.

Their captain approached the now visible Wesley. "My name is Bloggard. I am captain of the archers, my lord. We wish to accept your offer of mercy and to pray that you will intercede for us with his majesty. We were transferred to the Lady Sheriruth with no knowledge of his majesty's imprisonment. Only of late have such rumors reached us."

"Do you now swear fealty to the crown?"

"I do, my lord."

Raising his voice Wesley cried, "Let those who would serve his majesty now cry after me, 'Long live King Kardia!' "

With a mighty roar the archers responded. "Long live King Kardia!"

Wesley looked round at the others.

"I sense no treachery," Sir Nocham said remembering his own experience at the Castle of Authentio.

"You have done well in bringing them," said Chocma.

"Captain Bloggard, cause your men to fall in on our

right flank lest the Koach mistake you for our foes," Wesley ordered.

Minutes later the whole force, now greatly increased in size marched steadily to the Lesser Rocks. There would now be no one to fire arrows at them. Only the ghouls and ogres remained. The battle might be terrible, but at least their enemies would be of one kind. Moreover, the Koach whose sharp eyes had seen what was happening below were moving rapidly toward the largest of the Lesser Rocks where the evil ones were concealed. Meanwhile, Inkleth and his followers were advancing southwest toward the center rock.

"The Matmon will approach the exit between the second and third rocks," Wesley cried. "The distance between them is narrow, and but few of them at a time can pass through. We must catch them in a hail of arrows as they squeeze through the bottleneck. Captain Bloggard, position your men between the second and third rocks—to block the exit from there."

They were in position in minutes. Suddenly pandemonium broke loose. Howling and snarling the Koach descended from the rear on the ogres and ghouls from the west. By now they were experienced in the matter of attack. Within seconds monsters were running through the narrow gap between the second and third rocks only to be greeted by a deadly hail of arrows and a beam of blue light. More of them swept beyond, trying to move south, but Captain Bloggard's archers were awaiting them. Ogres and ghouls are ferocious (never mess around with them unless you have to) but they are undisciplined when they fight together. Harrassed by the Koach from the west, attacked by Matmon and human archers from the south, they turned to flee east, leaving their dead to liquify and sink through the ground. But as they turned east another hail of arrows met them from Inkleth and his Matmon.

Chocma was the first to understand what was happening. "It's Inkleth!" she cried turning to Wesley. "Look, the ogres and ghouls are running the gauntlet for the gates of Bamah." Their speed was faster than that of any of their enemies and within minutes the leading ogres had reached the gates.

The closed gates of the Ancient City proved no hindrance to the ogres. With incredible strength, they tore them from bars and hinges, flung them aside and crowded through the gateway, hurrying by instinct in the direction of the altar.

By the time the pursuing forces reached the gateway a strange sight met their eyes. The temple on the far side was enveloped in majestic flames rising high into the night sky. The ancient stone circle no longer existed. The monsters, still numbering thousands had crowded round the foot of the great altar. The enchanted knights were gathered under the walls of Nephesh. And far above them all they could faintly discern the fearful shrieks of the Qadar.

30

Gaal's Victory

Kurt and Gaal had watched the events taking place in Bamah from their vantage point on the city walls of Nephesh. (You must remember that in our own world at one time city walls were enormously thick, so thick that a road was often built on top of them. You could have driven a jeep on top of the walls of Nephesh.) Afterward Kurt said his experience was like watching a vast stage from the balcony. From the wall he had seen the knights with Kardia and Lisa pour out of the temple over on their far right. He had watched with growing interest their organized effort to harness their horses and pull down the circle of stones. One after another the stones fell ponderously to the earth.

His eyes had glittered in the light of the giant bonfire that was destroying the temple, and he had been excited when all the knights and the court officials had gathered beneath the walls of Nephesh on the south side of Bamah.

"Don't you think we should tell them we're here?" he asked Gaal.

"Not yet," Gaal had told him. "A lot more is going to happen before the night is over."

Then with a tremendous commotion the western gates of Bamah began to shift. In the moonlight they had seen gates being wrenched from the walls and flung aside, and hordes of ghouls and ogres scrambling madly through the opening toward the great altar. Soon a milling throng numbering several thousand surrounded it while just below where Kurt stood, the knights were helping one another to put on their armor and mount their horses for an attack.

Still Gaal made no move. Only when Wesley, Chocma, Sir Nocham, Gunruth and their followers appeared at the western gateway, did Gaal speak. The pigeon had fluttered onto his head, and quietly he placed it within his bosom. Then, without shouting, he called in a voice that would have awakened the dead, a voice that echoed round the walls of Bamah and all over the city of Nephesh. (Don't ask me how you can be heard that well without shouting because I have no idea how you do it.)

"Let no man be afraid. Let all those who are for Kardia, for Anthropos and for my Father, the Emperor, gather along the southern edge of Bamah, beneath the walls. There shall be no more fighting. I, Gaal, will now establish the supremacy of my Father, the Emperor, and of my servant, Kardia. Let the human children, his majesty, King Kardia, the lady Chocma, the Princess Suneidesis, the Matmon Gunruth and Inkleth, Sir Nocham, and the Koach Garfong come to me here on the walls of Nephesh."

Ghouls and ogres froze into stillness while knights turned in eager excitement to catch a glimpse of the speaker. Meanwhile the pursuing army of archers and dwarfs streamed along the south side of Bamah to join the knights. Soon Matmon, Koach, archers, horses, knights, and courtiers began to look like crowds mixing around the edges of a football field. The only difference was that they were gathering on one side only.

One by one, Lisa, Wesley, Kardia, Chocma, Suneidesis, Sir Nocham, Gunruth, Inkleth and Garfong ascended the stairway by the gate that connected Bamah and Nephesh to join Gaal and Kurt. Gaal greeted them all including Garfong with a warm embrace. They laughed. They cried. They chattered excitedly. They interrupted one another constantly (which was very understandable when you think of all the news they had to exchange and all the exciting things that had happened to them).

It was only when Kardia said rather loudly, "Let us cease our chatter! I doubt not that our Lord Gaal has summoned us here with some solemn intent," that their rush of talk abated. Gaal smiled at them all. Then striding to the ramparts of the wall, he called to the multitude below, "Let there be silence."

And silence there was. A silence in which you could hear plainly the terrible shrieks of the flying Qadar. As they stared they could see in the moonlight a great flock of circling black shadows that grew larger by the moment as it descended.

"Let neither man, Matmon nor beast move!" cried Gaal. "Let no arrow be shot nor spear flung!"

Every neck was craned upward to watch the sinister host descend. Somehow they knew that the final showdown was about to take place. Soon the swirling monsters were blotting out the sky and deafening them all with their shrieks. Then, as though drawn to the great altar like a magnet, they settled over and around it, jostling aside ogres and ghouls till the silence fell again.

The mound on which the altar stood was over a hundred fifty feet high, very much bigger at the base than at the top. It all looked as though it was draped with a mantle of black, flickering dull red on the right side with light from the flames of the temple. On the highest part, where Lisa and Suneidesis had once been chained, two tall figures stood. They were Hocoino and Shagah.

Shagah surveyed the multitudes contemptuously, his arms folded and his head flung back. Hocoino stood behind him and to his left. Somehow you knew, even though the distance was too great to see clearly, that Shagah was smiling and that Hocoino's eyes were full of fear.

Shagah's voice sounded across the distance to Gaal and his followers. "So you have all come to meet your doom. I felt it would be more appropriate to sacrifice you here than on the battlefield of your choice. I do not do battle with your kind. I brought you here. Welcome to your destiny! Welcome to the destruction of old Anthropos and to the birth of a new order!"

"Where's Gaal?" whispered Lisa to Suneidesis.

"Kardia, where is he?" Suneidesis repeated to the king. Gaal was no longer among them.

"Look, look!" Kurt cried pointing below them. A lone figure in a white robe was crossing the space that separated the two multitudes.

From the altar Hocoino pointed a trembling finger toward him as he spoke to Shagah. Shagah brushed him aside and stepped forward. With a swift motion he seized from the air a javelin of flame and flung it at the approaching Gaal. Yet as the spear flew toward him it shriveled and disappeared. Still Gaal walked forward. Still he showed no sign of hurrying. Before long he was halfway between the two groups. The stillness was intense.

Then from Shagah's mouth came the most terrible sound that any of them had ever heard. None of them knew what he was saying. Yet you could tell that all the power of ancient evil, all the stench of deepest vileness and the searing heat of a million hells poured out of his throat. He was uttering the last and greatest curse. Above his head came a clap of thunder. A flash of light tore the night in two. A fiery ball of dull red flame and smoke was suspended in the air above Shagah dwarfing him by its size. He lifted his hand and the sphere dropped to rest on it. Then it sped, as though he had flung it toward Gaal.

A gasp arose from all sides for the fiery sphere must surely swallow the tiny figure. Yet as it approached him, Gaal also raised his hand. The sphere stood still. Gaal advanced farther and pointed at the temple. The sphere shot into the midst of the flaming building with a clap of thunder that shook the ground beneath their feet. Sphere, flames and temple all disappeared. Only darkness remained where they had been. And Gaal strode on.

You couldn't help but admire Shagah—in a way. He remained standing, his arms at his sides now but his head still erect. Hocoino was lying flat on his face. Soft blue light surrounded Gaal. As he reached the ghouls and the ogres, an avenue opened up among them as if by magic, extending right to the altar steps. The Qadar, the ghouls and the ogres fell on their faces before him, cursing him as they did so. Slowly, his face contorted with hatred, Shagah himself knelt and bowed his head.

Gaal spoke softly, and once again (as I told you before, I don't understand how) his quiet voice could be heard in the remotest corners of Bamah. "I have come to proclaim among you my sovereignty and to set the captives free. Let them now be released!"

There was a crack as the altar split widely down the center, and a dull red light glowed from caverns beneath it. Stumbling into the moonlight came citizens of Nephesh taken captive over the years by Hocoino. Their faces were bewildered, yet as they saw Gaal, they knew somehow, even though they did not recognize him, that all was well. They hugged one another, laughed, cried, clapped one another on the back and began to walk and to run past Gaal to the walls of Nephesh. More and more of them poured into the open—children, old people, men and women of all ages and kinds—until they numbered not hundreds but thousands running across the wide area to join their fellow citizens. Only when the last of them had been released did Gaal quietly turn and follow them.

Around the altar it was as though all had been turned to stone. There was neither sound nor movement. No one saw it happen, but once again Gaal was beside them on the wall. Dawn was breaking in the east. He turned to Wesley, "Did you deliver the orb to his majesty?" Wesley looked startled. The orb?

His hands flew to his food satchel. He had forgotten all about it. But it was still there. How could he not have been conscious of something so heavy? With trembling hands he pulled it out and walked over to Kardia. Somehow he felt he ought to kneel. Bending down on one knee, he raised the glittering object to the king.

Kardia's face glowed. "Thank you," he said looking first at Gaal, then at Wesley, then at all three of the children. "Thank you all for what you have done."

"You must open the gates to Nephesh," Gaal said,

smiling gently. "Your subjects on both sides of the wall await you."

It was only then that all of them realized that not only on the Bamah side of the wall, but also from the whole city of Nephesh came the sounds of human voices and running footsteps. They could see that the streets of the city below were crowded. The noises from Bamah and the light of the fire had wakened the sleeping people. In nightgowns and nightcaps they were peering through their open windows and crowding the streets, talking pointing and moving toward the main gate that connected Bamah and Nephesh.

"Only one thing remains to be done," Gaal said, and turning again toward Bamah he called in that penetrating voice I have already told you about, "Let there be silence!"

Throughout the streets of Nephesh and across the wide spaces of Bamah, again a silence fell. Pointing his finger at the altar, where Qadar, ogres, ghouls and the two great sorcerers remained he cried, "Let death receive the dead and let the gates be sealed behind them!"

With a crash that could be heard for miles, the earth split from one end of Bamah to the other. Flames shot into the sky as the altar and all who were around it tumbled like a great truckful of garbage into a vast incinerator. Then with the clap of thunder the earth closed again.

Silence reigned.

Everyone able to see what happened blinked and stared in wonder.

Cautiously over the eastern horizon, the shy sun peeped to announce the day. People began to hurry to line the main street down from the gates. The town criers kept the people on the sidewalk by ringing their bells and calling (don't ask me how they knew), "Make way for his majesty, King Kardia of Anthropos!" From the royal palace, a coach led by four horses arrived at full gallop at the gates. So eager was the coachman, that I am amazed the coach never overturned. As for how he got both coach and horses turned around when the crowds were pressing so hard beside the gates would take far too long for me to describe.

Kardia, Suneidesis, Chocma and the rest were standing on the wall above the gates. Kardia stood with the orb in his hands and cried, "Thanks be to Gaal and the Emperor that Anthropos is free again! The tyrants that oppressed you are no more! The prisoners are set at liberty. I hereby proclaim a week of holiday and feasting and announce that in three days I will marry your queen-to-be, the Princess Suneidesis. Now let the gates be open and may they never again be closed!"

And the gates did open. And the people cheered.

And Kardia led the Princess Suneidesis down the stairway into the royal coach. The coachman cracked his whip, and the coach with king and princess waving through the windows rumbled magnificently (if somewhat precariously) over the cobblestones to the royal palace in Nephesh.

But as the children watched they saw something more wonderful that caused the tears to run down their cheeks and their faces to light with joy. Through the open gates came the former prisoners, and you could hear people saying things like, "There's George! It's George! It really *is* George! George! It's me! Mary! *George!*" or else, "Mummy, there's daddy coming through the gates. Daddy! Daddy! We're over here!" Or, "Jean, Jean—can that be little Jackie—yes it is! She's alive, sweetheart. She's alive! Look! Right over there! Jackie, Ja-a-ackie!"

It went on for hours. And eventually everybody found

everybody, at least everybody who was still alive; some, I am sad to say, went home weeping quietly for the members of their families would never be seen again.

Wesley and Lisa were so excited that they scrambled with Chocma down the steps into Nephesh, with Inkleth, Gunruth, Garfong and Nocham, and mingled with the citizens, the knights, the nobles, the horses, the Koach and the Matmon.

There never was such a morning. There was weeping and laughter, dancing and singing, embracing and hugging. People pulled their tables out onto the streets and gave tea and bread to perfect strangers. The doors and windows of every home were opened. The children had never in all their lives seen anything like it.

But as the sounds died away and the crowds moved down into the heart of Nephesh, Gaal and Kurt walked back along the wall together.

"So you wanted to be a great magician," Gaal said quietly.

"Please, Gaal, not anymore!"

"Power is not evil, Kurt—only dangerous."

"It was bad for me, Gaal. You know what it made me do. I didn't care what happened to anybody—even to you."

"Would you like power, Kurt?"

"I don't know what you mean."

"Power to do good."

"I'm not sure, Gaal. I'm frightened of power."

"Perhaps we could do something together, something good for the people of Anthropos."

"You could—not me."

"Kurt, I don't like working alone. I like to do things with people who love me and who love others."

Kurt blushed. He was too young and too embarrassed

to say the thing he wanted to say—that he loved Gaal.
Instead he moved a little closer to him and was glad to
feel Gaal's arm over his shoulder.

"Kurt, the city of Nephesh needs a defense on the
north side. It also needs a deep lake in case drought
comes again. And the whole country needs rain."

Kurt was not sure what Gaal was getting at. They were
now standing, looking at the dried grass growing over
the foundations of buildings that once had been the
Ancient City, but was now an empty circle nearly two
miles across.

"Let's make a lake here, Kurt."

Kurt looked at him not believing what he heard. "But
how?"

"Well, we could let the sloping land where the circle
of stones was sink down on this side for seven or eight
hundred feet and on the far side somewhat less."

"Are you . . . are you pulling my leg, Gaal?"

"I never pull legs."

Both of them stared silently over the brown waste of
grass. Quietly Gaal took the pigeon from his bosom and
placed it on Kurt's head. "Tell the land to sink, Kurt. Tell
it to do so because I say so."

Kurt hung his head. He thought with shame of the
keep on Geburah. "I don't like to."

Gaal put his hand under Kurt's chin. He raised Kurt's
flaming face to meet his own. "The past is gone, Kurt.
You belong to me now. And as my servant you must do as
I bid you." They stared into each other's eyes until Kurt
began to laugh.

"O.K., then. Land—*sink!* Sink because Gaal says so!"

Before his very eyes a circular crack appeared just outside the ring of fallen stones. Slowly, descending like a
vast elevator into the bowels of the earth, the center of

Bamah, more than a mile across, began to sink. On the far side it sank slowly while beneath them amid roars and crashes of fallen rock, the land sank rapidly. The middle crumbled into crazy shapes with loud cracks and great clouds of dust. It sank till they overlooked an immense cliff. On the far side, where the land was lower there was little more than a low rim of rock, a hundred or more feet high.

"Let it fill with water, Kurt!"

"D'you really mean it?" Kurt's eyes were wide and staring.

"Yes. Bid it do so because I want it to!"

Kurt wasn't sure how to put it.

"Fill yourself with water," he shouted. "Gaal says you have to!"

Suddenly on their left, two-thirds of the way up the new rocky cliff a great waterfall burst from the rock rushing and roaring down into the hollow alive with the gold of the morning sun.

"It will fill the lake to the proper level," Gaal said quietly, "then overflow gently where the dead tree lies into the River Rure. But there will always be cliffs on this side, to defend the city of Nephesh. Now we must bid the rains to begin. Shall we make it rain for a week?"

Kurt shook his head, not because he disagreed but because he thought he must be dreaming. In front of them the morning sun was shining—but behind them black clouds were almost overhead.

"You must command it to fall, Kurt, because I'm not going to!"

In a daze Kurt said, "Fall, rain! Fall for a week! Fall because Gaal wants you to!" Splashing spots the size of silver dollars began to spatter one after another, thicker and faster.

Down in the city people held up their faces and opened their mouths to feel the first rain in years. Those who were inside their houses ran out into the streets without their coats or hats and spread out their arms to feel the cool water. Soon it was raining in torrents with water rushing over the cobbles in streams and little rivers. But nobody cared.

And over the city of Nephesh arched the most beautiful rainbow anybody had ever seen.

3*I*

What Uncle John Found Out

Wesley, Lisa and Kurt sat crowded together in the window seat of Lisa's room in the royal palace looking over a great sweep of lawns sloping down in terraces to the river. Everywhere preparations were being made for a royal garden party.

"Thank goodness the rain is over," Lisa said. "Just think—rain for seven days without a break."

"Well it wasn't all heavy rain, not like the first day," Wesley countered. "And you must admit the country needed it."

Kurt said nothing. He had told his brother and sister nothing of what had happened on the wall, not even when everyone was talking about the sensational discovery of the new lake which they were now calling Lake Bamah.

"Still, it *might* have stopped raining for the wedding,"

Lisa said. "Just think of all those thousands of people standing in the rain just to watch the procession go by."

"I'm glad we got seats in the cathedral," Wesley said. "That was awfully good of Kardia!"

"Distinguished visitors from other worlds," said Kurt mischievously.

"Distinguished nothing," Wesley snorted indignantly. "Can you imagine a royal wedding in our world with people from a senior citizens home, school children, Koach, Matmon, poor people and nobility all sitting together at a royal wedding? Talk about democracy! Kardia had the right idea."

"Didn't Sun look beautiful?" Lisa said. "She was terrific!"

"The whole thing was terrific," Kurt said. "Man! Would I ever like to learn to blow one of those long trumpets which have flags hanging down from them!"

For a moment there was quietness as Kurt and Lisa stared at the preparations on the lawn and Wesley eyed the beautiful old tapestries that lined Lisa's room and the dark oak table where silver trays lay with the remains of their breakfast.

"How long before this thing starts?" he asked.

"The garden party? About two this afternoon, I think."

Lisa looked puzzled. "I thought garden parties were things where the women wore lace dresses, big hats and white gloves and the men wore tails and silk hats. You know, the sort of thing you see in movies—everybody very polite and bowing and sipping tea, and waiters going round with trays of hor d'oeuvres and...."

"You sound disappointed," Kurt teased. "This one looks much more fun!"

"I can't imagine acrobats and tumblers in royal garden

parties in our world."

"Oh, don't be stuck up, Lisa."

Lisa smiled. "I'm not really. It's just . . . different."

"Look at the clown practicing his tightrope walk!"

"And the performing bear down there on the right."

Wesley too was staring now. "I do believe they're setting up coconut shies! It's more like a country fair than a garden party."

"What are coconut shies?"

"Can you see that row of coconuts—balanced on top of the wooden cups? Well, you get to 'shy' five balls at them, and if you knock a coconut down you win a prize."

Everywhere on the lawn below them tents and pavilions were being erected and tables put up. Carpenters and servants ran hither and thither in what looked like chaos. The sounds of hammer and saw could be heard as a bandstand was being hurriedly constructed. "They're making *long* tables, not tiny little ones where you all sit round and talk politely," Lisa said.

"They'll never get it all ready in time."

"How many people will be coming?"

"Goodness knows. But it won't only be the nobles and the courtiers, but ordinary people and dwarfs and even some of the Koach."

"They say there's going to be a fireworks display on the far side of the River Rure."

"Why on the far side?"

"So people don't crowd too close, and so that you can see the reflections in the water."

"Sounds great."

Wesley frowned. "I wonder if we'll get to see it."

"Of course we will, Wes. Whatever d'you mean?"

"Oh, I don't know. Gaal said something about going back to our own world."

Strange feelings began to rise in their minds as Wesley spoke. It was not that they had ever forgotten. But somehow their adventures had made their own world seem remote and unreal. Now with a warm rush came the memories of Winnipeg and Grosvenor and the horrible school in River Heights with its detestable female principal (thin as a saint and six foot tall). But even the school was not enough to drown a rising love of home.

"I have a feeling this is to be our last day," Wesley said.

"I'm torn in two," Lisa said. "I can't bear to leave Kardia and Sun. . . ."

"And Gunruth and Garfong. . . ."

"Or Chocma—you know she's gone young again, all blond, blue and flowery."

"I would hate to lose touch with Sir Nocham. Did you know Kardia has given him the Castle of Authentio?"

"No, really?"

"And Inkleth—he's been so different since he met Gaal."

"Aren't we all?"

"It's Gaal I hate to leave most."

For a few moments they continued to look in silence through the window. Lisa said, "I don't think Gaal is the sort of person you can leave."

"What d'you mean?"

"He can't just belong to this world. He doesn't even belong to this age we're in now. He's too—too *big*."

"I've never heard of a Gaal in our world."

"Perhaps he's not called Gaal in our world."

They went on staring in silence.

"They're building an enormous platform under the window here." The noise of hammers, of saws and of men shouting began to get on their nerves a little.

"Let's get our cold baths. I can't say I'm used to them

yet, but I'm sure they're good for us. And we ought to put on some of the clothes they've laid out for us."

The children had never had such fun as they had that afternoon. Anthropos was the most unsnobbish place you could ever dream of. Lisa fell in love with an old lady in a wheelchair and insisted that the old lady throw balls at the coconut shy. And whether it was because of the delighted good will in the air or the poor quality of coconuts, I don't know, but with her third shot she not only knocked a coconut down, but cracked its shell wide open.

"Well," said the red-faced man in charge, "that's the first time in all my life I've seen anyone do *that*. I guess you win the first prize." He pulled from under the counter the prettiest silver teapot you could imagine. The crowd clapped and the lady began to cry. The red-faced man kissed her and Lisa kissed her, and before you could say, "Jack Robinson," half the people in the crowd were kissing her too.

Things like that kept on happening all afternoon. No tiny children seemed to get lost, or if they did they didn't seem to care. The band played and large numbers of the people sang folk songs of old Anthropos. Other people began to dance on the grass. There was laughter and lemonade and big men making speeches (to which nobody listened but which everybody applauded). There were circles of old men with long beards holding tankards of mead, smoking their pipes and saying to one another very solemn things like, "Now let me tell you. ..." Or, "Now when I was a little whippersnapper. ..." Or, "Fifty years ago it was! I never did see the like! It was even bigger than this. ..." And so on.

Another area of the garden party was more like a Sunday-school picnic. There were races for Matmon of three hundred years and older. There was bobbing for apples in barrels of water. There were knitting races for old women and young women. There was a pig-roasting contest (I have no idea what the rules were). There were fencing matches for armored knights with wooden swords and feather pillow fights for young boys. There was a crumpet-eating contest, a pie-eating contest and even (can you imagine it?) an eel-eating contest. Wesley's stomach turned inside out.

Chocma said while walking among the crowds with the three of them, "The simple joys are those that mean the most to our people." As Wesley thought of the artificiality of television and movies and Santa Claus parades, he couldn't help but agree. "I just hope you never get to see our world," he said quietly.

At seven in the evening a bell sounded for supper. The sun was getting low. Because of the many trees there was cool shade. Light was fading. Tables had been arranged so that everybody could see the great platform beneath Lisa's bedroom window. How people still had any appetite left, I don't know. But the tables were loaded with roasted pigs (with cherries in their eyes and apples in their mouths), chickens, turkeys, grouse, guinea hens, blackbird pies, fish, fruit pies, mince tarts, fruitcakes, cream cakes, grapes, pears, apples, oranges, nuts, cheeses, breads, creams, fresh butter, milk, wine and honey—and really I've forgotten half the things.

The marvel was that the guests ate the tables bare. People in Anthropos have big appetites. As soon as plates were emptied, filled plates took their place. People were still eating happily when Kardia and Queen Suneidesis stood on the platform of the pavilion. A trumpeter sounded his trumpet and the clatter of cutlery and the sound of talking died down.

"Queen Suneidesis and I are deeply grateful for the kind and loyal way you have welcomed us back. Because of the goodness of Gaal, things will never again be what they were in the recent past. I owe a great debt to all of you. I owe an unspeakable debt to her majesty, the queen. The debt I owe Gaal the Shepherd, Son of the High Emperor, is a debt I can never repay. But there is a special debt that all of us owe to three children from another world without whom this war would never have been won. I pray you, my Lord and Master, Gaal, to present their lordships and lady Lisa to the people of Anthropos."

Lisa, Kurt and Wesley stumbled awkwardly onto the platform. It was an empty stage and behind them was a smooth wall of what looked like black glass. Gaal stood at the front of the stage, gathered the three round him and smiled at the people at the tables.

"The greatest wars are not won by generals or mighty warriors but by weak and little people who have the courage to obey. The three who stand before you knew nothing of Anthropos before I brought them here, yet they went through weary nights and tiring days. They battled against treachery with trust. They penetrated the keep of Geburah by simple obedience. Time would fail to tell of all they have done. They fought your enemies and rescued your king. Let them be examples for you."

The applause and the roar that burst from thousands of throats moved and embarrassed the children. They were grateful, but in their hearts they knew that had it not been for Gaal, everything would have ended in tragedy. Suddenly they were being hugged by Suneidesis, leaped on by Garfong, embraced by Kardia, Chocma, Nocham, Inkleth and Gunruth. Then as the applause continued, they heard a sound which was strangely familiar and yet all wrong for the land of Anthropos. It was the sound of a Winnipeg front doorbell. When Wesley turned to look at the back of the pavilion, he saw that the black glass was not there. Instead—and all three children saw it at once—was the attic on the top story of the house on Grosvenor.

Dazed they walked with Gaal toward it. He was smiling and standing aside to let them pass. In their ears rang the cheers and applause of the citizens of Nephesh along with the ringing of a Canadian doorbell.

One by one they stepped into the attic. Immediately the sounds from Anthropos stopped dead. In the silence the doorbell rang again. They looked behind, but there was nothing but the attic wall covered with faded, old wallpaper.

"We'd better see who it is," said Wesley.

They hurried after him down the staircase. Halfway there the bell rang again. Wesley opened the front door, and in from the frozen night stamped Uncle John.

"*My,* it's cold out there," he said. "I was afraid you were in bed. I forgot my key and no one answered the phone when I called. Didn't Mrs. Janofski come?"

The children glanced at each other. "No . . . not exactly . . . I mean, Mr. Janofski had a heart attack and they had to take him by snowmobile to the Health Sciences Centre," Wesley said, frantically wondering why Uncle John was there, what day it was and how they could avoid giving themselves away.

Uncle John had removed his snow boots and dropped them in the rubber tray by the door. "I'm sorry to hear that. Is it something bad?"

"We don't really know, but he had to go on a stretcher."

"We're wearing our ordinary clothes," Lisa whispered

to Kurt—and indeed they all were.

Uncle John hung his coat and fur hat in the closet in the hallway. He went to the telephone where they heard him talking to Mrs. Janofski. As he talked the children spoke in whispers.

"It must be—but it can't be—the same night we left," Lisa murmured.

"Uncle John obviously never got away because he seemed to expect to see Mrs. Janofski here."

"Then that means it *is* the same night."

Their uncle's voice sounded loudly above their whispers. "Oh, I'm so glad . . . , no, don't worry about us, Mrs. Janofski. We'll be fine. . . . So they think it wasn't a coronary? . . . Well, a good rest will do him no harm. . . . Let us know if there's anything we can do. . . ."

He replaced the phone and glanced upstairs. All of them could see that the light was on inside the attic. There was an uncomfortable pause.

"Is that the light in the attic?"

The children looked at one another.

"Yeah, I guess it is," Kurt said.

Uncle John stared at the three of them for a long minute. "So you've made quite a discovery. I can tell by looking at you what's happened." They stared back at him not knowing what to say. Then Uncle John shrugged.

"Well, I suppose it had to happen sooner or later. Come and make me some coffee and tell me about it."

A warm sense of relief settled over them.

They sat for hours in the kitchen. Cup after cup of coffee was served. There's no point in my telling you what they told Uncle John for I've already told you most of the story myself. And I think I got it more in order than they did since Uncle John was forever interrupting them with questions to get things straight.

"Will we ever get to go there again?" Kurt asked.

Uncle John looked down into his fifth cup of coffee and said, "We'll have to see, won't we?"

But if ever they do, I promise you I'll let you know what happens.

Pronunciation Guide

(long o indicated by oe, as in toe)

---

aman   *ah-MON*
Anthropos   *AN-throe-paws*
Aphela   *ah-FAY-lah*
Authentio   *aw-THEN-tee-oe (th as in* thin)
Bayith of Yayin   *BAH-yeeth of Yah-YEEN*
Behrens   *BAY-rens*
Bereth   *BARE-eth*
Bilith   *BIL-ith*
Bloggard   *BLOE-gerd*
Bolgin   *BOEL-guin*
Borab   *BORE-ab*
Borglun   *BORE-glun*
Chakam   *CHAH-kum*
Chazak   *CHAH-zuk*
Chocma   *CHALK-mah*
Chosek   *CHOE-zek*
Dorab   *DORE-ab*
Duin   *DOO-in*
Ebed Ruach   *EH-bed ROO-ach (ch as in* loch)
Gaal   *GAHL*
Garfong   *GAR-fong*
Geburah   *geh-BOO-rah*
Gregorio Gaavah   *greh-GORE-ee-oe GAH-vah*
Gunruth   *GUN-ruth*
Habesh   *HAH-besh*
Hocoino   *hoe-COY-noe*
Inklesh   *INK-lesh*
Inkleth   *INK-leth*
Kardia   *KAR-dee-ah*
Koach   *KOE-ach (ch as in* loch)
Lechesh   *LEH-kesh*
Mashal   *MAH-shull*
Matmon   *MAHT-mun*
Nachash   *NAH-kash*

Nephesh *NAY-fesh*
Nocham *NOE-chum (ch as in* loch)
Norab *NORE-ab*
Numa *NOO-mah*
Pachad *PAH-chud (ch as in* loch)
Playsion *PLAY-zee-on*
proseo comai *pro-SAY-oe KOE-my*
Qadar *Kah-DAR*
Qava *KAH-vah*
qosht *KOESHT*
Quashash *KAH-shash*
Rinnar *RIN-ar*
Rure *ROOR*
Shagah *SHAH-gah*
Sheriruth *SHARE-ee-ruth*
Suneidesis *Soo-nah-DAY-cease*
tiqvah *TICK-vah*
Vilkung *VILL-kung*
Visgoth *VIZ-gahth*
Vorklund *VORK-lunt*
zabach *ZAH-bach (ch as in* loch)

The Tower of Geburah *and its sequel,* The Iron Sceptre, *are imaginative fantasies for young and old.* The Tower of Geburah *is John White's first major work of fiction. He is also the author of* The Fight, The Cost of Commitment, Eros Defiled, Daring to Draw Near, The Golden Cow, Parents in Pain *and* The Masks of Melancholy *(all published by Inter-Varsity Press). Prior to becoming an associate professor of psychiatry at the University of Manitoba, he was the associate general director of the International Fellowship of Evangelical Students in Latin America.*

The cover and interior illustrations here are by Kinuko Craft, a Chicago artist who was born in Japan. In addition to illustrating other fantasy books, she has contributed to Smithsonian *magazine,* Psychology Today *and the* World Book Encyclopedia.